ENSLAVED BY HER BEAUTY

Edmund Lanney—His seductive charm and exuberant confidence ignited Marie's love and deepest passion. But on the day he cruelly betrayed her, she vowed eternal revenge.

ENCHANTED BY HER INNOCENCE

Henri de Nemour—He saved Marie from shame and degradation. The desire kindled in a New Orleans bordello would flame in the glittering châteaux of Europe.

INSPIRED BY HER SPLENDOR

Paul Grillet—His nude portraits of Marie shocked the court at Versailles—and captured on canvas the elusive mystery of their insatiable passion.

IMPRISONED BY HER PASSION

Pierre Lanney—Edmund's bold, dashing son. He was hypnotized by Marie's beauty. When he asked for her hand, she was torn between infinite love and scorching scandal.

THE IMAGE AND THE DREAM

Chloe Gartner

A DELL BOOK

To Andrea, Linda, and Bill.

Published by
Dell Publishing Co., Inc.
1 Dag Hammarskjold Plaza
New York, New York 10017

ISBN 0-440-13226-6

Printed in the United States of America
First printing—August 1980

BOOK I

Mary

The shadows of buzzards flitted across the burial ground, but the buzzards didn't land. Not while the people were there. Only a speckled brown bird was brave enough to fly down to the heap of damp earth beside the grave and scratch for worms. When the gravedigger dug his shovel into the mound, the bird hopped back, cocked a bright eye at the child, Mary, as if to say, "I am not afraid," then returned to scratching as the gravedigger slapped the earth onto the slowly sinking coffins.

The grave was barely four feet deep, because at that point water had seeped in, filling the pit with a foot of water.

"No use trying to go deeper," the gravedigger had said. "It'll only get worse." He glanced at Mary, then said in an undertone to Frank Goodacre, "Good thing you drilled holes in the coffins or they'd float."

Bubbles broke the brown surface of mud. Mary tried to keep her mind on the bird and not on the brown water entering the coffins, soiling the bodies of her parents. They had died within hours of each other and now shared the same grave.

Last night she had wept until nothing was left but despair. Now she was dry-eyed, emptied of sorrow, steeling herself for whatever was to come.

I shall have to be like the bird, she told herself. *I must not fear anything. I too shall have to search for worms, for there is no one to take care of me.*

She sighed, and Frank Goodacre patted her shoulder awkwardly as if touching her embarrassed him, as if he knew no words to say.

Frank Goodacre had worked beside her father and carried her father home when he had dropped with fever and finally arranged for the burial. He had taken Mary home with him. His house was little more than a log shack thatched with palmetto leaves. Mary did not see how it could contain the brood of children, each of them as yellowed and hollow-eyed and gaunt as Frank and his wife. They reminded Mary of little animals. They had eaten like animals, acted like animals, staring at Mary in curiosity and distrust. No wonder. Mrs. Goodacre had refused to let Mary into the house. She had stood in the door, arms akimbo, and glared at her husband.

"You want us all to take the fever too? You want to see your children in the grave so you don't have to feed them?"

"It's not catching, Faith. The child's not taken it."

"How do you know it's not catching? The mother had it first, didn't she? Then the father? You wait and see! No use the gravedigger filling the grave to the top. You tell him that. They'll be putting her in it next."

"Hold your tongue. Don't speak like that in front of her."

"She doesn't understand. She's but a child. How old is she? Ten? Eleven?"

"Eleven. Before he died, Gavin Macleod told me she was eleven."

"Eleven. And in another two, three years she'll be on the street same as the brat daughters of that Frenchman who died. She's got that look about her. If she lives, that is. But she'd be better off dead."

"There was nothing else for those girls. If they'd had a home—"

"That one's not having a home either. Not here. Not with the fever in her."

"She could help you."

"My own can do that."

"What's to become of her?"

"What's it to you what's to become of her?" Mrs. Goodacre had given Mary a long, cold look. "She can sleep here tonight, but outside. After the burial tomorrow, you figure out what's to become of her. You brought her here. You take her away."

I wouldn't have stayed if she had asked me, Mary told herself.

Frank had given her a sour-smelling, ragged quilt, and she had wrapped herself in it and huddled against the house. She had slept little. Time after time the high-pitched cries of the night birds, the bellowing of the bull alligators, and her own nightmares had awakened her. She had not even had her doll, Flora, to share her loneliness and fear.

The gravedigger leaned on his shovel and wiped the sweat from his face. "Hot."

Frank nodded. Sweat trickled down his face from under his hat, and his faded shirt was soaked, clinging to his body.

It was early, but the sun was dazzling. The trees were limp with heat, and the stench of marshy earth and canebrake was so heavy it was difficult to breathe. Clouds of mosquitoes hung in the air and left a bloody smear when Mary slapped them.

The bird uncovered a fat worm, devoured it, then flew to a tree to sing as Mary watched.

"Praise God from whom all blessings flow . . ." Blessings! Why had she thought of blessings now?

From the distance came the sound of machetes slicing through the jungle foliage and the hum of men's voices. The French Canadians always sang as they worked; the black slaves sang too, accenting their singing with the beat of their shovels and the rattling of their chains.

The digging, the clearing, the trenching to drain the land were supposed to have been done entirely by slaves, but slaves were in short supply. The Indians were of no use as field hands. They bartered pelts for rum, drank until it was gone, then returned with more pelts. But they would not work. It was just as well. The Africans had no use for the Indians and didn't like working beside them. The white settlers feared them. Too many isolated families had been killed for their meager possessions. If the digging and clearing were to be done, the whites would have to work beside the blacks to do it.

"We might as well get on with it," Mary's father had said. "Sooner done, sooner we'll make our fortune." And he had laughed because he knew now he would never make the fortune he had hoped awaited him in the new territory.

"Fortune!" Mary's mother had mocked, but not unkindly. She had known how to make happiness.

"You have to have a dream, Betsy."

Canada had been a dream. They had gone there after the Jacobite rising in 1715, when the Macleods had fought on the losing side. Mary had only a vague recollection of Scotland and the dreadful sea voyage. She remembered Canada: the short hot summers and long snowbound winters, the howling winds, the hostile Indians, the hungry springs when the winter's food supply had been exhausted. She remembered her father's excitement when he had heard of the Louisiana territory.

"It's a gentle climate, Betsy, and the land's fertile. The Indians are friendly there, and there are riches to be had. It's being developed by the company of the Indies, which is run by a Scot, John Law, and a Scot wouldn't be telling lies."

"They've told lies before now—some of them—as you are knowing, to your sorrow."

But they had gone. Down through the wild lands, through Illinois territory, through bad weather and perilous Indian tribes to the swampy, tangled land of Louisiana. It was nothing like what the propaganda had led her father to believe. The "city" was a collection of huts, the church a dilapidated warehouse, the inhabitants the scum of the Paris streets and French prisons.

In 1722, the first year there, a hurricane wiped out not only the city but the house Mary's father had built, the garden he had planted, the tobacco he had hoped to sell. It was not a land of dreams, but of backbreaking work, fever, and death.

Mary looked around at the new graves sinking into the swampy land. It seemed there were more dead than living.

Water trickled from the dwindling heap of earth, and the bird flew down and drank from it. The gravedigger grunted and waited until the bird had flown away. "Wouldn't mind a drink myself, but something stronger than that. This is no kind of burial. Do better to heave 'em in the river and let 'em go down to sea. Pity there's no way of burying folk above the ground, but I guess if that was possible, the Lord would've fixed it that way."

He thumped the last shovelful of earth into place, wiped his hand on his trouser leg, and held it out. Mary shook it, but Frank put money into it.

"Can you—can you afford it?" she asked.

"It was your father's money, Mary. Out of his box, remember? Don't fret. There's a bit for you too. Now, if you're ready . . ."

Mary nodded. There was no point in saying goodbye to a heap of steaming earth. She looked quickly toward the grave and saw that the bird had gone.

"I been figuring," Frank Goodacre began, "trying to, that is—and all I can come up with is, there's the church in town. It's Roman, but I guess that won't matter. My wife says there's no difference between Roman and Episcopalian, which your father said he was. But she's Puritan and sees the devil everywhere. The priest, they tell me he's a good man. Maybe he'll know what to do with you. There's a new convent. Could be the sisters'd take you in. It'd mean making you into a Roman, I guess, but you've got no one left to object. We may as well go see."

"All right."

"Don't think too badly of my wife, Mary. She's a fearful woman, and there's never been enough food to go 'round. She hates it here. Hates the heat, hates the way we live, hates the snakes and 'gators and bugs. She says the town's a hell spot dripping with wickedness. She'll hardly go near it. But like I said—" He sighed. "You wouldn't've been happy with us anyway, Mary."

"I know."

"I hope you'll be all right."

Mary hoped so too, but she felt the need to reassure Frank. "I will be."

They fell silent after that. It was a long hot walk into town. Mary wished she had a hat. The sun beat onto her head, and after a while everything took on an unreal pinkish light. Sunlight bounced off the steep roofs and rippled over the streets and the river.

It was the hottest time of day, and the streets were deserted. Only a drunken Choctaw warrior lurched along the levee, his blue-tattooed face gleaming with sweat, his cheap blanket reeking, the tin ornaments hanging from the brim of his hat jingling and flashing in the sunlight.

Since the hurricane, a new levee had been built in an attempt to contain the river during the next, inevitable disaster. The town was being rebuilt, this time in an orderly fashion, laid out according to the original plans drawn up in Paris. The houses were of cypress logs chinked with a mixture of mud and Spanish moss, set in a garden, fenced and hedged with orange trees. Each lot was surrounded by a ditch to serve as drainage when the river flooded. It also served as a garbage and ordure dump. Every day prisoners wearing iron collars and dragging their chains cleaned the ditches, but the stench remained.

When they reached the convent gate, Mary tugged

at Frank's sleeve. "Aren't we going in?" In the garden the poultry flock nested in their dust baths in the shade of the orange trees. She too wanted to sink down in the shade to rest, to be comforted.

He hesitated, then quickened his pace. "No. No, Mary. We'll go to the priest first. He knows how to talk to those wo–ladies. I don't."

She thought, *All you have to do is explain to them. Ask them if I can stay*. But she was too weary to protest. She sensed he was anxious to be rid of her. She would be as glad to be rid of him. Somehow she felt as if she were the adult and he the helpless child. If she was not yet a woman in body, her parents' death had made her a woman in mind overnight.

The priest's door was shut and padlocked. A note nailed to the door fluttered as a sudden hot breeze caught it, then fell back limply against the door.

Frank studied it a long time. "Looks like he's not here."

"It's French," Mary said. "It says he's gone to visit the sick. He'll return for vespers."

Frank smiled at her. "I remember your pa said you could read. Even French."

"I learned in Canada."

"You keep at it and don't forget it. This town's French through and through, and that's the pity. You'll need that talk more'n you'll need to know how to read, I reckon."

"Father said everyone should know how to read. Even women."

"He had some rare ideas." Frank removed his hat and wiped his brow with his shirt sleeve. "But here's the thing, Mary, what'm I to do with you?"

"I could wait in the church." The door was open, and the dark interior looked cool and inviting. The church too was new since the hurricane.

Frank's face brightened. "That's it. Then you won't miss the priest when he comes back. You tell him what happened and ask him to help you. Here's your money, and this is the key to your cabin. I guess what's there belongs to you, though there's precious little of anything. I'll be getting on now. I'll try to look in on you sometime, wherever you are. Your pa'd like that."

Mary shifted the bandanna, lumpy with coins, to her other hand and shook hands with Frank. Then she undid the knot and took out a coin. "Buy some fruit for the children."

Frank turned red. "You don't have to do that, Mary. There's no call to do that."

"Please." She pushed the money at him. She looked like a miniature lady standing there, dignified and magnanimous. Some man would be after her in another year or two, but he'd have to be strong-minded to handle Mary. Neither sorrow nor fear of the future had managed to cloud the directness of her gaze. Frank had never seen the like of their color before, so dark a blue they were almost purple. But everything about Mary was unusual. She had her mother's white skin and rose-tinted cheeks; her father's dark hair, which curled in the damp heat, and his well-defined facial bones. She would never be soft and pliant in a man's arms, the way her mother must have been, unless she got some flesh on her. But Faith had been right about one thing. Mary had a look about her that made Frank know she'd give a man a good time once she learned how.

"All right, Mary." He grinned. "It'll be interesting to hear what my wife'll say about you givin' us money."

They shook hands again, then Mary went into the church, since Frank seemed to be waiting until he saw her safely inside.

The darkness was so deep and unexpected that she was blinded for a moment. She stood still, waiting for her eyes to adjust to the gloom. The church was not cool but stiflingly hot, smelling of candles and incense. The candle flames flickered like fireflies in the blackness. She could see the white cloth of the altar and the image of Christ, His body as gaunt, His face as hollow and white as her father's had been when he had died.

Mary had not seen her mother's body. She had fallen sick and died too quickly. It had happened during the night, and her body had already been taken away when Mary had awakened.

Close upon her first violent burst of grief had come the terror. What happened to orphaned children? Would the convent take her in? She was half-fearful that it would. She remembered the walled-in convent in Canada, the poor gathered at its gates, the sound of bells, and the nuns in their strange dark habits, their faces and hands raw with the cold.

Mary sat down and put her head in her hands. Her eyes hurt, her head hurt, and her stomach ached because there had not been enough to eat that morning. Nor had she eaten the night before. The floor seemed to whirl beneath her, and when she put out her hand to steady herself, she found she was trembling. She wondered if she were getting the fever too. It would be better to die, just as Mrs. Goodacre had said.

The heat outside had crushed the town into silence, but now the sound of footsteps penetrated Mary's troubled thoughts. She turned, hoping it was the priest who approached. But it was a woman in a dress the color of smoldering coals, with a lace mantilla on her head.

She glanced at Mary as she passed. Then she went to the altar. Once she glanced back over her shoulder and met Mary's gaze. As she left the church she looked at Mary again with eyes that looked black in the dim light. Her full red lips matched her dress, and a black patch at the corner of her left eye made her gaze more arresting. The way she walked showed off her body, and Mary knew that underneath that dress and petticoat the woman wore neither corsets nor a chemise. She was as naked as Mary was under her cotton sack. Her mother had said it wasn't necessary in this climate to wear petticoats so long as she stayed at home. She wasn't at home now, but there had been no time and no privacy to dress properly that morning. She hoped the nuns would understand. Anticipating their questions, she tried to frame the explanation in French. *Ma mère dit . . .* She could go no further. Her head ached too much, and she was too conscious of her hunger.

A long time passed, but still the priest did not come. *Ma mère et mon père est*—no, no,—*sont morts . . .*

The next person who passes the church will be the priest, she told herself.

But the next person passed with a jingle of tin. Mary pictured the Choctaw brave, still staggering about the town, ready to pull a bundle of otter skins from under his blanket to bargain for drink.

She moved restlessly, and her foot touched the bandanna Frank had given her. The coins clinked. She was a goose not to have thought of it before. With the money she had she could go to the market and buy food. She conjured up visions of shrimp stews and bananas, chunks of bread and spitted meat.

Her legs trembled as she stood, and she walked not unlike the drunken Choctaw. She was dizzy and had to lean against the doorway until the world stopped turning. The sunlight stabbed her eyes. The earth burned her feet through the soles of her clumsy sandals.

She crossed the Place d'Armes to the levee and walked along it, moving from one tree's shade to another's. If she remembered rightly, the market place was at the end of town. The dirty brown river swirled past on its way to the Gulf. Watching it made her head spin, so instead she looked across its mile-wide expanse to the dark green pine forest on the opposite shore. The forest appeared silent and mysterious and deathly still in the heat.

Everywhere she looked, everything she saw had a

dark center and a spinning halo. Even her own hands radiated light. Her stomach churned, and her legs felt as if they were melting. If she were not careful, she would fall into the river and be carried away like the branches and refuse that sped past, bobbing up and down with the current.

She crossed the street and sank down on the nearest doorstep. Even with her eyes closed tiny bursts of light sparkled and spiraled. At any moment she would be whirled off the earth, out into the glimmering blue-white sky, into the heart of the sun.

A figure bathed in an aureole of light came down the street and stopped in front of the house. Blinded as she was, Mary still recognized the lady she had seen in the church.

"What do you want?" the lady asked in French. "Who are you?"

Mary tried to summon her wits to reply, but the sunlight exploded, leaving a black void. Mary spilled into it, turning as she fell.

Céline

As soon as Céline was old enough to beg, she had been put on the streets of Paris. Her father was himself a beggar, who bound his legs like a cripple and had his own corner on the Rue du Bac, where he scraped away at a tuneless viol and whined for alms. Her mother, a laundress, had died of consumption when Céline was six.

Céline did not mourn her. Her mother had never lifted a hand to protect Céline from the beatings her father gave her when she did not bring home enough money. She had never caressed her daughter or kissed her. Her attitude was one of resentment that Céline existed at all.

Céline had watched her mother's death without compassion or pity. When her father had wept, she had sneered at him. She had no more love for him than she had for her mother and was only biding her time until she could run away.

She was old and wise by the time she was ten. Her father had bound his legs for so long he was losing the use of them. Some days he could not go out to beg but stayed home drinking the wine he sent her to buy for him. One night when he sent her out, Céline did not return. She slept under a stall in the market while rats and starving cats and dogs rooted and fought in the refuse.

She awakened in the predawn, when the farmers arrived with their fruits and vegetables, milk and freshly slaughtered beasts, cackling chickens, hissing geese, eggs, and cheeses. That morning she breakfasted on a bruised and wormy apple tossed to her by the woman who owned the stall, then spent the next few hours wandering through the market, filching a fruit here, an egg there, and a soup bone, which she gnawed like a dog, raw though it was. Later she sat on the riverbank watching the old fishermen and bargemen at work. In the afternoon she went to a *boulangerie* and begged an old loaf.

"I would have thrown it out anyway," the baker said with a shrug.

It was so hard she nearly broke her teeth on it. She took it back to the river and dipped it in the water to soften it, then ate it all.

That night she slept under the Pont-Neuf with some other homeless people. In the middle of the night one of the men raped her. She would have run away after that, but she was more afraid of the dark and the cutthroats who lurked in the narrow streets at night than she was of the man. So she stayed, and he put his cloak around her and said if she would be good he would give her money. Being good meant letting him do the same thing again. This time it did not hurt, and it was warm under his cloak.

When the sun came up, they looked at one another, and the man clutched his head and swore.

"Christ's bones! You're nothing but a child. I thought your tits were small because you were starving. They're small because you haven't grown them yet!" He had a country accent which Céline found difficult to understand.

He was young himself, with a straggly beard and curly hair and dark, lavender-blue eyes like the sky over Paris in the evening. Céline thought him the most beautiful man she had ever seen.

"Christ! I've never done it to a child before. I've got to go to a priest. God knows what he'll do to me. Damn me to hell, probably." He scrambled to his feet and started to put on his cloak.

"You said you'd give me money," Céline reminded him.

He stared at her. "You damned little whore!"

"I'm not. It was you who wanted it and you who promised. You know I'd never done it before. You found that out. See, there's blood on your cloak."

He flung the cloak at her. "Wash it and spread it to dry, and don't let anyone steal it. I'll be back after I've been to church."

"I'll steal it myself and sell it if you don't give me my money."

"What a little bitch you are! If you're such a bitch when you're so young, what'll you be when you're grown, eh?" He grinned suddenly and reached inside his shirt, fumbling for a moment. Then he brought out a copper. "Catch!"

She did and dropped him a mocking curtsy. "I'll wash your cloak this time, but I'm not a laundress any more than I'm a whore."

"Then what are you?"

"A beggar."

"And a damned poor one from the feel of your bones. What's your name?"

"Célestine, but I'm called Céline. What is yours?"

"Pierre Millet. From Troyes. Or the countryside nearby, to be truthful."

"It's best to be truthful when you're on your way to church," Céline said mockingly.

He shook his head. "How your parents came to name such a little bitch Célestine, I'll never understand."

"The same way your parents named a rapist of children after Saint Pierre."

He looked abashed. "*Touché*, Céline. See that my cloak is clean when I return." He went off laughing.

Céline washed the cloak. While waiting for it to dry she lay down in the grass beside it. It was peaceful, watching the river float past and the clouds forming and reforming overhead. The street cries of Paris seemed far away. The carved faces on the bridge grinned at her as if in fellowship.

She took out the coin Pierre had tossed her and turned it over in her hands, studying it. It was the first money she had ever had that she didn't have to give to her father. It was also more than she sometimes took home in an entire day. And all she had had to do was to lie there.

At midday Pierre came back, bringing with him a loaf of bread, a sausage, and a jug of wine. "So you didn't steal the cloak after all."

"I told you I wouldn't if you gave me my money."

"A young bitch but an honest one. Let's eat."

It was on the tip of her tongue to say, "Fix your own," but she was too hungry to be impolite. Pierre let her eat as much as she wanted and even handed her the last crust of bread, which should have been his.

"What did the priest say? Did he forgive you?"

"Yes. He said I should ask you to forgive me too."

"I forgive you. After all, you paid me for what you did."

"He said too that I should take you to a home for orphans. They'll take care of you and protect you from men like me, and they'll feed you every day so you won't have to steal."

"I don't want to go to a home. They'll make me work," she said. "Why can't I stay with you? I'll beg for you."

Pierre shook his head. "You can't stay with me. I'm going to the New World."

The New World. The words were magic. "Let me go with you."

"You can't. They want men without dependents, without wives or children."

"What will men like you do without women?"

"I'll get myself a redskin."

"And end up scalped one night."

He laughed. "By heaven, I'd take you if I could.

You make me laugh with your good sense. You're an old woman of a child, but I suppose that comes from living in the streets."

"When do you leave?"

"Tomorrow. Over a hundred of us. We march to the coast, where there's a ship waiting for us."

"Then you must take me to the home before you go."

Pierre sighed. "Yes, I suppose I must. It's a Catholic orphanage, not far. Are you ready?"

When they arrived, he told the Mother Superior he was Céline's brother, that their parents were dead and he was off to the New World.

"Now you'll have to be forgiven the lie," Céline told him.

He kissed her good-bye and wiped his eyes with his cloak. "I didn't cry when I left the farm, though my mother would have liked to see my tears. I don't know why I'm crying now." He sniffled and gave her a rough pat. "Be a good girl, Céline."

The Mother Superior waited in the door while Céline stood in the street waving until Pierre was out of sight.

The nuns taught her to cook, to read, to write, to iron, and to sew. When she was fifteen, they found a place for her in a seamstresses' shop. She was fortunate, they told her. "They sew for royalty. If your work pleases, perhaps you'll be taken into a noble household to do the mending."

The nuns reminded her to be virtuous, honest, and industrious, and gave her a missal with her name in it. Then the porteress accompanied her to the gate and watched until Céline turned the corner. The girl waved happily, laughing because the nuns had been foolish enough to trust her on her own.

She walked along the riverbank to the Pont-Royal and asked the first guardsman she saw to direct her to the nearest brothel.

"What's a woman want with a brothel?"

"I want to work there."

He looked her up and down, then ran his tongue over his lips and nodded. "Try Colette. She's not the best, but she's not the worst either. She'll like your looks." He gave her directions, and as she walked away he shouted after her, "How do you call yourself? I'll ask for you."

"Céline."

By the time she was twenty, she knew everything there was to know about pleasing a man, but Colette was tight-fisted, and Céline had not made as much money as she thought she deserved. One day she told Colette she was leaving, going onto the streets on her own, and when she made enough money, she was going to the New World. There was a man there . . .

Paris was hung with posters designed to lure settlers to Louisiana. The warm climate, the fortunes to be made, the beautiful city of New Orleans, and the friendly Indians were described in poetic detail. But applicants to emigrate were few.

To hasten the growth of the population the crown ordered all rogues and prostitutes rounded up, all prisons, detention homes, and orphanages emptied, all illegal salt makers and any man sentenced to the galleys deported. Along with these were a number of political enemies, merchants hoping to make a fortune, younger sons for whom there were no inheritances, and people unfortunate enough to have been wandering in the streets of Paris after dark, no matter how harmless their intent.

Céline had been wary at first, but lack of money and food sent her back to the streets one night. When she saw the band of men coming up the Rue du Bac one night, she ducked into the nearest doorway and might have escaped had the door been unlocked. Any decent Parisian would have helped even a prostitute escape deportation. But even decent Parisians feared that band nicknamed the Mississippi Thugs and barred their doors against possible invasion. Céline beat on the door as the tramp of boots came nearer, but the lone woman on the other side refused to unbolt it. "Forgive me, forgive me," her voice called as Céline was dragged away.

Céline found herself chained to five other prostitutes and loaded into a wagon bound for Port-Louis. The women were shrill in their anger, the food was no better than swill, the chains rubbed their flesh raw. It was a slow journey as the highways were clogged with countless vehicles. At night they slept in the wagon, burrowing into the straw like animals.

When they reached the port, the ship was not yet ready. It was ten days before it sailed. The quay was crowded with people, and there was neither order nor organization.

One day the prostitutes rioted. They mobbed the soldiers, kicking, scratching, biting, and beating the soldiers with their chains. Céline was dragged into the melee by her companions. It took gunfire to quiet them, and the woman chained next to Céline was killed.

A soldier held a gun on Céline while another released her from the body. He approached warily, rolling his eyes like a frightened cur.

"Do you think I took any part in that?" Céline asked. "Do you think I'd beat you? Get me free of that scum, and don't chain me to any other. Don't chain me at all. I'm glad to go to New Orleans. I had intended to go anyway. Tell the king he has my thanks for paying my passage." She rubbed her wrists, which were bleeding from the iron cuffs.

"So you were planning to go, were you, *poule*? And what will you do when you get there? Get yourself a hundred slaves to work your plantation?"

"Set up the best house in New Orleans."

"You'll have your pick of girls." The soldier gestured with his musket.

"There's damned few from this lot I'd give room to. I said the *best* house."

The soldiers picked up the body by its heels. "Say *adieu* to your friend, *poule*."

Céline spat.

The soldiers dragged the body to the edge of the wharf and kicked it into the water. A young gentleman who had been strolling about since the riot had overheard the exchange between Céline and the soldiers, and now he raised an eyebrow at Céline.

"I know you from somewhere." He opened his snuffbox and offered it to her.

Céline refused the snuff. "Colette's. I've seen you there."

"Ah, yes. Was her house raided?"

"I left her. She kept too much of my earnings."

"That is Colette. High-priced and tightfisted. How does it happen I never had you?"

"You had your favorites, M. Henri."

"You said you plan to set up a house in New Orleans? I don't think the king is sending you for that purpose or that Sieur de Bienville expects it. Bienville wanted women suitable for wives."

"Then the governor knows nothing about men."

Henri laughed. "He is perhaps idealistic. Like yourself. Do you have any money?"

"That has nothing to do with it."

"You will require money. I am going to the new territory myself, due to a misunderstanding between certain persons of authority. But I have money. Perhaps I can help you."

"I wouldn't refuse help," Céline said carefully. "But only as a business arrangement suitable to both parties."

"I like a shrewd woman. Very well. I shall see you when we land in New Orleans, providing we survive the voyage."

By the time *La Baleine* reached New Orleans, Céline had recruited her women. The first sight of

New Orleans was not reassuring, but it was such a relief to emerge from the disease-ridden, odiferous hold that Céline would have welcomed hell itself.

Within a week M. Henri had Céline and her girls installed in a house of their own. It was not what she had hoped for, but it was no worse than the other houses in the town, and it was set in an overgrown garden of orange trees that assured their privacy. The walls were whitewashed, and fur carpets covered the floors. The rooms were little larger than *garde-robes*, and there was no glass in the windows, but the sitting room was spacious. There was also a separate kitchen house.

They were located close to the taverns, directly across from the levee and docks. Since the ships came in the spring and didn't sail again until after the danger of the hurricane season had passed, business was brisk. Each girl got one fourth of what she earned. One fourth went into a common fund for food and upkeep. One fourth was repaid to Henri. The last Céline kept for herself. Any girl who didn't like the arrangement could get out and find herself a husband or walk the streets.

But the girls stayed because they shared Céline's dream. "There is a piece of land out by the ramparts. Nothing is there yet, but there will be. A house with a salon, music, crystal chandeliers, a black to serve wine, and us dressed in the latest court fashions. A card room and billiards for gentlemen who prefer a milder form of entertainment. Gambling whets other appetites."

"You're mad," Blanche said. "What about the sailors? Will they come all the way out there? They keep us fed."

"They'll find us. Tomcats have a nose for what they seek," Alixe said. "And we already have a slave."

Blanche sneered. "A cripple no one else wanted. Besides, M. Henri gave her to us instead of payment."

"Her legs went bad on the slave ship, and we do not

have to do our washing or cooking," Céline pointed out. "Unless you prefer to do your own, Blanche."

Blanche yawned and shook her head so violently that her breasts shook as well. "Never!"

"So, you see, it is a beginning."

"A beginning, but it is a big dream," Mimi said.

"Never do anything small."

Meanwhile Céline went every day to church to thank God for the blessings He had bestowed and to explain to Him about the house. The nuns had taught her religion along with sewing.

When she noticed the child sitting in the pew reserved for members of the Superior Council, she was startled. It was as if she were seeing a vision of the child she herself had once been. The same boney frame and gaunt look. But this child had eyes of the same violet color as Pierre's. Could she be his child? Was such a coincidence possible? It frightened Céline to think about it, and she could not keep her mind on her prayers.

She stopped off on the way home to examine the city register. No Pierre Millet was listed there. "That long ago," M. Henri had told her when she had confided in him, "he probably went to Canada."

When she reached her house, the child was sitting on her steps, like an omen. When Céline spoke to her, the child fainted.

Marie

Mary was first conscious of the smell of food, spicy and redolent with onions and garlic. She opened her eyes and found the woman she had seen in the church kneeling beside her. The mantilla was thrown back over her shoulders, her hands clasping her prayer book lay in her lap, and when she leaned toward Mary, there was a faint flowery smell.

A black woman knelt on her other side. She wrung a cloth out of a bowl of mint-scented water and sponged Mary's face before she laid the cloth on her forehead. When it grew warm, she replaced it with another, over and over.

The white room was dazzling with sunlight. Even the great chimney in the corner was whitewashed, though a smoke stain went up the bricks.

The light hurt Mary's eyes and made her headache worse. She closed her eyes and opened them again when the woman touched her wrist.

"Who are you?" There was a beading of sweat on her upper lip, and the mole at the corner of her eye was not real but a bit of black paper shaped like a heart.

"Mary. Mary Macleod."

"Ma-rie Mac—" The woman gestured helplessly. "You aren't French?"

"Scots. Canadian."

"Ah." The woman sat back on her heels. She was not really old, Mary decided. Younger than Mary's mother had been. Beautiful even when she frowned, as she was doing now.

"Why did you come to me?"

"I didn't come to you." It was difficult to think in French when her head was hurting. "I–I go to the market to find something to eat. I felt–" What was the word for dizzy? She gestured a circle with her hand, then touched her head. "I had to sit down, and your house was there. My head is sick."

"Sun," the black said.

"So. Yes, perhaps. Where is your mother?"

The tears she should have shed by the graveside came now, but whether it was sorrow or pain she didn't know. "Dead. My father too. They were buried this morning."

The black woman clucked. The other swore.

"Is that why you were in the church? You weren't praying," she added accusingly.

"I awaited the priest. Frank Goodacre, a friend of my father, said perhaps the priest would find a home for me. Perhaps the convent."

The woman studied Mary thoughtfully. "Yes, perhaps they would take you, but they're having trouble marrying off the girls they brought from France. They aren't quite suitable for wives, and no one knew the men here were satisfied with their Choctaw girls and their blacks. The men know French women turn into shrews and want to handle the money. I think the nuns may not want another girl. Not even a child."

"Then I have no place to go." Mary closed her eyes and began to cry silently, hopelessly as she explained about the journey from Canada, the fever, and the night she had spent with the Goodacres.

"There, I understand. Yes. I'll ask the nuns. They may say yes. Again, they may say no. They don't like me too much." She touched Mary's hand. "Don't cry, Marie. A place shall be found for you. For a little child, a little mourning, eh? Come, sit up and take some soup. Food heals, and you said you've had nothing." She got to her feet, shook out her dress, and put the prayer book and mantilla on the table. "I, Céline,"—she tapped her breast—"will help you. Once, I too was homeless. I was no older than you." She turned to the black. "Thank God it is quiet today."

"Too hot for men to be thinking that way." The woman ladled soup from the big caldron hanging over the fire and placed it on the table. Then she helped Mary to her feet. "The child's all bone. If she were a chicken, I wouldn't kill her for supper."

The soup was highly peppered and thick with vegetables and pink shrimp. Mary ate slowly while Céline sat across from her, watching her, drumming the table with her fingers.

"I know what you're thinking as clear as if you spoke the words," the black said.

"You always know, Sheba."

"It's wrong."

"Is it? Is it any more wrong than letting the nuns work her like a slave and then marry her off to some settler who wants a wife because marriage is cheaper than buying a black?"

"She's too young."

"Now, yes. But in a year or two? A good price is paid for virgins."

"Only once. Unless, like in some places, you sew her up again and pass her off as a virgin."

"I'm not a cheat. Besides, it is painful, that."

"You're too honest to ever get rich."

"I'll be rich. And you are so honest any other woman would sew up your mouth."

"You try it."

"Christ's bones, woman, I don't want to try it. Be quiet and let me think."

"Think! Your mind is made up. I see that. Does she know what kind of house this is?"

"Would she understand?"

"Ask her and find out. She might not want to stay when she knows."

"She has no place to go and damned little money in that filthy handkerchief."

Mary knew they were discussing her, but they spoke so rapidly she had difficulty following the French, and what she did understand made little sense to her.

The food was making her feel better. The hot, damp wind blowing through the open windows smelled of orange blossoms, and although the room was hot from the fireplace, it didn't matter the way it had mattered at home. There the roof had pressed down, trapping the air, and the canebrake shut off the draft. Clouds of mosquitoes had hung in the air, and the water and earth smelled rancid.

This place with its walled garden seemed remote from all her sadness. She wished the women would stop talking to each other and talk to her.

"Marie." Céline spoke suddenly, as if in answer to her wish. "Would you like to stay with me?"

"Oh, yes, yes."

"Huh," Sheba said.

"Do you know what kind of house this is? A place that is—how to describe it?—not quite nice. The friend of your father would take you away. Your father, he wouldn't approve. Nor would your mother. It isn't a house for daughters."

"I don't understand."

"Sheba, you explain."

"Child, do you know nothing of men and women? Some men, they have no woman and need one. Some men have a woman and need another." As Mary still looked blank, she demanded loudly, "Have you never seen animals, child?"

Suddenly things which had puzzled her fell into place. The talk of the men around the campfire on the journey from Canada. The sly laughter. The frowzy Indian women who would appear in camp and go into the bushes with the men.

Her face burned, and she looked into the empty bowl. "Yes. I know, in a way."

"So, Mme. Céline and the other ladies, that's what they're here for. Those men we're talking about—you don't have to see them, because you're a child. You can live here, but don't expect anyone in this town to speak to you. Still, it's better than going homeless and hungry. It's better than the convent, where all you do is pray and work so long and so hard the devil hasn't a chance to put evil thoughts in your head. But it's a strange place for a child to live."

Mary still did not quite understand. She did understand that these women were kind and Mrs. Goodacre had not been kind. She was welcome here. She had not been welcome there. Céline was beautiful, and Sheba, young as she was, had a comforting strength which Mary needed.

"May I stay?"

"Perhaps it's destined," Céline said.

"Where else would she go?" Sheba asked. "That offal, making her sleep outside like a dog. A mother that woman calls herself? May all her girls turn bitch."

"Don't bring down curses, Sheba. It's bad luck."

"May I stay?" Mary repeated.

"Yes, stay, stay. There are certain problems. She must sleep out here with you, Sheba. The house will not do. Where are your clothes?"

"At my house. My doll too. Flora. I'd like her."

"Mon Dieu! A doll. Yes, we must fetch her too but tomorrow. Today you must rest until your head is better."

They fixed a pallet for her in the corner of the kitchen and rigged a mosquito curtain over it. Mary was sure she wouldn't be able to rest, but she was asleep almost as soon as she closed her eyes.

When she awakened, the shadows had moved across the room. Sheba was taking loaves of bread from the oven in the wall of the fireplace and laying them on a trivet to cool. She hacked a chicken apart with a shining cleaver and threw the pieces into the caldron. She took handfuls of rice from a stone jar and dribbled them through her fingers into the pot.

Mary watched from under the netting, content to lie there a little longer and watch Sheba work. Despite her limp, there was a kind of gracefulness to her movements, as if she did everything in one smooth, flowing motion.

"Sheba."

She whirled around, then smiled. "I forgot you. How is your head?"

"Better."

"Food and sleep. They've been known to cure even broken hearts."

Mary got up. "Shall I help you?"

Sheba thought for a moment. "You get some water from that bucket out there and wash yourself. Wash off the fever. Then you can help, if you aren't too fine to work alongside a slave."

"I'm glad to help." She took the bowl Sheba held out to her. "My father doesn't—didn't—believe in slavery. He said it's a wicked practice."

Sheba stared at her, ladle poised in midair.

"Was he white?"

"Yes."

"Pureblood?"

"Of course."

"Then he must have been crazy. Crazy with the fever."

"Do you believe in slavery?"

"You go wash off the fever before you go crazy too."

It was good to wash and let the warm wind dry her. The shadows were heavy on the tangled grass, and the vine covering the fence lifted its golden trumpet-shaped flowers in the breeze. Along the base of the house the whitewash had flaked off, revealing the moss and mud between the split logs. The shutters of the main house were open, and through the windows the sound of women's laughter rippled across the garden. It was rich, easy laughter, as if those amused had no cares in the world. Mary smiled. Perhaps she too would have no cares if she stayed here.

Sheba issued an endless stream of orders, and Mary had no time to do other than obey, but she obeyed willingly. She had always helped her mother, and taking orders came naturally to her.

When the meal was ready, they carried it on wicker trays covered with mosquito netting to the other house, where Sheba entered without knocking. Céline and three ladies dressed in India calico wrappers were seated around a table. They were drinking wine, and one of them seemed a little tipsy.

The floor was covered with fur rugs, and the tipsy lady was wriggling her bare toes in the fur. The entire room and high ceiling were whitewashed. On one wall someone had painted a green lattice with a vine of trumpet flowers winding through it and on the top crossbar a bird, its head back and its throat swelling, its beak open so Mary could almost hear the notes it was singing.

All the ladies stared at Mary, and she lowered her eyes, because their gaze was so open and so curious it was like an assault.

"Marie, look up," Céline ordered. "This"—she gestured toward a lady whose blond hair tumbled out of the ribbon holding it off her neck and whose enormous breasts seemed about to tumble out of her wrapper—"is Blanche. This is Mimi, and this Alixe. Marie is going to join us."

"Join us!" Blanche grabbed a chunk of bread from the tray and stuffed it into her mouth. "A child join us? What kind of house is this? Selling children!" Her words were muffled as she chewed.

"She will not be sold. We are her protectors."

The tipsy lady—it was Alixe—giggled and rolled her eyes and winked at Mary. "She's funny, Céline is."

"You'll sell her eventually," Blanche said, reaching

for another piece of bread and dipping it into the soup Sheba had put before her. "I know."

"Not until the time comes. Kindly oblige me, Blanche, by eating and not talking."

"She's pretty, considering what a scrawny little pullet she is," Alixe said. Her head drooped slowly to one side as she considered Mary. "And she is not that much of a child, are you, Marie? The little breasts are beginning. Come, let me feel them."

"Keep your hands off her, Alixe. Save your perversions for M. Henri. He appreciates them. I do not."

"I wanted to judge her age."

"You can judge by asking her. She is eleven, and I don't want you ruining her. Tomorrow we are going to her house to fetch her things and her doll."

Alixe laughed. "Her doll! With breasts like that she wants a doll? What she needs—"

"What you need," Céline interrupted, "is a slap in the mouth. I regret the day I asked you to join me."

"You knew what you were getting. What did the authorities write beside my name on my papers? 'Given to all vices.' I am useful to you with all my vices."

"Can I go with you tomorrow?" Mimi spoke for the first time. She didn't look much older than Mary. She was slight with velvety eyes and a face the shape of a fawn's. "I like to walk in the country."

"You like the men to stare at you," Blanche said. "And you like to stare back, so when they come they ask for the young one, the little one. It excites them because you are so young, so innocent. Like Marie here."

"Take Marie away and give her dinner, Sheba. This talk isn't for her ears. After this, when Marie is with us, there will be no such talk."

"No, we'll recite psalms," Blanche said. "You've landed in a nice bucket of slops, little Mariette."

They made a strange procession when they set out the next morning. Céline wore a gray homespun skirt, and her hair was braided and wound about her head so she looked like a country woman. Sheba held a black parasol over her. Mimi tripped behind wearing a straw hat held in place by an immense green ribbon tied in a bow under her chin. She kept tilting her head to peep out from under the brim and smile at Mary. A hat had been found for Mary too, but it was too large and kept falling over her eyes. They all carried baskets on their arms and looked as if they were going marketing.

A small wind off the river ruffled the trees. The smell of urine and garbage in the gutters mingled with that of blossoms, and over it all was the smell of the river land and swamp and heat.

If it had not been for where they were going, Mary would have enjoyed the walk. She longed to talk to Mimi, but could think of nothing to say. The nearer they got to her home, the more her grief surfaced. If Mimi had spoken to her, Mary would not have been able to reply, she was so choked by unshed tears.

The neighbors came out to stare when they neared the house. Then they scowled and shut their doors. It didn't matter to Mary, but Céline sniffed disdainfully. "They'd rather see you starve."

The house was stifling and smelled of sickness. Mimi stayed outside and held her skirt to her nose until Sheba opened the shutters. Céline took in everything with a glance. She selected a few garments from the clothes chest and told Sheba to bundle them together. She examined the bedding and rejected it. "The fever," she said.

She looked at Mary standing helplessly in the middle of the room, tears wetting her face, and laid her hand gently on her shoulders. "Get your doll. Get your doll, and we will go."

"Is there anything we can sell?" Mimi asked, wrinkling her nose at what she saw.

"Marie must take what she wants. The rest we leave."

Mary came back from her tiny bedroom carrying Flora.

Céline smiled and took the doll by the hand. "*Bonjour, Mlle. Flora. Comment ça va?*"

Mimi answered in a tiny voice, "*Je vais bien, Mlle. Céline. Et tu?*"

Mary laughed.

"She's beautiful," Céline said. "She *is* a flower. And with a dress of satin. Finer than your dress, Marie."

"She came from France to Scotland and from Scotland to Canada to here."

"A lady of the world. She shall ride in my basket."

"In that chest, Céline, there's a plaidie. My father would want me to take that and his dirk. It's the Macleod tartan, and it saw the '15.'"

Céline was bewildered by the Scots word *plaidie* and stared curiously when Mary took out the ragged woolen, faded and worn thin, and folded it reverently. The girl laid a buckhorn-handled dirk on top of it, as well as a small silver brooch of two hearts intertwined, and a lady's silver comb.

"That's all, I think." These things remained, and her parents, who had worn them, were gone.

"What is that carved box?"

"Oh, yes, I should take that. It's my father's money box, but the money went for the—the coffins, and to pay the gravedigger."

"Do you have the key?"

"Yes, but it's empty."

"Still, it's a fine box. You may have money of your own to keep in it some day." Céline opened it. "What's this paper?"

"Accounts."

Céline studied it thoughtfully. "These are the names of the month in English, yes? And these are sums. Sums are the same the world over, except in truly foreign parts where they write in bird scratchings. Who opened the box, Marie?"

"When?"

"To take out the money to pay the carpenter and the gravedigger."

"Mr. Goodacre. He asked if there was any money, and I showed him."

"Your friend, Mr. Goodacre, I think, was not such a friend if these figures mean what they say. I never heard of a carpenter costing so much, and as for the gravedigger—is Goodacre a fool?"

"He can't read."

"So that's it. We shall see about Mr. Goodacre. Do you have everything you want from here?"

Mary nodded.

"So we'll lock the door. From now on, no looking back. We've closed the door on your old life. We'll ask M. Henri if the house can be sold when the fever has died out. If it sells, he will not cheat me, and I will not cheat you, as Mr. Goodacre has done. I shall see that man someday. Sooner or later they all come to Céline, and when I have him naked—" She threw back her head and laughed. "He shall pay."

As Céline dropped the key into the basket under Flora's skirts Mary thought, *That's the end of Mary Macleod. From now on, I'm Marie.*

She was not quite sure what Frank Goodacre had done except take more money than was needed. But it shocked her to think of him naked, and she hoped he would never see her at Céline's.

Frank Goodacre

The coin Mary had given Frank burned in his hand. He had recoiled from taking it. He suspected that Mary's giving him that money had been a form of revenge for the way Faith had treated her. She wasn't a fool, Mary wasn't. He would have to be very careful.

As he walked along the levee he was tempted to fling the coin into the swift muddy water. But there was no sense in parting with good money.

Good money. *Good money*. The words made a kind of rhythm that accompanied his steps. *Good mon-ey, good mon-ey.*

The leather bag tied in his trouser leg thumped against him. It too burned him, and for a moment he was tempted to go back to the church and hand it to Mary.

But money would be of no use to a child. The priest or nuns would get it away from her quickly enough. It was better for him to keep it than to have people like that get their hands on it.

He stopped and watched a tree trunk turning in the current. Would Faith have let Mary stay with them if she had known about the money?

No. Not Faith. She'd take the money, say she spent it on food to feed Mary, and when it was gone, she'd put Mary out because they couldn't afford to keep her anymore. Well, Faith wasn't going to spend this money on food. She wasn't going to know about it—not unless she found out about it the same way she had sensed something about Mary that he hadn't realized until she had told him.

He had worried about Mary sleeping outside and asked Faith why she wouldn't take her in. Faith had given a grunt of laughter.

"I saw the way you were looking at her. Not now, maybe, but in a year or two you'd be feeling her, and she'd be rubbing up against you. She's got that look, and I know your look, and I know what would happen."

"That's a lie, Faith." But even as he had said it he had remembered the shape of Mary's small breasts when the wind had flattened the thin cloth against them. Until Faith had put it into his mind, he hadn't wanted to touch Mary any more than he'd touch his own daughter. But patting her shoulder, there at the graveside, his hand had burned just as it burned now, holding the coin. Yes, it was best to get rid of her before he did something he'd be ashamed of. Something worse than taking the money.

The money. He had to think carefully what to do with the money.

He sat down in the shade and watched the river. The day was so hot that the shade did nothing to cool him. But it was as good a place as any to think, away from work, away from Faith and the brats.

Macleod had been saving for a larger piece of land and a better house. He had told Frank so. Well, he had a smaller piece of land now, six feet by three feet with running water, and a new pine house just his size. All that saving hadn't done him any good.

Money, good solid coin, was scarce in Louisiana. Paper money, card money, notes, negotiable only when French ships were in port, letters of credit, barter by produce, that's what was common here, not coin.

What Frank had in that bag made him nearly a king. With it he could buy a big passel of land beyond the ramparts and start his own tobacco plantation. He could build a bigger house. He could buy blacks to do the work. Faith would ask him where he got the money for all this. Maybe she'd laugh when he told her, and maybe she'd make him give it all back. He never knew what Faith was going to do. So whatever he did, he'd have to do it secretly, slowly, so there'd be no questions asked by Faith or anybody else. Meanwhile he damned well couldn't walk around with that bag hanging down his legs like a bull's balls.

What he ought to do, he figured, was to go to that frog-eater, Henri de Nemour, put the money in his trust at interest, or arrange to have him get the land for Frank. He could tell Faith he was hired by M. de Nemour as manager, with the understanding that half his wages were to go into purchase.

Maybe de Nemour would go for a tricky plan like that, and maybe he wouldn't. From what Frank heard about him he wasn't straight as an arrow. Got sent over to the new territory by the king himself after some funny business in France. His family sent him money on every packet that came, paying him to stay away from France.

He had a finger in every business in New Orleans. He had set up a whorehouse, he owned a land grant near Lake Pontchartrain, he had shares in the tobacco factory in Natchez, he bought skins off the Choctaw, he bought slaves and sold them at barter. In spite of all that he did little but sit around playing bagatelle and drinking wine all day, with a black boy fanning him to keep him cool.

Yes, de Nemour would be the man to deal with, but Frank couldn't French it too well, and he didn't know if de Nemour could English it. Still, he might as well try.

As Frank crossed the Place d'Armes he saw one of the town prostitutes advertising herself in her red dress, going into the church. Fine place for a whore, the church was.

He wondered if Mary was still there. No matter. He didn't have time to worry about Mary. He had to hurry and get his business done and get home, or Faith would be accusing him of God knew what.

De Nemour's house was new since the hurricane of 1722. Its steep bordeaux roof extended out over the banquette that led to the front door, and was supported by carved columns. The door had wrought iron hinges, and the windows were grilled with iron bars which twisted and turned in an intricate pattern. In contrast to the dazzling whitewashed walls, the shadow cast by the overhang seemed dark as indigo.

Frank felt a moment's shyness and almost walked on by. But when he felt the bag thump against his thigh, he made up his mind. He had rapped on the door before he realized that the iron lion's head decorating it was a knocker.

Henri de Nemour opened the door himself. He was younger than Frank had expected, probably not over twenty-five. His cheekbones were high like an Indian's, his nose thin and aquiline. Faith would have called it aristocratic. Maybe it was, for all Frank knew. The goatee and mustache were silky black and looked as if they had been combed. But his clothes! He was dressed like a heathen in an Indian cloth, and on his feet he wore loose open clogs which left his toes exposed. He took a long pull at the thin cheroot he held, and as he exhaled the smoke he raised an eyebrow and said, "*Alors?*"

Frank cleared his throat. Faith didn't hold with smoking, but at the moment he wished he had a cheroot of his own to suck while he collected his thoughts.

"Well, it's like this, monsieur." Frank pronounced the word *monsewer*. "See, I don't speak your language, but if you can speak mine, I've got some business to do with you." There. He'd got it out.

"I speak English. What is your business?"

"Money. I've some money to invest."

"Ah!" De Nemour stepped back from the door and gestured for Frank to enter.

Kicking the dust from his boots as best he could,

Frank stepped into the room. He had never seen such a place. He wished he could tell Faith about it, but he'd never be able to.

The carpets shone as if they were made of silk dyed with melted jewels. Frank tried to avoid stepping on them because to do so would be sacrilege. The table was polished wood with gilt trim, the chairs had satin cloth on the backs and seats, and the bed behind the netting was as big as a skiff, and it too was gilt-edged.

A turkey feather fan was suspended from the ceiling, and sure enough, a black child scarcely older than Frank's son Jackie pulled away at the line so the fan moved back and forth.

De Nemour indicated that Frank should sit in one of the chairs near the table, then seated himself opposite. "And so?"

"I've come into this money, monsieur. Hard money. Not paper, not letters of credit. I figure I can do something with it. But I need advice and"—he hated admitting it—"I need help. The help of somebody who knows what he's doing."

"Why don't you go to Sieur de Bienville or the Superior Council or the Company of the Indies officials?"

"I don't put much trust in governors and officials."

The scimitar eyebrows went up. "Sieur de Bienville is an honest man. Perhaps too honest."

"Look, monsieur, men like me, we're the spittle of the earth in the eyes of officials. Sooner or later the owners of the big land grants will wipe us out. If life's chancy now, what'll it be then?"

"If it's land you want, the land grant concessions must come from the company officials. If Bienville were to go to the Superior Council for you—"

Frank interrupted. "I don't want to go to Bienville, and I don't want to apply to the council or the company. I wouldn't have a chance, because I'm not French. But if I'm going to deal with Frenchmen, I need a Frenchman to represent me." Frank leaned across the table and tapped its polished surface. "If you don't want to deal with me, monsieur, say so, and I'll go 'long. Maybe I was a fool to come here in the first place." He got to his feet, his face reddening with anger and humiliation.

"Sit down, man. Calm yourself. It's too warm for temperament. What do you propose?"

"I'm not sure. I've these ideas, see, but I don't know which is best." Frank resettled himself. De Nemour was interested, he could see that. "There's tobacco, indigo, buying pelts off the Indians—" Frank ticked them off on his fingers. "Pitch and tar, lumber—"

"And bricks."

"Bricks?"

"New Orleans needs bricks. Haven't you noticed that the houses rot in the dampness? The timbers rot sitting on the ground. The moss and mud used as plaster disintegrate. Bricks. That's the answer. Tobacco—" He shrugged. "The market is flourishing now because it's easy to grow, you don't need much land and no cultivation. But British tobacco is still preferred abroad. Indigo requires too much land, expensive machinery, and a large crew. And slaves are a scarce commodity. I think it must be bricks. The ones we import from France are too costly, and the ones the prisoners make at La Balize aren't made in sufficient quantity. Now, any fool can make a brick. Even children. You make them, I sell them."

"Bricks, eh?" The children could make them, could they? Keep the little buggers busy. Make 'em pay for their keep.

"How much money do you have?"

Frank fumbled at the ties and brought the bag to the table. He emptied it slowly, piling like coins with like. De Nemour remained expressionless, looking at the money.

"There. That's the lot. Is it enough?"

The Frenchman touched each pile of coins lightly with his finger tips and seemed to be calculating.

Then he stared hard at Frank. He blew a cloud of smoke toward the ceiling, where it was dispersed by the fan. "It is enough. Yes. I will apply for a concession in a suitable place, set up your house and brick works, and dispose of the bricks as your agent. You should get rich if you work hard and make good bricks, sound bricks, dependable bricks. No cheating. Bricks that will stand up against this miserable climate."

"I won't cheat." Didn't de Nemour know Frank would be afraid to try to cheat a Frenchman?

"We'll draw up the papers now. You're willing to leave the money with me? You trust me?"

"I have to." That was the devil of it.

"You'll have a copy of the paper, signed by both of us. If ever you think I am cheating you, all you have to do is take that paper to Bienville or the council."

"I reckon there won't be any need for that."

De Nemour had taken paper and quills out of the drawer in the table and was writing away at a furious rate. The fan moved back and forth. In the garden a bird sang the same few notes over and over as the shutters creaked in a sudden gust of wind.

De Nemour pushed the papers toward him. "So. In both French and English. Satisfactory?"

Frank studied the spidery writing, wishing he could read. As if the other man knew what he was thinking, he said, "My script is difficult. I'll read it to you. 'Received of Frank Goodacre this day. . . .'" It sounded airtight. Safe. "And here we sign our names and the date." He signed with a flourish and handed the quill to Frank.

Frank flushed. "I–I'll have to make my mark, monsieur. I never had time to learn to write."

De Nemour shrugged. "Take my advice, Mr. Goodacre. Learn to write and learn to read. You cannot trust everyone."

Carefully Frank folded his copy of the paper. "I'll try." He got up and took a last look at the stack of money. As he had said, he had to trust de Nemour, and if that was the last he ever saw of the money—well, he hadn't any right to it anyway.

"Come back in two weeks," de Nemour was saying. "I should have some news by then. Meanwhile keep your mouth shut. The English aren't popular around here, especially in business."

"I'm not rightly English. I'm Canadian."

"Whatever you are, you aren't French."

Henri

Henri bolted the door behind Frank Goodacre, then returned to the table and stared thoughtfully at the money. He wondered where the man had stolen it. Men like Goodacre did not save that amount of money. It was a *pot-au-feu* collection: shillings, livres, doubloons, guilders, issues of Canadian and American colonies, Spanish pillars and reals. All good money in a busy port. Henri would have less trouble getting rid of it than he would have getting rid of the current paper money and letters of credit issued in New Orleans, but still it would take time. It was a curious business.

But none of his concern. If the need ever arose, he could say he had taken the money from Goodacre in good faith. If it was stolen, it was Goodacre who should hang for it. Whatever Henri's other faults, he was blameless financially.

What his father paid him to stay in the New World was sufficient for survival. What Maman sent him from her estate allowed him to live as luxuriously as was possible in this uncivilized hole.

Henri often thought of framing the *lettre de cachet* which had catapulted him out of the paradise of Paris into the limbo of Louisiana as a reminder that one's sins always found one out in the end.

Not that he considered his affair with Minette a sin. If Henri hadn't amused her in the afternoons, someone else would have. It was unfortunate that the old capon, her husband, had come home when he did. It was unfortunate that the old capon should be a cousin to the regent and had no more pride than to go whining to him, demanding that Henri be deported. He should have thanked Henri for amusing Minette and teaching her a few things which would make his own life more interesting.

Recently Maman had hinted that with the new regime in power it might be possible for Henri to return. She would approach Papa very cautiously. But Henri did not want to go back to Paris. He had grown accustomed to New Orleans and had learned that limbo had its advantages.

Maman also enquired if there were not a *gentille belle jeune fille* with a nice dowry who would be a suitable wife. Marriage, Maman assured him in her rippling script, was beneficial to the health and gave one a tranquil mind.

There was no doubt that Maman was healthy, but if she had a tranquil mind, Henri had yet to see evidence of it. She was a gadfly, a bee, buzzing from flower to flower in what she romantically described as her garden of children. Nevil, the eldest, would certainly inherit most of the estates, but the others must have their share of pollen—even poor Henri, so unfairly deported. He would have her family château when she died. Meanwhile he received the taxes collected from the tenants on the estate.

Papa, the beekeeper, did not know the distances his bee distributed her pollen, even to an uprooted flower like Henri. Flower? Papa would say *weed* was more appropriate. For Papa had agreed with the regent, had seen the justice of the deportation. The old capon was a friend of his. Papa had stomped, as if he stomped on Henri himself, declared he was disgraced. But the good God alone knew why. *Papa* hadn't been found with little Minette and her sister in circumstances any imaginative man might find himself in. What none of them understood was that if Henri had remained in Paris, he soon would have tired of Minette and her giggling friends and their pretty little bodies and eager little mouths.

Sighing, Henri began to sort the money properly, not by size as Goodacre had done. Henri swept the bag which had contained it off the table with the back of his hand, loathe to touch it. He would dispose of the pillar dollars and reals when the next ship came from the Indies.

The afternoon breeze had risen, and the shutters creaked as they bent with it. Henri poured a glass of wine. He had not been able to bring himself to drink with Goodacre. Now he sipped it and looked at the money.

When it came right down to it, he didn't give a damn about making bricks or selling bricks or tobacco or pelts or anything. Not so long as the taxes were paid in France and the ships came safely to port.

He dealt in pelts and tobacco simply as a safeguard against those times when the ships did not come or brought no money. To relieve his boredom. But his house stank. He should consign the pelts and tobacco to one of the new warehouses, but there was too much pilfering there, too much underhanded dealing. They were both crowded to overflowing anyway. The tobacco sat on the quays, exposed to sun and rain. The pelts deteriorated because the Indians only half cured them. At least bricks neither spoiled nor smelled, and he could always sell them to ships for ballast if no one else wanted them.

Henri lifted the mosquito netting and flung himself onto the bed. He would sleep until evening. Then he would walk along the levee and decide how best to approach Sieur de Bienville.

It was easier than he had anticipated. All Bienville asked was assurance that the land would not lie idle as did so many choice sites along the river and St. John's Bayou.

"The company officials in France stake out large

claims for themselves and never put them into operation." Bienville scowled and jabbed at the map over which the two men were bending. "There, there, and there. Look at the size of them. Idle land when we need meat, vegetables, products we can export, yes, and bricks. All necessary to keep the colony going. The German colony up the river is doing more to feed us than our own Frenchmen.

"This is the piece of land you had in mind?" He tapped the area. "And you give me your word it won't lie idle as, I must remind you, does your own grant on Lake Pontchartrain?" De Nemour nodded. "Good. Leave it to me.

"It is a shame that France is so unconcerned about us. Ignorant of the entire situation. I ask them for wives for my settlers, and they send bawds. I ask them for colonists, and they send criminals."

"I too came under a *lettre de cachet,*" Henri reminded him.

Bienville smiled. "I have not forgotten, monsieur. But you come of good blood and good family. You had the misfortune to make the wrong enemy. Show me a man without enemies, and I will show you a saint. I think we are both a long way from beatification."

His business with Bienville done, the remainder of the day stretched before him, heat-filled, monotonous, meaningless. The drainage ditches steamed and stank. The wooden planks of the banquette were scorching. The buildings seemed to bulge and contract in the heat waves.

Henri decided to stop by Céline's, not for sex but for conversation. Sometimes he thought the heat was killing his sexual appetite. He would end up a capon like little Minette's husband. That would be a pity. But the thought of his body touching another, both slippery with sweat, repelled him.

It was strange that he enjoyed talking to Céline. She did not recognize that her social stratum was so far below his own that in Paris she would have been less than a scrap of refuse on the street. She treated him as her equal, her business partner, her friend.

He liked the company of women. They had a cutting honesty and impatience about important matters and a delightful deviousness about the unimportant.

Yes, he would visit Céline and tell her about the bricks. She wouldn't care where the money came from or whom Goodacre had cheated to get it in order to go into business. But she would probably laugh and demand free bricks to improve her house.

Blanche opened the door, her face fixed in her false professional smile, which changed to one of sincere welcome when she saw Henri and then faded when he said he had come to chat with Céline, not to employ Blanche's favors.

She yawned and stretched, her thick, soft white arms raised above her head so the loose sleeves of her sack fell back.

"Céline's not here. She and Mimi and Sheba have gone for a walk in the country." She laughed at his expression. "Yes, and not on business. They went with the child, Marie. She's an orphan Céline's taken a fancy to. They've gone to fetch her doll."

"Where did Céline find an orphan?"

"Orphans aren't difficult to find if one wishes to look for them. Brats of Indians and soldiers and sailors. This one fainted on our doorstep. Céline said it was an omen. God knows why. Shall I call Alixe and fetch some wine?"

He started to say no, but the idea of Céline with a child amused him. It was a side of her he had never seen. It would be interesting to be there when they returned.

He had almost given up waiting. Alixe and Blanche were boring company when they were not in bed. But even as he was rising to leave he heard their footsteps on the banquette and Céline complaining as she always did about the stink of the gutters. As if the gutters of Paris smelled any better.

She kicked off her clogs as she came into the house and limped across the room, holding out her hands to Henri.

"My feet! They are blistered from walking and as black as Sheba's with dust and dirt. Give me some of that wine, Blanche. My throat is parched. Henri, did you sense that I wanted to see you? You haven't been around lately. Has someone else been taking care of you? Some Choctaw girl with a savage little cunt? You want to be careful, Henri. They've been rolled in the forest by every settler here. You never know who's entered the door before you." She sat on the floor like a child and began to massage her feet. "Run along with Sheba, Marie, and she'll give you a tisane to clear the dust from your throat. Bathe your head so you won't have another attack of sun. Curtsy to M. Henri, then go."

Marie pulled off her hat and pushed her hair out of her eyes. She dropped a curtsy to Henri, then took the basket with the doll and ran from the room.

Henri's gaze followed her. "That is your orphan?" He had expected a child of three or four, not a girl nearly as tall as Mimi, budding into womanhood. She had given him only a quick glance before she had lowered her head, but he thought he had never seen such beautiful eyes.

"Blanche told you about her? Yes, that is Marie. She is bearing up well considering her parents were buried only yesterday. The shock will come later. I think the house and plot of land can be sold. I want to know how to go about it. Marie must have the money to replace what her father's friend stole from her. A man who would steal from an orphan is no better than *merde*. Oh, yes, Blanche, we found a money box and Marie's father's accounts with dates and entries and amounts exceeding that which Marie had wrapped in the handkerchief he gave her. Perhaps I should set the law on M. Frank Goodacre."

"Goodacre!"

"Yes, a strange name for a bad man, *n'est-ce pas?*"

"A bad man with a bitch of a wife," Mimi said, fanning herself with her hat so its green streamers fluttered. "She forced Marie to sleep outside. Imagine, Monsieur Henri, a little child sleeping outside with reptiles and wild dogs and savages everywhere, and newly sorrowed as well. A very bad woman."

"But now Marie is in our care," Céline said.

Alixe laughed. "She doesn't yet know what awaits her."

"Céline pretends now that she will not, but she'll sell Marie when the time comes, M. Henri. You see if I am not right."

"Is that what you plan, Céline?"

"My God, no. Not without her permission. I am going to send her to school." She turned to Blanche. "Tell Sheba to bring us more wine. Henri's glass is empty, and my throat is as muddy as the river."

"I'm going, Céline." He needed time alone to think what to do about the money. Now that he knew who owned it, he should rightfully return it. But there would be an awkward explanation to Bienville, awkward difficulties with the law and Goodacre and the problem of Céline keeping a child in her house. Besides, he suspected the child would not benefit by the money. Céline would use it to further her dream of a grand establishment, and New Orleans was not ready for such a house yet. Let her continue to save, and when the time was right, he would help her.

She followed Henri to the door, urging him to return another day and advise her about Marie's house.

"Do you really propose to do as Blanche said?"

She widened her eyes in pretended innocence. "What was that?"

"Sell the child?"

"You make her sound as if she were a slave. I do not mean to *sell* her, Henri, but virgins are in great demand. She is only eleven. Later—who knows? If she is not unwilling, I may 'sell' her, as you and Blanche put it. I would say, introduce her to a profession."

"You're shameless."

"No one of quality will marry her, and the other kind of marriage isn't worth a peach pit. Did you notice her eyes? She could make a fortune for herself, and for me."

"I noticed them. When that day comes—*if* that day comes—Céline, remember I saw her first. Save her for me."

"You'll make it worth my while to save her?"

"You have my word."

To Be Alone

Céline was right. Marie's sorrow caught up with her. It was worst at night, lying on the lumpy pallet in the loft over the kitchen where the supplies were kept. Céline had decided it was not proper for Mary to sleep on the kitchen floor with Sheba, and there was no other place to put her. "But we shall remedy that soon," Céline promised.

Meanwhile Marie climbed the ladder every night to the loft, so narrow it was scarcely more than a shelf. The air was stifling next to the bricks of the chimney, and the roof was too low to stand upright. It smelled of rice and flour, meal and sugar, spices, dried fruit, peppercorns, and garlic. But there was a window, and Marie would open the shutters and crouch beside it to look down into the dark treetops or up into the sky dotted with stars.

She knelt there, aching with the hollowness inside her that only sleep could fill; the pain that distorted her dreams; the sorrow and loneliness that all her tears could not relieve.

It was at night that she remembered that she was Mary and not Marie. It was at night that she whispered her sadness to Flora and dampened the hard pillow with her tears until at last she slept. She longed for her father's gaiety and the stories he had told, the songs they had sung together, the smell of him, his protectiveness. She longed for her mother's tenderness, the way she had tucked in the covers at night and kissed Mary before dropping the mosquito netting into place. Mary tucked the blanket around Flora and told her to sleep peacefully.

She told Flora, "I must not forget who I am." But more and more she felt as if Mary Macleod had been buried in the watery grave along with her parents. Soon there were more nights when she fell asleep without crying. With every day that passed it became more difficult to recall her parents' faces. Every day she fitted more easily into the new mold of her life.

She began to take pleasure in small things: the oranges hanging like round golden lanterns among the dark and shining leaves, the spicy scent of Sheba's cooking, the trips to market with Sheba, the pirogues and flat boats. She began to enjoy the sight of Indians and farmers in their small crafts surrounded by their produce and to look forward to the days when a company ship came in and the waterfront swarmed with seamen. There were always peddlers, black longshoremen who called out to Sheba, making her toss her head and laugh, and merchants. Sometimes planters came with their wives in enameled carriages, the women shaded by ruffled parasols. Often M. Henri was there. He always bowed to Marie and looked at her in a way that made her feel like a young lady and quite as elegant as the planters' wives.

She liked the sudden storms when the day darkened and clouds scuttled over the rooftops. Lightning pierced the sky, and thunder rolled along the river and echoed over the swamplands as the rain crashed down on the thatched roofs and turned the streets to running streams.

After a storm, frogs set up a deafening chorus which lasted throughout the night. It wasn't safe to walk outdoors unless you kept your eyes to the ground, because what appeared to be a harmless fallen branch might be a moccasin with a white venomous mouth.

There were things Marie did not like: the nights when a ship was in and candles burned late in

Céline's house and there was talk and raucous laughter and the wooden banquettes echoed with footsteps till dawn. There was no serving an early breakfast the morning after; the ladies slept until noon. They spent the day lounging in their sacks, yawning and talking but always falling silent when Marie came into the room.

There were other things she did not like. When a slave ship came to port, Sheba always went to the quays and talked in Kimgombo, an African dialect, to the sick and frightened blacks. The ship's master always tried to drive her away, and she would pretend to put a curse on him. It was on one of those days, after they had been to a slave auction, that Marie learned that Sheba's real name was Quasheba. It meant the day of the week on which she had been born: Sunday.

Sheba told her stories about Africa and sang strange songs, beating out the rhythm on the wooden tabletop. She brought tears to Marie's eyes when she told her how the slave traders came, about the ship, the slave camp where they were broken and trained, and the auction.

"I'll set you free one day, Sheba," Marie would say at the end of these stories.

"How are you going to do that? You'd have to buy me from Mme. Céline."

"I'll buy you."

"How'll you get the money? The same way Madame and the others get it?"

Marie's face burned. "I'll get it. I don't know how." But she did know. She would get it from Frank Goodacre.

Sheba was her friend more than Céline was, but it was Céline who decided Marie should go to the nuns for instruction. "Knowledge is a greater weapon than being a woman is," Céline said. "If you have both, then you are formidable! But like everything else, such weapons must be used with discretion."

The nuns were strict but, underneath their severity, kind. It was exciting to be learning, to feel her mind growing as her body was growing, to become adept at French so she no longer had to stumble through a sentence, groping for words.

The students were a strange assortment of both white and Negro. There were orphans who had come from France with a small dower from the government, daughters of the French settlers of both noble and common birth, slave girls being trained in deportment and fine sewing and instructed in French so they would become suitable house servants and ladies' maids.

Céline was proud of Marie's advancement. She showed off the girl's handiwork, her copybooks, and her French lessons to M. Henri. When he looked at Marie, his eyes were so dark it was impossible to read his thoughts, except to know that somehow she was being appraised and approved. Then his gaze shifted to Céline. "You are amazing, Céline. How did you persuade the nuns to accept her as a pupil? I am astonished they let you in the door! I heard a rumor they plan to have every townswoman of ill repute set upon wooden horses and flogged by soldiers."

"It was simple. The priest approached them. Besides, the lost sheep are always of more importance than the ones in the fold."

"Do they know where she lives?"

"Do you think the priest and I are fools, Henri? They know only that she is an orphan. She is treated well and is learning her prayers."

"She will need more than prayers if they become curious."

"Don't make difficulties, Henri. Besides, in another year—or two, perhaps—we will fulfill our agreement. You have not forgotten our agreement, have you, Henri?" Céline suddenly remembered that Marie was present. "Go, Marie. Do your studies."

Marie curtsied deeply and gracefully, the way the

nuns had taught her. Henri watched her as she walked out the door.

"You have not forgotten, have you, Henri?" Céline repeated.

"I have not forgotten."

"A little virgin, Henri, to be trained to your own tastes. Fresh, unspoiled, tender, shy at first, but once broken, eager and insatiable. It is always so."

Henri stood abruptly and began to pace the room. "Yes, so I have been told, if they don't freeze completely."

"You will know how to handle her, Henri."

"And afterward?"

"How do you mean, afterward? She will be here for you, and when you tire of her—if you tire of her—there are always other men at Céline's door."

"Sacred God, Céline, you are shameless. You would do that to her?" He grimaced. "But I too am shameless for striking such a bargain. At times I hate myself."

"Why? You are not a monk."

"Nor ever could be."

One day near Christmas Marie was called from her lessons.

"There is a—" Sister Josephine hesitated over the word. "A gentleman here to see you. He said he knew your father."

Her skirts whispering along the floor, she accompanied Marie to the small dark sparsely furnished sitting room where new girls were received, business was conducted, and accounts done. Sister Josephine sat down and bent over her account books, but Mary knew she was listening.

The man stood nervously near the door, as if at any moment he would change his mind and bolt. It took Marie a moment to recognize Frank Goodacre. His skin no longer hung on his bones as it had six months ago, and he wore new buckskin breeches. He looked uneasily at Sister Josephine as he said, "Uh–Mary. Do you remember me?"

"Of course. How do you do, Mr. Goodacre."

"You're looking well, Mary. You've fattened a bit. I see they took you in. I worried some after I left you that day, Mary."

But not enough to come back and ask if I were here, Marie thought: "Yes, I am here."

"And they're"–he leaned forward to whisper–"good to you, Mary?"

"Yes."

"Have they forced you to convert?"

Sister Josephine's chair scraped the floor, and her papers rustled.

"Everything is all right, Mr. Goodacre."

He nodded, visibly relieved. "That's fine, then. I've been wondering."

I should ask after his wife and children, Marie thought, *but I won't. I don't care about them, and I don't care about him. He stole from me. Father's money. That is why he has new clothes.*

She stood unbending, dignified, and haughty, waiting, torturing him, she knew.

"That money you gave me, you remember, Mary? The children liked the fruit I bought with it. And Mrs. Goodacre said–" Faith had said, "Who does that brat think she is, offering us charity?" ". . . said it was kind of you to think of others when you were sorrowed."

"You took me in that night." Marie watched his face mottle. So he had not forgotten how his wife had stood at the door, preventing Mary from entering the house.

"The reason I came, Mary–it's getting toward Christmas, and I wanted to give you some remembrance. Your father would have wanted it, see? So, here, I thought you could use this." He thrust two silver coins into her hand. They were damp with his sweat.

She looked at them. He was giving her her own money to salve his conscience!

"Thank you, Mr. Goodacre. It is kind of you. I have nothing to give in exchange. I didn't expect you."

"It's all right, Mary. It's not a child's place, really. Not that you won't soon be a young lady. That's plain to see. I'll be going now, Mary. I'm glad to see you keeping well and growing and all." He edged toward the door, wrenched it open, and stepped outside. Then he winked. "Don't let them force you to spend it on candles, Mary. Buy yourself a pretty."

Marie closed the door and went to the table where Sister Josephine had ceased work to watch her. Marie laid the coins on the papers where the sister's quill lay.

"This is for candles for my parents, Sister Josephine. And this"—she touched the other coin—"is for the poor box."

"That is generous of you, my child." Sister Josephine did not look at the coins or touch them. "But one would suffice for both. Don't you want to keep one for yourself or for your foster family?"

"I am not being generous. I do not want his money. I hate him! I hate him." *And one day I'll get even with him,* she thought.

"Hate, Marie, and judgment—"

"I know," Mary interrupted. "They should be no part of mortal man. They should be left to God. I shall try to hate Mr. Goodacre less, but I *do not want the money.*" She curtsied stiffly and left the room.

Sister Josephine sat looking at the coins. It had been a curious incident. For the first time since Marie had come to them, she began to wonder who the child's foster parents were. She must remember to ask the Reverend Mother.

But the Reverend Mother did not know. "Father said they wished to remain anonymous. It is something to do with money they receive from France. If it were known they have taken in an English orphan instead of a French one—"

"Is charity only for the French?" Sister Josephine demanded, her eyes flashing. "Would they let her starve because she was born on the wrong side of the Channel?"

The Reverend Mother shook her head. "You are too idealistic, Sister. You do not know the evil that is in the world. Father said we must make every effort to urge Marie to become a novitiate."

"She is not suited," Sister Josephine said. "She is hardheaded and strong-willed under that demure exterior."

"She is one of our best students."

"Not of religion. You should have seen her staring down that poor man who came to ask after her welfare. I did not need to know English to know she insulted him. You should have heard her tell me that she hated him. She would be a troublemaker."

"We shall wait and see if God chooses her, Sister. We shall wait."

Céline closed her doors to business on Christmas Eve, and everyone went to mass. Céline made Marie go in alone, ahead of the others, and sit alone. It made the girl sad to see the families celebrating together, and tears came to her eyes as she remembered Christmas celebrations with her parents.

When they returned home, they had a cold supper with champagne and exchanged small gifts. Mimi had made a new dress for Flora. Céline gave Marie ten livres. Alixe and Blanche gave her a new sack, and to Marie's surprise there was an ivory fan, exquisitely painted, from M. Henri.

"Why me?" Marie asked, opening and closing it.

"He likes orphans," Alixe said, winking. "Some like them old, some like them young, some like them a different color, some like orphans."

"And some like women who hold their tongues," Céline said.

In the spring Céline had a house for Marie built in the garden.

"Is she too good to be in the same house with us?" Blanche asked.

"She is too good and also too big to go on sleeping in the loft. She must have a place of her own. In another year or two she will be ready."

"She's ready now. Men pay dear for a child," Alixe said.

"I manage this house, Alixe. Not you. M. Henri's tastes do not run to unripened children."

"She's to be his, is she? I hope he is paying a good price."

"For an exclusive property?" Céline rubbed her fingers together as if the gold coins were already in her hand.

When the house was finished and the interior whitewashed, Marie said hesitantly, "There is just one thing, Céline—" Céline raised her eyebrows and Mary added quickly, "Perhaps I should not ask."

"Ask."

"I would like a painting on the wall like you have."

"Um. I don't know. The house is very small, Marie."

"And very bare. Like a nun's cell. Please, Céline."

Céline shrugged. "So. A painting, Mimi, if you please, for Marie."

"Mimi painted it?"

"That is why it is so primitive," Mimi blushed.

"But it is beautiful! I can almost hear the bird sing."

"You shall have a bird. Let me think. Because the room is small, I think it must be a little scene opening out. Yes, that is it."

No one was allowed to enter the house until the painting was finished. Then they all crowded in.

Mimi had painted at each corner a French door opening onto a garden which rose from the banks of a narrow green river. In the foreground five ladies picnicked on the grass, their skirts full blown about them like the petals of peonies. Beside them stood a black woman with a tray of bread and fried crayfish. A bird watched from an orange tree, and in the distance was a magnificent building. The sky reached up, spilling blue onto the ceiling, where cherubs supported puffy clouds on their shoulders.

"It is us, don't you see?" Mimi explained. "That is Céline with the hat with pink ribbons, and that is you, Marie, with Flora beside you. And that is Blanche—"

"I look like a nursing sow."

"That was not my intention, but your breasts got too large because I kept getting one larger than the other. That is Alixe watching the gentleman in the distance—"

"Wondering whether to accost him," Alixe said. "And that is you, Mimi, painting the scene?"

"Certainly."

"It's beautiful, Mimi. You should go to the convent and take lessons. Why, the ladies even look a little like us. And such a lovely house in the distance!"

"It is Versailles. A gentleman took me there once. We rode in his carriage and—" Mimi broke off, choked with laughter. "It was too funny. Bumpety-bumpety-bump, all the way. In a carriage! Imagine!"

Céline glared at her. "And the gentleman in the picture, Mimi? Is he the gentleman with the carriage?"

"That is M. Henri. You see, he is looking at Marie. His eyes are a little crossed. I could not do eyes at the angle his head is turned."

"Why is he looking at me?"

"Because—" Mimi caught Céline's eye and turned pink. "To see if you are carrying the fan he gave you at Noël. It is there on your lap."

"Enough of this. We have seen the picture, and Marie must do her studies."

Left alone, Marie sat a long time gazing at the picture. Crude as it was, it gave her a feeling of happiness and sun and the scent of flowers. Her gaze lingered the longest on the distant figure of M. Henri. There was something about all that which she did not understand and was afraid to think about.

Now that she was no longer in the kitchen with Sheba for company, she withdrew more into herself. She liked her isolation. It gave her more time for introspection and daydreaming. The introspection, however, was largely gloomy. What was to become of her? She did not want to stay at Céline's forever. As much as she liked Céline and Mimi—and she did like them—she found their profession distasteful, and she knew if her acquaintances at the convent found out where she lived, she would be ostracized. Not that any of them mattered that much. They were just acquaintances, not friends, for she held herself aloof, afraid of how much she might reveal to a real friend. Nor did she want to become a nun, though she was glad of their teaching. She saw no future for herself, and it worried her.

Her daydreams were limited by her experience. She wished for a man who would love her as her father had loved her mother; a child to cherish as her mother had cherished her; a house; a garden—but not here. Not in New Orleans, where the heat weighted the very passage of time, spun webs of languor about the mind. She did not know where she would choose to live, nor did it matter, for it was only a dream.

One morning Céline brought her a handful of money. "There! It is your first payment."

"What do you mean?"

"From your friend, your kind friend, M. Goodacre. There will be more. Alixe made him very happy."

"He came here?" Marie asked, and Céline nodded contentedly.

"It's disgusting. I don't want it."

Céline made a hissing sound. "Look, *ma petite*, it was your money to begin with. Whether you want it or not does not matter. Put it in the little box like a good child. We'll get back all he took from your father and more, with interest!"

"How do you know he will come back?" It made Marie ill to think of Frank Goodacre and Alixe. Wasn't his own wife good enough? Weren't his children skinny and ill-clad enough?

"He will come back. All men do. Take the money. Who has money has power. It is the best revenge."

Marie touched it thoughtfully. "Very well. I will take it. Some day I'll make him sorry." But how did one buy revenge? It was so personal a thing that the taking of it should be personal as well, searing the hatred in the heart.

In 1726, with the end of the regency in France and the return of Louis XV to power, Bienville was recalled as governor, and there was a shake-up in the Superior Council. Under Bienville the French had maintained a chain of outposts from Mobile to Fort Toulouse, across to Natchez, and up the Mississippi to Illinois country. These outposts were intended to protect Louisiana and isolate the Choctaw Indians from British influence. They also protected the tobacco factory at Natchez; the large tracts of claimed but still uncultivated land; the timber yet to be cut; the furs to be taken from as yet untrapped animals; and the small farm gardens which kept the colony fed.

But it was a sprawling territory. There were an enormous number of adverse circumstances. There were too few settlers, too few slaves, too little money. Like any other man of vision and strength struggling against overwhelming odds, Bienville had enemies whose voices clamored in France more loudly than his own.

"What will happen now?" Frank Goodacre asked Henri as he wiped his dripping face with a handkerchief. The handkerchief was new, Henri noted. A few months ago Frank had used his shirt sleeve. Was money actually making this sow's ear into a silk purse?

"Nothing, or very little, will happen. A new governor will come. Things may even improve for a while. Bienville's enemies hindered him in everything he tried to do. They may cooperate with a new man, even if he is a fool. I mean, even a fool can see the land is rich, waiting only for the Midas touch."

Goodacre heaved himself to his feet. He had put on weight, he had not rid himself of his shambling gait or his air of unease, which was always intensified in Henri's presence.

"Then we'll wait it out. I wouldn't like to see all we've put into the brick business go floating down the river, so to speak. But if you think everything's going to be all right, I'll go on same as I've been doing."

"Please do."

"Not that I like all this money on paper. Letters of credit. Notes. It's not like good hard coin. Every day it gets harder to cash them in." Goodacre hesitated at the door. "Maybe we should have hung on to the real money while we had it."

"Everyone's in the same situation. It's accept the letters of credit or not sell the brick, isn't it?"

"All the same—" Goodacre shrugged and closed the door.

Doing business with Henri de Nemour always left Frank feeling frustrated and inept. He could see that the Frenchman barely tolerated him. The day when an honest Canadian wasn't good enough for a Frenchie was one hell of a day. Yet they were bound together in business, and they were profiting.

Frank had a decent house now, out by the brickworks. Not that two rooms and a loft could be called fancy, but it was better than the shack they had lived in before. The children were fattening up despite the fact that he worked them hard. Good little buggers they were, making bricks as if their lives depended on it, and their lives did. Faith, now—it was a funny thing about Faith. Instead of being grateful to him, she made him feel as if he'd ruined her life, moving her out of that run-down hut. She spent all her time reliming the walls and scrubbing the plank floor and destroying the spiders and other crawling things. When she wasn't cleaning, she was washing and boiling and ironing clothes until he told her she'd wear them out with so much soap and scrubbing.

She kept the door bolted because she was afraid of Indians. She complained she was lonely with no other womenfolk nearby. And worst of all, she wouldn't let him touch her. Faith, who'd always been hot-blooded, was cold as an Atlantic oyster.

"I'm not having any more brats! That's final."

"We could be careful, Faithy."

"Careful! You, careful? I've heard that before, and look at the result."

He went to the whores because she'd driven him there. That girl Alixe didn't give him any lip about being careful. She made him feel like a real gentleman, and a roguish one at that. After his first visit to Céline's he hadn't returned until morning, and Faith had never asked him where he'd been. She had just looked at him as if she knew. Just as she had known about Mary before he had known himself.

There was another cold oyster. He had gone with the best of intentions to give her money for Christmas. She had no call to dislike him after what he had done for her when her parents had died. There was no way she could know about the money, yet he would almost swear that she did. Women were witches. She had just stood there and looked at him in the same way de Nemour did.

She wasn't the scrawny little thing she had been. Even under that drab, shapeless, homespun sack the convent girls wore it was plain to see she was developing a fine figure. Frank had never seen eyes like hers before nor lips, which looked as if she had painted them, though of course the nuns wouldn't have allowed that.

Faith had known what she was doing when she had made him get Mary out of the house. With the way Faith was acting these days he wouldn't have been able to keep his hands off Mary. Probably there never would have been a chance to get at her, but if there *had* been . . .

He shuddered. No. She'd probably stick the meat knife in him.

Marie and Henri

Céline was fond of Marie. The girl was no trouble, it cost almost nothing to feed her, and she had a mature dignity that Céline admired. Nevertheless, she regretted promising to save Marie for Henri's exclusive use. She had offered Marie to him as a child, and he had made a face. "I am not that perverted. Let her become a woman first."

Girls matured early in that hot and humid climate, but it seemed to Céline that Marie was taking a long time to begin to menstruate. Marie had lived with them a year and a half now. She was a valuable product going to waste. So Céline was greatly relieved when Sheba told her Marie's periods had finally begun.

It was then that Céline announced to Henri that Marie was ready for him.

"You have told her?"

"Not yet. You will give me a day's notice, and I shall prepare her for you."

"Will she be agreeable?"

"What else can she be after all I have done for her?"

"She could refuse, Céline. She could run away."

"Pah! Where would she go?"

"To the convent to ask refuge of the sisters."

"My God, so she could," Céline admitted. "But I doubt it."

"I think you will need more than a day to prepare her. I think you do not know Marie as well as you think you do. I'll wait a little longer."

"You still want her?" Céline's voice was anxious.

He hesitated. "Yes . . . I still want her."

"And you will pay?"

"I will pay, Céline." He would have to pay. He had agreed to that long ago. He could not expect the child—well, she was no longer a child—the girl to knock at his door and ask to become his mistress. He could not meet her socially and make one of those discreet arrangements. If he was to have her, it must be arranged by Céline, and Marie must be bought as any whore was bought.

A distasteful thought. Céline had done her job of maintaining his interest too well. In showing him Marie's school work, displaying her accomplishments in music, French, drawing, and fancy work, she had presented him with a side of Marie that had nothing to do with what he had wanted of her in the beginning. She was intelligent and talented. She spoke French now almost entirely without accent. Her pencil sketches and watercolors of New Orleans made him see the city with new eyes. The shadows were blue-black, just as she had colored them, the sunlight tawny, the roofs of the houses exaggeratedly steep, the bayou water wrinkled by its own slow movement. She had caught the lurch of a drunken Chickasaw, the strut of the seamen, the sullen hauteur of a newly arrived slave, the avaricious eyes of a beggar.

Marie moved with a grace and elegance that showed good breeding. He wondered about her parents. They could not have been common like Goodacre. He would ask her about them one day. Meanwhile . . . meanwhile, he would wait.

Céline did not wait. She went to Marie's house that evening when the sky seemed to reflect the color of the evening river and moths fluttered around the candle flames.

"I must speak to you, Marie."

Marie looked at her warily. "You—aren't going to turn me out, are you?"

"What made you think that?"

"Sister Josephine said I would soon be ready to take a position as governess. She said my French and drawing and music are good enough, and some of the people on outlying plantations would be glad to use me for the little ones too young to attend school. They would give me a room and food and clothe me and treat me as a member of the family, she said. I must be a burden to you. Another mouth to feed."

"Ridiculous! And Sister Josephine is ridiculous as well. It's plain to see she's spent all her life on her knees in her cell. To be a governess is no better than being a slave. No, I'm not going to turn you out. On the contrary." She pointed at Mimi's fresco. "It is M. Henri I want to discuss. He would like to have you."

"Have me? Have me how? He doesn't need a governess."

"Governess, governess! Forget governess. He wants to have you in the way any man wants a woman. He wants to bed you. To be your lover. He will pay, and I will share the money with you."

"What!" Marie's voice rose to a shriek. "You'd sell me the way you sell them, in there?"

"Don't scream. They'll hear you."

"Let them! They are as shameless as you are, or they wouldn't lend themselves to any filthy seaman who comes to your door. Nor will I!"

"M. Henri is not a filthy seaman. He is a gentleman of noble birth. You would be his exclusively. No seamen, Marie. No lonely government officials, no drunken plantation owners, no M. Goodacre."

"Holy Mother, I should hope not."

"Don't use profanity, Marie. It does not become you."

"Does it become me to sell myself to M. Henri?"

"It is an honor that he wishes you to be his sole property."

"If he wishes that, why doesn't he marry me? To be bought is no honor. It's slavery. I'd rather be a governess. That, at least, is respectable."

"You little fool! The first thing you knew, the children's father would be slipping into your bedroom at night, and you wouldn't dare to shout or object. You'd have to submit to him. And once he had you pregnant, you'd be dismissed in disgrace. Where would you go then, little Marie?"

"Now it is you who are being ridiculous."

"It happens. I have seen it."

"I hate you! To think all the time you were being kind to me you were planning this." Marie began to cry.

Céline shrugged. "It seemed not such a bad fate for you." She wanted to ignore Marie's tears. She got up and looked out the window into the depths of the dark green hedge. The scent of orange blossoms was almost too sweet. A bird sang deep within the branches. "A better fate than I had. If I could have gone with Pierre, I would not be shameless. It's strange, Marie. M. Henri also told me I was shameless. Perhaps I am. I'm sorry. I don't want you to hate me. You won't believe me, but I think of you sometimes as the daughter I might have had."

"If I *were* that daughter, would you do this to me?"

Céline flinched. "That is an unfair question." She turned from the window and met Marie's eyes. "I don't know, Marie. Believe me, better than have her become a governess, I would wish her to become the mistress of M. Henri. It is, as I said, not such a bad fate, and you've little choice."

"Everyone has a choice. I am not your chattel to sell, and I will not be sold."

"I'll leave you to think about it."

Now Marie understood why Mimi had painted M. Henri into the mural. They had all known and were waiting for the day when Céline would tell her. She wished there was someplace she could go, someone who would help her. But she was as alone as she had ever been.

She avoided Céline for the next few days. Late one afternoon Mimi tapped timidly at Marie's door. "I wanted to warn you. Céline's coming for an answer this evening."

"Why didn't you warn me before of her plans for me? I thought you were my friend, but you betrayed me too. You knew all along."

Mimi sighed and dropped her head to one side. "I supposed you knew that if you lived in a place like this then sooner or later . . ." She made a *moue*. "I didn't realize you were so innocent. Couldn't you have guessed from the interest M. Henri took in you? The fan he gave you? He didn't give us any gifts. Just you. He bought you paints . . ."

"Mimi, what shall I do?"

"*I* would say yes. You've no place else to go, have you? You may not think it's nice, but lots of things aren't so nice, Marie. It's better than what I have to do."

"Mimi, is it true what Céline said about governesses?"

"I've never been a governess, but I think no man would be able to keep his hands off you. M. Henri intends to pay well. Make Céline share it with you. If you save it, eventually you can go away."

"Where could I go?"

"You see how it is, Marie? You don't have any choice."

When Céline came that evening, Marie still hadn't made up her mind.

"I can't stay long," Céline said. "Is it yes or no?"

"If it's no, will you put me out?"

"I'm not such a devil as that, but you can't expect me to provide for you forever. We'd have to find someone for you to marry, which shouldn't be difficult considering the shortage of women here. The trouble is, the kind of man I meet isn't the kind you'd want."

"The convent could probably find a husband for me."

"Then go and ask them for one instead of a position as a governess." Céline shrugged and opened the door. "Henri will be disappointed, but no matter."

"It doesn't matter to me that he will be disappointed. I should never have stayed here."

Céline's lips curled. "Christ's bones, have you no gratitude? You were an orphan who'd been refused shelter and robbed by your father's friend. Hungry, homeless, and defenseless as a newborn kitten. Oh, you could have gone to the good sisters. Perhaps that's where you belong. Take the veil, Marie, since men are so repugnant. Yes, by God"—Céline's eyes flared like coals—"get out of here! Better an honest whore than a sanctimonious Puritan, I always say." She stalked across the yard.

Marie began to cry. She ran after Céline and caught her arm. "Céline, I didn't mean I'm not grateful. I am. You're my friend, and I love you. But I'm frightened. It seems wrong to—to sell myself."

"It's a business transaction," Céline said coldly. But then her voice softened. "You're right, Marie, you never should have stayed here. It's better that you get out."

"Mimi said he would pay well."

"He will pay very well."

"You will share it with me?"

"Half to each of us."

Money was power, power to buy revenge. Marie took a deep breath. "Very well. How is it done? How does he 'have' me?"

Céline came back into the house and sat on the bed. She told her in detail and in the only terms she knew. "It is not so unpleasant as it sounds," she added hastily. "You will find, in time, that you like it."

"I do not think I will like it, but as you said, I have

no other choice. I don't want to become a nun, a governess, or the wife of a man like Frank Goodacre. Once I have enough money, I can choose my own fate."

"Certainly. Open a little shop. Make hats and lingerie and petticoats for the planters' wives."

"And go blind from sewing fine seams."

"What in the name of the devil do you want then? To live on dreams? Life is not made of dreams, Marie. It is made of hard work and money. Dreams are for sleep, but when you awaken, there is the flesh, the mud, the hunger, the fight to live. You would find out soon enough if I turned you out, as any other woman might do. You'd even be glad of one of those filthy seamen when you were hungry enough."

Even after Céline sent word to Henri that Marie had been informed and was agreeable, he stayed away. His reluctance puzzled him. He felt as if he no longer knew himself. Unbeknownst to him some metamorphosis had taken place.

One day he saw Marie shopping with Sheba. Their baskets were laden with fruit. Marie's swung from her arm while Sheba carried hers on her head. They were smiling and chattering away, and once Marie tipped back her head and laughed so that her bonnet slipped off the back of her head and hung from her throat by the wide cerulean ribbon. Sheba reached out and shoved it back into place. As the girl reached up with her free hand to straighten it she caught sight of Henri. The laughter faded, and she blushed. Then she bowed and, turning her head away, dismissed him.

He understood then why he'd hesitated to fulfill his bargain. Marie was no ordinary woman one purchased for an hour or two. She was something fine, and he desired her because he desired that fineness, as if possessing it would purge and revitalize him.

He sent word to Céline that he would be there that night.

* * *

The candle flame fluttered in the evening wind. Marie leaned on one elbow, her head against the pillow, the sheet drawn across her breasts, her shoulders rose-tinted by the candlelight. In the dim light her eyes had lost their color, so Henri could not read whether she was afraid, contemptuous, or simply resigned, like a trapped animal. She looked frighteningly young, yet in France girls became wives at thirteen.

He had never felt so eager or so afraid. His hands trembled as he removed his coat. This was a new experience in every way. He was no longer the man who had enjoyed the depraved games Alixe and Blanche played or the man who had bargained for a virgin child. He felt as if he were wielding the knife at a sacrifice, but he could not turn back. He wanted that sacrifice as he had never wanted anything else.

He had made love to so many women that he thought he knew every way of arousing them, but Marie lay cool and unresponsive. It made him feel foolish, as if he were kissing a statue.

"Embrace me, damn it," he said, his lips against the hollow of her throat.

Obediently she put her arms lightly around him. She brushed his forehead with her lips, and encouraged, he kissed her mouth again, forcing it open, gently teasing her tongue with his, flicking it in and out like the tongue of a snake.

Yes, he was the serpent in the child's Eden.

He sat up, releasing her. "I can't do it. I can't defile you. I am wicked, but I am not that wicked."

"You made a bargain with Céline."

"Before I knew you as I know you now. Don't worry. Céline will have her money. I think half of it is to go to you."

"Yes."

"Forgive me, Marie?" He touched her hair, smoothing it back from her forehead. Even his desire was ebbing. "Forgive me. I'll not come here again."

"Céline will be angry."

"The devil take Céline." Would she force the child to take someone else, money-hungry bitch that she was? "Why don't you go live at the convent, where you would be safe?"

"And spend the hours when I'm not on my knees scrubbing floors on my knees before an altar?" Her scorn astonished him. One of his sisters, who was a nun, washed the sores of lepers, cleansed the poor of their lice, fed paupers and cripples, and all the time her face shone with radiance because she was doing the work of God.

"Have you no relatives?"

"Perhaps, in Scotland."

"Then you must go back to them."

"I wouldn't know how to find them, even if I had the money to go there. Please, you must do—what Céline said. You must come again, if I please you. You see, I've little choice. Céline made that clear. To be a governess—Céline said that—" She stopped.

"I can imagine what Céline said. Possibly she is right. A man would have to be a saint to resist you, and there are damned few saints in these parts."

"And if it is not you, she might force me to take someone else. Please, it is all right. She promised there would be no one but you. She said I was very fortunate."

He pinched out the candle and lay back beside her. She turned and drew him to her. "It is all right, you see; because of what you said, asking me to forgive you. I will try to do what I am supposed to do. I hope you will be pleased." She pressed her lips against his, timidly touching his tongue with her own. She stroked his back, inflaming him again so it was all he could do to prevent himself from plunging into her immediately.

By the time he had completed the preliminary rituals, he knew she was as eager as he was. It was frustrating not to be able to enter her, to find his way blocked. She whimpered as he tried to push inside her.

"Shall I stop?"

"No, no. Please, no. Do that again." She guided his hand to her breast, and then said, "Do what you did before." As his lips plucked at her nipple she sighed. "Céline is right. That much, I like." She pressed hard against him. "Now try again. This time it will be better."

They rocked together and suddenly he was inside her. "Yes, yes, yes," she whispered. "It is all right. Do not worry, monsieur."

They did not speak afterward but lay quiet and apart. Once he touched her face to see whether she was crying. To his immense relief she was not. The moon had risen, filling the room with light, tracing the pattern of the hedge against the wall.

At last she said, "Did I please you?"

"Immensely. It has never—you must believe me, Marie—it has never been so pleasurable before."

"You will tell Céline I pleased you? So she will know I fulfilled my part of the bargain?"

"Damn the bargain. It was wrong of Céline and wrong of me. But it's done now. But listen, Marie, you did not sell yourself. Do you know why? Frank Goodacre came to me with the money he stole from your father. I didn't know then that it was yours, though I sensed he had stolen it. Later I learned the truth from Céline. I invested it for him. We are partners, he and I—"

"Partners with that man?" she cried.

"Hush, listen. The money will be repaid to you. What I give you, that is your money. What I give Céline, that is my money from France. If I had not taken the money from Goodacre, you would never have got it back. Now you shall, and with interest. You'll be rich. You can go away from here. I will give you some money tonight, but you are not to tell Céline. She has enough, and she'd find a way to get it away from you. It is our secret. Yours and mine."

He wondered at her sudden, Sphinxlike smile, not knowing that she was thinking that Céline too was returning Frank Goodacre's money, and with interest. She would indeed be rich, though in a way her parents would not have approved.

Henri leaned over and kissed Marie gently. "I should go now and let you rest, or the good sisters will wonder at your shadowed face tomorrow."

"I'll tell them I didn't sleep well for worrying. Now that I have refused to become a governess, they are trying to find a husband for me. They are also trying to find out who my foster parents are so they can persuade them to put pressure on me."

"Mon Dieu! A husband! They'll succeed too. Some backwoodsman who'll work you to the bone. We must prevent that."

"I can refuse to marry just as I refused to become a governess. I am my own person. If they are too insistent, I'll leave the school."

He laughed inwardly, wondering if the sisters knew how strong Marie was. As he threw back the sheet to leave the bed she threw her arm across his shoulders and drew him back.

"You may do it again before you go. That is, if you wish."

"Do you wish it?"

"Yes. Perhaps this time I will be more expert. I must learn to please you." *If I am to be rich,* she thought.

He hated the inflection of obedience in her voice, but he took her again because he found her irresistible. He was, to his astonishment, a changed man, purified.

Edmund

Six months later, on her thirteenth birthday, Marie left the convent by mutual consent. *Insubordinate,* Sister Josephine wrote on her report.

The truth was, all the sisters, and the Reverend Mother as well, were puzzled by Marie and especially by the recent change in her. She was guilty of at least one of the Seven Deadly Sins: pride. Sister Josephine suspected she was guilty also of a second, anger. And even the loose sack could not disguise her developing voluptuousness, so she would most certainly, in a place like New Orleans, fall prey to lust, her own or someone else's. Sister Josephine knew the look too well, having worked with the prostitutes of Paris. The convent was probably well rid of her. They had failed her only because Marie had failed them.

A new governor had not yet come to replace Sieur de Bienville, and now that the hurricane season was approaching it would be fall before one could arrive.

But a score of petty Company of the Indies officials had come and reorganized the Superior Council. Bienville's friends were replaced, price controls were set on all goods exchanged between the company and the colonists so that control of the commerce passed into the hands of the company. Prices were raised on imported goods and lowered on colonial produce. And although the colonists complained that agriculture could not advance when there was insufficient labor, the company set prices on slaves and refused to sell them at all to planters who still owed for their last shipment. How could they pay, the planters demanded, when there were no goods to export? The company, they protested, did not foster the production of silk, indigo, lumber, pitch, tar, hides, furs, hemp, flax, waxberries, or cotton. It paid no attention to tobacco. What were they expected to produce and how could they thrive when they could barely eke out a living?

Yet survive they did. By now there was a network of plantations struggling for survival around the city, and they lived more graciously, though they did not know it, than did their English counterparts in the colonies in the North. They had brought their fine furniture and court gowns from France, and they carried on the customs they had followed at home.

There was no difficulty in finding husbands for their daughters. The difficulty was in providing a dowry which did not consist of notes of credit or paper money, the value of which dropped with every new issue. Not that a dowry was a great consideration in a population where men outnumbered women by more than two to one. The problem was the girls themselves. With so many men to chose from the girls could be somewhat particular. Backwoodsmen, common soldiers, and common seamen weren't even considered.

Henri de Nemour, at first thought to be a catch, showed no interest in even the most eligible young ladies. Fortunately not every man was so aloof. Most of them were quite openly hunting wives, and among them was a recent arrival from France, Edmund Lánney.

The Lanney family had no *de* before their name and not a drop of noble blood, which, Lanney père said, probably accounted for their success. They had arrived at their position by hard work, shrewdness, good marriages, and good fortune. They had no scruples about dealing with the English and the Spanish, no matter what national policy regarding both was at the time. Where other men had lost fortunes backing John Law's Company of the Indies, Lanney père had waited to see whether the company would succeed.

He could afford to wait. He had what the company and the settlers in New Orleans would need: ships, a slave trade, and access to supplies and markets.

Whereas in noble families the eldest son was destined for the army or navy and the second son for the Church, Lanney père disregarded convention. The services already had more applicants from the noble families than there were ranks. An abbé had to scramble for a position at court or the favor of some royal personage who would confer a living upon him. The Lanney family had a better place for its sons. The two eldest boys were sent to sea as soon as they were old enough to leave home. When they had served their apprenticeships, Lanney père outfitted a ship for each, underwritten by English maritime insurance. Paul became a slaver; Léon a West Indies shipper. One sister had married a Paris banker, another had married a La Rochelle merchant, and the third, with the assistance of a six-hundred-thousand livres dowry, had married into the aristocracy. By the time Edmund was born, Lanney père had become a deputy to the Council of Commerce, a body responsible only to the crown.

Edmund was twenty years younger than his eldest brother, who referred to him as the Surprise. He was also known as the Little Uncle, as his nieces and nephews were all older by some years than he. His mother called him her dear one, and even his father could not conceal his pride.

"A special place must be found for him," Lanney père would say. A special place for the dear one, the Little Uncle, the Surprise. What would it be? A ship? A bank? A warehouse in La Rochelle?

His mother said, "He is so beautiful he will surely find favor at court."

When Edmund was twelve, he was sent on a voyage

with Paul, contracted African fever from the cargo of slaves, and spent six months recuperating. His next voyage was to the Indies with Léon. Léon returned him to their parents in disgust. Edmund had been seasick the entire voyage, showed no aptitude for sailing or command and no interest in bargaining. "*And* he has no judgment about anything!"

"Then he must learn judgment."

Edmund had liked the Indies, the green, flowering islands, the warm winds, the jewel-toned seas, but he knew he could never make a life as a seafarer. His stomach would not have it.

It was his sister Adele's husband Gustave, the merchant, who came up with the solution. "Send him to New Orleans. He can be our merchant for their products: tobacco, pitch and tar, furs and skins, indigo, wood for ship building. We need someone there to receive our imports and distribute them, someone to gather the local produce to be shipped to us, but most important to collect payment. Not a merchant in France wants to trade with those people because it's too difficult to collect from them."

"He has no sense of value," Léon warned. "No head for haggling. He overpays. And if *you* can't collect payment, how do you think this one can?"

"He will learn after he's been cheated a few times," Gustave said. "He has a mind like a thistledown, but the seeds of a thistledown will implant themselves and grow, mark me. After all, he is a Lanney, is he not? It will be good for him to be out there where life is none too easy. And he is handsome enough that he should be able to manure his field well."

"Such a vulgar expression for the beautiful sacrament of marriage," Lanney mère protested, her nose wrinkling in disgust.

"It is no more vulgar to marry for money and live well than to marry for love and starve," Gustave replied.

"A good marriage is an obligation, and vulgar or

not, a marriage is as manure to a man's future," Lanney père said. "If there is love as well, as in my own case"—he kissed his wife's hand—"all the better."

"I approve of Gustave's idea," Léon said. "Edmund is no sailor. A good seaman can't spend all his time puking over the rail."

Edmund listened and smiled and waited. He knew he was helpless in the hands of his family and must accept whatever decision was made.

"First there must be an apprenticeship," Lanney père decided.

"Certainly," Gustave agreed. "With me in La Rochelle. I am a good teacher . . ."

And an exacting one, Edmund found. Gustave forced him to memorize prices, to judge the quality of the cargoes, to criticize or approve the manner in which they were shipped, to sort and assess letters of credit, to decide which goods were most profitable to send on consignment.

"But how can I know that until I have been there?"

"Precisely. Now I must judge for myself without being there. You, once you are there, will inform me."

His apprenticeship lasted three years. The first year Edmund felt as if he were in prison. His evenings were spent with the studies Gustave assigned, his days as a general flunky. Even after mass on Sundays he had to accompany Adele and Gustave on a round of boring visits during which the talk inevitably turned to business. In Paris people would have danced or listened to music or gossiped about society. Often he was so homesick and pitied himself so thoroughly that he had to blink back tears of frustration.

When he went home for Christmas, his appearance shocked his mother. "So thin, so pale! It is terrible! Does Gustave think you are his slave?"

The second year Edmund was given one free evening a week. He knew no one but Gustave's business associates and their sons, who, like most of the rest of France, spent their spare time gambling. Edmund found it an exciting pastime. With luck a man could become rich in a single evening. He listened to Gustave's warnings with half an ear.

He made money and lost it, won it back on borrowed funds, and lost all he had made a month later. By his third year of apprenticeship he was so deeply in debt that his father had to come to his aid. Lanney père extracted a promise that Edmund would gamble no more.

Edmund's chagrin at being treated like a child and having to avoid his companions was painful, but he kept his promise. He was glad when the time came for him to go to New Orleans.

He was given enough money to live on for a year, and he was to be allowed to keep a certain percentage of the debts he collected and the receipts from imports sold. The rest was up to him.

Edmund was eighteen when he sailed. He was excited by the prospect of his new life and filled with self-importance, marred only by the fact that his stomach was already reacting to the lift and fall of the ship as it slipped away from the quay. But he had to laugh in spite of his queasiness, for the last words of farewell that carried faint but clear across the widening expanse of water were Gustave's, saying, "Remember, Little Uncle, manure your field well."

It was not until they reached the translucent waters of the Caribbean that Edmund began to enjoy himself, and this despite daily lectures from Léon.

Léon recommended frugality and caution in all dealings, whether business or courtship.

"You must be as astute in your wooing as in your business dealings. There are twice as many men as women in New Orleans, so you'll have to outbid your competition." He looked at his young brother critically. "With your looks and the Lanney name you should have no trouble winning the best of the lot."

"I am too young to marry. I have not lived yet."

"You are very nearly too old. I was married at fifteen and was a father at sixteen. You can do your living afterward. A wife is an asset. Men trust a married man more quickly than they trust a bachelor."

"It would be easier if I were provided with more money as well as looks and a name. Father doesn't trust me."

"You failed in every apprenticeship he set for you, and gambled away all you earned."

Edmund flushed. "That's not true. I did not fail with Gustave. Damn him for a liar if he said that I did."

"You've yet to put to test what Gustave taught you."

"At least I know what's needed. A warehouse so the merchandise doesn't sit exposed on the docks; suitable packing; low prices for good quality; an open ear and a closed mouth."

Léon tapped his temple with his forefinger. "Now, you begin to think."

"But how the devil I'm to get a warehouse with so little money I don't know."

"That will be your first challenge."

At La Balize they took on a river pilot, but strong northerly winds and water too low for the ship to cross the bar delayed them for ten days. Edmund shivered in the cold and cursed the fog and his boredom. There was nothing of interest ashore but a fort garrisoned by fifty men and a handful of miserable prisoners.

The jerk and toss of the ship at anchor brought back Edmund's seasickness. At night he dreamed of warehouses of every fantastic size and shape, filled with chained men, neatly crated, awaiting shipment to La Rochelle.

One morning the wind veered around to the east, dispelling the fog. With a squeal of the capstan the anchor was lifted, and the torturous journey upriver began.

Edmund's excitement returned. He spent all his time on deck, standing at the prow, waiting for New

Orleans to come into sight. It was a long time coming. There were sand bars and reefs, sudden jutting points of land, barriers which broke apart as the ship rammed them and proved to be stinking composites of drift wood, slime, sediment, dead animals, and rotting logs.

The marsh grass and rushes gave way to willow and canebrake, which in turn gave way to cypress forests and water oaks draped with Spanish beard.

There was water everywhere. Edmund could see no clear division between the brown, muddy river and the brown, muddy land. Ducks swam among the tree trunks. Egrets waded in the shallows. Islands of lily pads rose and fell in the wake of the ship, and blue masses of water hyacinths were like bits of fallen sky. Everything lay silent in the oppressively heavy air, and it felt to Edmund ominously like the calm before the storm.

Then the river widened, and traffic increased, slowing their progress, and unexpectedly they eased up to an artificial bulk of land and dropped anchor.

"New Orleans." Léon waved his arm at the arc of land.

Edmund gazed in dismay at the roofs sprawled below the levee. This could not be the place he had been sent to prove himself and make his fortune. It was worse than Africa. There one did not *expect* civilization. True there was a church tower, but . . .

Léon clapped him on the back. "Well, Little Uncle?"

"It will require a miracle."

It was usual for vessels to remain in New Orleans if there was a possibility of a storm coming but Léon decided to leave at once and lie over in Martinique. "The sooner you are on your own, Little Uncle, the better."

Edmund watched *La Belle Amie* fade out of sight and then went desolately to his rented room. At any rate he would no longer be called Little Uncle.

He spent one homesick evening watching cockroaches explore his belongings and listening to the wire-thin whine of mosquitoes outside his netting-draped bed. He tossed and turned and sweated and cursed his fate. Homesickness was more difficult to bear than seasickness, for it produced nothing but unmanly tears.

The next day he walked the length and breadth of the town and found it both worse and better than his first impression. Léon had provided him with letters of introduction, and Edmund lost no time in using them. He was determined to spend as little time as possible in the bug-ridden room that was the best the city had to offer.

Within a fortnight he was one of the most popular young men in New Orleans. His curling red-gold hair and sparkling eyes, his exquisite manners and supreme self-confidence in combination with the Lanney name brought him invitations to almost every home of distinction in the area. He seldom had to buy any meal other than breakfast and never spent an evening alone.

He danced superbly and paid delicious compliments to mothers and daughters alike, making the mothers feel he would really prefer them but knew full well he was too young for them to take notice of him.

The fathers also approved. Edmund was ambitious and knowledgeable. He spoke of building warehouses, running a retail store, and distributing imported goods throughout the colony as far up the river as Illinois.

The only problem was money. His father was conservative and overly cautious. He had not yet been to the New World, and the reports he had received from the colony were not encouraging. So his advice was to wait until the new governor was appointed and had taken up residence; wait until they decided on a principal export; wait until the letters of credit had been paid off. Edmund would explain all this with shrugs and a rueful smile and say, "That is Papa."

There wasn't a planter in the area who wouldn't have loaned Edmund the money for his ventures if any of them had had it to spare.

"Perhaps we should finance a warehouse for him," Frank Goodacre said to Henri. Goodacre had taken Henri's advice and was learning French. It was halting, basic, and ungrammatical, but he had made more progress than Henri had expected. Plainly the man was not stupid.

"Why should we? His own father won't do it."

"The old man doesn't know the situation here."

"Is that what Lanney told you? His father knows very well what the situation is here. The Lanneys aren't fools or they wouldn't be where they are today. They aren't nobility. They're damnably shrewd middle-class people who have a talent for marrying well and making money. How did you meet Lanncy?"

"His brother needed bricks for ballast, so he came out to the yard himself. He's a great planner. Seems to me New Orleans needs a young man like that." Not someone like de Nemour, who laid around dressed like a Hindu and yawned all day. Frank lapsed into English. "I wager he'll end up owning half the town."

Henri shrugged and yawned, not knowing how his yawning irritated Goodacre. "Perhaps. If he marries wisely and doesn't accumulate gambling debts." The heat was so heavy that the fan barely stirred the air. Henri wished Goodacre would go. His head ached, and every time he moved it was all he could do to keep from wincing from a pain in his back. He had felt so well that morning—it was the heat, the oppressive, all-enveloping heat. His skin felt as if it were being slowly parboiled. He leaned back and closed his eyes but opened them again hastily, for the room whirled so violently he thought he would be thrown from his chair.

Frank Goodacre looked at him anxiously. "Are you all right, monsieur?"

"It's the heat. It has given me a terrible headache."

Goodacre stood up. "The fever starts with a headache. You'd better get to your bed."

"I don't have the fever. It's the heat."

"It's not particularly hot today. There's even a bit of breeze. You get to your bed. I'm going."

Henri was too weary to see him to the door. He sat dully in his chair, wishing he had the energy to move. He had planned to be with Marie that night, but that would have to be postponed.

Marie had become an important part of his life during the past months. Passionate in body, she aroused and satisfied him as no one had ever done. Yet despite their intimacy she was an enigma, aloof, secretive.

Sometimes he wondered if she hated him for having corrupted her, and was afraid to ask for fear of her answer. Once he had offered to try to find her relatives in Scotland if she would give him whatever information she had about them. She had stared him down with those enormous eyes, which had darkened so suddenly they were almost purple. "Do you think I could go to them *now*?"

He was horrified to think what he had done, but there was no way to remedy it. Nor could he stay away from her. He could never have enough of her, even if she loathed him.

He loved the delicate bones of her ribs under the ivory flesh, the small rose-tipped towers of her breasts, which responded so quickly to his kisses, the taut thighs already moist when his fingers explored them, the taste of her. He had taught her well, and she had been an apt student. She was obedient to any of his wishes. And no doubt she loathed him.

The fear of that haunted him, and now, with his head throbbing, his back aching as if he were being racked, and vomit rising in his throat, he thought he could bear any pain if Marie loved him. If she would forgive him as a priest would forgive him. But a priest would command him to sin no more, and he knew he would return to Marie again and again.

That night he dreamed he had gone to her and found the house empty, the bed bare of sheets, the shutters closed and webbed by spiders, a vase of dead flowers on the shelf where the doll, Flora, had stared with her glass eyes.

He awakened moaning and immediately afterward began to vomit. By morning the vomit was streaked with blood, and he was out of his head with fever.

The wind freshened, and a transparent veil of cloud shimmered in the sky, giving the light a watery tone. The mosquitoes disappeared, and the lizards that scuttled across Marie's roof at night disappeared also. The grove of orange trees was full of birds which alternately chattered as if in alarm and suddenly fell silent. The swampland and bayou, usually loud at night with frogs and alligators and the lonely, haunting cries of night birds, were as still as if all life had deserted them.

Henri had not been to visit Marie for nearly a week, and Céline accused her of having offended him.

"I did nothing of the kind," Marie retorted. "You have no right to accuse me of such a thing. I do everything he asks." And more. Things she had thought of herself, to her shame. "Everything." She walked up and down the room. Céline sat in the only chair, the chair on which Henri put his clothes when he undressed. Céline's sack was open to her naval, and sweat ran in rivulets between her full, round breasts. She fanned herself violently and kept pushing her damp hair back from her temples.

"I please him," Marie added, unable to stop defending herself. "He told me I do, and he told you."

"Then why has he not been here?"

Marie had unconsciously picked up Céline's habit

of shrugging, and she shrugged now. "Perhaps he has got engaged to a planter's daughter."

"It is impossible! No. Something is wrong. Sheba must make an enquiry. I would go myself, but I do not wish to compromise him by appearing at his door."

Marie laughed. "He compromised himself long ago."

"The nuns are right. You are insubordinate. You are only what—thirteen?—and you act like a bitter old woman."

"Why should I not?"

"Christ's bones. I don't know, but it is not becoming."

"I don't have to worry about that. Not anymore. You have seen to that, haven't you? And don't ask me again what I would have done without you. I don't need to hear that again. The sisters could have found me a husband."

Céline wiped the sweat from between her breasts and lifted them to fan beneath them. Marie wondered if Henri would like her breasts better if they were as round and heavy and dark-nippled as Céline's. She decided he would not. Céline was saying, "Yes, they could have found you some lout who wouldn't pay you but would take what Henri takes and consider it his right. This way—"

"I know." Marie stopped before a window, hoping some stir of breeze would cool her. "I will have money of my own. I know." More money than Céline guessed. It was a secret between her and Henri. "When is Sheba going to his house? I'll send him a message."

"Very generous," Céline said, her voice heavy with sarcasm. "How will your note read?"

"'Céline accuses me of having displeased you. Please come to her house and tell her it is not true.'"

Céline closed her fan with a snap and got up. "You are a little cat. Keep your claws for scratching Henri's back, Marie. Men like that. Or perhaps you have learned?"

Sheba returned almost before Marie realized she had gone, her eyes wide with fright.

"It's the fever. The woman said he's yellow as citrine and throwing up so much blood if you cut him he wouldn't bleed. He's off his head too. He'll die. They always die."

"Not always," Céline said. "Not if they don't die at once."

"Should I go to him?" Marie asked.

"And risk catching it yourself? Do you think because you did not die when your parents did that you are immune?"

"My father said it comes from the heat and the water."

"Nevertheless you must not go to him. I forbid it."

"Very well." Marie shrugged. "I thought it was part of my duty to him. I don't want to go. I remember how the fever smelled. It's nothing to me if he dies." Except that there would be no more money."

"That is unkind. The man is ill."

"Is it necessary that I love him? Because I do not."

"You should pity him."

"I do that. Yes. He is a lonely man, a man without a purpose. I wonder what will become of him if he doesn't die. I mean, when he is old."

"He could go back to Paris now that the new king has come of age and taken over the rule."

"Then why doesn't he? Why would anyone want to stay in this place that stinks of fever and death?" She had never forgotten the stench of sickness in her parents' cabin, the putrid seepage in the grave.

"You've never smelled the streets of Paris." Céline wrinkled her nose. "Sometimes I miss that stink."

"Perhaps you should go back as well."

"Mon Dieu, Marie, I've no desire to go back. This is the good life. I'll have a big house one day, with crystal chandeliers and elegant furniture from France. I'll make a fortune, for I'll take only gentlemen. You'll be glad then that I took you in."

"Why should I be glad? I'll not end up as one of your girls. When I've saved enough money, I'll leave you. And leave Henri too."

"You need not threaten," Céline said. "I'll let you go."

Meanwhile Marie managed to remain her own person. She did not even take her meals with the others but had Sheba bring them to her own small house.

Sheba was as full of advice as Céline. "You make that man marry you if he lives," she would say. "Then you get away from here, and I'll go with you."

"I don't want to be married to him."

"He's gentle-born. Rich. Handsome. You don't have to love a man to marry him. Marriage is better than this house."

Was it? Once she had thought she wouldn't mind working hard as her mother had done, making a home, having a child to love; had thought it would not be so bad to marry one of the young militia men who had been transferred from Canada. Now she was not so sure. But neither was she sure that there was anything else for her.

Was it too late to return to the convent and ask Sister Josephine to find her a husband? Sister Josephine would have no time for her. A new shipment of "casket girls" had arrived during the summer, their caskets being the dower given them by the government in France. Until they were married off, Sister Josephine would ignore her. "Insubordinate," she would say. "How can I recommend you as a wife?"

So she would wait. She could afford to wait. Céline was right. She was like an old woman. She had grown up the day they had buried her parents, and Henri had been her matriculation into life. Sometimes she wondered why she wanted to be free of him.

He had awakened her to a sensuality she had never dreamed existed, despite her close association with

Céline. It had never occurred to her—and the convent had done nothing to enlighten her, naturally—that the men who came to Céline's did so for anything other than relief, as from a need to urinate.

She had begun by accepting the fact that if she were to survive she must be the instrument of Henri's relief, for it had been almost in such terms that Céline had described what she must do. But after the first time, she found herself longing for him to return. He had become her instrument as well. The nights he did not visit she imagined he was there. She touched herself, to remember his touch, which only made her long for him all the more. She hated herself for it. It would be different, she told herself, with someone she loved. In what way "different" she was not sure.

One morning she awakened drenched with perspiration, feeling as if all the air had been sucked away from the earth. The sky was pale as smoke, and the day was deathly still except for the distant mutter of thunder. No birds called, no leaves stirred, no shutters creaked, for there was no breeze to move them. The all-pervading odor of the bayou was heavier than usual and overlaid with the smell of salt water, as if the ocean had invaded the lowlands.

It was too hot to dress. Marie walked to the kitchen in her nightgown. Sweat streamed down Sheba's face, and her sack clung damply to her body. Sheba handed Marie a glass of wine, tepid as bathwater, and cold rice cakes.

"Too hot for cooking. That smell, that's a mean storm brewing."

When Marie went back to her house, she paused in the garden and looked at the sky. A wall of clouds wreathed the place where the river ran, swirling up and up toward the meridian, cupping over it as she watched. She did not feel frightened, although she knew hurricanes took their toll of injury and death.

She ate slowly. The rice cakes were good, and the wine made her feel drowsy. Perhaps that was what

Sheba had intended. If they drank enough wine, dying would not matter. She took her money box and Flora, wrapped them in a blanket, and put them under the bed.

The orange trees shivered, rustling their leaves. Wind stirred the inert air. A flash of lightning blanched the landscape, followed by a crack of thunder which shook the walls. It ripped the clouds apart, letting loose the rain. The rain did not start gently with a few hesitant drops but as a deluge, blanking out the world, hitting the earth with such force that it bounced up to fall again. Once, through the sound of pelting rain, Marie heard the bells in the church ringing as the wind swung them, but then the sound was lost in the shriek of wind which rattled her roof, carried foliage and timber in a wild carrousel. Even the floor seemed to heave underfoot.

Marie wondered why she found it exhilarating. She felt a part of it, as if the energy loosed were her own. She wished she had such force and could sweep away the world in which she lived and, in the calm which followed, begin the world anew.

She stood at the window, watching until the wind-driven rain made it imperative that she close the shutters. That she found frustrating, to listen and not to see, to feel the fragility of the walls and watch the shutters bulge and strain at their hinges.

She wondered if the storm penetrated Henri's fever-dulled mind and if he felt fear, being helpless and ill. She felt no pity, only curiosity.

Soon she began to pace the floor. Suddenly unable to stand the isolation, she decided to go to Céline. The wind tore the door out of her hand and sent her staggering into the yard. It took all her strength to go back and force it shut again. By then the house was drenched. The wind threw her to the ground, and she crawled through the rain, which had turned the garden into a shallow pool, to the steps of the main house. She pounded on the door for what seemed a long time before Céline realized it was not the wind that made the rapping sound. It took both Céline and Sheba to hold the door while Marie crawled into the room. She stood up, dripping, her nightgown plastered against her, her hair streaming rivulets down her shoulder.

"Little fool, why didn't you stay where you were? You could have been picked up by the wind and hurled to death!"

"I like the storm." She laughed. "It didn't pick me up. It tried to beat me into the earth." Her laughter died, and she paused, embarrassed. A young man was in the room, staring at her with the greenest eyes she had ever seen. Like jewels, she thought, like emeralds. He smiled at her, and she felt a spasm of desire.

"Madame—" Edmund Lanney bowed slightly toward Céline—"you asked me a moment ago if I wished to amuse myself while taking refuge from the storm. I refused, but I did not know then that you made a specialty of mermaids. May I reconsider?"

Céline frowned. "You mean Marie? It is impossible, monsieur. She is spoken for. She belongs to someone. A special arrangement, you understand."

"What a pity for me and what a delight for the gentleman who owns her. I am sure Mademoiselle"—and he bowed to Marie—"is his most precious possession."

Looking at him, Marie thought, *He's beautiful as an angel. Saint Michael of the Golden Light.* Her body tingled under his gaze. She knew she had been drawn to Céline's because he was there. She wanted him as she had never wanted Henri.

"Monsieur, Céline is mistaken. I belong to no one. It is true, there is only one gentleman. I am quite virtuous, you see. But I am also free to choose my companions. Will you brave the wind with me?"

"With you, mademoiselle, I would brave death."

"It may be that." Marie laughed. "The wind may pick us up, hand in hand, and blow us to Illinois."

"I will not allow it!" Céline exploded.

"I am not your slave, Céline, nor M. Hen–*his*. Give me a bottle of wine to take with us, Sheba."

"Disgraceful!"

"It was you who set the example," Marie said.

Laughing, she and Edmund clung to one another, thrown this way and that by the force of the wind, falling, struggling to their feet again, and finally reaching Marie's house. Once inside, they embraced, covering each other's faces with kisses.

"Take me, take me," Marie whispered.

He gripped the neck of her gown and ripped it apart. She stepped out of it, her body glistening with rain. Edmund gasped and closed his eyes. Then he laid her gently on the bed and stretched out beside her. He traced the shape of her eyes, her face, kissing the trail left by his fingers. He would not be her first, yet her aura of innocence made him hesitate. Her touch on his back was as light as the wings of a butterfly.

Suddenly her nails dug into him and ripped. He shuddered as she rolled over, pulling him with her so he mounted her.

The suddenness of her attack, her expertise, her violence astounded and inflamed him. He had never known such love-making as this, so uninhibited, so satisfying, as if this girl knew all his secret desires and wildest imaginings.

For Marie it was all that it should have been with Henri but was not. It was inspiring and satisfying because she felt the first inklings of love.

The wind was an endless shriek which rose and fell, crashing against the house. The shutters were never still but rattled like a series of musket shots. The sound of the storm intensified their ardor, as if they drew energy from it.

When at last they lay back, exhausted, they were aware of the sudden silence. The wind had ceased. The shutters were still, the rain no longer slashed at the roof.

"The silence is as deafening as the storm," Edmund Lanney said.

"The storm isn't over. This is the eye. It will begin again."

"Again? Mon Dieu! The storms here are as violent as your passion, mademoiselle."

"I thought to please you."

Edmund flung himself back on the pillow. "Please! Dear heaven, I have never been so pleased, as you choose to call it." He laughed.

"Are you new here?"

"But yes. That is why I have never experienced one of your storms. I am from La Rochelle. A younger son, you understand. My father sent me here to further my fortunes and that of our firm. And, I suspect, to test me. *Parbleu*, I don't know how he expects me to succeed when he doesn't heed my advice. He has never been here, so he believes nothing I tell him. He is a cautious man, conservative, tight-fisted, suspicious. But do not misunderstand, he's a fine man. We are a very important family."

Marie smiled to herself. How young and voluble and vain, and how charming! And lonely, or he would not talk so much.

"I should like to build a warehouse on the wharf where the goods for shipment to France could be under cover instead of exposed to the sun and to storms such as this. I'll not be surprised if I see every packing case on the wharf either crushed by the wind or tossed into the river. But my father said no, we must wait. You see, he doesn't understand this country. But why am I telling you all this?"

"Because I find it interesting."

"Do you? Yes, well then, I suggested a retail store where we would sell imported goods over the counter instead of by order, as it is done now. He discouraged that as well. I thought to put under contract the small voyageurs to distribute goods up the river. Again my father says no." He sighed.

"They sound like wise ideas to me, but I know very little of the situation. The convent did not teach us business but prayers."

"You attended the convent? Yes, I thought you were educated and not like Madame Céline. How did you come to be in this—this place?"

"It's a long story," she said. "If your father won't give you the money to start your ventures, won't some of the local people? It would be to their advantage, wouldn't it?"

"Certainly. There's not a planter who wouldn't help me, but they have no money either. Only letters of credit. This entire colony is run on letters of credit! It is a wonder to me it runs at all. I thought for a time a M. Goodacre was going to help me, but in the end he refused. A strange man, M. Goodacre. Not *quite*, if you understand my meaning."

"I know M. Goodacre."

"*He* is not your gentleman?" Edmund leaned on one elbow to look into Marie's face.

"Never! I know him . . . because he gave some money to the convent."

"He would have done better to give it to me to build a warehouse. God helps those who help themselves."

"That is not what the nuns taught me."

"They are not very worldly, the nuns, eh?"

The shutters drummed, and the wind moaned.

"Here it comes again," Marie said. "It will not be so violent this time, for we will have only the fringe. It will have moved further inland." Before she had finished speaking, the rain hammered at the roof.

"There is no leaving now. But then, I am very content here with you in my arms. How are you called?"

"Marie. And you?"

"Edmund Lanney."

Céline was furious. She railed at herself for having brought Marie to this, she railed at Marie for betraying Henri, she railed at Sheba for having provided wine, at God for having sent the hurricane, and most of all at Edmund. "He tried to tell me that you said there would be no charge."

"I told him there would not be."

"That, Marie, is not the way my business is run, and I told him differently. Do you think we offer free service to a man because it rains? Pah! We should charge him double for sheltering him as well as pleasuring him."

"It was I who did the—the pleasuring and—"

"And you are in my employ."

"That I am not. I never asked to be, I never said I would be, and I never will be! I will not become another Alixe or Mimi or Blanche."

"Little bitch," Blanche said. "Too good for us? Just wait. You've taken the second step. Two men, not one."

"There is a difference." Marie turned on Blanche in a fury not unlike Céline's. "I love this man."

"Christ's bones, what do you know of love?" Céline said.

Blanche broke into peals of laughter. "Love! After one afternoon of fucking? Little one, you are a fool."

Céline frowned at Blanche. "We will continue this talk in your house, Marie, where there is privacy."

The yard was ankle deep in leaves torn from the trees, in ruined birds' nests, branches, thatch, bits of rag, refuse of every kind. The sodden ground sank with every step, and the land was loud with frogs and anguished birds whose nests had been destroyed.

"It must have looked like this after the Flood receded," Céline said, holding up her skirts and picking her way through the debris. "I wish never to experience a hurricane again. I thought the house would fall down upon us, and I had not had Absolution."

Good, Marie thought. Her anger is receding like the Flood waters.

But she was wrong. Céline began again once they

were inside, pacing the floor, swearing, reviling her. "Blanche is right, Marie. Next it will be still another man who catches your fancy, then another, and another. It is always so. You will end up like those you despise, taking anyone because the urge will be there."

"That's not true."

"I know better than you, Marie."

"There won't be another."

"Not at once. This one is coming back. He said so. Ah, that pleases you, does it? And what about Henri?"

"What about him?"

"It is unfair."

Marie pouted. "He need not know."

"That is a deception and not in accord with the agreement."

"Your agreement, Céline, not mine."

"Yes, by God, my agreement! You are being well paid for my agreement."

"And am I being paid for my pleasuring of Edmund, since you insisted that he pay?"

"The usual percentage. The same I give to the others."

"I'll accept that."

"You have no alternative but to accept."

"I would do it for nothing, but since you charge—"

Céline interrupted. "If you would do it for nothing, you are a great fool, and you do not do it for nothing in my establishment."

"Céline, shouldn't we go to see if Henri is all right? See that his house is standing and he was not injured?"

"Does your conscience prick you?"

"Perhaps. It is Christian charity, is it not?"

"Like your charity with M. Lanney?"

"That was for love. How long did you know your man, Pierre, before you loved him?"

Céline's shoulders sagged. She looked almost old. "A night. An afternoon."

"So love can strike as suddenly as a hurricane."

"He won't have you, Marie. I know that type. Not quite nobility and twice as haughty. A nobleman might set you up in luxury, but a bourgeois, never! Someone might find out and gossip."

"He knows I am different."

"Does he? He may say so, but you are still a whore to him."

Damn Céline! Céline knew nothing. Her standards, her opinions, her attitudes were as low as her profession.

"Wait and see, Céline," Marie said tersely. "Meanwhile we should go to Henri."

"Yes, yes, to ease your conscience."

But Céline would have nothing to do with going to a house where there was fever, so it was Sheba and Marie who set out with a basket of food.

The damage in Céline's garden was small compared to that in the streets. The banquettes were half under water, the higher sections serving as a refuge for snakes, toads, baby alligators, bedraggled cats and mongrels, birds and gulls with broken wings, all huddled in mutual misery waiting for the waters to recede. Shutters sagged on a single hinge or had been torn off altogether and flung into the slow-turning whirlpool of mud in the roadway. Roofs had been ripped off, boats flung ashore, their hulls crushed.

Despite the heat again settling heavily over the town, Marie shivered. Such disaster was depressing, and she wished she hadn't come out. A few slaves worked listlessly at clearing the docks, flinging broken branches, thatch, and garbage into the river, which was already clogged with refuse.

Henri's house was nearly undamaged. A small black boy opened the door, letting out the fumes of sickness. Sheba talked to him in their native language.

"Monsieur is still alive," Sheba told Marie. "Not vomiting anymore. The boy's gone to tell him you're here."

After a few moments Henri called to her from inside, his voice feeble and strained. "Marie, my dear, don't come in. There may still be contagion. I am past the crisis but very weak. It will be days before I'll have the strength to leave my bed. Thank you, my darling, for caring enough to come to visit me. A thousand kisses, Marie."

She was silent, wondering how to answer. That he had interpreted her concern as love was terrible. "Take care," she called. "Yes, a kiss for you until—" She thrust the basket of cakes and fruits into the hands of the boy and turned away. After Edmund she could not bear the thought of Henri touching her again.

"You listen to me," Sheba said. "I tell you once more, you make that man marry you."

"I've told you a dozen times, Sheba, I don't want to be married to him."

"You want to end up like the others? First one man, then another and another?"

"You sound like Céline. You heard her say that."

"It's the truth."

"I want only M. Lanney."

"All right, then. If you want to be a fool. I'll make a gris-gris for you. You keep it under your pillow, and maybe, just maybe, you'll have him. Then again, maybe not. Maybe he has a gris-gris of his own, and he wants something else."

"What is a gris-gris?"

"A charm. They make all kinds of magic. A gris-gris to get rich, a gris-gris to get your man, a gris-gris to bring bad luck to your enemy. Whatever you want, you make a gris-gris."

"Then make one for me, Sheba, so I'll have him always."

"You won't be able to set me free if you marry him. He smells of poor luck."

"Nonsense. He's going to be rich."

"You'll see. But I'll make a gris-gris because that's

what you think you want. Sometimes you get what you want, and you find you don't want it anymore."

"I want him."

Sheba gave a sniff of contempt. That evening she brought Marie an odd-looking ball covered with feathers, smelling of saffron and some other odor which was very unpleasant. Marie wrapped it in a scrap of cloth and put it under her pillow, as directed by Sheba. Her father had told her that charms and potions were powerless superstitions, but if you believed something hard enough, it would happen. She dared not throw the gris-gris away no matter how it smelled, for Sheba would notice it was missing when she made Marie's bed.

Whether or not it was the power of the gris-gris, Edmund returned late that evening. Céline's first impulse was to turn him away, but fearing Marie would find out, she admitted him and sent Sheba to see if Marie would receive him. "I've lost money during Henri's sickness, and if he should die"—she paused to cross herself—"we should seek his replacement."

Marie had been asleep, but she brushed her hair, removed her nightdress, and bathed with scent. Then she lay back against the pillows, her heart thumping with excitement.

Edmund paused at the door, then knelt beside the bed. "You are more beautiful than I remembered. An ivory goddess. I thought it was the storm, the madness of the wind, but it is true. All day I have thought of you."

"And I of you. I ached with longing for you."

The joy of giving herself to him and at the same time pleasing him swept her into extremes of passion which surpassed those of the day before. Afterward, lying in each other's arms, they talked; rather Edmund talked, and Marie listened. Henri never talked to her but took his leave when he had exhausted himself, looking grave and guilt-ridden.

Edmund spoke of his ambitions, of the dull party he

had attended where everyone told what *he* had done during the storm. He gave an amusing imitation of Mme. Arnolie showing off her daughters, "who are pretty in the way a dairymaid is pretty."

"I know," Marie said. "I was at convent with them."

They made love once more before he left. "Your Mme. Céline will make me pay through the nose for this." He laughed. "She is hard, that one."

"I'll return the money to you," Marie whispered.

But when she offered it to him as he was dressing, he closed her fingers over it. "My darling, if need be I would spend my father's fortune on you."

"If you could get it away from him," she teased.

"Yes, there is that."

It was the same the next night and the next. Always he was passionate, amusing, and adoring.

One night a mockingbird in the orange thicket sang all throughout their love-making. Its song, filling the room, became a part of the act, engulfing Marie as Edmund's arms enfolded her. Her body seemed to blossom with beauty and happiness, unfurling as a flower might unfurl. She was no longer one person alone but an extension of Edmund, a completion of him, as he was a completion of her.

This is what true love is, she told herself, and sank into the bliss of giving herself to him.

Afterward, as he prepared to leave, he leaned out the window and whistled, trying to recall the bird to song.

"It has flown," Marie said. "I heard its wings and the leaves shaking. Listen."

They heard it again, farther away. *Near Henri's,* Marie thought, and wondered if he was awake and heard the bird as well.

Edmund sniffed the air. "I am beginning to like this country. In time I may grow accustomed to living here. At any rate I dare not return home until I've proven myself." He laughed. "So far I have done little but play. Soon I must become serious. A businessman."

"Can you be serious?"

He drew himself up and put on a solemn face. "But certainly. Perhaps when winter comes." He relaxed. "Meanwhile, do you know what I should like? A picnic! Would Madame let you out of here for a day?"

"She has nothing to say about what I do."

"Then you aren't entirely her girl?"

"How can you think that?"

"I was not sure. Tomorrow then?"

"It will be wonderful. What time?"

"Early. Before it gets hot. When it rings nine. I'll buy fruit and wine at the market. I know of a little pirogue I can hire, and we'll go up Bayou Piquant to Lake Pontchartrain."

Marie clapped her hands. "Lovely! I'll ask Sheba to pack something nice in a basket to go with the fruit. Oh, Edmund, I am excited."

He chewed his lip for a moment. "You understand, I can't call for you here in daylight. It is a place where I should not be seen. You must meet me at the market."

Marie felt a twist of pain. "Of course. You're right. I hadn't thought of it. You can't be seen coming here. It wouldn't do."

"Uh— No one knows you, I suppose? No one will recognize you?"

"No one will recognize me, Edmund." There was an edge to her voice, but she was as angry at herself as she was annoyed at his concern. "I told you, I am not one of Mme. Céline's girls." She must leave this place. Edmund must marry her and take her away.

"Good. At nine then." He twinkled suddenly. "Shall I recognize you, dressed?"

"As easily as I'll recognize you, dressed."

He came back from the door and kissed the tip of her nose. "Naughty!"

* * *

Mimi pouted wistfully when Marie told her. "How lovely! Oh, Marie, you do have good luck. It is so much nicer in nature. So much more pure. So innocent."

"I wish you could come."

"You must not even think of it. You must be alone with him. Such a *beau* man! He will make love to you, and the crushed grass will smell sweet, and you'll lie back and watch the clouds overhead and the birds flying."

"Mimi! You have a wicked mind!"

"No. It will happen. It always does." She sighed. "Sometimes I remember the smell of new mown hay and fruit ripening and the sound of bees, and I almost weep. Instead I have a little glass of wine and think, Ah, well, this is not so bad. I smell the orange blossoms at night even over the stink of drunken soldiers. And I remind myself that farm work is hard for a woman. Calvings, milking, mowing, preserving for winter. Here, if it is a gentleman I am with, I do very well for him. I make him think he pleases me as much as I please him. If it is a soldier a tiny bit drunk, I've but to give a little bump now and again. I can sleep all day and drink wine, and Céline is good to me."

"I wish there were something better for you. A man like Edmund."

Mimi smiled and shook her head. "Perhaps one day if I do not get the whore's sickness. Go, Marie, and if he asks you to marry, say yes, yes, yes!"

"Yes, yes, yes!"

They laughed and hugged one another.

But Céline snorted when she was told.

"I suppose you didn't have the brains to name a price."

"A price for going on a picnic?"

"For the pleasure of your company. And for spreading your legs in the grass."

"Céline! You and Mimi think alike. He won't do that."

"You don't know men, Marie. All right. Let him have this one as a bonus. It serves me right for not having named a higher price in the first place. It's too late now. Go on your picnic, and if he offers to pay, it's two hundred sols. Take the money."

"I won't take it. He'd think I was a whore."

Céline started to speak. Instead she shrugged and waved Marie out of the room as if she were an annoying insect.

Marie paused at the door. "I know what you're thinking. It's not true."

She saw Edmund before he saw her. He was pacing back and forth along the levee, silhouetted against the golden blaze of morning sky. While she watched him he paused once or twice to shade his eyes and scan the market place, looking for her. She was almost beside him before he recognized her in her bonnet and Mimi's shawl. She detected a moment's hesitation before he bowed.

"I—thought you might not come."

"Am I late? The bells are just now sounding nine."

"Well, then, shall we go?" He glanced around nervously, but no one was watching them.

The pirogue rocked and scattered gold-flecked water as Marie stepped into it. Edmund had placed a blanket over the bow seat where Marie sat, and another under her feet, for the bottom was damp. He removed his velour coat, folded it, and handed it gravely to Marie. "Please." He rolled his lace-cuffed sleeves to his elbows and dipped the oars into the water. They jerked forward and stopped, bobbing on the current.

"You forgot to untie it."

Edmund blushed and laughed. "So I did. No wonder my brother would not have me as a seaman." He called to a slave sitting on the levee and asked him to untie the boat.

The man pulled them back so the rope hung slack

and undid the knot, holding them fast against the tug of the river. Expertly he coiled the rope and slung it into the pirogue at Edmund's feet. The current took them, but Edmund soon had command of the craft, jerky as his movements were. Marie opened her parasol as protection against the sprays of water that showered over them at every lift of his oars.

"Good." Edmund nodded in approval. "I don't want my coat to get wet. Velour spots."

"So do I." Marie laughed.

"But on you the water glistens like diamonds. It is adorable."

When they slipped into the limpid water of the bayou, Marie thought she had never been so happy. She began to sing a Jacobean song she had learned from her father: "It was in old times when trees composed rhymes, and flowers did with elegy flow . . ."

On such a day it did seem as if the wavering reflections of the trees were poetry. Marie could see through the shallow water to the silvery sand strewn with cockle shells, which gleamed as the ripples passed over them. An alligator lumbered off the bank and slid heavily into the water after they had passed. It lay there, half-submerged, blinking in their wake.

Edmund wiped the sudden sweat from his forehead. "Mon Dieu! It had not occurred to me there would be beasts."

"And snakes." Marie pointed out a moccasin, still as a fallen branch on the bank.

Edmund gave a soundless whistle. Marie continued her song: ". . . a rose and a thistle did grow . . ."

"You must translate for me." Edmund was breathless from his exertion.

Translation was difficult. She did not know the French word for thistle, and she could not make the words rhyme. When she had finished, Edmund said it must be very subtle, because it did not seem to make sense.

Marie tried to explain about Scotland and England

and the uprising for the Stuarts in which her father had fought. She sensed that he did not understand that either and was little interested in England's political situation, but he kept glancing at her with growing admiration. When she had finished, he nodded. "Then you are 'born.'"

"Born? Oh, you mean nobility? No. No, Edmund, and even if we were, my father was sent into exile. We had no money. Highlanders never do. My father had saved some before he died, but—" Somehow she did not want to tell him about Frank Goodacre. "But I used most of it to bury him. Recently I sold the concession to his land grant here, but that took a long time because it had to go through France. You see, I had nowhere to go after my parents died and very little money. Céline was kind to take me in, and I was—am—grateful to her, no matter what kind of house it is."

"I understand that, but such a place, Marie." He made a face. "And the danger of your becoming one of them."

"I would never do that."

"Mme. Céline takes money from me after I have been with you. Isn't that being like them?"

Marie's face burned. "I can see why you think so. But you are different, and with you it is different. Don't you understand?"

"I know you are lovely, and I do not mind that I must pay. And today, aha! There will be no pay for Madame."

"Is that why you asked me out?" She spoke teasingly, but he blushed.

"Not for that alone. I truly wanted your company. Most young ladies must be chaperoned and guarded as if they were jewels. I wanted to enjoy myself. With you I do enjoy myself. You do not giggle or simper or pretend. You are very womanly and lovely. The parasol casts a shadow on your face, yet still your face and eyes are luminous. You are like a painting. I am a tiny bit in love with you, Marie." He said it shyly.

"And I with you." She threw him a kiss, which he pretended to catch and put it on his own lips. Doing so, he rocked the pirogue dangerously.

"Look," he said. "That is the back of the Arnolie plantation. It fronts on St. John's Bayou. It's a large grant and only half cleared, but already he's talking about acquiring more land. After all, he has three daughters to provide with dowries."

"You seem to know a great deal about the Arnolies."

"They have been kind to me. It is pleasant to go to their house because my room"—he wrinkled his nose—"is rather unpleasant, and it is expensive to eat out, and tavern food—bah! You see, it is to my benefit to visit them. It is the same with all young unmarried men here, Marie. We compete for invitations and wives."

"Are you looking for a wife?"

"One must marry, Marie. But before I marry, I must establish myself. After that I shall think of marriage. I won't have to think very hard. I suspect I have found the wife I need."

"Is her name a secret?"

He laughed. "Yes, a secret. But I suspect she knows." He stopped to rest, leaning on the oars. Sluggish as the current was, the boat drifted backward. "Do you never think of marriage, Marie? What about your gentleman?"

"I never think of marrying him."

"I am glad. I don't approve of him and his arrangement with you."

"I had no choice."

"You would make a very fine wife, Marie. You are sympathetic and understanding and sensible and passionate and very, very beautiful."

"You'll turn my head with your flattery."

"It isn't flattery. You are all those things. All and more."

Now he will ask me, Marie thought.

Instead he spit on his hands and began to row again. "Mon Dieu, my arms ache. I hope we are nearly there."

Perhaps a pirogue was not a proper place to propose. Or Edmund was too shy. Perhaps she was expected to know from the things he had said. Perhaps it was her turn to say something, but she wasn't sure what to say.

"You–" She hesitated. "You will make a very fine husband, Edmund."

"Do you think so? I am a little young."

"Not at all too young."

"We *are* nearly there. The current is stronger."

The bayou widened and deepened. The tangle of moss-hung trees ended. Before them lay a shining lake, so vast it looked to Marie like an ocean.

"Oh, Edmund! It is glorious."

He glanced hastily over his shoulder, then smiled back at her. "It is, isn't it?"

"It's like floating in the sky." Marie trailed her hand in the water rippling the reflection of the clouds.

Edmund beached the pirogue and removed his shoes and hose before stepping out into the water. Then he lifted Marie out, swinging her in his arms, and planted a kiss on her mouth before he set her down. She gazed around in delight.

Spreading liveoaks, mulberry trees, wild figs and wild peaches, myrtle, and palmettos grew in profusion. Wildflowers bloomed down to the edge of the lake, and tall wild grass waved in the wind. It was like Eden.

"It's beautiful," Marie whispered. "I never dreamed any place could be so beautiful."

"Yes, it is beautiful. It's a huge grant. One of the best. A M. de Nemour holds the concession and, like a fool, does nothing with it. It's a pity. Such rich land and such a view. I wish it were mine. What I could do with it! Perhaps some day I'll be able to buy the grant from him. Here, can you carry the wine while I bring up the baskets?" He had not even noticed the start of surprise Marie gave at the mention of Henri's name.

Edmund led the way into a clearing. The lake spread out before them. "Here is where I'd build my house," Edmund said. "With wide galleries where I could sit in the evening and watch the color of the lake change in the sunset."

As Marie unpacked the baskets she wondered if Henri had the same idea, if he would ever give up the land. She broke the bread and spread it with the shrimp pâté Sheba had made for her, while Edmund opened the wine and poured it into pewter tassies. "I have to return them to the tavern. Don't let me lose them."

They toasted one another, they toasted the picnic, Lake Pontchartrain, and the pirogue. Edmund juggled cherries, trying to catch them in his mouth, then tossed them at Marie for her to catch. They washed the tassies in the lake, then waded in themselves, Marie holding her skirts high.

"What legs!" Edmund knelt in the water and kissed her knees, then stood up and embraced her, kissing her at such length they nearly toppled over. "Um, you taste of cherries. Marie, I must have you. Now! Do you know, you drive me mad?"

Mimi and Céline had been right after all. As Mimi had said, it was purer here, more innocent. "Where? Not in the pirogue."

"That tree. See how the Spanish beard grows down to the ground. Under it. No one can see us there."

The oak was old, wide-boled with low, spreading branches. The gray-green moss hung in heavy curtains. It was like a dim, secret room, green-lighted, sun-dappled, subtly fragrant. Birds sang, water whispered against the shore, and the moss swayed in the breeze.

Marie had not brought the cotton packing which Céline had taught her how to use or the thin silk sheaths for Edmund. But what did it matter? He had said that she was beautiful, that he had found the wife he needed. Nothing mattered but pleasing Edmund.

The sun was low beyond the lake when they awakened. Wild turkeys were roosting in the treetops, and the frogs answered their echoes across the water. The bayou was a dark tunnel, for the sun no longer reached through the trees. In the dim light rotting stumps and Spanish beard moving in the wind took on ominous shapes. The water, moving sluggishly over the white sand, held the dark reflections of the trees.

Marie did not sing this time. Neither of them spoke much, as if afraid to hear their own voices. It was a relief to emerge into the light of the open river, scarlet with sunset.

"It is not night after all," Edmund said. "You will be safe walking to Mme. Céline's alone."

"Of course." But she wished he could offer to walk with her. When they reached the levee, he handed her the basket and parasol and held her hand a moment before he let her go.

"Marie, thank you for making me so happy." He laughed. "I shall never forget you lying in our little room under the tree with your skirts spread out around you. You are an enchantress, Marie. What a wife you will be."

"Yes."

"Then, until soon!"

"Don't forget to return the tassies!"

She walked slowly through the town, swinging her basket. The streamers of sunset tinted the roofs, set flame to the cross on the cathedral.

Mimi met her at the door. "I can't wait to hear! Did he ask?"

"Not in so many words. But he said—oh, Mimi, the things he said made me sure. He will ask. I know it."

They caught one another's hands and whirled

around in a little dance. Blanche watched them and yawned. "So the little virgin will be leaving us, is that it?"

"I'll believe it when she walks out the door," Céline said.

Marie smiled at her. It was sad that they were so cynical, so jealous. If she were able, she would make each of them as happy as she was. Especially Mimi.

The next morning Marie and Sheba went to market. On the way Marie caught sight of Frank Goodacre supervising the unloading of bricks onto the levee.

"Wait here, Sheba. I want to speak to that man."

"Speak to him when he comes to the house."

"You think I want him to know I'm *there*?"

She left Sheba to select fruit from the slaves who had brought it in from the nearby plantations, and crossed the street. Frank Goodacre didn't recognize her until she spoke his name, then his eyes widened in surprise.

"Mary! Well, look at you! I heard you'd left the convent. I went there to see you, but the sisters didn't know where you'd gone. Back to your foster family, they said, but they didn't know their name. Surprised me some. I thought they knew everything there was to know about their girls, especially since they must have placed you."

"They don't know. It was kept from them deliberately." She hurried on because a frown of puzzlement was gathering on his face, and she didn't want to give him the chance to question her. "Mr. Goodacre, you too have changed. You look quite prosperous these days. I hear you are in business."

"That's so, Mary. Bricks. Bricks for ballast. Bricks for building."

"I know too where you got the money to go into the brick business." She said it quietly and let the words lie there.

He reddened and bluffed, "I'm a partner of M. de Nemour. It was lucky for me—"

"Lucky for you you had my father's money to offer him in partnership."

He gulped and took off his hat, then wiped the sweat from his forehead with his sleeve. "Mary, that's not so, Mary. I wouldn't steal from a child. That's all you were. A child."

"I found the money box and my father's accounts. I learned how much a burial costs."

"Burials cost dear when it's fever. Most men won't touch fever victims. There was just enough money to cover the coffins and the burial."

"That is a lie, Mr. Goodacre."

"Mary—" She had grown beautiful, and the wind off the river flattened her dress against her the way it had done when he had stood beside her at the grave. Then he had wanted to touch her budding breasts. Now he wanted to do more than that. It was strange that this cold-eyed, haughty little girl could arouse him in that way. "Mary, there may have been a little money left over, but we were that poor and—"

"I want that money, Mr. Goodacre. You aren't poor now, and I need it."

"It wasn't that much, Mary."

"Perhaps you would like me to tell Mrs. Goodacre of your visits to Mme. Céline's establishment."

His jaw fell. "How would you know about that?"

"You just told me."

"That's trickery, Mary. Trickery and blackmail."

"I know. But I want the money. I want to invest it. I have to think of my future, Mr. Goodacre."

He sighed and gnawed at his lip. "How soon do you want it?"

"Tomorrow."

"That's not giving me much time, Mary. Most business here is run on letters of credit."

"I know all about the letters of credit. I also know there is some cash in the colony. You have had more than two years to repay me. I think you never would have. You thought I didn't know about the money."

"Where shall I bring it?"

"Here. Tomorrow. This same time."

He glowered at her as if she were a moccasin he feared and wanted to kill. "I'll bring it."

That night she told Edmund she was going to give him a sum toward starting his warehouse. "Not give, exactly. It will be a loan."

"But, my darling, are you so well paid by your other patron that you can do that?"

"It is money my parents left me. I'll have it tomorrow. So you must come again tomorrow night."

"It will be late. The Arnolies are having another dinner. You would think they feared to be alone with one another."

"The family with the dairymaid daughters?"

"The same."

Marie put her hand under the pillow and touched the gris-gris. "You won't be marrying one of them?"

"I'd as soon marry one of their slaves."

"And you will come to me afterward?"

"You are like opium. I can't stay away."

I will have him yet, Mary told the gris-gris.

With the partial repayment Frank Goodacre had given her, what Henri had given her secretly, and what she had earned from Céline, Marie was able to give Edmund two thousand livres. She kept back a small sum for herself, feeling guilty that she was not giving it all to him, but there was an element of caution in her, a Scottish thrift, that made her dread being utterly penniless.

She and Edmund, love-making done, sat cross-legged on the bed, and she solemnly presented him with the money. He kissed her, counted it, kissed her again, and recounted it. Then he asked for a bit of paper, on which he wrote an IOU.

"I don't need that."

"But you do. And I shall pay you profits as well when they begin to roll in."

She folded the paper and put it in the money box. When she came back to the bed, he drew her to him and kissed her. "I love you, Marie. I'll never forget what you have done for me. You've done what my own father would not do. How strange it is. What a strange way to have laid the basis for my fortune." He looked wonderingly around the room. "Nor shall I ever forget this room. Nor you, my darling."

"You sound as if you're bidding me farewell."

"No, no. But tomorrow I shall be busy with this." He tapped the money. "My business may go on until quite late. Besides, I am exhausted. Give me a night to rest so I can make you happy in the way you like me to make you happy. You are inexhaustible, Marie, but I—any man—must revitalize."

"The night after, then?"

"The night after."

For three nights she waited. Each night she saw Céline's house go dark, heard the last footsteps on the walk, watched the moon rise and grow white with the dawn. Still Edmund did not come. She invented excuses for him which did not convince her. The third night she wept for him and cursed herself for having been a fool. She remembered the dairymaid Arnolie daughters. She touched the gris-gris and prayed to it. Then, feeling guilty, she knelt beside the bed and prayed to God.

Blanche mocked the dark hollows under her eyes. Mimi whispered, "Did you quarrel?"

"I gave him money to invest," Marie whispered back. "He is busy."

"*Sacré Dieu!* Take, take, take and take again, but never give! Once you give, you lose them."

"Don't tell Céline."

"She would kill you. She is very stern about such matters. Gave him money?" She shook her head. "Poor Marie."

"He didn't ask for it."

"That kind doesn't have to ask. That kind, women always give to them."

"Was I a fool then?"

Mimi looked at her with her head on one side and made a *moue*. "Yes. But you are inexperienced. It's to be expected. Especially with one like that. I should have seen it coming and warned you."

"It wouldn't have done any good."

"No, that is no doubt true. You wouldn't have believed me. Never mind, *ma pauvre*, he'll return. He must have some honor. The best of them get the itch sooner or later."

Only Céline made no comment, studying Marie through narrowed eyes, almost, Marie thought, as if she suspected the truth.

"The gris-gris isn't working," Marie said to Sheba.

"You don't know that. It works underground the way the alligator swims under the water. Be patient."

The fourth night he came, his green eyes sparkling with mischief, as hot-blooded and impatient and enthusiastic as ever. He didn't seem to hear Marie's wistful, "I have missed you." He brimmed with self-importance.

"It is all going as I planned. Now that I have money, real money, in my hands, half the men in the colony are eager to finance me. There will be not only a warehouse, Marie, but possibly a store. Edmund Lanney is a very important man. A man to be reckoned with."

He stayed only a short time, and his love-making was like a duty performed to satisfy himself rather than an adoration of Marie. "I have business meetings tomorrow. I must be brilliant, and that I cannot be if I am sated as a bee in a honey jar."

Would he have come oftener if she had not given him the money? Marie wondered. But she was content he had come at all, and it pleased her to know that she was the power behind his success.

The next day a brief note arrived from Henri saying he was well and would be joining her that evening.

All day Sheba cleaned the cabin "of *him*," jerked from the bed the sheets on which Edmund had lain, to wash and boil them and bleach them in the sun. Marie bathed and rubbed herself with perfumed oil, and Céline sent chilled wine and brandy to her house along with a tray of cala cakes.

"What if Edmund comes?" Marie asked.

"He will be turned away. He has known all along you have a patron."

Henri was thin and yellow with fever. His hands trembled when he lifted his wine glass, and he closed his eyes as he drank, as if it were painful. He asked Marie to sit at his feet, and he stroked her hair and made little move to take her.

"It is good to have you here. I dreamed of you in my delirium. Always it was to come here and find you gone. Have I wronged you, Marie? Did I sin, taking you?"

What could she answer? "I suppose it would have happened sooner or later, living in this house. I should never have stayed here."

"You do not regret me?"

"Of course I don't." For if she hadn't stayed here, she wouldn't have met Edmund.

"And you forgive me?"

"I forgive you." *I do not forgive Céline, but a part of the money I gave Edmund came from you,* she thought. *Edmund, did you come tonight? Edmund, Edmund . . .* It was all she could do as Henri embraced her to keep from crying out Edmund's name.

One morning when the ground steamed from a rain which had fallen at dawn, filling the air with smoky humidity, Marie sat listlessly, attempting to eat her breakfast. The smell of the hot rice cakes fried in grease turned her stomach. The musky odor of the melon made her head ache. The wine soured in her stomach. She felt tired and heavy-eyed, although she had been alone for two nights. Henri had said jokingly that the one night he had spent with Marie had set him back two weeks in his recovery. He came every afternoon to take a glass of wine with her, but there was nothing more between them, and she was glad. Edmund's visits were infrequent. He was busy with negotiations conducted at apparently interminable dinners.

Céline entered the house without knocking and surveyed Marie, arms akimbo. "So! It is true, what Sheba said. Damn that Lanney!"

Marie stared at her. How could Sheba have known about the money unless Mimi had told her? And Mimi had promised.

"I suppose you were so moon-struck, so love-drunk, you did none of the things I taught you to do."

"What are you talking about?"

"Sheba said you were pregnant, and I need only to look at you to see she is right. The eyes. The pinched look. The color. Toying with your food. It does not taste so good, eh? Christ's bones, what a little fool you are!"

Marie's mind reeled. Pregnant? It could be true. It must be true. What a goose she was not to have guessed. A child of her own. To love. To be hers.

She smiled at Céline, who did not return the smile.

"What in the name of the devil am I to tell Henri?"

"The truth." That I am pregnant and shall be married to Edmund.

"The devil take the truth! We shall tell him nothing until we approach that damnable Lanney. You are so convinced he'll have you, let us see if he'll have you now. I'll send for him at once."

"You'll do nothing of the kind. I'll tell him myself the next time he comes. Let me handle it, Céline. It is my affair."

"Pah! I let you handle it in the first place, and look at you."

"It will be all right. And I am happy."

"What of Henri? He will not be happy. He will be devastated." Céline glared at her. "And what of me?"

"You shall be the baby's secret godmother."

"It will have to be secret. Lanney and his big business affairs would never tolerate me openly. Oh, your friend is very busy now, Marie. He has found a backer for his damned warehouse. He preens himself. He struts. He tells everyone he will end by owning New Orleans. Not unless he makes a brilliant marriage, he won't. He has the brain of a cock rooster."

"How do you know so much?"

"Men talk, little fool, and Céline listens. That is why I know he will not marry you. There isn't a mother of a daughter in New Orleans who wouldn't like to make a match with Lanney. He's turned every female's head and convinced the men that the Lanney money in France is behind him."

"What a disappointment for the mothers when he marries me." And if she could tell those men whose money really was behind him, they would not be so impressed.

Céline's lips curled. "On the day he marries you I shall weep for them." She banged the door behind her.

"She is jealous," Marie said to Flora. "Will you be jealous when I have the baby, Flora? If it is a little girl, you will have a new playmate." Marie took the doll from the shelf and rocked it against her breast, wishing she already held the child which was barely started within her and that its pink lips sucked at her breast.

That night she cradled Edmund in much the same way, seeing in his face the face of their child. After they made love, not once but twice, Edmund looked down at her in wonder. "You are more magnificent than ever. Always you are a surprise to me. Every time is different."

"How was this time different?"

"It was as if—let me think—as if you were a woman deeply in love."

"I am in love."

"And your gentleman, is he in love as well?"

"How should I know that?"

"When you say to someone, 'I love you,' it is customary that they admit their love as well."

"I cannot tell him that I am in love with you." She touched his smile and was startled to feel it fade beneath her fingertips.

"It is with me you are in love?" He fell back and stared at the ceiling.

"Of course. Why else would I have given you the money?"

"I thought because you had a head for business."

"I hope I have that, and love besides. Edmund, I am pregnant." A cold foreboding chilled her where she imagined the child lay.

"*Sacré Dieu!* By me or by your gentleman?"

"By you. The day of our picnic. My gentleman has been ill and has not been here. There has been only you."

"Does Mme. Céline know?"

"Yes."

"And she can do something? Perform the little operation?"

"I do not want 'the little operation.'"

"You want the child? You must be mad."

"Don't you want the child?"

"Want the child! Want the child! What in the name of God would I do with it? I could never acknowledge it. And I suppose you would expect me to pay for its upkeep, its schooling, give it a little dowry if it is female, take it into my business if it is a male. Want the child? Do I want my foot in a trap? Do I want a stone around my neck? Do I want, in short, a bastard? No! No! No!"

"It would not be a bastard if we married."

He sprang out of bed, leaping halfway across the

room, and stared at her as if she were crazy. He hugged his arms about his chest as if to keep himself from beating her.

"Marry! What an idea!"

"But you said to me you had found the wife you needed. You said—I recall the words exactly—'What a wife you will be.' You said I made you happy."

"Yes, yes, yes. I said those things. I *have* found the wife I need. You *do* make me happy, but not in the way you mean. Happy in my body, joyous at the way you make love. The man who has you for a wife won't need to go whoring. He'll have the perfect woman in his bed. Your gentleman trained you well."

"But you said you loved me."

"In a way, yes. A man always loves his mistress for the pleasure she gives him, and in a way you've been my mistress, I suppose. But marry! I cannot marry a whore, Marie. Think of my family, of my future. Think of my business associates. Think of my position in New Orleans."

Marie sat up shivering with anger. "Think! I shall think about you every time I look at the child. I shall think what a fool I was to love a despicable, strutting, conceited cock of a man. No wonder your father sent you to the New World. He was ashamed of having such a vain, thimble-headed son. No wonder he does not trust you. You have no honor! You must sponge off whores to make your way. Yes, whores, whores, whores. One day I shall not even lower myself to spit on you!"

"A little convent schooling does not make a lady of a whore."

Fury such as she had never felt before mounted within her. As she got out of bed the gris-gris rolled from under the pillow, and she flung it at him. It broke open, spilling feathers and herbs and dog ordure.

"I am not a whore, but you are a whoremonger! It was whoremongering that got you the money to build your damned warehouse, and I want that money back. *Now!*"

Edmund was scrambling into his clothes, his face contorted with anger. "Bitch! I can't return your money. It is invested. I haven't a centime to call my own. Because you were so careless as to get pregnant, you are determined to ruin me."

"It is you who are determined to ruin me."

"Ruin a whore? It is impossible! I laugh to think of it."

"Bring the money tomorrow, Edmund. At noon tomorrow."

"I cannot, I tell you. The ship I sent to France for M. Arnolie's furniture was wrecked."

"Only a fool would have sent it out in hurricane season. But you are a fool. Bring . . . me . . . my . . . money!"

"I'll bring the militia to close down this house."

"You do and I'll go to M. Arnolie and tell him where you got the money to build your warehouse and outfit a ship."

"You are a shameless slut!" He jerked open the door. "I rue the day I ever set eyes on you."

"You'll pay for those words, Edmund Lanney," she screamed after him, then fell to the floor sobbing.

It was there Céline found her, helped her to her feet and to her bed.

"So, the bastard wants no part of you? He threw the money at my feet and slammed out of the house as if the devil were at his heels. A less practical woman would have thrown the money after him. We don't need his kind."

"You were right, Céline. To him I am nothing. He does not even want the child. He said you could perform an operation. Can you?"

Céline swore under her breath. "He would have you risk that?" Her dark eyes blazed with anger. "I could, but I will not. There is too much danger of infection."

"What am I to do?"

"Marry Henri." Marie started to protest, but Céline hurried on. "He will believe you if you tell him it is his. I will tell him what a little fool you are—and you are, Marie—not to have followed my instructions. He has nothing to lose by marrying you, and he has pride enough to outstare anyone who questions what he does."

"Will he want to marry me?"

Céline shrugged. "That is the question. We can try."

"And do I want to be married to him?" Marie spoke more to herself than to Céline.

Céline rose and readjusted her breasts over her corselet. "Be practical. What will become of you if you stay here? Sooner or later, as Blanche said, there will be another man, and then another, and another. What about the child? Do you want it to grow up in a nest of whores? Think of the future, Marie. It would be wise to marry Henri whether you want him or not."

There was little sleep for Marie that night. The dull pain of sorrow and anger, the humiliation of Edmund's rejection tortured her. Over and over she repeated the words he had hurled at her like poisoned darts. To him she was a whore, and it was true. She had said she wouldn't take his money, but she had taken it when Céline had brought it to her. She had given it and more to him with her love. He had accepted it with what she now knew was contempt.

A whore, yes, and an idiot to believe what she wished to believe. It would be better to risk the operation than to live with the truth, even if death robbed her of her revenge on Frank Goodacre and Edmund. Better to risk the operation than to bear a child who would remind her of Edmund and the fool she had been. Better to risk the operation.

As the church bell began to toll noon a black boy who had been loitering on the banquette in front of Céline's stood up, stretched, and before the note of twelve rapped at the door.

Céline gaped at him and started to say, "We do not serve Negroes, and furthermore you are too young," when he thrust an envelope into her hands and with a sly grin and an obscene gesture skipped away.

The envelope was addressed to Marie. Céline took it to her and waited for Marie to open it.

"It's from Lanney, isn't it?"

Marie nodded.

"Perhaps he has changed his mind."

"I would not have him if he had. I know what it is. It's something he promised to me."

Céline raised the black crescents of her brows. "Then no doubt it is nothing but paper. Worthless."

Marie was determined not to open the packet in front of Céline, but Céline was equally determined not to leave until she had satisfied her curiosity. Finally Marie shrugged and broke the seal.

A few crumpled bills were wrapped in a letter of credit along with a new IOU and a scrap of paper on which was scrawled, *This is the best I can do on such notice. You'll have your money and your pound of flesh, but you'll have to stew for it.*

Céline laughed scornfully. "I suspected as much. I suspected when he suddenly had enough money to talk big and brag about his importance. I knew he had been to Henri, who turned him down. I knew Arnolie, who is courting him as a son-in-law, had nothing but paper to offer. But you, *ma petite folle,* had cash in a pretty little box and Lanney between your legs. And you gave away both the money and the honey pot."

"Céline, I have decided to risk the operation."

"The devil you will. I'll not perform it. Henri will marry you. You'll see."

It was Céline who broke the news to Henri. She had calculated carefully how best to do it and decided if she herself seemed displeased it would throw his sympathy to Marie.

When he called two evenings after Edmund's flight, Céline detained him before he went to Marie.

"Sit down a moment, my friend. I have some unfortunate news."

Henri eyed her speculatively but did not speak.

"The little fool—but wait. You must understand, I instructed her carefully. I gave the best advice. The most foolproof methods. I should have guessed that, being young, she would be careless. She did not always—perhaps she found it more exciting, more stimulating, not to—"

Henri frowned. "What are you trying to tell me?"

"The evening you were here after your illness she admits she did not bother to take precautions. The short of it is she is pregnant."

Henri laughed and wiped his brow with his handkerchief. "Could you not have come right out with it instead of trying to excuse yourself? One would think you had never known a pregnancy before."

"Oh, I have known them. The house in Paris was full of children, miserable, unwanted little brats, and nothing for them to do but to follow in their mothers' footsteps. But you did not bargain for a pregnant calf. It will ruin your pleasure, bring the bargain to an end." Céline gestured hopelessly. "I can only apologize. And tomorrow, if she will allow it, I will do the operation. If she will not allow it, Sheba can drug her with wine, and when she wakens, *voilà*, no baby."

"Name of God, woman, hold your tongue for a moment and let me think. No. No operation. Not even if she wishes it."

"Oh, but she does not," Céline lied. "She is pleased."

"I too am pleased."

"Christ! I see it makes you feel like a man to have made a baby. I know that type, but I never thought that you, Henri—"

"Do you think she will marry me?"

"But that is not necessary. You would not wish to marry her."

"She is charming, intelligent, a constant pleasure to me. I will see her now, and tomorrow I'll see the priest. It must be done quickly. I wonder I didn't think of it long ago instead of leaving her here for you to turn into a whore."

"I would not."

"You know damned well you would. You wouldn't be able to resist it."

"You insult me."

"Nonsense. I am a realist, just as you are. And now I shall see Marie."

The filthy bills and the note Edmund had sent her had worked like a purge. His calling her a whore had stung and sickened her. Had he brought the money himself, had he apologized for the paltry amount, she might have softened. Not softened enough to love him again—that she would never do—but softened sufficiently to understand that his vanity and ambition had led him to act the way he had. As it was, if he expected her to demand a pound of flesh, that was precisely what she would do. That and take a revenge so subtle he would never forget her or what he had done to her.

To be married to Henri and gain respectability was the first step. So when Henri arrived, took her into his arms, told her how delighted he was with the news, and begged her to marry him, she responded to his embrace and accepted him.

She was able to make love to him as passionately as she had ever done with Edmund, as if by doing so it would make the child Henri's. But all the time it was as if her mind and body were separate entities, and the real Marie was someplace else watching the pretense.

They agreed that the wedding should be private. Marie did not even want Céline.

"Céline will be furious," Henri said.

"She will understand."

"What do you want for a wedding gift?"

"Sheba."

Henri laughed. "That *will* make Céline furious. She isn't likely to get another slave. Too few are being brought in, and the planters need them."

"But they can't pay cash, and Céline can. She'll manage, if I know Céline."

"I'll bargain with her," Henri agreed. "You are very determined, Marie. You will be good for me. My mother would approve of your firm hand."

Marie had never thought of Henri as having a mother and father. It put him in quite a different light.

"What is she like, your mother?"

"Papa calls her his *petite abeille*, his little bee."

"She stings?"

"Maman? Never. She buzzes, but she is as gentle as a butterfly. She has wanted me to marry. She said it would give me tranquility of mind. She is right. Already I feel happier and at peace. Marie, you are my angel, my good fortune. I will do everything I can to make you happy."

Tears gathered in her eyes. She did not deserve such love. She had betrayed him and was marrying him only because there was no alternative. But no one had been so kind to her since her parents had died. She would do all she could to make him happy, and she promised herself he would never know the child was not his. Yet she knew it was a weapon which she, or even Edmund, might use in anger.

The next day she packed her few possessions into a basket and with Sheba following, the basket balanced on her head, set out for Henri's house.

Céline stood in the doorway to watch them go, crying unrestrainedly. Mimi too had wept and laughed and kissed Marie and wished her luck. Blanche had pouted, and Alixe had said Marie was a small loss since she was such exclusive property.

"But I shall see you all again," Marie promised.

"No, no, Marie. It would not be proper. But don't forget us."

Clouds wrinkled and curled across the sky. Their reflections floated on the river. The wind was so gentle it scarcely lifted the dust. An old Indian woman hawking wildflowers thrust a bunch of blue lilies at Marie, who started to brush past but then stopped and gave the woman a few coins and took the flowers. A bride should have a bouquet.

An open cart came slowly toward them. Marie looked up to see Edmund at the riens, and at his side, leaning possessively against him, a young lady. His eyes were startled when he saw Marie, but before he could turn away, she nodded and smiled a greeting. His face flamed, and the young lady looked from Marie to Edmund and back again.

Sheba laughed. "She's asking who you are. I hear her plain."

"You have sharp ears. But your gris-gris didn't work, Sheba."

"It worked. You got him. In your belly."

"Don't ever let M. Henri know."

"I'd sooner cut out my tongue. He won't know, and I say it's a good thing the gris-gris worked as it did. That M. Lanney wouldn't have bought me from Céline, because he wouldn't have had the money. And if it weren't for the baby, M. Henri wouldn't be wedding you, and the first thing you know you'd be no better than them back there. Don't you believe the gris-gris didn't work. It worked. It knew better than you what was right for you. You're going to be rich, and you're going to be happy, and that M. Lanney, he is going to be neither."

"How do you know that?"

"Because he defied the gris-gris."

They were married at noon. In one of his trunks Henri had found some lavender tissue silk with a border of fleur-de-lis worked in gold thread. From this Sheba fashioned a garment more like a toga than a dress, but there was no time for sewing anything more elaborate. The veil was of the same material, and Marie carried the lilies she had bought from the Indian woman.

Henri was enchanted and gazed at her as if she were a goddess. Marie too was pleased. It seemed right that her life as Henry's wife should be completely different from her former life and that it should begin with a fancy dress that transformed her into someone totally new.

As the priest raised his hand in benediction she remembered Edmund's face turning scarlet because she had nodded to him. If they had met at any other time, under any other circumstances, it might be Edmund standing beside her now. She looked up at Henri, wishing she loved him as she had thought she loved Edmund. He smiled at her and gave her hand a reassuring squeeze.

Then the ceremony was over, and he was kissing her. She was Marie de Nemour. Until death.

To Be a Wife

Frank and Faith Goodacre did not talk much these days. When Frank attempted to make conversation, Faith answered with shrugs, sniffs, and grunts. Gradually he stopped trying.

After supper was cleared away, he sat at the table with his two elder children and studied. They were learning reading, writing, numbers, and French. If a man was going to succeed in this country, he had to know these things. Ambition had Frank in its grip as firmly as any drug could have had. The more he learned the more he wished to learn; the more he succeeded the more he wished to succeed. He wanted to see every building in New Orleans built with his bricks. Then he'd move on to Natchez and Mobile and "brick them." He wanted a solid business to pass on to his sons, so they had to be transformed from scrawny, ragged, ignorant children into well-bred, clear-thinking youths who would carry on what he'd begun. He would see to it that they married well. There wouldn't be a mother in New Orleans who wouldn't be willing to have one of his sons wed her daughter. None of his boys would end up with a common, sour woman like Faith.

It was strange about Faith. There she sat at the far end of the room, not mending though their clothes needed mending, not scrubbing or cleaning or doing anything but sitting there, watching the boys do their lessons with eyes full of contempt. Sometimes Frank thought she would rather be back in the bug-infested shack, living from hand to mouth, than where they were now.

She sneered at his new clothes, she sneered at his attempts to speak properly and deliberately answered him as ungrammatically as possible just to annoy him. Most of all she sneered at his learning French. "Isn't your own tongue good enough for you?"

He had learned to ignore her, ceased to care what she thought, no longer made tentative fumblings when they were in bed. One day they'd have an even larger house, and he'd have his own bedroom. Then perhaps she'd be satisfied, and he would be free of her and her rank-smelling body, which still excited him for all their mutual contempt.

Tonight his mind wasn't on French grammar. He stared at the pages with unseeing eyes.

"Pa." Charlotte prodded him with her slate. "It's your turn to read."

He rose from the table. "You take my turn, Lottie. I have to speak to your ma—*ta mère*—about something."

He dragged his stool across the room to the corner where Faith sat. He faced her, elbows resting on his knees, and spoke softly so the children wouldn't hear.

"Something happened today, Faithy. I know you don't care a centime for what happens in the town. You'd as soon see it flattened by a hurricane and have us go back to scraping dirt for a living. But I think you'd like knowing about this." She wouldn't like it. He was telling her to taunt and punish her, but also because he had to share the news with someone.

"I went to see M. de Nemour today."

Faith sniffed.

"When I went into the room, there was a lady there."

A flicker in Faith's eyes betrayed her interest.

"First off I didn't recognize her. Her hair was done up, and she was in a silk dress and fancy shoes—mules, the Frenchies call them. Even when de Nemour introduced her as his wife, it took me a minute to see who it was. You'd never guess who it was, Faith. Mary Macleod! Marie de Nemour she is now, and you'd never know she'd been that pinched-faced child we took in when the fever carried off her parents."

"*Mary?*"

"The same."

"I don't believe you have met my wife, M. Goodacre," de Nemour had said to him. "My dearest, this is Mr. Goodacre, with whom I do some business in bricks."

Marie had tilted her head and smiled. Frank knew mockery when he saw it. "But I do know M. Goodacre. He was a"—she had hesitated ever so slightly, but Frank had caught it—"a friend of my father. He arranged the burial for me. Isn't that true, M. Goodacre?"

She even pronounced his name the French way, and butter wouldn't have melted in her mouth. A person would think she hadn't been hounding him, threatening him, blackmailing him to get back her money. How the devil she had met de Nemour and got him to marry her was something Frank would give fifty sols to know.

"I had no idea you were acquainted," de Nemour had said. "We must have a glass of wine together for the sake of old friendships."

"Where'd she meet the likes of him?" Faith asked.

"Maybe the foster family that took her in knew him. She's pretty enough to have turned his head."

Faith sniffed again. "Then she's changed since we had her. It wasn't beauty got her a husband. It was that look. I told you she had it. The kind'd rub up against a man."

To Frank's way of thinking de Nemour was damned lucky to have her rubbing against him. She was a woman now. A sensuous woman. It must have been marriage that had changed her. She was different from the way she'd been that day she had come threatening him. That day she had seemed like a petulant, angry child who would stamp her foot and burst into tears at any moment. Now, by God, he sensed she'd as soon spit on him as not. He'd pay, oh, yes, he'd pay rather than risk what she might expose him to if he did not. He forced his thoughts back to the scene in de Nemour's house.

"It's not the same now she's there. The house," he added, seeing Faith's bewilderment. "I suppose it's her doing. The bed's been moved out. And the place doesn't stink of hides and tobacco anymore. De Nemour said it's all been moved to Lanney's new warehouse. Fool thing to've done. The warehouse is only half finished. I don't suppose he means to ship through Lanney. That lad's not learned enough yet, though he's talked somebody into outfitting a ship for him. I doubt it'll ever get across the Atlantic. Might as well be a pirogue." He was thinking aloud now. He had not admitted to de Nemour that Lanney had talked Frank into selling him the bricks for the warehouse on credit. It was a big debt, and with Mary—Marie—bleeding him . . .

Marie had excused herself after drinking her wine, leaving Frank and de Nemour to settle down to business, with Frank wondering the whole time how much de Nemour knew. Didn't wives tell their husbands everything? If she had told de Nemour about her father's money, he had given no sign of it.

Maybe she hadn't told him. Tight-lipped, vindictive little bitch. Where the devil had she met de Nemour? What family had taken her in? She might have connections that could make or break the likes of Frank Goodacre. He must tread as gently as if he were crossing a stretch of swampland where moccasins with their white, poisonous mouths lurked in the underbrush.

"You must admit the man has improved," Henri said after Frank's visit. "He speaks almost correctly, and he has learned to wear clean clothes."

"His accent is atrocious. I don't know how you tolerate him. I will never forget what those people did to me."

"Marie, what the Goodacres did no longer matters." He sounded righteous to his own ears. "Isn't it better that they did not take you in? You said the woman hated you. You would have been hungry, ragged, despised. Céline would never have found you. *I* would never have found you. By now you'd have married some common soldier to escape them, be living hand to mouth, carrying his child . . ."

Instead of Edmund's child. Edmund. His ghost haunted their bed. She tried to imagine it was Edmund she embraced; Edmund, not Henri, she kissed. But her imagination could not supplant one with the other. They were too different.

Edmund was lost except in nightmares when, his face contorted with anger, he shouted, "Whore, whore, whore," so loudly that it awakened her. She would lie there burning with hate and shame until morning came, soft and reassuring.

She tried to love Henri. There was no denying that she enjoyed their physical relationship. Together, but separately, he and Edmund had fully awakened her body, just as Céline and Mimi had taught her to be unashamed of physical passion. But Henri had yet to touch her heart as Edmund had done.

If he knew she did not love him, he pretended not to. He was entertaining, carefree, and adoring. Her pleasure was his sole concern. She had but to wish for something and it was hers. Only a woman of stone could have failed to respond to such kindness, and stone Marie was not. She even found it difficult to maintain her resentment of his having bought the child Mary from Céline. It was all so long ago.

The first weeks of their marriage were spent remodeling Henri's house. Originally he had eaten, managed his affairs, and slept all in one room. Now he had the partitions removed between two of the four ground floor rooms, creating two large rooms only. The back one, facing the garden, they made into a dining room and furnished it with a cypress wood table and straw-bottomed chairs made by a local carpenter. Sheba sanded and waxed them until they shone. A slatted door opened out onto a trellis passageway into the garden, the kitchen, and the slave houses.

The loft had been windowless. The steep roof absorbed and trapped the heat. It was here the tobacco, pelts, and spices had been stored. Even after windows had been opened onto newly built galleries, and the walls and floors had been limed, the rank odors lingered. A tobacco stain kept reappearing on the floor like a bad conscience and finally had to be covered with a Turkish carpet. The elaborate bed and armoire were moved to the new room, and a lacquered screen across one corner formed a dressing room for Marie. Here she bathed in an enameled hip bath, kept her few treasures in an ivory-inlaid table, and dressed her hair before a silver filigree mirror inlaid with coral and lapis.

There appeared to be no end to the treasures contained in the great chests Henri had brought from France.

"I can produce almost anything but a carriage and horses to draw it," Henri said, smiling when Marie marveled at their contents.

When the house was finished, there was nothing more to absorb Marie's time. She felt shy and awkward in Henri's company and could think of little to say to him. It was like living with a stranger.

Henri was not the only stranger. She was a stranger to herself. She studied her face in the silver-framed mirror, saying, "You are Marie." The hyacinth blue eyes mocked her, and a voice in her mind said, "You are Mary Macleod."

She was two people in one body. Mary, still a child, but a child of lost innocence, a child who was woman enough to be carrying a child. A woman, cold-hearted and vengeful. And Marie, compliant, smiling, obedient, and passionate in bed, beloved.

Mary had work to do against her enemies. To accommodate her life to Henri's was one thing. He was her weapon and her shield, just as Marie was Mary's mask. Mary was confined to a private part of Marie's mind where she brooded, remembered, and schemed. Marie set about the business of being Henri's wife.

It was lonely at first. She missed Mimi and Céline. Henri thought it improper that she should see them.

"It wasn't improper for you to go to Céline's before we were married," Marie said.

"That is quite a different matter."

Marie wondered why it was different. A few days later she was returning from market with Sheba when she saw a familiar figure hurrying across the Place d'Armes toward the church.

"There's Mlle. Mimi, going to pray for her sins," Sheba said.

"You go on, Sheba. I want to speak to her."

"What will Monsieur say?"

"He won't know. Anyway, he can't object to my going to church."

"He doesn't know you got a sin to pray for." Sheba laughed soundlessly.

Mimi was kneeling near the rear of the church, her face in her hands, whispering to her beads as she passed them through her fingers. Marie knelt beside her and whispered, "Mimi."

Head still bowed, Mimi lowered her hands enough to glance sideways. "Marie! Oh, I am glad to see you. Are you alone?"

"Yes. I saw you come into the church, and I followed."

"I am so glad! I think about you often. Are you happy? Is marriage nice?"

"I'm lonely. I miss you."

"Oh." Mimi sounded disappointed. "You should not be lonely with M. Henri. He is so lovely."

"I miss you. And Céline."

"Don't you have friends? Other nice wives?"

"No. Henri said all his friends left when the government changed, and there is no one here he cares about."

"Then he must be lonely too. But no, he has you."

It was like a conspiracy, the two of them kneeling, whispering.

"Sometimes I feel like his prisoner."

"Oh, Marie! Isn't he kind to you?"

"Very kind. Too kind. And the house is nice. I wish you could see it. I have my own dressing room with a beautiful little bath with cupids in blue ribbons chasing one another around the rim, and a silver mirror—"

"It's like Versailles!"

"Not quite, Mimi. How is Céline?"

"The same as always. She doesn't change. I wish you could come to see us."

"He won't allow it."

"*He* came often enough when you were there. Does he think Céline will sell you again?"

"I don't know what he thinks. Oh, Mimi, we must meet sometime, someplace where we can talk."

"Where? Every soldier in the militia knows me, to say nothing of—" Mimi tossed her head, then lowered it again hastily and rattled her beads. "Of course I could wear a veil and wrap up a pillow like a baby and sit on a bench and look like a nice wife. Should I make the pillow a little bonnet to wear?"

They stifled their giggles.

"I'll send a note by Sheba saying when I can get out and where to meet. I'd better go now." They squeezed one another's hands. "Oh—Mimi, has there been anything from Edmund?"

"I don't think so. Céline hasn't mentioned it. *Au revoir,* Marie."

When Marie got home, she found Henri waiting for her. He had brought a cypress wood cradle which he had had made as a surprise. The headboard was beautifully carved with a thistle and a fleur-de-lis encircled by a heart.

A month of thunderstorms followed, drenching the shallow land. The bayous rose, seeped across the fields. The garden flooded, and mud oozed up between the boards of the banquettes. Between rains the earth steamed, and the heat was oppressive, enervating.

While they were confined by the weather the beginning of a companionship grew between Marie and Henri. He taught her chess and the dances of the French court, and he read aloud to her while she hemmed sheets for the cradle. In spite of trying to remain aloof, she felt herself taking root in this house, easing into Henri's style of life, absorbing his contentment.

"It's your condition," Sheba said when Marie told her. "You nest-make when you carry a child."

"It's the heat," Marie said. "I never noticed it before I got pregnant. Everything sticks to me. It's hot all the time. I can't sleep."

There were days when Marie didn't bother to dress but lounged in the negligées Henri had had made for her, "after the French fashion."

His own sack amused Marie, but it suited him in a way his white silk hose and red-heeled shoes and ruffled shirts did not. "You look like a Turkoman," Marie teased. "Soon you'll be wanting a harem."

"I have a harem, all in one woman. As for my dress, it's far more sensible in this climate than brocaded vests and knee breeches. You should be glad I don't go around in nothing but paint and a string like the Indians. That's the real dress for this heat."

"Isn't Paris hot in summer?"

"Stifling. The gutters reek, and all the perfumes from Gras couldn't cover the stench of sweating bodies at court. We go to the country in summer. The old stones of the château are cool, and the river reflects patterns on the ceilings of the rooms."

"Are you homesick? You never talk about why you left France."

"Sometimes I miss it. Not so much now as I did at first. You have made this place tolerable." He frowned. "I could lie and tell you I was one of those poor damned unfortunates kidnapped by the bandits as we called the Mississippi thugs. They rounded up anyone incautious enough to be on the streets at night. The truth is, I was asked—forced—to leave. I was handed a *lettre de cachet.*"

"But why?"

"How can I explain it to you? What I did was nothing worse than others have done. I took a mistress. In France it's the alternative to divorce. No gentleman expects his wife to be faithful, just as no lady expects her husband to be. My mistress had been married at thirteen, through family arrangement, to a man of sixty. Unfortunately he expected her to confine her attentions to him alone. There's a saying in Paris: He wanted to deny the light of her sun to more capable men. My sin was getting caught. He was related to the regent, had the regent's ear. That's all that was needed. Are you shocked, Marie?"

"No."

"The woman to whom I had been betrothed at the age of seven died a few weeks before we were to be married. I was still young, hot-blooded, and bored."

"Did you love her—your mistress?"

"Love had nothing to do with it."

"And your betrothed? Did you love her?"

"I scarcely knew her. No. Believe me, Marie, I have never loved until now."

"What was your mistress's name?"

"Does it matter? Come, let's have a game of chess."

Why did some women insist upon torturing themselves with their lover's past and long-forgotten affairs? When a woman no longer mattered, she no longer mattered. There were damned few affairs in which affection or desire lingered past the moment of pleasure.

Minette had been nothing more than a pawn, less than the pawns he was now arranging on the board. The memory of her sister, Sophie, still distressed him. In that alone Henri felt he had been wrong, for Sophie was not yet married, and as her irate brother-in-law had pointed out, it would be the very devil to marry her off now unless they sewed her up again. Well, the old fool should never have taken her from the convent until the day of her marriage. Any mother in France could have told him that. A girl had to be kept in a nunnery until the day of her marriage if she was to go as a virgin to her husband. Henri had accused first Minette's husband, then the regent himself, of wanting to deflower Sophie, thus giving another turn to the screw which had led to the *lettre de cachet*.

"Her name doesn't matter," Marie said. "I only wondered."

"Her name was Minette. There! White or black."

"White."

"Why do you always choose white?"

"You may have it if you wish. Why do you ask me to make a choice if you want white?"

"My darling, we are quarreling."

"Are we?" Marie reached across the board and touched his hand. "I'm sorry. For a moment I was jealous."

He kissed her palm. "If you are jealous, in time you may even come to love me."

She drew her hand away and moved a pawn. "I—do love you." Yes, she must learn to say such things.

She had never said it before, and he did not believe her now, but her jealousy had given him hope. His only triumph over her was that she carried his child and that she had agreed to marry him. Considering her alternatives, though, it was not much of a triumph. He would do all he could to make her happy, but what could he do to make her love him? He wanted her love as he had once wanted her body. He, who had never loved.

They had played in silence for only a short time when Marie announced, "Checkmate."

Henri stared at the board. "By the saints, Marie, you've won."

"I know." She was as surprised as he was. "Did you let me win?"

"I did not. You outfoxed me completely. Come, let's try again."

Marie was tired, but there was nothing else to do. Another thunderstorm had rattled the house and deluged the streets that morning. The air lay like a weight on the town. Baptiste's face dripped as he pulled the cord to the turkey feather fan. He too looked tired, and Marie wondered that his arms didn't ache. Ache or not, the thick air must be kept in motion.

As Henri set up the pieces, Marie picked up the white queen. The face looked a little like her own, with prominent bones, a delicate pointed chin, a broad forehead, and her carved hair piled high, as if to keep her neck cool. The queen could move in any direction she liked. She was all-powerful. The ebony pieces were not her slaves but her foes, black of heart, and she was pitted against them. She would move across the board, up and up against the black king until she could cry "Checkmate!"—which Henri had told Marie had originally been *shah-mat*, "the king is dead."

Her hand trembled as she replaced the queen on the board. Did she want Edmund's death or only his disgrace?

This game she played as if it were life itself. She forgot the heat and her physical discomfort, forgot it was Henri against whom she played.

He was puzzled by her set, intense expression, and

had an uncomfortable feeling that her savage concentration had something to do with himself. When at last she shrilled, "Checkmate!" he felt as if he had been struck. She beat the table with her fist. "Checkmate! Checkmate, Henri!" She burst into tears.

"My darling, what is it?"

"It's nothing." *Edmund dead.*

"You're tired. We shouldn't have played the second game. It's hellishly hot. Lie down, and I'll send Sheba to bathe your head and fan you."

"It's nothing, I tell you. I'm crying because—because I'm sorry I defeated you again. You see, it is a stupid nothing."

"Stupid, indeed. I am the one who should weep. Instead I'm laughing because my wife is so clever. Too clever for me. No more chess until I regain my cunning. I'll teach you hazard instead. At that I excel. The sweet little dice, they always fall right for me. You'll see. Your generalship will do you no good in that game. You must listen to the inner voice telling you what to call."

"Pooh! It's stupid to sit here all day playing games." She pushed the board away. The white queen toppled over at the feet of the black king. Would she too fall at Edmund's feet if he beckoned to her?

Henri stretched and yawned. "You're right. It *is* stupid and stupefying." He smiled at Baptiste. "Run along, *petit garçon,* and rest your arms. Ask Sheba to make you a cooling tisane. We can do without the fan for a while."

The air sank around them. Marie had not moved from the table, where she sat with her head in her hands.

"You need a friend," Henri said. "Were there no young ladies at the convent you'd like to see again? Someone you could gossip with about babies and husbands?"

"If there were, why should I want to gossip about either?" Marie's voice dripped with scorn. "I am not like other wives. No, there was no one. I kept to myself. I was afraid they would find out about Céline."

"And find out about me?"

Marie lowered her hands and looked at him in surprise. Could he read her thoughts so clearly? If so, she must never again let Edmund's name cross her mind.

"Yes. And you."

"But you do forgive me?"

"Yes, yes, yes! I have told you a thousand times. I forgive you. But Céline—I have not forgiven her. Yet, in a way, she is my friend. Please, Henri, may I go to see her?"

"In this heat?"

"Why not?"

He took a long pull at his cheroot and blew out the smoke slowly, watching it layer in the air. "I have told you before, it is no longer suitable."

"*Why* is it no longer suitable? Because you have made me a wife instead of a whore?"

"Don't ever call yourself that, Marie." He began to pace the room, pausing at each window to look out.

"But I was bought, just as Mimi and Alixe and Blanche are bought, as Céline herself is bought." Her voice was shrill with anger, and she struggled to control it because she hated the sound. "How am I any different?"

He gave the cord of the fan a pull as he walked past it, so the air stirred and the smoke writhed and dispersed. "You were different to begin with."

"You and Céline saw to it I did not remain different." Her voice was under control now, but Henri's broke as he cried out, "But, Marie, you forgave me! You have said so again and again. Only a few seconds ago you said so."

She stood up. She should go to him, put her arms around him, hold him, ask forgiveness for herself. It was thinking of Edmund that had started the discussion. Always Edmund. "You *are* forgiven, Henri. I am sorry that I cannot forget. And now, I am going to see Céline."

"Then wear a mask as ladies do in Paris. Take Sheba with you, and don't stay too long."

"And do you also want to dictate what we may talk about?" She forced a teasing tone into her voice.

"Would you obey me if I did?"

"No." She picked up the white queen and placed the piece in its original and rightful square on the board.

No breath of wind stirred the air. Heat waves undulated through the streets so ships' masts, houses, and trees changed from shape to distorted shape, as if they were made of rippling gauze. The earth steamed as if it vented hell.

Cattle had been slaughtered in the market place that morning, and despite the rain the air smelled of blood. Sheba had brought home a fresh, still dripping haunch and put it down in spices and wine.

We need a cold room like we had in Canada, Marie thought. But where would one find a cold room in this country? It was hot under her mask and hood. The parasol Sheba held over her head did little against the glare of the sun. She wished now she had not come, but even this was better than the stifling boredom at home.

She wondered how Henri could bear it. But Henri had his business affairs. He went out at least once a week, and it seemed to Marie that trappers, tobacco dealers, and planters, were always pounding at the door, forcing her to absent herself while Henri talked to them. She did not mind. She looked forward to the times when she was alone. She enjoyed sitting on the upper gallery, looking down into the garden, sewing clothes not much larger than those she used to sew for Flora. Sometimes she wished she were still sewing for Flora. But Flora was put away, wrapped in a silk cloth, lying in a carved and brass-bound camphor chest.

"If it is a girl, I shall call her Flora," Marie thought, but she spoke aloud, and Sheba said, "And if it's a boy, what? After *him* or him?"

"After my father." But he would look like Edmund, whose half-finished warehouse on the levee they were now passing.

There was more activity there than anywhere in town. Three lanky boys were unloading from a handcart. Even from a distance Marie recognized them as the Goodacre children, although they were less underfed and fever-ridden than they had been the long ago night when she had thought of them as little animals.

It took her longer to recognize Edmund standing, arms akimbo, watching the boys work. He had exchanged his knee breeches and silk shirt for buckskin pantaloons and the striped shirt of a seaman. His hair was tied back, and a flat-crowned, wide-brimmed straw hat shadowed his face. He looked hot and dusty. Picking up a brick from the pile, he examined it carefully, weighed it in his hand, then replaced it precisely.

More bricks being bought with her money, which she would collect from Frank Goodacre, with interest from Edmund. The corners of her mouth curled into a smile.

"I thought you were a businesswoman," Edmund had said.

So she was. A better businesswoman than he had guessed.

"Why are you smiling? You glad to see him?" Sheba's voice was tinged with suspicion.

"He's changed," she answered, hating the unwanted desire she felt whenever she saw him.

"Changed?" Sheba's laughter rose from deep in her throat. "Changed his dress, not his heart. Not that one. M. Henri now, he's changed."

* * *

"You've changed." Céline surveyed Marie critically. "But that's inevitable, *n'est-ce pas?* You are older, a woman now, not that pretty child we knew. Are you happy, Marie? Wasn't marriage the right thing? Have you forgotten your handsome fool who took his fun and didn't want to pay?" Céline fanned herself vigorously. She was lying on a chaise, her sack open to her naval, her body gleaming with sweat.

"How can I forget him in my condition? Is there anything to drink? It was hot in the sun."

"It's hot everywhere. Why did you come out? Not that it isn't long past time you came to see me."

Marie had forgotten how shabby the room was, and it had grown shabbier during her absence. "Boredom."

"The universal ailment. Sheba, go to the kitchen and tell Estella to bring some wine. The good wine, not that swamp water I serve to seamen. Estella's my new slave. A Chickasaw with some unpronounceable name. She was all I could afford after you took Sheba from me. Blacks come dear. Indians are cheap."

"Henri paid you enough to buy a black."

"There aren't enough blacks, no matter how much Henri paid me. The plantations swallow them."

"What did you do with the rest of the money?"

"Ordered new beds. We need them. Maybe the militia and seamen don't deserve them, but there's no reason we should break our backs. I promise you, Marie, one day I'll let no one through that door who isn't an officer or a gentleman—not that they aren't all alike with their breeches down. One day I'll have a salon as grand as any in Paris."

"Do you have a letter for me?"

"Aha! I was waiting for you to ask. I knew it was more than boredom that brought you here." Céline pointed her fan at the clothes chest. "It's right on top. Too thin to contain anything but air."

Marie tore open the note without even breaking the

sealing wax. No money came out, only a sheet of paper with two sentences scrawled across it.

I can give you no money this month. I am marrying and need every sol.

The writing blurred before her eyes. The heat pressed in around her, suffocating her. She closed her eyes and felt herself swaying, then Céline's arm supporting her, guiding her back to her chair.

"Marie, what in the name of God? Are you ill? Here." She held the wine glass to Marie's lips. The wine tasted bitter as iron. She pushed the glass away. "I'm not ill. Here, read it."

"Bah!" Céline tossed the paper back to her. "Of course he's marrying. Did you expect him not to? It's for that you frightened me so I thought you were losing the child?" Her tone changed. "I'm sorry, Marie. I thought you had heard. Henri must keep you prisoner just as Mimi said, if you hear no gossip."

"I'm not interested in gossip."

"A good thing. Better you heard it here than from Henri. What would he have thought of your little performance?"

Marie folded her hands in her lap, clenched them into fists so Céline would not see them shaking. "Who is she?"

"One of the Arnolie daughters. M. Arnolie has a plantation on St. John's Bayou. He isn't one of my customers. The family thinks Lanney is a fine catch, and he thinks he's making a wealthy marriage. He'll find out there's not much money there. Arnolie has three daughters and damned little good hard coin. That dowry will be nothing but paper, letters of credit, notes, card money."

"He was always talking about the Arnolies. He called the girls dairymaids."

"Then he should set them to milking cows that give gold like the goose of the golden eggs."

"He needn't think taking a wife will excuse him from his debt. I'll grind him into the mud."

"You're finally learning, eh? Squash him like a scorpion, Marie, but take care Henri doesn't know it was the scorpion's tail that stung you."

"Henri doesn't suspect."

"Keep it that way. What does Henri hear from Natchez, by the way? Fort Rosalie?"

"I think he has some tobacco interests in Natchez territory."

Céline dismissed the tobacco with a wave of her fan. "I'm talking about the Indian trouble. Estella, I told you, is a Chickasaw. She's heard—God knows how they communicate, these savages—there's trouble brewing between the Natchez tribe and the commandant at Fort Rosalie."

"If Henri has heard that, he hasn't told me. Natchez is a long way off, isn't it?"

"Two or three days by river, I think. But if the Natchez rise, the Chickasaw will join them. They're allies. And God knows what the Choctaw will do."

"The Choctaw are our allies, aren't they?"

"And know damned well we've cheated them out of their land. The English are arming the Natchez and Chickasaw and salting their wounds. The English would take off their clothes and paint themselves red if they thought they could drive the French out of Louisiana." Céline stiffled a yawn. "My God, Marie, doesn't Henri tell you anything? Doesn't he know there's a mind along with that succulent body?"

"Of course he does. I beat him at chess."

"I could think of better things to do with you than play chess if I were Henri. I could have made an expert whore of you, Marie, and shipped you off to Versailles, where you'd have been a morsel for the king. But I'm a woman of scruples." Marie laughed. "It's true. Go home to your man, Marie, and be thankful I arranged a nice marriage for you instead of another future."

"You would have arranged that other future if I hadn't got pregnant, just as you arranged for Henri."

Céline surveyed Marie through narrowed eyes. "Do you hate me for that?"

Marie shrugged. "I suppose not. I'm grateful for all you did, just as I'm grateful to Henri. But I know what you would have done, just as I know what would happen to me if I lost Henri. Don't worry, Céline. I'll do my best not to lose him. You see, I'm something of a whore after all."

She tore Edmund's note into small pieces and dropped them into her wine glass. She wished it were as easy to destroy Edmund himself, but even if she were to take a knife and stab him, the love and the hate, two faces of the same coin, two passions of equal intensity, would remain. The child would be there, like an evil talisman.

Despite the heat, Marie shivered.

A Wedding

The next morning Henri said, "I've been thinking about what you said about the stupidity of our lives. I have a surprise for you. I've arranged to borrow a horse and cart, and we are going into the country for a drive."

Impulsively Marie clapped her hands, causing Henri to smile.

"So, at last I please you."

"You do that always."

"Not always, my dear. I'm not such a fool as to believe that. But I think this will please you. There is something I want to show you."

"A surprise?"

"Not exactly a surprise. Some land on Lake Pontchartrain that my father arranged to have granted to me. Eventually I may put it into cultivation. Up till now I haven't wanted to be bothered. I've been out there only once. If it's as I remember it, I think you'll like it. If you don't, I may sell the grant if I can get cash instead of worthless paper."

"It sounds—lovely." But she knew it was a kind of punishment. Perhaps God always punished in small ways, in painful pricks of memory, like darts thrown at a captured beast.

"It is lovely. It overlooks the lake, and there's a rise which would be a pleasant site for a house sometime in the future."

She knew the lake front and the rise, the secret hollows beneath the bearded trees, the smoke from the distant Indian village that drifted across the water; knew the reflection of clouds and the beat of heavy wings and the rustle of leaves as the turkeys came to roost at dusk. Knew it better, she thought, than did Henri. She doubted he had waded in the water and felt the sand come up between his toes or lain beneath the trees with someone in his arms.

What a fool she had been.

The morning mists had evaporated and the blue burned from the sky when they left the house. They followed the road which ran between the river and the marshy forest edging the town. The recent rains and the flow of traffic had rutted the road. Dark puddles stood in the deeper ruts. The cart jolted, the wheels splashed sprays of water, the shafts squeaked. But it was a vast improvement over the streets of the city with their ill-smelling, refuse-filled ditches, the crowded market, and the heavy air. On the river small service crafts rode the current. Those coming down from the German colony rode low in the water under their neatly stacked piles of produce, plump melons, russet yams, grapes so purple they were almost black. The Choctaw canoes were carelessly loaded with pelts. Marie noticed one Choctaw who wore a bear claw dangling from his pierced ear.

They passed slaves bringing vegetables to the market from the plantations; a boy driving a herd of rebellious cattle which bawled and shook their horns at the cart; prisoners, their chains clanking, dragging a sledge of newly felled trees to be shipped to France for masts of merchantmen; a woman balancing a basket of golden bananas on her head and a black baby on her hip.

The smell of resin, the musky odor of bananas, the steam rising from fresh cattle dung blended with the scent of river mud and water and greenery. In the ditch the indigo plants thrust up their spikes of red, white, and purple flowers, and birds swooped and darted and dived into the depths of the trees. Smaller roads, scarcely more than well-worn paths, branched off from the main artery, leading to plantations and their squat cypress wood houses and outbuildings. Once, in one of those sudden silences which fall, they heard the creak of a tobacco press.

Henri named the owners of the homes they passed, and some Marie recognized, the daughters of the family having been at the convent, among them the Arnolies. "His grant joins mine."

Their house was larger than the others, with a gallery built the length and width of it, and a shed-shaped second story. The ground-floor windows were shuttered against the sun, giving the house a secretive look. From the upstairs gabled windows gaily colored quilts were hanging out to air. As Marie watched, a girl appeared and dragged them in, one by one. She caught sight of the cart and shaded her eyes to watch it pass.

A little way past the Arnolies', Henri pointed his whip at a tangle of jungle. "There was a trail there once, but it's grown over. A pity I haven't come here more often."

Black oak, water maple, dogwood, mulberry, and pine trees vied with one another for roothold and sun. Wildflowers bloomed where the sun drove spikes of light through the leaves. The long wild grass said, "Hush, hush," as it bent beneath the carriage floor boards, and the air was perfumed as the wheels crushed the flowers into the earth.

Marie folded her parasol. There was no need of its shade in this corridor of interlaced branches. The motionless air was green-smelling, green-tinted. It was a place in which her mother would never have let her venture alone for fear of snakes, drunken Indians, renegade militia men, or escaped criminals. But Henri appeared to be unafraid.

The ground rose, the vegetation thinned, and the vista opened onto the lake. Marie gasped as a flock of water fowl left the lake with a thrumming of wings, shattering the surface of the water into diamond-bright ripples. The horse whinnied and moved to the lake's edge to drink at the very spot where Edmund had let the pirogue drift ashore.

There was a hummock where they had eaten lunch, the rise where Edmund would like to build a house, the liveoak where the child had been made. She had been so happy . . .

"All the land we came through since we left the main road is mine, and all the lake front to that tree in bloom. It's one of the largest grants in the area. I don't know how my father managed it, or why. Perhaps he thought it would keep me out of mischief if I turned planter."

They picnicked close to the lake's edge on a fresh baked loaf filled with river shrimp and shallots, wild berries, and wine. They threw crusts to the ducks which swam back and forth before them, watching with their shiny eyes.

They walked to the hummock, where Henri spread a feather quilt. Marie stretched out and folded her arms under her head. There was none of the intoxicating happiness she had felt with Edmund, but she did feel surprisingly content. Content and secure, as if no harm could ever touch her.

"Henri, I want a house here." To make Edmund jealous.

"It's very remote, my dear. I had forgotten how wild it is."

"But it's peaceful and beautiful. You said yourself it would be a pleasant place for a house."

"You'd be lonely."

"With you?"

"It would be quite an undertaking to clear the land, put it to use, bring the materials out from town."

"You're hedging."

"You really wish it? All right. I promise to consider it." He looked at the sky. "I think another storm is coming in. We'd better start back."

As they passed the Arnolie plantation a man hailed them. He wore buckskin knee breeches and worsted stockings and boots and no coat over his plain shirt. His hat brim was turned down, shading his face. He was stocky, broad-shouldered, and years older than Henri.

"Monsieur, Madame." Marie felt his sharp, curious gaze as he nodded to her. "My daughter saw you go by earlier. Speaking to you here will save me a trip to town. I'd begun to think I'd missed you."

"Good day, M. Arnolie. Do you know Mme. de Nemour?"

"A pleasure, madame." Again that stabbing look.

"My daughter's to be married, monsieur, and she's set her mind on your land for a home. Her fiancé and I have tried to talk her out of it. It's far from his business, and I can't spare the slaves to clear it. Not that it shouldn't be in cultivation, if you'll pardon my saying so. But Annette has set her heart on it, so I promised to speak to you."

"No!" The word came out before Marie thought. The men looked at her in surprise, and Henri laughed.

"You can see Madame has set her heart on it as well, M. Arnolie."

"Then you are planning to use the land?"

"Not immediately. Not until after Madame's confinement."

"Ah." The eyes appraised Marie's figure. "You'd find it isolated, madame, but we'd be glad to have you as a neighbor. I've two more daughters who'd enjoy your company."

But she wouldn't enjoy theirs.

"Should you change your mind—" M. Arnolie gestured. His hands were fleshy, hard-working peasant hands. "If I know Annette, she'll not be satisfied long living in a wing of Lanney's warehouse."

Bile rose in Marie's throat. Lanney's warehouse indeed! It was *her* warehouse, and one day she would have it.

"You'll come to the wedding party, of course," M. Arnolie went on. "Annette would like that. She might even persuade you to part with your land. She has a way, my Annette has. I had another husband in mind for her, but no one but Lanney would do. I gave in, in the end. Not that I don't like him, but he's young. He's of a good family and will make something of himself."

"Yes, I've met him. We'll see you then, M. Arnolie. It will be a pleasure for Madame to meet some of the local society." Henri flicked his whip.

"I won't go," Marie said when they were out of M. Arnolie's hearing. "Why did you accept without consulting me? I don't want to go to that—that dairymaid's wedding party."

"Nonsense. You were complaining about the monotony of our lives. It will be good for us. You will make friends—"

"I don't want that kind of friends. I don't want to go. If you insist on going, go alone."

Henri stopped the cart and laid down the reins. He turned and took Marie by the shoulders. "I will not go alone, because you shall go with me. I love you. I am proud of you. I want to dance with you. And I want to talk with the men and learn what's going on in the town. I want you to make friends. We are going to the wedding party, Marie, and I expect you to accept my decision in good grace."

She sulked the rest of the way home. She longed to spit out the truth. "I will not go because Lanney, not you, is the father of this child. I loved him, and he wouldn't have me, and one day I'll have his hide, but I won't see him marry someone else." But she knew she could not.

They ate dinner in silence, then Marie went upstairs, leaving Henri at the table with the brandy bottle. Sheba followed her.

"You have trouble?"

Marie explained what was wrong.

"Something bad about that gris-gris," Sheba mused as she helped Marie out of her clothes. "You wanted him, you got him in every way, except he's going to be in somebody else's bed."

"Damn your stinking gris-gris! I wish I'd never asked for it."

"Too late. Nothing left but to put a curse on him and her." Sheba began to brush Marie's hair. "You get some hair, like in this brush, see, or a nail paring, even some spit or pee—"

"Ugh! No more voodoo. Look what happened last time. You're supposed to be a good Catholic, Sheba, not a heathen savage."

"All the same, priests and obeah men are no different. Miracles, they're magic. Voodoo is stronger, that's all."

"You'd better not let the priest hear you say that. And don't make any more spells. Help me into bed and get out."

"You going to say your prayers?"

"No."

"You want your stomach oiled?"

"No."

"You ought to oil it every day now. You're stretching."

"I wish I had let Céline get rid of this brat."

"You think if you were still at the house he'd come visit you? He's got a wife now to keep him. No time to go whoring."

Marie grabbed Henri's pillow and threw it at Sheba. Sheba caught it and tossed it back. Her laughter echoed as she descended the stairs. Damned insolence!

Marie pretended to be asleep when Henri came to bed. Before he snuffed the candle, he leaned over and kissed her eyelids.

"Marie, we must not go to sleep on our anger. I'm sorry the idea of a party displeases you, but you must indulge me by going. I think it would be best, for both of us."

She leaned on her elbow, her eyes blazing. "I know how it will be, even if you don't. They'll ask questions, those women. Who am I? Where did I come from? Where did I meet you? Who are my parents?" And she would have to smile at the bride and groom and wish them happiness when she wished them both dead.

"Ah, so that's it. Then we'll invent a little romance. We met on the ship coming over. I knew your brave father in France after he fled Scotland with his rightful Stuart king after the failed revolution. We lost contact with each other after settling here. It was only recently I found you again. Let me think . . . yes, I saw you at mass and recognized you. I asked for your hand . . . My word! I almost believe it myself."

In spite of herself, Marie smiled. "What a liar you are."

"Not at all. That's the way it should have happened. If we believe it enough, it will be true."

A white moth with brown eyes upon its wings circled the candle. Henri extinguished the flame and drew the mosquito netting into place.

"All right, Henri. I'll go to the party with you." There was nothing else she could do.

Marie leaned against the pillows sipping a concoction of hot chocolate, milk, and coffee from a china cup decorated with a long-tailed scarlet bird. The sound of church bells soared across the roofs of town. The wedding mass was over. If she had a chance to speak to Edmund alone, she would demand full payment of her loan. *Congratulations, Edmund.*

"Up, my dear. You're not going to excuse yourself by pleading a headache or fatigue." Henri came from his dressing room more elegantly clothed than Marie had ever seen him. His hair was dressed high and powdered, his shirt front was lace ruffles, his mulberry velvet coat was fastened with ruby buttons, and he carried a cane with an enormous amethyst knob.

"You're very grand. I'm awed."

"I thought it would please you."

She studied him a moment. "Yes, it does please me," she said, thinking of the impression it would make upon Edmund.

The length of lavender silk in which she had been married had been made into an overdress, caught in front by diamond buttons, flowing out in pleats from her shoulders in back so the gold border flowed out like a peacock's tail as she walked. It opened over a gold petticoat. Her hose was pale pink silk, and her embroidered shoes purple velvet with gilded heels.

As Sheba was fastening a velvet band around Marie's throat Henri brought her a diamond fob. "Fasten it to the ribbon. No, here, I'll do it. And a patch at the corner of your eye—a crescent moon, I think. A bit more rouge?" He looked at her, his head to one side, then laughed. "You'll outshine the bride, Marie. I scarcely know you myself, for I've never seen you with your hair powdered. I'll flirt with you at the party, and if it leads to seduction, so much the better."

"It led to that long ago, as everyone will be able to see. Nothing can hide the fact that I have a shape like a pigeon."

"The men will envy my success."

There was one who would not; one who would know it was not Henri's success. Perhaps Edmund would not recognize her in her new finery. She would soon jog his memory. She smiled into the mirror.

"Why are you smiling so enigmatically, my dear?"

Quickly she thought of a lie. "The Arnolie girls will never recognize the orphan student, Mary Macleod. I was wondering whether to remind them of her or allow Mary Macleod to disappear forever."

"She has disappeared forever, Marie, and with it all her sorrow."

So you think, Marie answered silently.

Only one thing marred Edmund's happiness: that his family, so given to advice and constructive criticism, was not at his marriage. He would have liked to show them how wisely he had manured his field. They would never have guessed he could do so well. He had been in New Orleans five months, and he was a man of importance, a bridegroom, and the owner, if one overlooked his debts, of a warehouse.

His father-in-law had one of the largest land grants on St. John Bayou and owned ten slaves. The bottom land was in rice and the rest in indigo. M. Arnolie, at Edmund's suggestion, had built brick processing vats for the indigo. Edmund had negotiated with Frank Goodacre for the bricks, and Goodacre had paid him a small commission as go-between.

"They don't like dealing with someone who's not French," Frank had admitted to Edmund.

"Change your name, monsieur. Become M. Bonarpent. That would be the translation."

Frank hadn't answered, but Edmund had seen his lips moving, saying the name over to himself. Mon Dieu, did the man take him seriously?

Edmund's bride was one of the prettiest girls in New Orleans. Perhaps not tall enough and too wide-hipped for some tastes, but those wide hips would carry babies well, and Edmund thought her size perfect. She had a temper, but what woman did not? She had shown it when her father had told her M. de Nemour would not sign over the land on Pontchartrain because his own wife wanted it. Annette had stamped her feet and sobbed and beat her father's chest with her fists, as if he were responsible for her disappointment.

"Who is she, anyway?" Annette complained. "I didn't know he was married. He certainly wasn't married when he came to dinner here, because you kept telling us what a grand catch he would be when we were of marriageable age."

"I don't know who she is." Her father grabbed her wrists and held her at arm's length. "Edmund, can't you control your bride? Whoever she was, she's Mme.

de Nemour now, and she's pretty enough to turn any man's head."

"You're saying that to make me angry. I'll wager she's ugly as a witch."

"You'll see for yourself. They're coming to your wedding feast. And if you behave, you may talk her or him around to your way of thinking. *I* doubt they'll ever use that land. He's too much of a gentleman to turn farmer."

"We couldn't afford the land now anyway," Edmund said, laughing at Annette's tantrum. "We have no slaves to clear it and no money to build a house. Everything must go into the business first."

"You promised—"

"I promised, yes, in time. In time, my pet."

"Papa could lend us slaves."

"Papa could not," her father answered.

"You could. You have more slaves than anyone in New Orleans. Almost."

"I need every hand."

"I don't want to live in that smelly warehouse on the river forever. Why can't we live with Maman and Papa, the way all other young couples do?"

"There is no room and no privacy. And I must be close to my business."

"I think it would be grand to live in town," her sister Claudine said. "To see all the sights, the people going by, the traffic on the river, the floating shops, the market. It would be a lot better than being stuck out here, where you never see anything. She's being hateful, Edmund. You should have waited another year and married me."

But Edmund had been of no mind to wait for anyone. The long period of enforced celibacy on the sea voyage and the encounter with Marie had aroused all his youthful sexuality. He wanted no more to do with whores who demanded to be married because they had no better sense than to get pregnant. He cringed every time he remembered the scene with Marie.

Annette would settle down once they were married. She would soon grow to like town life. She would like having him within call. He would teach her to do the accounts, and when there was little work to do, he could always walk into the wing where they would live and take her to bed. She was going to be a passionate bedmate. Once when they had been walking, chaperoned by Claudine and Angela, she had persuaded them to leave her and Edmund to themselves.

Giggling, the sisters had agreed, and no sooner had Annette and Edmund outdistanced them than Annette had wrapped her arms around him and pulled his head down to kiss him. Her ardor had astonished him, especially when she had taken his hand and guided it into her bodice. He had worked one breast free and kissed the pink nipple before Claudine and Angela grew tired of waiting and called they were coming out.

"Edmund, I can hardly wait," Annette had whispered as she had rearranged her clothes. Her face was as pink as her nipple. "I know what to do, and I'll make you happy."

Edmund could hardly wait either. Often he dreamed Marie was in his arms. The night before the wedding he had dreamed he stood at the altar. When he placed the ring on his bride's finger, he had looked down into Marie's face. The dream had frightened him. He hadn't dared take his eyes off Annette during the ceremony in case a transformation took place. He had been so absorbed in willing her not to turn into Marie that the priest had to prompt him to repeat his vows.

When Marie and Henri walked into the Arnolie house, it took Edmund a moment to recognize her. After all, he had not often seen her clothed. His face went white when his father-in-law presented the de Nemours. Edmund saw the triumphant mockery in Marie's eyes. He saw too that she was still pregnant.

He stammered out a greeting which probably made

no sense. It didn't matter. Annette, remembering her father's advice, was making herself sickeningly charming to M. de Nemour, to Marie's obvious amusement.

When the de Nemours joined the other guests, Claudine said, "You see, Annette, Papa was right. Mme., de Nemour isn't ugly. She's beautiful. Edmund thought so too, didn't you, Edmund? His eyes were popping out as if he were seeing a goddess." Annette gave him a quick, narrow-eyed look.

Claudine prattled on. "I'm going to have a dress like that after I'm married. That same color, like water hyacinths, and a gold brocade petticoat."

"You'll look ugly as sin in it," Annette snapped. "Who does she think she is? The dauphine?"

Angela said, "You're just jealous because you won't look that pretty when Edmund's given you a baby." She giggled. "Look at him blush!"

"And you're jealous because I'll be sleeping with him tonight instead of with you—you children."

"Sleeping!" Claudine laughed. "He'll be kissing you you-know-where, like he did the other day when you thought we weren't watching." Claudine whirled away as Annette reached out to box her ears.

At that moment the music started, and Edmund took his bride firmly by the hand and led her to the center of the room. There were times when he wished Annette weren't so childlike. She was the same age as Marie, but Marie was a woman. Damn her! Damn her for a whore. What right had she to come to his wedding?

The dance was a galliard. Marie and Henri did not dance. Perhaps all that jigging and high leaping was dangerous for a pregnant woman. Edmund could not keep from looking over Annette's head at Marie. She was a magnet drawing his eyes back to her. He remembered her as he had first seen her during the hurricane, her hair dripping ringlets, her nightdress plastered against her body, the color of her flesh visible through the wet garment. He remembered ripping the fragile cloth so she stood naked before him, her small breasts moist and gleaming. A rivulet of rain had trickled down her body into her navel, where it stopped, trapped, shimmering like a translucent pearl.

He wondered if he would ever experience such passion again. For all Annette's boasting that she knew what to do, she would never be what Marie had been. The thought saddened him. No matter how much he hated her, no matter what she had been, he would remember that lust, that satisfaction, forever.

He lusted for her now. She was more desirable in that elegant gown than she had been naked. It frightened him that he longed to undress her, lay his head between the breasts which were no longer small, lay his head on her swelling body, lie between her thighs and fill her as he had once filled her, again and again.

Annette sank into a deep curtsy at his feet, her eyes adoring him. Did she have to open them quite so wide? If she weren't careful, they would pop out of her head. He was unaware that he was frowning until Annette reached up and smoothed his forehead.

"Our guests will think you're angry if you glower like that. They'll be saying I must dance like a cow to make you frown so."

"I dislike the galliard. All that leaping about is exhausting."

"You told me it was your favorite dance."

"I've changed my mind."

"Well, I like it, and if you don't want to dance it with me, I'll dance it with Captain Leclerc—if I can get him away from Claudine. It's disgraceful the way she's hanging onto him. I must speak to Maman about her."

The galliard was followed by a gavotte, and that by a minuet. Edmund announced pompously that the minuet was going out of favor at court, but no one paid any attention to him. The ladies liked it because it showed off their gowns and didn't leave them sweating and breathless.

Edmund noticed that Marie and Henri danced the minuet as if it were a ritual of love. She was a witch to snare men like that. De Nemour was obviously besotted with her.

Annette gasped as the music ended. "Dear husband, do you worship me as he worships her?"

"Who?"

"You know who. You were watching them too. Everyone was. Oh, please say that you do."

"You know I do or we wouldn't be celebrating our marriage."

"You might have married me for my dowry and because Papa is rich."

"Your dowry, my sweet, is a lot of paper notes. And your papa is rich only when the rice and indigo are shipped to France and paid for there."

"Edmund, that's cruel!"

"I'm trying to tell you I married you for yourself. You are the most beautiful, most charming young lady in New Orleans."

"Not so beautiful, I think, as Mme. de Nemour."

"Without her paint and patches and gold brocade, she'd be nothing," Edmund answered carelessly. He remembered with an ache in his loins how beautiful she was without her gold brocade.

"Edmund, they're coming." She clutched at him as Henri bowed.

"Madame, with your husband's permission, I beg a dance with the bride. Can you spare her for so long, monsieur?"

"Not to do so would be denying you a great pleasure," Edmund answered. Now was Annette's chance to try to persuade de Nemour to part with the land on Pontchartrain. He gave her a quick glance and saw she had the same thought. Obviously she had inherited some of her father's business acumen.

"I've told my husband I knew you—ever so slightly, of course—at convent." Marie smiled at Annette. "You don't remember me. I was one of the orphan students that Sister Josephine anguished over."

Annette frowned. "I think I do remember. But you look so different."

"As do you. Those gray sacks made us look like prison inmates."

"But how ever did you meet—?" Annette bit back her words. It was unthinkable. Orphans were usually charity students, and for one of *them* to have made such a marriage was preposterous!

"I knew her family in France, where they were refugees at the exiled Stuart court," Henri explained.

"You're royalty?"

"Not at all. My father was an officer in our poor king's defeated army."

"There is the music, Madame Lanney. Ah, a pavane. One of the most civilized of dances." Henri led Annette away, leaving Marie smiling at Edmund. There was nothing to do but dance with her.

"Well, Marie, I scarcely expected to see you here."

"My husband insisted that we come. And I agreed because it is better to speak to you here than on the street. I want my money."

Edmund suppressed a groan. "You know damned well I can't give it to you now. I wrote to you, explaining."

"Marriage doesn't excuse you from your debts."

"Marriage involves certain expenses. My wife's family thinks—"

"I'm not interested in your expenses or what they think. That IOU you gave me—"

"Which you didn't want to accept."

"I admit I was a fool. That IOU said you would repay me with interest and a share of the profits. I know you have had profits. I know what goes on in this town."

"I had to build on a wing for a home. You can't expect that I would take my wife to that dingy room in M. Brun's. I could scarcely sleep there myself. It's fit only for roaches and spiders."

"I find it impossible to pity you."

"You'd rather bleed me."

"Of *my* money."

"I'll pay next month, somehow."

"All of it."

"As much as I can."

"If you don't, remember, I'll tell M. Arnolie where the money came from."

"Do that, and I'll tell M. de Nemour whose child you carry. He must know where *you* came from, so it will be easy for him to believe."

"Poor Edmund. Do you think you are the only man capable of impregnating me?"

He missed a step and cursed under his breath. "Then you had the operation?"

She smiled so beautifully that anyone watching them would have thought they were exchanging compliments. "Do you think I wanted to bear your bastard?"

"You were anxious enough when you thought I'd marry you."

"You should have married me, Edmund. I would have lived at M. Brun's willingly. Or in a wing of the warehouse, which I hear your dairymaid objects to doing."

"Damn you."

"And damn you, my dear Edmund."

"Was that true about your father? You told me you came from Canada."

"From France to Canada. From Canada to Louisiana. I was a baby, of course."

"Was M. de Nemour your gentleman?"

"Of course."

"Is it his child?"

"You'd like to be certain, wouldn't you, Edmund? I think, to torture you, I'll not say yes and not say no. It will ensure our mutual silence."

The dance ended and Edmund bowed over her hand, but his lips did not touch it, as was the custom. His own hand was shaking, and although the pavane was a slow, stately dance, he was sweating.

The wedding feast was served on trestle tables in the garden. The Arnolie slaves and those borrowed from neighboring plantations kept the wine glasses filled and the plates replenished from the mountain of pink shrimp, the numerous oyster loaves, the cauldrons of venison stew, the platters of fish poached in wine, wild turkeys bulging with Indian corn and grape dressing, the variety of conserves, cakes, and liqueured fruits.

"I shall be sick," Marie whispered to Henri. "It is too much. They must have slaughtered every deer and turkey in the area."

"There is certainly enough food to feed the entire city. What did you think of the bridegroom? You had never met him before, had you?"

She was saved from answering by another toast. By now all she was doing was touching her glass to her lips. She set down her glass and prodded a shrimp with her fork, but then decided she didn't want it. "He's arrogant."

"You were having a lively conversation. The bride could scarcely take her eyes off you long enough to try to persuade me to part with the land at Pontchartrain."

"Poor little dairymaid."

"Why do you call her that?"

"She's plump and pink-cheeked the way I imagine a dairymaid is."

"A dairymaid is more apt to be sallow, underfed, and mud-bespattered. What *did* you and Lanney talk about?"

"Are you jealous, Henri? We talked about Paris, which of course I don't remember, having been either a child in arms or not yet born. I couldn't do mathematics in my head quickly enough to decide which, but I don't think he noticed. He's not only arrogant, he's very uncertain of himself in a way and very anxious to be the success M. Arnolie expects."

"He'll succeed. He's done damned well already. Made a business for himself and got backing for it. No one knows who financed him, and he's close-mouthed as an oyster about it. He's made a fortunate marriage, is still young—"

Marie cut in scornfully, "So he's taken you in, as well."

Henri frowned, puzzled. "You really do dislike him, don't you? That's interesting. I wonder which of us is right; you with your feminine intuition or I, who think I know men."

That night Marie wondered if Edmund and Annette too were locked together and if Edmund enjoyed his dairymaid as much as he had enjoyed her. She gasped with unwilling pleasure as Henri took her, then bit her lips to keep from crying out Edmund's name.

Seeking Vengeance

The day after the wedding Marie began drawing plans for the house at Pontchartrain. The sooner it was built the less chance there was of Henri's being swayed to part with the property. He knew she liked the property, but every time she had mentioned it he had pointed out obstacles to their building there any time in the near future. They would need transportation, and there weren't twenty horses in all the area, and certainly none the owners would part with. It would be difficult to keep slaves so far from town, even if he could get them. He had no desire to be a planter of indigo, tobacco, rice, cotton—in short, a planter of anything. "It is not my *forte*, Marie."

"A summer house then. Very little clearing need be done for that, and it would be cool on the lake."

A summer house, Henri conceded, was a possibility now that the canal connecting Pontchartrain with the city was completed.

So Marie's plans went forward. Marie had done little painting since her marriage except for some sketches of the garden and the house. Now she was busy every day with floor plans, scenes of rooms, the house from every viewpoint, the lake, and the garden which would lead down to the lake front. She even planned a mooring with a red boat casting its reflection on the water.

"Sixteen rooms!" Henri said, looking over the plans one evening. "What will we do with sixteen rooms? Where will we get the furniture to fill them?"

"Have it made here or send to France for it."

"You may have to use some of your money for this project, Marie. I swore to myself I'd never touch it, but the tax money from the estate in France has been slow coming in."

"I'll pay for the furniture." By then she would either have collected from Edmund or she would own the warehouse herself.

But before the plans materialized, the Natchez tribe attacked Fort Rosalie. Only about twenty people escaped. All the males except for the young boys were killed. The women who were not pregnant and the children were taken as slaves. The fort and the buildings in the surrounding settlement were burned.

It was all the fault of the new governor, Perrier. He had not protested when the Company of the Indies had decided to close all the forts north of Rosalie. The troops had been withdrawn, and the posts were falling into decay, leaving the English free to woo the tribes. It was Perrier who thought it a foolish expenditure to placate the Indians with gifts. Perrier who had appointed that fool Etchpare as commandant of Rosalie. Let him deal with the refugees who were pouring into New Orleans with tales of horror.

A family not twenty miles from New Orleans had been scalped and their house fired. It was discovered by a neighbor who had been alarmed by the heavy smoke rising where there should have been only a thread from a cook fire. He had lost no time in bringing his own family into the safety of New Orleans. It meant abandoning everything he had worked for, but better that than their lives.

But what safety did the city have? the citizens asked one another. There was no stockade, no fortification, only a handful of soldiers compared to the number of savages. Fresh rumors circulated every day, each new one sworn to be true: The Natchez chief said there would soon be no French left along the lower part of the river. The Choctaw at Mobile had risen and beseiged the port. A slave who had had her ears boxed for insolence had shouted that the French wouldn't be beating the blacks much longer. Fort St. Claude had been wiped out. A Jesuit celebrating mass in the woods had been killed. And so the panic spread.

"It was bound to happen sooner or later," Henri told Marie. "All it takes is the stupidity of one man to set the blaze that destroys a city."

"Céline said she had heard there was going to be an uprising."

Henri looked at Marie, one eyebrow raised. "You said nothing to me."

"I didn't think it important. Fort Rosalie is—was—a long way off. Could you have prevented it?"

"Probably not, but that settles it. No house on Pontchartrain until the danger of Indians is put down."

"Do you seriously think there will be any trouble here?" She wished Henri would stop pacing the floor. "And if there should be, do you think drafting every slave in the area to dig a moat around the city will be any protection? I don't. Particularly with the troops gone off to try to defeat the Natchez and rescue the prisoners."

"To try to defeat . . ." he repeated. "Yes, that is about it. They've been idle too long, but perhaps some action will bring them back to life. Truthfully, Marie, I think the civilian militia that's been formed is more dangerous than the Indians. It's certain some fool will get excited and kill an innocent person."

"Not necessarily a fool. Even someone like you. You're no more suited to being a soldier than to being a planter."

"I admit it. I may not be a fool, but I feel like one, drilling in the Place d'Armes with the other recruits. Any warrior worth his salt could scalp the lot of us while we're trying to muster."

Marie laughed, but laughter did not keep her from

listening at night for the stealthy step, the shot that would signal the church to ring the alarm, the ear-splitting yelp of the Natchez war cry. She wondered how Henri could sleep so peacefully. She had nightmares woven of the tales told by the refugees, of the pregnant women who had been slashed open and the children they carried ripped from their wombs and thrown to the dogs. She did not want this child, but she wanted neither it nor herself to die in such a way.

The soldiers returned without having put down the Natchez tribe. Instead they had negotiated with them, allowing them to retire across the river in exchange for the release of the prisoners the Natchez had taken at Fort Rosalie. They had also taken a Natchez woman captive.

The townspeople lined the streets to cheer the freed prisoners. But their sympathy and charity soon cooled. The people had to be cared for and fed. It was fairly easy to place the boys; the plantations could always use more hands, especially when the price of slaves rose with every shipment. The Ursuline nuns accepted the orphaned girls into the already crowded convent. The widows of the murdered men felt they deserved compensation for their suffering. Two of them were pregnant with Indian bastards and half-resented having been rescued, for who would want them now? Some of the women openly admitted they were in the market for a new husband. The remainder turned to prostitution.

The weather had turned chill. Winter winds whipped up waves on the river and drummed at the shutters. The kitchen with its huge brick fireplace was warmer than the house, so when Henri went to drill in the Place d'Armes with the other civilians, Marie took her paints or her sewing there.

One day as she was returning from a drive into town she stopped to speak to Baptiste, who was cleaning the ditch around the hedge. Scowling, he grumbled a reply without meeting her eyes. He was unusually sullen these days. He was nearly as tall as Marie now. Perhaps he thought pulling a turkey fan and gardening stupid work for someone soon to be a man.

Henri too was scowling. "Do you know what that imbecile of a governor has decided? He wants to hold a public torture and burn the Natchez woman the soldiers took. Do you know the effect that will have? The Choctaw are teetering on the brink of rebellion, the slaves are ready to revolt, and we're going to burn an Indian!"

"What is that supposed to do? Compensate the widows and orphans for their suffering?"

"They're howling for revenge all right. Mainly I think Perrier hopes it will serve as a warning to the Choctaw. I think it will make them hate us all the more. A woman! Not one of the warriors guilty of murder, but a squaw whose only sin—if it was that—was having been the wife of one of them." Henri paused in his pacing to pound the table. "I loathe and despise public executions. I am too civilized to enjoy the sight of some poor devil put to death in the vilest manner possible, his agony observed by a pack of fools." He shuddered. He poured a glass of wine and raised it to his lips, but before he drank, he looked into the glass with distaste, then opened the shutter and threw it out, glass and all. "It looks like blood." He laughed nervously. "Why do you stare at me, Marie?"

"I am wondering if I will ever really know you. You surprise me constantly. I did not know you were such a gentle man."

"Why?" His voice was harsh. "Because I was sent here by *lettre de cachet*? Because I bought a girl just come into womanhood for my licentious pleasure? Because I am indolent and hedonistic—" He interrupted himself, took her by the shoulders, and drew her to her feet. "What *do* you think of me, Marie?"

"I think you are a very moral man at heart, and that you should remember that self-loathing is a sin."

He pulled her close so their bodies touched. "It is you who changed me, Marie. I did not know it was possible to love and to love so deeply. Try to love me, my darling, instead of resenting what I did and being grateful that I righted the wrong. I want more than your gratitude. Please, try."

"I do love you, Henri."

He kissed her eyes, her face, her lips. "One day you'll say that and mean it. And now I'm going to see the governor to try to persuade him to forestall the burning. Not that he'll listen to me. Not that I have much hope, but I must try."

The execution was held on the levee. Marie and Henri could hear the crowd and see the thick smoke plume into the sky. The pine faggots burned fast and hot, and the heavy odor of resin almost disguised the stink of burning flesh.

A few days later a company of soldiers brought in seven more captives. A week of executions followed. Smoke hung over the rooftops. Ash blew in the streets and into the doors, powdering the floor. Peddlers sold charred bones as souvenirs.

The town was drunk with blood. The soldiers had been rewarded with an extra round of brandy. The Choctaw were surly, and the black slaves openly carried firearms. When Henri ordered Baptiste to mend a broken shutter, the boy refused. Henri gave him a cuff that sent him sprawling, and as he fell a dagger dropped out of his waistband. Before Baptiste could retrieve it, Henri kicked it out of his reach.

When Baptiste refused to answer his questions, Henri went into the house for his whip.

"Don't, Henri! You've never whipped him. Don't start now."

"I must."

Marie covered her ears to shut out the sound of the whip. It did not take long for Baptiste to confess.

"We rising," he sobbed. "When they give the signal full moon night, white blood going to flow. I don't want to kill you, M'sieur, or Madame. But white men gonna burn us. I don't want to burn. I saw it. I don't want the fire."

"All right, Baptiste. Tell me the names of the leaders, and I won't flog you anymore."

Baptiste named ten men, supposedly trusted slaves on various plantations.

"You'll be rewarded, Baptiste, for having told me, but I'll have to betray your friends. They'll be punished, and you damn well deserve to be for having got mixed up in the filthy business. Go to the kitchen and stay with Sheba and Calla until I return. If you try to run away, I'll send the militia after you and see you broken on the wheel." Henri flung the whip aside and stamped into the house.

"It wasn't so bad, my dear," he told Marie soothingly. "I didn't even raise welts. But there's no end to this disaster. When I come back from seeing Perrier, I'll have to question Sheba and Calla too. They must have known about this. The slaves know everything that goes on. Nothing is secret. Nothing except a plot to murder us all in our beds."

Alone in the house, Marie was frightened. Nearly half the population of New Orleans was black slaves. Alone, they could raise havoc. Banded with the Choctaw who had been armed and marched with the militia against the Natchez, they would dangerously outnumber the whites. It would be a massacre. The plot had been formulated and ready to put into effect four days hence, and no one had known, because the slaves were trusted as Henri had trusted Baptiste.

She wished Henri had not left her. Every sound startled her, a footfall on the banquettes, a bird rustling in the hedge, a sudden rippling of wind against the linen covering the windows. The barking of a dog was taken up by others, answering one another across the town. A stealthy step made her whirl around. It was Sheba bringing her a tisane.

"Why did you sneak in like that?" Marie demanded.

Sheba opened her eyes wide so the red-veined whites showed. "I didn't sneak. I walked like always."

"Did you know Baptiste had a knife to kill us?"

"He's too much of a coward to kill anybody."

"You knew and didn't tell us? You knew about the plot?"

The lids came down. Sheba stared at a corner through narrowed slits. "I knew."

"And didn't tell us? After we gave you your freedom?"

"I knew the first slave to draw a knife or gun would be dragged off to the stake on the levee."

"I thought you were my friend. You would have let us be killed."

Sheba held up her hand and spread her fingers wide apart. "You see that little finger? That's the slaves. You see these other fingers? That's the whites. You think that little finger could conquer all those other fingers? If you think that, you're crazy. Like them planning the revolt. They're crazy too. Drink your tisane. I made it nice for you."

"How do I know it isn't poisoned?"

"*I'm* not crazy. If I was crazy enough to poison you, I wouldn't poison the tisane with *him* away. I'd poison your food at dinner. But I'm poisoning nobody, and I'm making no gris-gris against you. You took me from Madame. You gave me freedom. I know what I owe, but I didn't speak because I didn't want the burning."

"All right. I believe you. Monsieur doesn't like the burnings either. But the men who planned the uprising will probably be punished, Sheba. He can't prevent that or keep the governor from doing what he wants."

"White man's justice." Sheba shrugged. "That governor, he likes killing."

All afternoon Marie waited nervously for Henri. When sunset purpled the sky, Sheba came to light the candles. She seemed surprised that Henri had not returned.

"The stew's ready. You want to eat?"

Marie was always hungry these days, and she was hungry now, but she decided to wait rather than sit alone at the long table in the shadowy dining room.

It was almost dark when he tried the door which Marie had bolted. A cold gust of air entered with him.

"Have you been with the governor *all* this time? I've been worried and frightened." Her hair had come loose during the afternoon, and she followed him across the room like a small, snake-haired Fury.

He smiled at her anger, thinking her beautiful. "No, my dear, I have not. I finished with him quickly, but I've been busy. I've made arrangements for us to leave New Orleans. We're going to Paris, Marie. I refuse to stay here and see you murdered."

"Paris? But how? But—but when?"

"There's a ship sailing in three days' time. I secured passage for us. It will be a rush, but it may be our last chance. God knows what will happen next. The Choctaw may rise now that they're in possession of arms. The Natchez may sweep down here with the English to back them. The slaves may make another try. I'm sick of the worry and sick of the reprisals and sick of Perrier's bungling. No matter what he does, it's sure to be wrong."

"But—Henri, I'm not sure I should travel at this time."

"Nonsense, you're only three months along."

She knew it was longer than that, but she dared not tell him.

"Of the two dangers I think the sea voyage is the lesser."

"What about our house? Our things?" The money Edmund owed her. Edmund himself. Her revenge.

"It's all arranged. The furniture will be stored in

Lanney's warehouse for safekeeping. M. Lanney and his little dairymaid will move in here."

Marie stamped her foot. "That is outrageous! You know I dislike them."

"For no good reason. You are utterly unreasonable in that respect, Marie. Lanney was delighted, and so was his wife. They will take over Calla and Baptiste. As Sheba is free, she can stay or come with us as she chooses. I hope she will come."

"You did these things without consulting me—"

"I did what is best for us."

Once before she had heard that deadly calm in his voice. Without wanting to, she began to cry. If she came back, she would never be able to live here, where Edmund and Annette had lived. The walls would bear their invisible imprint, the bedroom would echo with their love-making, the scent of their flesh would linger like the odor of the hides and tobacco lingered, their child would sleep in her child's cradle.

She paced up and down the room, sobbing, wringing her hands in agony. When Henri tried to comfort her, she shoved him aside. "Don't touch me! I hate the Lanneys, and I hate you! You have no understanding."

"I confess, I do not. You puzzle me, Marie. When you are ready to tell me why you dislike the Lanneys, I'll be ready to listen. Meanwhile, madame, I suggest you call Sheba and start packing your things. You are going to Paris with me, where I trust you'll behave better than you are behaving now."

"If you're afraid I'll disgrace you, you should leave me here."

"That I won't do. You go where I go. Céline warned me that you had a temper, and by God, she was right. You can be *douce* eyed and agreeable when you have your way, but you turn into a Fury when you do not. Come, Marie, what is it about the Lanneys you so dislike?"

"He is an arrogant fool."

"That is his wife's problem, isn't it?"

"She was—rude to me in convent."

"Schoolgirl nonsense! She is not rude to you now. She envies everything about you. Your beauty, your pregnancy, your position, your home, the land on Pontchartrain. She told me she had hoped to be friends with you."

"I do not hope to be friends with her. At least I can escape that by going to Paris."

"She might teach you how a wife behaves."

The tears gave way to rage. "If you wanted such a wife, why didn't you marry her when you had the chance? You would have had your virgin and not had to buy me!" No sooner had she screamed out the words than she wished them back. Henri's face was terrible, as if an awful mask had fallen over it, a mask of white porcelain with exaggerated lines from the nostrils to the twisted mouth, the reflection of candle flames picking out the eyes, dark with anger, in their sockets.

A cockroach clicked across the floor, and a chill draft swirled through the room, wreathing the candles with smoke. Marie waited, expecting Henri to strike her. He did not move, but he held her locked in his gaze as firmly as if he had gripped her.

"You damned little *poule*. I've half a mind to send you back to Céline. You'd soon learn what it's like to be bought. Bought by half-drunken soldiers, by seamen poxed by every whore from here to Ceylon, by some man past his prime who can take you only if he beats you first or after you've mouthed his unclean parts! That is how it is to be bought, Marie. Night after night after night until you take to opium like Blanche and Alixe or dose yourself with wine like Mimi."

"You wouldn't dare!"

"Wouldn't I? As you accuse me of having bought you—"

"You did. You can't deny it."

"—you must assume that I own you as I own a slave. And if I own you, I can do what I wish with you—body, mind, and soul. If you think of yourself as chattel, then chattel you are and shall be treated as. I'll sell you to the highest bidder after the child is born. You'll fetch a higher price without a bulging belly. Besides, I fancy having a child to rear according to my tastes."

"It's not—" The dinner gong interrupted her. It was a large gong from some heathen land, and its deep, hollow brass tone reverberated throughout the house. It drowned out Marie's words, startled her so she only whispered "yours" and added quickly, still in a whisper, "It's mine."

Henri seemed not to hear. The gong had startled him as much as it had her. The mask vanished from his face. He jerked his head toward the dining room door. "She'll have heard us. My God, how I long for privacy."

"You'll have it when you're rid of me." She whirled away from him and sailed into the dining room, head held high. Sheba gave her a warning look and shook her head. Marie made a face, a child's face, at Sheba's back as the woman turned to curtsy to Henri.

They ate in silence. Marie's temples throbbed, and she could scarcely force down the food. Bile soured her throat and rose in her nostrils. Anger, shame, fear, and sorrow were like a tempest within her. Sorrow that she had spoken to Henri as she had. Sorrow for the way he had spoken to her. Just when she had begun to feel that she might come to love him, he had destroyed that love. As Edmund had destroyed it. As Céline, whom she had trusted, had betrayed her.

She went to their bedroom directly after dinner, undressed in the dark, and climbed into bed, but she did not sleep. She had not thought of her parents for a long while. She thought of them now, saying over and over, "Mother, father, come back to me." How different her life would have been. She thought of the grave and the slowly sinking coffins, and of Frank Goodacre standing beside her in his sour-smelling clothes. She remembered Mrs. Goodacre barring her from the house; the filthy quilt they had tossed to her to cover herself with that night; the grief and despair; Céline in her red dress in the church.

Everything that had happened since was woven together by the sable thread of her parents' death. Even Edmund had been no more than a shooting star, a brief golden trail of light, then darkness. She pressed her thighs together, remembering him between them.

After a long while she heard Henri climbing the stair. Twice he stumbled and cursed. He had not brought a candle with him and cursed again when he tripped over the heap of clothing Marie had dropped on the floor. She sensed, rather than saw, him throwing off his own clothes and felt the bed give as he got in. He jerked her to him, rolled her over onto her back, and came down on her, forcing her legs apart. He smelled of brandy, and she turned her head away.

"Since you are a bought woman"—the voice in her ear was thick with drink—"I'll show you how drunken officers treat bought women. You must learn to like it before you go back to Céline's. I'll train you well."

She tried to beat him off, but he grasped her hands and pinned them above her head. She tried to bite, but he laughed and bit in return, and she cried out as he drew blood on her neck.

"Your blood is sweet, *ma petite poule*. Not tainted yet with pox."

Then he raped her, slowly but not gently. The more she tried to draw away from him the more violent he became, thrusting into her more and more deeply. She gasped, "Henri, you'll injure the child!"

"The child that isn't mine?" he shouted. "Were you and Céline cheating me all along? Taking money from some other fool? Selling the little virgin body again and again?"

"No! No, I swear it. There was only you. I swear, there was no one else."

She expected the roof to explode and Lucifer's black wings to sweep her to the bowels of hell in a hurricane of air. But nothing happened except that Henri laughed, plunging again and again and again, covering her neck and breasts with bites, until suddenly all the anger that had fired him emptied into her, as if he had been chaste for years and all his manhood had been saved for this moment.

He was still at last, but he did not pull away from her. He continued to hold her, and at last he spoke. "What have I done to you? What have we done to each other? What have we said that we will never be able to withdraw? I am always asking you to forgive me, Marie, and I must ask it again. Forgive me, forgive me."

He kissed her bruises, licked away the blood, loosened her wrists and smoothed her hair, touched her eyes to see if she was crying.

Reluctantly her arms encircled him. "Henri, don't send me back to Céline. Please don't. I will do whatever you ask."

"Do you think I could be parted from you? Do you think I could live with the thought of what would happen to you there? Do you think I could live with the thought of you in someone else's arms? God forgive me for even having voiced such a threat."

"And you love me still?"

"I adore you, worship you."

She touched his body as if feeling it for the first time. He was not Edmund with his dancing eyes and exuberance, his arrogance and laughter. But she belonged to him. He was her salvation, and she must never put that in jeopardy again.

France

Day after day for almost four months there was the unchanging, ever-changing sea. Every day, every creak of the ship's ropes, every swell which lifted the ship, every wind that bellied the sails carried Marie de Nemour farther away from her past.

Marie had gritted her teeth and welcomed the Lanneys into her house. Annette had run from room to room, squealed, exclaimed, lifted the lid of the soup kettle in the kitchen, and acted like the silly girl Marie considered her to be. Edmund had followed her, very stiff, very correct, speaking only to Henri, avoiding Marie's eyes.

He had not been stiff and correct the day Marie had gone to the warehouse to supervise the storage of their goods. She had managed to be alone with him only for a moment, but it was enough.

"You will send a payment to Céline every month. She will hold it for me until we return."

"I will pay what I can and when I can, and the devil take you."

"She will let me know if you don't pay, and a letter to your wife will demolish you."

"I wish to God I could demolish *you*. I wish to God I had never seen you."

"Ah, but how you enjoyed it when you did." She had laughed because he had turned scarlet. "You haven't forgotten, have you? You don't know how fortunate you are, Edmund. Don't you know there's a law here which requires all unmarried pregnant girls to declare their condition before the registrar and name the father, or be punished? Had it not been for Henri, I would have been forced to name you. You wouldn't have liked that."

"I doubt that law applies to whores."

"Even to whores, Edmund. As we'll be sailing tomorrow, I'll tell you now, I did not have the operation. It is your child."

"Name of God! You *are* a bitch!"

"Would you have had me sin?"

"You were already steeped in sin."

"It's you who sinned, Edmund. I offered you my love."

Then Henri had come in, following the workmen carrying the enamel hip bath in which was packed the silver mirror. Marie had spoken no more to Edmund beyond a gracious, "*Adieu,* M. Lanney. Enjoy our home."

Just before they had sailed, Marie and Henri had gone to church for Absolution. For the first time Marie confessed everything to the priest: her sin, her lies to Henri, her deep hurt and resentment, and her desire for revenge.

"You have carried these secrets all this time, daughter? That was wrong. They are festers in your soul."

"More like a heavy burden which I can never put down."

"I command you to put it down. To renounce your hatred. To wish ill to no man. To be penitent. To cherish your husband. The child, then, will be as your husband's child, and no evil will come of your erring way."

She promised to try, and as she promised the burden seemed to lighten. It lightened each day of the voyage, and she almost forgot her secret terror of giving birth on board the ship. She felt the change. It was a different Marie who nursed Sheba when she became seasick; washed Henri's shirts and hose; dressed her own hair; and took pleasure in every new day. She came to accept the inevitable—whatever would happen, Henri would be by her side. And meanwhile, everything delighted her, the green islands of the Caribbean, the dark, steep, stormy waves which tossed the ship like a piece of bark, the boxlike cabin where they bumped into one another constantly, which gave Henri an excuse to take her in his arms.

He was aware of the change without knowing what had caused it or in what way Marie was different. He knew he was more deeply in love than he could have imagined was possible. There was no more rape, but tenderness, doing all he could to bring the melting softness which darkened her eyes until they were like violets and her mouth clung to his. Her nipples, dark as garnets as she neared her time, were sweet in his mouth, her thighs trembling, welcoming. The intensity of her passion surprised him.

Often it was Marie herself who instigated the lovemaking, sometimes by asking if he loved her still, even though she had grown fat and ungainly, sometimes by only a touch, a look. For Marie it was a desperate attempt to love Henri as he loved her, to accept the happiness he offered, to forget Edmund forever.

They felt the land swell two days before they reached France. It lifted the ship, almost repelled it, aided by the seaward wind.

The second morning a low gray mass grew on the horizon. Gulls screamed, circling the mast. The smell of earth mingled with that of sea. The land rose slowly, taking jagged shape against the darkening eastern sky. The sinking sun glinted off a rooftop. A light winked at them. "La Tour de la Lanterne," Henri said. "The lighthouse to guide us in."

All night the ship rolled at anchor outside La Rochelle's quay, since a chain barred the harbor after dark. Henri and Marie did not sleep but lay in each other's arms as if their passion would suffer a land change and nothing would ever be the same again.

They were up early to watch the ship enter the harbor, protected on one side by Fort Saint-Nicholas with its crenelated walls and on the other by the Tour de la Chaine. Already they smelled the narrow streets with their odors of tar and brine and human waste. On the crowded wharf people cried out for news of the colony.

Peddlers, vendors, prostitutes, and innkeeps called the prices of their wares and services, and the ever-present beggars whined underfoot. Like a pack of hounds the crowd yelped at the passengers, jostled them, caught at their sleeves.

A seaman tried to clear a pathway, but Marie and Sheba were separated from Henri. A legless beggar grabbed the hem of Marie's shirt and held it. As she tried to jerk free a sharp pain sent her staggering. She would have fallen if Sheba hadn't caught her. Gasping, she leaned on Sheba, her eyes closed. The stink of fish and sea-soaked pilings nauseated her, and she thought she was going to be sick. Then, as suddenly as it had come, the pain left her, and Henri was hurrying back, calling them, looking for them.

"What happened?"

"For a moment I didn't feel well."

"Land sickness." Henri dismissed it. "Travelers often feel it after a long voyage. You can lie down when we reach the inn."

They could not get there fast enough to suit her. The cobbled streets were slippery with grime, and though the wind chilled her to the marrow, sweat beaded her lips. She was so long accustomed to gauging her walk to the rolling of the ship, the earth seemed to rise and fall beneath her feet. She clung to Henri to keep from falling.

The inn was flanked by tall buildings built out over arcades which were overlooked by carvings of leering gargoyles and allegorical figures. The room smelled of mildew. Icy air seeped through the leaded windows. Beyond the uneven glass a gargoyle stuck out its tongue at the street below.

Marie sat down on a stool by the fireplace and stretched out her hands to the cold ash. After a quick inspection of the room Henri went off to fetch the innkeeper. While he was gone the pain struck Marie again. When Henri returned with the innkeeper, the innkeeper's wife, a coal boy, and a maid with an armload of clean linens, they found Marie hunched over, moaning and biting her lips in pain.

The innkeeper looked at Marie in alarm and with lifted eyebrows glanced at his wife, who gave a brisk nod. "Is it her time, monsieur?"

"No, no. It's two months away."

"I had my first at just over seven months. The voyage may have brought hers on early. It can't have helped her any." Marie heard through the pain, and relief flooded over her. "Get the bed ready, girl. Madame may be needing it soon. You, boy, stop staring and get the fire going. I've been in stables that were warmer than this room! You'd no business letting the fire go out when you knew a ship was docking. There, madame, it's passing, isn't it?"

Marie straightened and tried to smile at Henri. "It's gone, yes. Don't worry, my love. I think it's nothing but indigestion. You know yourself the meat on the ship had turned," she said.

"Are you sure you're all right? I have to go back to the docks to see to our luggage and get a letter off to my parents warning them of our arrival."

"Go, monsieur," the innkeeper's wife advised. "You'd only be in the way. You, boy, when you're finished there, run around to Mme. Martin and tell her she's needed. A midwife, monsieur, madame. One of the best in La Rochelle. I'd trust her with the queen herself."

Sheba helped Marie undress, and she huddled by the fire until the pain sent her pacing again. When she walked toward the wndow, the unevenly blown glass made the gargoyle seem to move as she approached, shrug his shoulders, grin, and shift position. It made her dizzy, and she turned her back so she wouldn't see him. He was grinning at her pain, which she deserved for having been unfaithful to Henri.

"Sheba, are babies sometimes born at seven months?"

"You heard the woman say it."

"Do they look different from nine month babies?"

"I never saw one, and I doubt Monsieur has."

"You must warn the midwife. There's money in my purse to help her hold her tongue."

"I'll speak to her."

She had no idea how long Henri was gone. The pains were bad now, and she bit the sleeve of her velvet dressing gown to keep from screaming. Once, through glazed eyes, she saw Henri holding out a cup of steaming liquor. She gulped at it gratefully. It seared her throat as she swallowed, and her stomach churned. She thought she was going to vomit, but then the warmth of the brandy spread through her, and she drank some more.

By the time the midwife arrived, Marie was drunk. Sometimes she bit her hands, sometimes, to her surprise, Henri's. He blotted the sweat from her forehead and supported her when she paced the floor.

When the midwife ordered him out of the room, Marie wept. But somehow he was gone and she was in bed and Sheba and the midwife were kneading her stomach. She had a towel to bite now. Her body churned. She was torn apart. A scream which not even the towel could muffle rent her throat. Darkness closed over her. As she drowned in it she said, "Thank God," but she didn't know if she said it aloud.

When she awakened, Henri was sitting on the bed, smoothing her hair from her forehead. He kissed her when he saw that she was awake.

"My darling, we have a beautiful daughter. A minx

to have made her mother suffer such hell." He put a velvet box into her hands. "This will help to relieve the pain. Peridots are said to have magical powers."

The stone was the size of a hazelnut, cut so the light turned it to green fire. It was set in the gold claws of a loop too large for any but Marie's forefinger. Henri slipped it on and kissed her fingertip.

A daughter. A girl. A boy might have looked like Edmund, kept his memory alive, perhaps betrayed her infidelity. She twisted the huge ring on her finger. It was the color of Edmund's eyes. "I don't deserve it." Green like the light that came through the leaves and the hanging moss of the liveoak tree.

"I say that you do. What shall we name her?"

"Henriette." To make her more truly Henri's child.

"I protest. Why not Mariette?"

But his delight was so obvious that Marie smiled. "You protest and I insist. She shall be Henriette or have no name at all."

"Very well. Henriette she shall be."

The two weeks they stayed at the inn seemed like two months to Marie. Rain coursed down the uneven panes, and the gargoyle wept.

A wet nurse had been hired, a giggling girl named Eloise, plump and, of course, unwed, with a pink porcine baby. She was eternally pulling her breasts out of her bodice to thrust a dribbling nipple into the hungry mouth of one or the other of the babes. Sheba was jealous and snatched Henriette away as soon as the baby was fed, but Eloise only laughed good-naturedly.

The thought of going to Paris delighted Eloise. It was a lucky day, she said, when she was hired by M. de Nemour.

Marie's own breasts were bound, so there was a new pain added to that in her swollen and bruised loins. She felt as cold and stonelike as the gargoyle. She suffered Henri's kisses and dreaded the time when she must again submit to him, when his arms would hold her and his fingers invade and stroke her.

She felt no relationship to the child, no wish to hold it, but she spent long minutes gazing at its sleeping face, trying to find some resemblance to Edmund and fearing that she might.

Henri adored the child. He looked in on her a dozen times a day, extending his finger for the minuscule fingers to curl around, dancing with her, singing to her, and teasing Eloise until she turned scarlet with laughter, warning her not to mix up the children and forget which belonged to whom.

"And how could I do that, monsieur, when they have different fixtures?"

"How, indeed. I had forgotten there was a difference."

"Oh, monsieur, a gentleman like you'd never do that!"

Two weeks after the child's birth Henri's mother's own silver coach arrived in La Rochelle to carry them to Paris. With it came letters to Henri and gifts for all. Henri's father congratulated him on having been sensible enough to marry at last and prayed that he would conduct himself as a husband should. His mother urged them to make haste to Paris so she might have the joy of holding her grandchild in her arms.

For Marie there was a sable-lined cape and a string of pearls that reached to her knees; for the baby a lacy wardrobe and down-filled blankets; for Henri a purse of money.

"Thank God for that!" Henri tossed it in the air and caught it again so the coins clinked as he walked up and down the room. "I was wondering how we were going to pay our bill here. We might have had to use your money, Marie."

Thank God, indeed, Marie thought. Henri didn't know how little of it there was, thanks to that damned Edmund.

"We'll leave as soon as you're strong enough. I'm so anxious to show you Paris! The ballet, the theater, the opera, the salons. I didn't realize how dull I had become in that hellhole of a colony."

"I told you often how dull we were."

"But you resisted making friends."

"Who wanted to be friends with people duller than ourselves?"

"You won't find the Parisians dull. They catch hold of every new idea and worry it as a terrier worries a bone until it's sucked all the nourishment from it."

"I'll never fit into such a society."

"You've nothing to do but smile and listen."

Marie doubted that smiling would suffice. With every league they traveled, every turn of the wheels, her apprehension increased. She was not ready for this life with strangers who sent gifts of pearls enough for three people.

It was difficult to share her anxiety with Henri. During the day there was no privacy in the coach. Eloise and Sheba would have been too interested in anything she had to say. At night she was so weary that she fell thankfully into bed after she had eaten. If she had been able to share her doubts, what would she have said? "I am afraid"? She didn't even know exactly what it was she feared.

She almost wished the journey would never end, though the roads were miserable, mud-rutted, and at times almost impassable. Every evening Marie discovered new bruises from being tossed about. By midday the mud and dust had turned the silver coach as brown as a walnut shell and the grays that drew it muddy as a peasant's donkey.

But castles, cathedrals, and old stone towns topped the rounded hills already springtime green, and eventually the road they had followed turned onto the Rue Saint-Jacques, the ancient Roman road that went straight into Paris to the Ile de la Cité.

The shadow of the coach and the plumed horses

raced along beside them now. Rocked by the motion, Sheba, Eloise, and the babies slept. Henri held Marie's hand, his fingers interlaced with hers. Now, now, she should speak, say, "Henri, I'm afraid." But she knew he would answer her with a laugh and empty reassurances. It was different for Henri. He was going home.

The city became a silhouette against the sky, gradually taking on the shape of windmills, towers, spires, domes, peaked roofs, and chimney pots. Soon they were in the midst of it, bouncing over the cobblestones, halting, easing ahead, backing, jerking forward again as the coachman brandished his whip and shouted insults to get through the astounding press of traffic. Carriages, coaches, sedan chairs, and men on horseback and afoot vied for the right of way.

Sheba and Eloise awakened, and Eloise crowed with excitement. Once, as they were squeezing past another coach, a brandy merchant jogged along beside them, beat upon the window, shouting, "*La vie, la vie!*" The babies awakened and howled. Not even Eloise's proffered breasts silenced them. Henri winced and closed his eyes as if in pain.

There was another delay for a company of acrobats in particolored tights. Marie leaned forward to watch them. A juggler tossing tarnished gilt balls into the air pretended to throw one to Marie, winked, and showed the tip of his tongue to her. She blushed and drew back against Henri. Eloise gurgled with laughter.

"He's bold, madame. He'd toss you in his bed if you gave him a nod."

Henri groaned.

They crossed Pont-Notre-Dame, but it was impossible to see the river because of the gabled houses, art shops, and stalls that lined the bridge. The excitement of Paris began to penetrate Marie's doubts. There was a vitality here which New Orleans lacked. She felt her mind quickening, as if it darted in and out among the crowds, peeked and peered into shop windows, explored the twisting lanes. For a reckless moment she wished she were a part of it. These street people she could understand as she was sure she would not understand the society Henri had described to her.

She wished the babies would hush so she could think clearly. She was very close to some new knowledge of herself. As if in answer to her wish Henri said, "Give me the child, Sheba. I can comfort her."

The instant he took her, Henriette stopped crying and gazed up into his face with her blank baby eyes as if she actually saw and recognized him.

"Would you like Guy too, monsieur?" Eloise giggled, jouncing the screaming child so violently it seemed to Marie that he was in danger of flying out of her arms.

"If you wouldn't throw him about so . . ." Marie said.

They left the traffic behind, turned and turned again through such a labyrinth of streets that Marie wondered how the driver knew the way. They passed walled gardens with only the tops of trees showing over them and beyond the trees a slated roof, turrets and towers, a curl of smoke from a chimney, an ornate gable. The afternoon light was fading, the sky turning from blue to lavender, when the coach stopped before a wall covered with a lacework of budding vines. Beyond the wall the trees were coming into green leaf, and they too were like lace against the lavender-tinted sky. Through the grill of the double gate Marie could see the house, all the windows glowing with the gold of candlelight.

"At last," Henri sighed.

"*This* is where you live?" All her apprehension became understandable. "Henri, I don't belong in such a place. It's like a palace."

"Nonsense. It's a very simple, old-fashioned house." He handed Henriette back to Sheba. "For God's sake, keep her quiet. We don't want to arrive sounding like a circus."

As Henri helped Marie down from the coach the door of the house flew open and a woman tripped down the brick path, arms outstretched, a rustle of taffeta and silk rosettes, a flutter of pink ribbons and silver lace trailing behind her.

Marie shrank back against the coach, wishing she could escape. The woman flung herself into Henri's arms so forcefully that he staggered, and she covered his face with kisses. Unbidden, tears came to Marie's eyes. Her parents had never lavished such demonstrations of love on her.

"You're a good lass," her father would say and tug playfully at one of her curls. Her mother would give her a pat of approval, a good night kiss on her forehead, a loving smile. But neither of them had ever held her as if they could not bear to let her go. Perhaps it was because they had never been parted until the fever took them. If they could return from the grave, she knew she would hold them in that way.

"Maman, Maman, you throw me off my feet." Gently Henri loosened the embrace.

"But I must. My youngest one, my dearest one. I thought I would never see you again! And you have returned to me twofold—or is it threefold? With a wife and a little one. Where are they?" A frown wrinkled her forehead under its powdered ringlets.

"Marie." Henri beckoned her forward.

She was conscious of her dusty clothes, her hair tied back beneath the hood of her cape, her face, from which all trace of powder and paint had vanished long before they had sighted the walls of Paris, and her shoes, mud-stained from the times they'd had to walk beside the coach so it could be freed from the mire. How much better it would have been to enter the house in secret, bathe and change, and meet Henri's parents looking less like the peasant she felt she was.

Mme. de Nemour caught Marie's hands and drew her to her, scrutinized her face as if Marie were a painting, judged her, looked, Marie thought, into her very soul. And then she smiled and embraced her. In the warmth of that embrace some magic passed from Mme. de Nemour's body into her own. Appearance, travel-worn clothes, did not matter. It was Marie herself that Henri's mother saw.

"You're very beautiful, *ma petite.* Beware, Henri! She'll have every man in Paris desiring her."

"It is you who are beautiful, madame. Even more beautiful than Henri told me." She had Henri's dark eyes and finely boned face, but she was rounded, almost plump, and exuded energy and the scent of tuberose. She gasped slightly as she talked, as if her laces were too tight, and her Parisian accent, so different from the drawling patois already developing in New Orleans, was difficult for Marie to understand.

"Tush! Beautiful! I am fifty, my dear. The babe. Where is she?" She looked uncertainly from Eloise and Guy, who had subsided into startled silence at the first gust of cold air, to Sheba's pink cocoon.

"But of course!" She gathered Henriette into her arms as if she had been a wet nurse all her life. Again came that dark and piercing scrutiny and the pleased smile. "She is lovely. The picture of—I wonder?"

"My mother," Marie supplied quickly. "Henriette has her coloring. She too was beautiful." Before the hardships of exile, before the heat of New Orleans had faded her. Or so Marie's father had told her, though Marie had no memory of it.

"Of course. The Scots are fair, are they not? The next little one will perhaps resemble Henri's maman, yes?" She trilled with laughter.

"I hope so, madame. I hope Henriette isn't a disappointment."

"A disappointment? You cannot believe, Marie, how I longed for such a baby, blond and pink and blue-eyed. All my children were dark as Egyptians. I smothered them in powder, but all it did was to make them look like little ghosts. But what am I thinking, prattling away like this? We must go in. Your father has been waiting just as impatiently as I, but of course dignity would not permit him to come down to the garden to meet you."

Still carrying Henriette, she led the way up the path between green spikes of iris and tulips and blooming daffodils.

Dignity had not prevented Henri's father from waiting in the doorway. Marie's first thought was, *That is how Henri will look when he is old.* Grave, disdainful of life, with an eye which took in everything at a glance and dismissed that which did not concern him.

Henri pushed Marie toward him. She started to curtsy, but he drew her up and embraced her, kissing both cheeks. "Welcome, daughter. Welcome, my dear. I can see Henri chose well."

He embraced and kissed Henri too, then half-turned away to wipe his eyes. He coughed to clear his throat of tears but did not quite succeed. "It is good to have you home, Henri. I have missed you."

"I have missed you too, Papa. I am grateful for your welcome after my—disgraceful departure."

"Enough, enough!" his mother interrupted. "We will all be weeping, and it is a time for joy. Come, dear man, admire our granddaughter."

M. de Nemour accepted the child into his arms, examined her closely, and nodded approval. "Well done. It is not too early to start thinking of her dowry, Henri. We want her to marry well."

In spite of herself Marie laughed. "She's scarcely a month old."

"High time she's betrothed." But the dark eyes twinkled, and a smile tilted the ends of the mustache upward.

It's going to be all right, Marie told herself. *I needn't have been afraid after all.*

Later, standing at the window of their apartments, which overlooked the river in the direction of the squat towers of Notre Dame, she thought that but for

Edmund she would not be here. She could almost find it possible to be grateful to him. At this moment he seemed very close. How foreign, how ugly, he must have found New Orleans. How wide the Mississippi was compared to this narrower river reflecting the amethyst sky and the lights of the barges.

Henri came up behind her and put his arms around her. "Well, Marie?"

It was not Edmund but Henri to whom she should be grateful. This was his world. She had been accepted, welcomed into it with a love that had been there, awaiting his wife.

"It's lovely, Henri. I am very happy."

She could scarcely believe it.

Henri too was happy. He had been welcomed home like the Prodigal Son, and Marie had been accepted as a daughter. He and his father were companionable as they had never been before, and his mother was making a project of Marie. It began with shopping, because, Maman declared, her clothes were shockingly provincial and out of fashion.

"They will be gone the rest of the day, and I'll be the poorer when they return," Papa observed. "However, we cannot have your wife appearing in society like a drab."

"She would never be that even if her dress were out of fashion. My God, Papa, you must admit she is beautiful."

They were sitting in his office, stretching their legs toward the marble fireplace, drinking a morning brandy and eating thin, crisp sweet cakes. Henri's father gazed at him thoughtfully and finished chewing before he spoke. "So, you married her for beauty? Has she a dowry?"

"I married for love. She is an orphan, as I explained in my letter. She has a small sum of money of her own, and I have not touched it, nor will I if I can avoid it. I would have married her if she hadn't had a sou."

"Then we're bound to go on supporting you from the estate taxes. Have you developed the grant I obtained for you?"

"Not yet."

"Why?"

Henri shrugged. "It's remote and lonely. I'd need slaves to clear the land. It would be expensive to build there. I wouldn't think of it until the Indian problem is solved."

"From what I have learned from the maps I've studied Pontchartrain is a main artery to the Mississippi, and there are landing stages there. I understand tobacco growers are given first choice of the slave shipments."

Henri shrugged again. "The price of slaves is high. The bidding goes up and up. Furthermore, I distrust the tobacco trade. They can ship more cheaply from Virginia. I'll use the land eventually, Papa. Marie likes it. She wants a house there. I usually try to please her."

Henri's father sipped his brandy and rolled it around on his tongue. "Good. Perhaps exile has taught you to lead a blameless life after all."

"To do that in New Orleans one would have to be a stone pillar in the church."

"Humph. I'm an old-fashioned man, as you know, Henri. I've never considered marriage—even an arranged marriage—as an unpleasant necessity. I have a deep respect for marriage. It is a sacrament and should be lived as such. While you are in my house I expect you to behave accordingly. No affairs, no dalliances, no flirtations to relieve your boredom." His words were harsh but not his tone.

"Papa, in that way I have changed. There have been neither affairs nor flirtations since I married Marie. If you ever suspect me of being unfaithful, you may send me to the block."

"I hope there will be no need for the ax. And I hope you will impress my attitudes upon Marie. There will be temptations. With those eyes and that gentle air she'll be game for every fop in Paris. The more she resists the more persistent they'll be to claim the honor of being the first to win her favor. You must warn her. She is still young and unaccustomed to society."

"Marie is faithful. If I'd thought she would ever be otherwise, I wouldn't have married her."

"That is settled then."

"Papa . . . what became of Minette Devereaux after I left?"

"Ah. Her husband forgave her grandly, convincing himself that you had seduced her and led her into evil ways. She found someone to take your place and someone after that. She has children, which the old gentleman parades as his, but anyone at court will tell you that is impossible, and they are scarcely likely to have been fathered by the Holy Ghost." Papa chuckled. "She's a bad lot, like all the other petticoat tails at court, but I suspect it was you who introduced her to her downfall."

"I was her first lover after her marriage, and I'm no longer proud of it. But it would have come to that sooner or later, wouldn't it have? What of her sister? Sophie?"

"Just as you predicted. she became mistress of the regent. When he discarded her, she entered a convent."

"That's rather a pity."

"Is it?" His father's voice was dry. "We might say you gave that soul to God, Henri. You deflowered her."

"Please, Papa." Henri closed his eyes. It was not a pleasant memory. It had never been a pleasant memory. Minette, her sister, the little harem of girls that had fluttered around him. And Marie. Was there no end to his sin? Had exile been enough, or was greater vengeance yet to come?

"*Eh bien*, it is past. We will bury it. I regretted afterward that I was so hard on you."

Henri got up and stood with his back to the fireplace, hands behind him to warm them. Beyond the leaded diamond-shaped panes a gray drizzle began to fall. Upstairs a child wailed for a few minutes, then was silent. He pictured Eloise baring her breast and guiding the huge nipple into the pink birdlike mouth. Was it his own Henriette or Guy? He could not tell their cries apart.

He wished Marie and his mother would return. He felt lonely without Marie, hungry for her. He had not possessed her since the child had been born. They lay side by side in the huge gilt bed never touching one another. Henri waited for the time when she would say she was ready for him again. Too many nights had passed already.

The drizzle turned into a violent downpour. For a panic-stricken moment he imagined he would never be allowed to possess her body again.

Marie thought of their years in Paris as the time when she grew up. Until then she had acted as a child, obedient to the commands and whims of her elders. The affair with Edmund had been like a schoolgirl infatuation, she realized. Even after she had become mistress of the house in New Orleans, she had never ceased to remind herself that it was Henri's house and that she was there through his charity.

It was not the birth of Henriette that matured her but Paris itself, the swarming street people brawling for survival; *le monde*, the elegant society with its exacting code of manners; the coffeehouses where conversation bristled with ideas and arguments and knowledge; the glittering illusion of the fairyland of the theater, the opera, and the ballet. All these awakened her mind so that she almost felt it stretch and grow.

Maman, like the Cinder Maid's fairy godmother, transformed Marie into a member of this world. When Henri asked sardonically where her glass slippers were, Marie laughed and Maman took it as a compliment. Henri had not meant it as one.

Marie and Henri seldom saw each other alone anymore. They took their morning rolls and chocolate in their apartments in the morning, but there were always milliners with hats for Marie to try, and Maman standing by to give advice, to nod approval or roll her eyes in horror that such a hat should have entered the house; merchants with gloves of Russian leather and samples of shoes; lacemakers, hairdressers, silk merchants; Eloise with the baby, which Henri held and admired because Marie had no time. Always there was something to distract Marie and prevent Henri from exchanging a private word with her. Sometimes, but not often, he was brought into the discussion to express his preference as to the silks and satins and brocades. Those he picked were not always the ones chosen in the end.

Breakfast over, Marie and his mother would go off in the silver coach to the Rue Saint-Honoré, where the best dressmakers set the fashion not only for Paris but for the rest of Europe as well.

As Henri had known she would be, Marie was an instant success at every salon, always surrounded by nearly all the gentlemen present, which did not win her many female friends. More than once Henri had glanced around a room seeking her and not recognized her when he found her.

In a society where everyone played a part, where everyone talked continuously and flirted with a passion and where wit was highly prized, Marie was something new. Henri had told her she needed but to smile and remain silent. She had a repertoire of smiles which he wondered if she practiced in secret before her mirror. There was the beguiling smile, the skeptical smile, the innocent smile, the interested smile, the wiser-than-you-think smile, the smile hidden by her fan. Gossip had it that Marie de Nemour said more with a smile than any other woman said with words.

"It's fortunate I *can* smile." Marie said to Henri. They were in their coach returning home after a supper party which had lasted for hours and at which there had been as much talking as there had been eating. "I am ill-read, ill-informed, and nothing like any of those people. I didn't even understand that young man's poetry when he recited." Henri laughed. "You needn't laugh. I suspect it was not very good poetry, and he was allowed to recite only because he is Madame's lover. And I suspect the only reason he is her lover—witchy old thing—is because she allows him to recite."

"You're becoming very witty, Marie."

"No, I'm not. I refuse. I don't want to be like those peoole. They are all so sickeningly polite, and underneath that perfect politeness there is malice. Their gestures are studied, their *bon mots* are studied, their looks are studied, as if they were constantly changing masks."

He took her hand. "And to think, Papa was afraid you'd be swept away by it all and that I would lose you."

"How could he have thought such a thing?"

"Because you are inexperienced."

"I may be inexperienced, but I feel infinitely old and infinitely wiser than any of those ladies. I doubt if any of them has ever had a real emotion. They wouldn't know how to behave if they did have. They'd turn it into a clever little story to amuse their friends and destroy the real feeling, sweet or sad, suffering or joy, whatever it was." She sighed and leaned against him. "Henri, I know when we are in society we must pretend not to care for one another, but do you love me still? You don't wish your former mistress back?"

"My God, no!"

"Have I met her?"

He hesitated. "Mme. Devereux."

"Her! With that old ape of a husband? And those silly young men carrying her fan, her parasol, her purse, and fetching her sweets while he grimaces in the background and scratches his fleas? My God!"

"She was charming once."

"Does she want you back?"

"Not for an instant. She looked at me and laughed and called me *mon vieux.*"

Marie laughed too. "Bitch. I didn't like her even before I knew."

That night she changed into a robe of such exquisiteness that Henri gasped. "That cost Papa a sou or two."

"Maman insisted we buy it. She said"—Marie gave the amused smile with one eyebrow raised—"that you would need temptation in the bed chamber as well as in the salons."

"The only temptation in the salons, my dear, is you."

"And in the bedchamber?"

"Come here, Marie. You have forced me to be celibate long enough."

She went willingly into his arms and lifted her face to be kissed. It was not one but many kisses. Then he picked her up and carried her to the bed.

Afterward he asked, "Why? Why did you make me wait? I thought you had ceased to love me."

"I couldn't stand the thought of being touched. I had to forget the pain first. And I don't want another child, not yet. But when I am ready, Henri, we'll have another. Yours and mine."

As he was falling asleep he thought it was a strange thing to have said. What was Henriette but theirs?

* * *

In July the household moved, with mountains of luggage and an exhausting flurry of activity, to the château in the country. It was, Maman explained, to restore one's tranquility after the carroussel of *le monde*. Otherwise, one would have the breakdown.

"One has the breakdown merely by making the move," Henri teased.

"Tush! It is all done by servants."

From the moment Marie saw the château she loved it. It was reached by a hump-backed bridge straddling a moss-green tributary of the river. The turrets and tall leaded windows, the ivy-hung stones and rustling poplars were mirrored in the water. River reeds waved and bent in the wind, an orchard shed its last late blooms, a lush garden awaited Maman's pruning shears.

The ground floor apartments were somewhat damp, as the land tended to be marshy, and at high water the river lapped the foundations. But the rooms were airy, paneled in apple green, citron, or rose. The walls ripped with the reflection of the sun on the river. Instead of the ornate gilt furniture which overcrowded the Hôtel de Nemour in Paris, the chairs here were pale wood with natural homespun coverings.

Marie found it a great relief to be away from Paris, where a feigned smile paralyzed her face, her corselets stifled her breathing, and even if she were not wearing a heavy silver wig, her powdered hair made her head ache. Freed from the demands of society, she wore a plain loose garment of brown or blue homespun, sabots, and a peasant's straw hat which she sometimes garlanded with flowers.

Maman too wore the simplest of gowns. There were still a great many ribbons and small silk flowers around the hem, which was so short that her ankles showed. The costume was so amusing Marie could scarcely keep from laughing, for on her feet she wore sabots as she pottered in the garden. She was out before the dew had dried gathering bouquets for the château so every room was like a garden itself, pruning, kneeling on a cushion to plant or transplant, grafting, watering, and consulting with the two gardeners, who followed her with their wooden rakes and spades.

There were picnics in a grove where a statue of Ceres inclined its head over their feast and on an artificial hill, a mock Grecian temple between whose columns swung strands of ivy. The ivy curtained the real reason for the temple's existence: a privy.

There were days when Marie and Henri rowed an ancient scull down the sluggish stream to the Loire and drifted past the greater châteaux of royalty; days when Marie did nothing at all beyond playing a game of chess with Henri or Papa, or half-dozed in the grass while Henri, who had discovered Voltaire, read aloud to her. "*'Tous les coeurs sont émus de ma douleur mortelle . . .*"

And when no one was around to watch her, Marie painted. Everything seemed to cry out to her to be rendered in watercolor so she would never forget it, the red poppies polka-dotting the meadows, the peasants fishing, the view of the marshes from her turret windows, Maman amongst the roses, the château itself. Her portfolio bulged.

In August the peace was broken. Henri's brothers and their wives and children, his sister Laure and her husband and their children, and all their servants joined them. Even Sister François, the de Nemour daughter who had become a nun, came. She looked as thin and ascetic as her namesake until she frolicked with the children or hooted with laughter at some bawdy joke.

One morning Henri's sister Laure announced that she had asked the de Montforts to a picnic. Their château was on the Loire. They would arrive by boat, stay the day, and depart by lantern light.

The kitchen had already been informed, and preparations were underway for the feast. Rugs and cushions and parasols had already been carried to the grove along with tubs of flowers, which "denuded the garden," Maman scolded. "You might have consulted me, Laure. I can't think why you want to entertain such common people."

"They're not common, Maman. They are aristocracy and live at Versailles."

"And can talk of nothing but the latest scandal at court," Maman sniffed. "She is certainly not aristocracy. I happen to know her father, M. Lanney, bought her way into that marriage with a shockingly large dowry."

"M. Lanney is a deputy to the Council of Commerce, Maman. No small position in itself. Anyway, we must entertain them. My husband is angling for a favor—no, never mind what it is until de Monfort can whisper in the king's ear."

"I have no patience with such doings."

"If you had, Maman, you and Papa would be living at Versailles yourselves instead of in that run-down old hotel in the Marais. That quarter is no longer fashionable. It embarrasses me to give directions to the coachmen when I visit you."

"Oh, come, Laure," Henri said. "You're becoming a snob."

"I was born one," Laure said proudly. "So were you until you turned into a colonial. Speaking of that, I hope you and Marie will dress properly for the picnic. They'll take you for a peasant in that homespun bag, Marie. And, Maman, pray wear your mules instead of those horrid sabots."

Marie, Henri, and Maman exchanged looks, but they agreed to respect Laure's wishes.

Marie felt so secure these days that the prospect of meeting Edmund's sister made her curious rather than apprehensive. Everyone had accepted Marie's statement that Henriette took after her family, and Henri had never suspected her relationship with Lanney.

Days had passed without her thinking of Edmund

or Frank Goodacre. Once, when she had wanted an exquisite little brooch in the shape of a thistle, Henri had teased her about being close-fisted. "Buy it," Henri had said. "It's a fitting thing to buy with the money from your father's house." How could she tell him that this money and all he had given her and what Frank Goodacre had repaid her had bought a warehouse in New Orleans? In the end Henri had bought the pin and threatened to demand repayment one day. She scarcely dared to wear it for fear he would remember.

No, she did not mind meeting Edmund's sister. Marie had nothing against her, and her own plans for vengeance had been put aside until she returned to New Orleans.

Marie was still dressing when the de Montforts arrived in three sculls, gilted, cushioned, and upholstered in royal blue bearing the de Montfort crest in gold thread. Marie, watching from the curved window of the turret, groaned. "Henri, you must see this. It's like the barges of Cleopatra. Can you imagine such a sight on the Mississippi?"

"Thank God we don't often see such a sight here when Laure doesn't visit. I suppose I should have forbidden her to invite the de Montforts, if she had given me warning."

"*You* forbid her?"

"It is my home and my land."

"I thought it belonged to Maman."

"It's my portion of her estates—or at least it will be mine when Maman dies. We could live here always if you wished. Would you prefer it to New Orleans?"

"I don't know. I'm so astonished. I have always thought that one day we would go home. New Orleans *is* home, Henri. But in a way, so is this. Must I choose now?"

"Good Lord, no. All you have to choose now is which jewels to wear to impress La Montfort. Colonials have their pride, you know."

"Yes, we must not disgrace Laure."

The entire de Montfort family acted like a group of strangers thrown together by some strange coincidence. M. de Montfort treated his wife with formal gallantry and addressed her as "madame." In return she spoke to him with gracious condescension, as if she did not think him worthy of the six hundred thousand livres dowry she had brought him.

Her resemblance to her brother Edmund was slight. Her eyes were hazel rather than green and her hair a darker shade of gold, so rich that Marie suspected it was dyed. But she had the same arrogant tilt to her head Marie had sometimes seen in Edmund, and when she smiled flirtatiously at the gentlemen, the same cherubic dimples appeared in her cheeks.

Her daughter, Eulalie, was Marie's age, a pallid, unhappy-looking girl with a baby a little older than Henriette. Eulalie's husband, Comte de Deffand, seemed completely uninterested in either his wife or child and spent most of his time taking snuff, smoothing his mustache, and ogling Marie.

Bored by the whole affair, Marie retreated to her enigmatic smiles without attempting to take any part in the conversations. Presently the gentlemen went for a stroll along the river. Laure and Mme. de Montfort began to gossip about mutual acquaintances, Maman dozed over her needlework, and Marie tried to make friends with Eulalie.

It was a hot, still day, and Marie suggested they go wading in the river. Eulalie turned paler than she naturally was and stared at Marie as if she were insane. To occupy herself Marie wove flower-chain chaplets for the babies while Eulalie watched with disdainful curiosity.

When the chaplets were finished, Marie called Sheba to bring Henriette. "There is one for your little girl too." Marie smiled tentatively at Eulalie.

"Oh, well, I suppose she may as well wear it. Jeanne, bring my baby."

The children were propped against cushions on a carpet and the chaplets placed on their heads.

"They're really quite sweet," Eulalie said. She called to her mother, "Madame, look. Baby is wearing a little crown like a dauphine."

Mme. de Montfort interrupted her flow of gossip to give the babies a glance. Then she stared.

"But they could be twins! Look, isn't there a startling resemblance? Tell me I do not imagine it. Why, your little Henriette could be my own grandchild. I remember the Little Uncle—my brother, we call him that to tease him—was the very picture of her when he was young. Everyone mistook him for a girl."

Marie's stomach lurched, and she felt sick. There really was a remarkable resemblance between the two babies.

Eulalie made a face. "Oh, madame, all babies look alike. They are all so boring. And I am *enceinte* again."

"Eulalie, what a time and place to announce it! And why, may I ask, why? One would think you would be more cautious."

"About announcing it or about getting that way?" Red spots mottled Eulalie's pallor. "I knew you'd be angry. That's why I told you now. So you couldn't scold. There are no gentlemen present"—*Thank God,* Marie thought—"so it's really not so shocking."

"Quite shocking enough." Mme. de Montfort turned her attention to Marie. "Perhaps you know my brother? Our father sent him to New Orleans to look after our business there. We hear he's doing very well. Do you know him? Edmund Lanney?"

It was an effort to speak naturally. "Yes. We were at his wedding celebration."

"Ah! Then you can tell me about his bride. The family. Are they 'quite'?"

"Quite?" It was difficult enough to concentrate with her stomach churning without having to think in riddles.

"Their background? One hears such dreadful rumors about the colonials. Their reputations. Their reasons for being there. Abduction by the Mississippi Thugs. Released criminals. Evaders of taxes. Some disgrace which led to a *lettre de cachet*—" Maman's gasp interrupted her, and Mme. de Montfort's face reddened under her paint just as Eulalie's had done, as she remembered Henri's reason for being in New Orleans.

"Oh," Marie said, "you mean, madame, is her family 'born'? I don't know the Arnolie family well, madame. My husband could tell you more about them. My impression is that they are peasant stock and went to Louisiana to make their fortune. We don't have the rigid social structure there that you have in France."

"Peasant! Name of the Virgin!"

"It was only an impression, madame." She picked up the flowers from her lap and hoped no one noticed that her hands trembled as she began another chaplet.

"Undoubtedly a wrong one." Mme. de Montfort's voice was vinegary. She too had recovered. "Ah, the gentlemen are joining us."

Marie shot Sheba a warning look.

"My pet." Mme. de Montfort tapped her husband's arm with her fan. "Do you remember the Little Uncle as a babe? Will you look—"

Only Marie saw Sheba pinch Henriette, who shrieked with anger, drowning out Mme. de Montfort's words. Sheba carried the child away, the cries dying in the distance. Before Mme. de Montfort could recover from the insult of being interrupted by a child, Marie stood up, spilling flowers from her lap.

"Henri, take me for a walk? The wine has gone to my head, and I'm horribly dizzy. You'll excuse me, won't you, Mesdames, Maman, Laure?"

She didn't wait for an answer but fairly dragged Henri away. Eulalie's voice drifted after them. "Maybe she's *enceinte* too. The wine always makes me sick."

* * *

When the de Montfort family left, quiet returned to the château but not peace for Marie. Mme. de Montfort's remark had upset her more than she realized. Every time she looked at Henriette, she saw a reflection of Edmund and wondered that Henri didn't see it as well. Henriette's eyes were even beginning to turn the color of the peridot.

Marie had had little sense of Henriette's belonging to her, no sense of motherly possession. She had grown the child in her body and produced her in pain, but Henriette was not hers. She was a separate entity, a thing apart, just as the ghost of Mary Macleod was a thing apart from Marie de Nemour.

As the weeks went by the sun rose later, and the dusk came earlier. The hay stood in stacks "like *brioches*," Marie said to Henri. Day after day there were flights of geese and ducks and small birds going south. "It is going to be an early winter," Papa said. "We should return to Paris."

Marie was sorry to leave the château. The last morning she stood at the curved window of the turret and watched the shadow of clouds on the marsh and the undulation of reeds in the water. She turned to Henri with tears in her eyes.

"You asked me once if I wanted to stay here. Now I can answer you. Yes."

"My dear, it is cold in winter."

"It's cold in Paris too."

"The heating—"

"You don't want to stay."

"I've promised to assist Papa in some dealings."

"Never mind."

"We'll spend Christmas here."

"Promise?"

"Promise."

But they did not.

Paul

They returned to Paris in drizzly weather. Chill winds swept the fallen leaves along the streets and dropped them in drifts in the gutters. The hotel was airless from being closed all summer and because of the sudden change of weather took several days to heat.

Eloise came down with a cold and gave it to both babies. The odor of medicinal vapors drifted from room to room on the nursery floor. Henri got up a dozen times each night to see if Henriette was all right, to hold her over his shoulder so she could breathe more easily. The child vomited, coughed, screamed, and burned with fever.

Maman lighted a candle every morning after mass. That done, she took Marie shopping to refurbish their wardrobes for the new season. One day they returned home to find Papa pacing the walk in front of the house. He didn't wait for them to alight from the coach but rushed out to them and announced, "Henri is ill."

"I knew he would take Henriette's cold," Marie said.

"It is not a cold. It is a sickness I have never seen before. It came on very suddenly. He complained of a headache, then began to shudder with chills. He had to be carried to his room. He is vomiting, burning with fever."

"Oh, no! It's come back. The fever. He had it in New Orleans when I—when I first knew him." Her face betrayed her anxiety so plainly that Papa felt compelled to help her into the house. "I'm all right, Papa, thank you. I'll go to him. But you must not. You must not come near him. It is very contagious. Very serious."

She smelled it as soon as she entered their bedroom, the foul, hot stench that had preceded the death of her parents and lingered after their bodies had been removed. Henri didn't hear her enter, nor was he aware of her until she put her hand on his forehead. It was like putting her hand in a fire. He opened his eyes then, the pupils dull with fever.

"Go away, Marie. You mustn't risk getting it. Get out. Get out at once."

"I want to stay with you. I'll nurse you."

"Don't be a fool." He shuddered and struggled up onto one elbow and leaned over to vomit in the commode beside the bed. Already the bile was streaked with blood.

"Get out, get out, get out." He fell back on the pillow.

"Henri, Henri . . . please don't die."

"I'll . . . try not to, my dear." He closed his eyes. "I make no promises. Get out."

As she closed the door he called after her. "Take care of Henriette."

When she rejoined Maman and Papa, her face was so grave that Papa asked bluntly, "Will he die?"

"It's too soon to tell." She sat down because her legs were too weak to hold her. "It strikes so suddenly. It kills suddenly. Or slowly. You never know until it happens. My parents . . ."

The sorrow she had kept under control all these years welled up in her. She told them of her family's exile, the long journey through the wilderness down the river from Canada, the deaths, the burials, even of the night spent outside the Goodacres' door.

Maman sobbed, and Papa wiped his eyes and blew his nose.

"It was Henri who took pity on me, who loved me.

And I have learned to love him. And now I can do nothing for him."

A servant was sent to fetch a nun from the nearest hospital. There was nothing for Marie to do, so she kept what she considered a promise to Henri and joined Sheba at Henriette's bedside. The smell of vomit and excrement made her gag, but she forced herself to stay with her daughter, dosing the child with medicine, more than half of which spilled because Henriette spit it out as soon as it was in her mouth. Marie bathed the child with cool water to bring down the fever, but Sheba could do that better than Marie. In her opinion Maman's candles were as effective as the surgeon's powders.

All the perfumery and potpourri lavished about the lower apartments of the Hôtel de Nemour could not disguise the pest house stench. The noxious smell was a mixture of the vinegar with which Henri's room was doused daily, the tar burning in an iron pot outside his door, garlic and herbs, the steaming vapors from the nursery, and foul diapers and chamber pots which could not be emptied often enough. It was a wonder to Marie that the rest of the household did not take ill.

But Papa found business to keep him away from home until bedtime each day. And Maman spent so much time on her knees in church that she developed a stiffness in her joints from the damp stones and had to apply hot compresses in the evenings.

The garden was filled with racks to air their clothes. It looked as if they had mustered an army of scarecrows. There were no more shopping expeditions, no visiting *le monde,* and not even family was received, though they sent around daily inquiries which had to be answered in writing.

Night after night Marie lay awake, staring up into the rose-red brocade canopy above the bed in the room to which she had moved, wondering what would become of her if Henri died. She supposed she would stay in Paris, be taken care of. But the thought of Paris without Henri depressed her.

Perhaps she would go back to New Orleans to the house she and Henri had created. Every day she would walk past the warehouse so Edmund could not fail to see her. Finally he would be able to stand it no longer. He would come to her, beg to become her lover and— Here her imagination failed. If she were strong, she would sneer at him, reject him, shame him. But Mme. de Montfort's casual words had reawakened the memory of him. Marie remembered his lips on her breasts, his enormous, plunging, eager manhood, and she longed for him, against her will. Perhaps it wouldn't be the same, not after all these months of contentment with Henri. But to have him beg for her, to take him from that goose, Annette, would be in itself revenge.

Why do I think such things? she wondered. Edmund no longer mattered. New Orleans did. She was homesick for the heat and the forest and the watery land, for the wide tawny-colored water of the Mississippi.

Henriette recovered first and bloomed as if she had never been ill. She was growing and changing so rapidly that the resemblance to Edmund passed, and with it, Marie's fantasies.

Henri too was recovering, and though he was too weak to go out, Maman insisted that Marie relax her vigil and get some fresh air every day. There was a purpose behind the proposed outings.

"Laure is right, you know, Marie. The *quartier* Marais is no longer fashionable. It is possible to live here still and be genteel, but one should change with the times. We must move."

At first they explored Faubourg Saint-Germain on the Left Bank. The nobility had started moving there during the reign of the old king. But prices were high and, in Maman's opinion the less one had to do with the nobility the better. "It isn't that they are the nobility, which is quite all right. It's that they are so *aware* of it."

She settled finally on a spot just north of the Champs-Elysées in Le Roule on the Rue Saint-Honoré. They visited the site day after day, walking about, planning the garden, the size of the house, the wall. Maman discussed her plans at such length that Marie began to visualize herself. She made a series of sketches of the house and garden, which delighted Maman.

"You are so clever! This is exactly how I thought of it all myself. When I show these to my darling, he won't be able to resist my plan any longer. To show him a piece of land is nothing. To show him a completed plan is everything."

They found the gentlemen in Henri's boudoir, where he was lying on a chaise longue. The sketches were thrust into Papa's hands, and he gave them an impatient glance. "So"—he raised his fierce eyebrows—"you are so determined that you had plans drawn?"

"Not really plans. Just little sketches by Marie."

"Marie did these?" He gave her a sharp look, and she nodded. He went through the sketches again slowly. "Very skillful. Look at these, Henri."

"I know how skillful she is." He was very pale still, his eyes very black in his thin face. "Marie, have Sheba fetch your portfolio."

"They don't want to see those daubs."

"I think they will. Besides, they should see the ones you did in New Orleans. Our house, the garden, the levee. I like the one of the market place. I don't know why we didn't think of it before. There is even a painting of the Pontchartrain grant, Papa. You'll see how wild it is and the difficulties involved."

Marie's paintings of New Orleans shocked Maman. "You lived in that, my dears? Such a barbaric land, and I imagined it like Paradise."

"She must have instruction," Papa said. "I'll look into it. Would you like that, Marie?"

"I'd like it very much. Sometimes I ache to show a thing but can't make the perspective come right. And the color. You see this one? The shadows are too purple. An actual shadow should give the feeling of purple, but I don't know how to mix the paint to do it." She stopped, embarrassed.

Papa looked at Henri. "She is clever, our Marie. We must take her to see M. Crozat's collection, and at the same time I'll have a little word in his ear. He has thousands of drawings, Marie. Rembrandt, van Dyck, Titian, everyone of any importance in the Dutch or Italian school. It will be a feast for you."

Later Marie said to Henri, "I never heard of any of those artists Papa mentioned. You see, I *am* stupid. It isn't enough to smile."

"The sister who taught you drawing should have taught you the Old Masters."

"Perhaps she did, and I paid no attention. What were names if I couldn't put a picture to them? Besides my French was very simple in those days, and Sister Thérèse lisped."

Henri laughed. "So that is why you lisped when Céline had you display your drawings? I always wondered. I thought it was shyness."

"It was both. Dear God, what an innocent I was," she said. "I'm glad you're well again, Henri. Maman and I prayed very hard. I don't know what I would have done if you had died."

He reached out to her, and she took his hand. "I love you, Henri."

"I believe at last you mean it."

Below on the river in the silent evening air they heard a bargeman call. Marie could not hear his words, but his voice sounded like the voice of Edmund shouting, "Whore, whore, whore."

How could she have imagined that she desired him?

* * *

Thanks to Henri's illness and slow recovery they had avoided the society of *le monde* throughout the autumn. When Marie became a student at M. Condé's atelier, they continued to avoid it. Marie didn't know how Henri felt about her lessons, but she was glad. At last she had something worthwhile to do.

She felt almost like Mary again in the homespun gown and peasant's smock which became her uniform. She left her hair unpowdered, caught up on her head with a black ribbon.

Her dress, her dedication to her classes, and her enthusiasm amused and pleased Maman and Papa. Henri complained, not too seriously, of being replaced in her affections by a paint brush.

At first Maman's coach delivered her to M. Condé's atelier in Saint-Germain-des-Prés, but the silver coach and plumed horses were so conspicuous that they became an embarrassment to Marie. The street performers who put on daily shows revised their dialogue to comment on the princess who arrived in the silver nutmeg. Once an acrobat leapt from his tightrope to the back of one of the grays and rode, standing in arabesque, to M. Condé's door, while the crowd cheered. Then he had the gall to jump down, open the door for Marie, and hold out his hand. She put a coin in it and wished it were spit.

After that she insisted on being left off at the Pont-Neuf. "I can walk. I shall be quite safe."

"It is too far. And there is the danger that you will be accosted," Papa said.

Family pressure forced her to compromise. She could walk, but a servant followed at a discreet distance until he saw her safely in the door. He was there again in the afternoon, lounging in the square, watching the jugglers and dancers or being gulled by the card sharks. He slouched along after her, back to the Pont-Neuf, where a carriage or sedan chair waited her.

Marie had chosen M. Condé's atelier herself after

visiting drawing masters of the Flemish, Italian, Dutch, and rococo schools. Actually she had been most attracted to the work of a M. Boucher, and he would have accepted her as a pupil, but Maman had vetoed him as unsuitable.

"His models come from the Opéra. Perhaps Henri hasn't told you, but it is known as the national brothel. The poor girls receive no wages, you see, so they're forced to support themselves any way they can. And what is easier than whoring? I suppose if it were a choice between that and starving, I would take it up myself."

"Maman!" Marie was shocked.

Maman blushed. "Well, perhaps not."

It was also common gossip that the models not only received pay for their modeling but also for certain favors they granted Boucher. "I suppose his wife shrugs off that kind of thing just as the better born do."

M. Condé belonged to the Chardin school, specializing in ordinary objects and simple domestic scenes. This appealed to Marie. None of those dimpled nymphs and mythical figures for her. She wanted to record what she saw and felt, so one day her children would see the world as she had seen it.

As a painter M. Condé had never gained sufficient recognition, but as a teacher he excelled. He also specialized in the reproduction of Old Masters, for which there was a good market. "There are always those who want them but cannot afford the real thing, you understand," he explained to Marie.

He had an assembly line of students who had been studying under him for years. One specialized in faces, another skies, another clothing, another hands, and so on. They earned three livres a week, plus a supper of soup, free instruction in class, and "excellent training in technique," as Condé put it. 'To copy is to learn. In time they develop their own style through the knowledge of others'."

The studio was the entire top floor of a tall, ancient building. The north wall was windows of real glass from floor to ceiling. The assembly line worked here, moving up and down the row of easels as their special technique was required. There was a stage for the models, males one week and females the next. Marie wondered if they came from the Opéra. There were tables with still-life arrangements, easels, stools, a smoky stove, and two walls of the students' paintings nailed up for critical admiration.

M. Condé danced about the drafty studio on his rather dainty feet, moving from easel to easel, correcting a line here, the color there, with special attention to Marie, who didn't know that Papa had paid more for her instruction than was demanded from the other students.

"You must make an old jug so beautiful it looks like a jewel. You must make the fruit so tempting the viewer longs to bite into it. You must make us smell the soup in the kitchen, hear the lullaby in the nursery, the squeaky wheel of a cart.

"Shadows vary in color. The ordinary eye does not see them as color until we artists point it out. A shadow in the snow is the blue of crystal. In the shade of a tree on grass it is brown. A white parasol casts a lavender shadow on a lady's face. I don't know the color of shadows in your New Orleans, so you must teach me. Indigo? So? And deep purple. Ah, yes, it is the heat and the brilliance of the sun. But paint them so they do not look false. A picture is not a set for the Comédie Française. That is what you must learn.

"The movement there, pardon, madame, but you have not quite caught it. It is not only the lifted foot but the fall of the clothing. Let me see, we cannot use the model, as he has no clothes on to wrinkle. Ah, here, Paul, you are the right size. Leave that burgher's hand and come here. Take a step and hold it midway, so. You see, madame, how I do it?" He took the brush from Marie and with a few swift lines captured the pose perfectly. If the viewer glanced away for a moment, it seemed, the figure might walk right off the canvas. "It is the swing of the coattail, the wrinkled knee of the hose. All right. Back you go, Paul."

Marie rewarded Paul with a smile, and he looked at her picture and nodded as if he liked it. "It's warm there, in your home?"

He was a solemn, tangle-haired young man with a face all plains and angles and large dark-blue, heavily fringed eyes. His mouth was wide and sensitive.

"It is hot."

"We could do with some heat here." He blew on his paint-stained fingers. The windowpanes rattled loosely in the wind, and today even snowflakes drifted in.

Marie longed for that enervating heat these days. She wondered how the assembly line could move their fingers so deftly when they were so cold. Perhaps they didn't stop to think about it any more than she did when she really moved into a picture. Into the heat of New Orleans.

M. Condé was having her repaint in oil all her early sketchy watercolors of New Orleans, to learn by her mistakes. Three of the new ones he considered good enough to place in a small shop on the Pont-Notre-Dame. They were sold immediately to someone who had been a government official in Louisiana under Sieur de Bienville. To celebrate, Marie bought wine and cakes for everyone in the atelier. Paul climbed to the modeling stage and proposed a toast to "La Belle de la Louisiane." Even the praise Marie received from the de Nemours was not so fine as that celebration.

There was another feast a few days before Christmas. Maman was responsible for this one. She sent hampers filled with roast duck, breads and cheeses, pâté, chopped venison in flaky pastry, preserves, marzipan biscuits, and little pastel-iced cakes. Some of the best wines from Papa's cellar accompanied the hampers.

Marie sat on the floor with the rest of the students and ate as heartily as they did. Paul sat beside her. He handed her pastries and sweets, spread bread with cheese, filled and refilled her wine glass until she protested that he would make her drunk. "Here, you have the rest of mine," she offered.

She would have poured the wine from her glass into his, but he took it from her. "I will drink from yours, where your lips have touched." He looked at her over the rim of the glass as he drank, and she found she could not look away. It was romantic and rather silly, but he was a very appealing young man. When he took her hand and kissed the palm, she felt an aching in her loins, shameful, because she should not feel that for anyone but Henri.

She took a holiday over Christmas. Henri was almost fully recovered now. Nevertheless they decided not to go to the château. "In any case, I shouldn't be gone from my classes so long," Marie said.

As they came out of mass on Christmas Eve, bells were ringing all over Paris and snow was whirling down out of the black sky. Snow would be sifting through the windows of the empty atelier, Marie mused.

As they rode home, Marie's head nodding sleepily, her hand in Henri's, she wondered how Paul was spending Christmas. When she closed her eyes, she could see his face very clearly, hear him saying, *I will drink where your lips have touched.*

"Henri, are you too tired to make love to me tonight?"

"Not if you want me, Marie." His hand tightened over hers. "We must make up for the weeks that I was ill. I wonder if I'll ever be rid of that damned swamp fever. You wouldn't think it would recur here."

"No." Not so far from the heat and damp. *It's warm there, in your home?* "When are we going home, Henri?"

"We're nearly there, my dear."

The snowflakes, whirling as if they danced to the sound of the bells, isolated the coach from the rest of the world.

"I mean New Orleans."

"Oh, that home. Not until the Indian affairs are settled."

"They are not, after all this time?"

"No. You *are* happy here, aren't you, Marie?"

"Yes." But she was afraid of herself with Paul. He kept intruding into her thoughts, unbidden. She remembered the sudden readiness of her body when he had kissed her palm. She felt herself drawn to him like metal to a lodestone. It was the thought of Paul that had kindled her passion that night.

Spring was early that year, but Marie scarcely noticed. She was busy living two separate lives. Often she felt like the Cinder Maid when she came home from the atelier, doffed her "costume," and dressed for supper in the shimmering taffetas that changed color when she walked.

Le monde had never seemed so suffocatingly elegant, so false, its glitter so brassy as it had since Christmas. At more than one supper Marie remembered the feast on the paint-spattered floor of the atelier. As she watched the guests nibbling at the rich food she remembered the hungry students who had devoured every crumb of Maman's feast and had shouted after Marie as she left, "A thousand kisses, a thousand thanks to Madame *votre mère*." Such a memory made *le monde* almost intolerable.

Marie could do more than smile now. She could discuss art. Even M. Crozat with his enormous collection was impressed. Mme. Devereaux, Henri's former mistress, was overheard to remark that Henri's little colonial seemed to know more about art than was absolutely necessary. The simple little thing was actually taking painting lessons, as if she feared Henri would lose his estate or, more likely, that she would lose Henri.

"The only thing Mme. Devereaux can paint is her face," Marie said to the young gallant who had reported the gossip. "And I don't doubt she hires an artist to do that. He probably paints more than her face while he's about it, if all I hear about her morals is true."

The young man had laughed and hurried off to repeat Marie's quip. For days afterward there were jokes about the color of Mme. Devereaux's nipples and a rumor about an interesting scene on an intimate section of her body which Mother Nature had certainly not put there.

"How *could* you have, Marie?" Henri asked, half amused, half angry. They were at breakfast after a late evening during which Henri had heard for the first time the origin of the rumors.

"All I said was that she couldn't paint anything but her face. Someone invented the rest, but I shouldn't wonder that it's true. Why don't you reprove her for what she said about me?"

"I wouldn't lower myself to such trivia."

"Trivia? To say that you may leave me?"

"You know damned well I would never do that."

"Or take a mistress like everyone else?"

"Nor would I do that."

"I hate those people." Marie shoved her cup of chocolate aside. "Thank heavens I have something better to do than gossip and paint my—" She paused and smiled wickedly. "My face."

Henri's mouth twisted with amusement. "I thought you were going to say something else."

"So I was, but I decided it would shock you." She got up and dropped a kiss on his brow. "I must go. M. Condé hates it when I am late."

"I see very little of you these days."

"You should be glad I'm doing something—in case

you lose the estate—instead of being disgracefully idle like you."

"I may appear to be idle, but in truth Papa and I are constantly busy with estate matters, to see that we don't lose them."

"Pooh!" Estate matters seemed to consist of sitting before the marble fireplace in Papa's office and drinking Spanish wine. She was critical even of Henri these days and often found herself wondering how he would look dressed in a smock and country brogues like Paul.

It was more often Paul than M. Condé who helped her mix paint or correct her perspective now. He always understood what she was trying to do and would explain how other painters did it. He tossed around the names of the old and contemporary greats, describing techniques and color and use of subject until Marie was dizzy.

"You must study Picart," he would say. "He paints the street people of Paris just as you paint the street people of your home. Yes, yes, and you must stop in at M. Gersaint's shop. It is on the Pont-Neuf. Tell him you are a student of Condé. He likes Condé and takes the Old Masters we paint for his less discriminating buyers. Be sure to take a look at his signboard. Watteau painted it. He died in Gersaint's arms." Paul made a rueful face. "Ah, if I were to die in Gersaint's arms, I'd know I had arrived.

"Monsieur is glaring at me. I must return to the hands of Charles I. We are doing van Dyck today. Very beautiful, van Dyck." He lingered a moment longer, his eyes brimming with desire. "But better to lie in your arms than to die in Gersaint's."

"You must not say such things, Paul." She lowered her eyes, bewildered, shaken by the undisciplined desire he aroused in her.

It was M. Condé who was responsible for what happened next. He came to examine the picture Marie was painting of an Indian woman displaying her fruit at market.

"Madame, the hands are like claws. She would hold the fruit tenderly, not as if to crush it. Paul, come here, show Madame how to curve the fingers."

The assembly line all looked over their shoulders, grinning as Paul walked toward her. Their hands touched as he took the brush from her, and a shock went through her body.

"No, no," M. Condé called from across the room. "Guide her hand."

Paul gave the brush back to her and put his hand over hers. The line went jagged because their hands were shaking. Paul looked at the ruined line, looked at Marie, and tightened his hand on hers.

"Madame, I have ruined the picture."

"It was not your fault. My hand trembled when you tried to help me," she whispered.

"It was my own hand that trembled, as my entire body trembles when I am near you, when I think of you, when you come in and scent the room with your perfume."

"I know."

"You know? You know that I adore you? That I must have you? Do you—is it possible that you want me as well? That I may hope?"

She shook her head.

He sighed and went back to the assembly line.

Marie sat motionless, staring at the picture. Paul had put into words what she had dared not admit to herself. She did want him. She wanted him to hold her, press her against his lean body, which was so different from Henri's. She wanted to touch his face, trace with her fingers the high bones and hollows of his cheeks, the black brows, to push the tangle of dark curls back from his forehead, to kiss the full, curved lips. She wanted their bodies naked, touching.

Until now Henri had satisfied her completely. Not a man she had met in Paris had tempted her, though many had tried. But if she were not married to Henri, this would be the mate she would choose. This young man with his burning eyes, his passion for art, his simplicity, his skill at turning a phrase. *Better to lie in your arms than to die in Gersaint's.*

Better to lie in Paul's arms just once . . .

M. Condé stood beside her, pursing his lips at the picture. "That line. Surely that isn't meant to be."

"My hand, when he guided it, didn't go the way he intended that it should."

"I see, ah, yes, I see. A pity. Scrape it and begin again. I will help you myself this time."

When she left that afternoon, M. Condé followed her down the stairs. "Madame, I must speak. I have seen what is happening with Paul, but I have not been alarmed. It is good for an artist to feel emotion and to feel it strongly. I had not realized the feeling was returned. In your stratum of society, I realize, it is of course accepted for a lady to take a lover. But I beg of you, do not injure Paul. Do not take him lightly. He is very serious, very sensitive, very talented. Now he paints hands, copying Rembrandt or Vermeer or van Dyck. One day he will be as great as any of them. I do not want him destroyed."

"I've no intention of destroying him. I was destroyed once, M. Condé. I wouldn't wish that suffering on anyone."

"Thank you, madame. I will have a fatherly talk with him. Warn him that nothing can come of this passion he feels. If you become his mistress—"

"M. Condé, I love my husband."

"Pouf! When has love ever interfered with desire? If you become his mistress, would it be possible for you to help him financially? He is very poor. He would advance more rapidly if he could afford paints, canvases, and better food."

"Perhaps I could do that without becoming his mistress. I'll ask my husband if we can establish a fund to help some of your students."

M. Condé nodded. "That would be more subtle and less injurious to Paul's pride. He would not want to think you were buying him."

It was Maman who promised the money as a gift. She was so delighted with Marie's progress, so proud of her talents, that it pleased her to be bountiful. "In the new hotel we'll have one of the students do a series of panels. I fancy some little beasts, dogs, cats, monkeys, and so on in human dress cavorting in society. A monkey as a judge at the trial of a dog who has stolen sausages. A cat courtesan with cat musicians entertaining her. A dog smoking a pipe before the fire, dreaming of the wars and seeing his memories in the flames."

"Maman, how imaginative!"

Maman nodded. "And amusing, I hope."

"Papa has agreed to the new hotel, then?"

"He protests and makes a face, but that is pretense," she said. "He and Henri are going to Versailles to see about the land. Perhaps Henri will take you with him. It would be an experience to see the court."

"Must I go?" Marie asked Henri. They were having a game of chess before dinner.

"Not if you don't want to. There'll be another time, and I'll be busy in any case. You're taking your art classes very seriously. Your admirers miss you at the salons."

"I'm sure Mme. Devereaux doesn't miss me, nor do I miss her. Or the salons or the little supper parties. If I weren't married to you, Henri, I'd go live on the top floor of one of those drafty old houses in Saint-Germain and spend my life painting."

"And starving."

"I suppose that goes with it unless one becomes a favorite at court. Do you know what I wish? That Mimi were here to take lessons. She's far more clever than I, and she would learn so much. *She* would become a favorite at court. Not only for her painting, of course. She'd probably end up painting the king."

"And being one of the royal mistresses. For a lady, Marie, you have strange tastes in friends. Sheba, a whore, and a flock of art students."

"But those people are real, and your friends are not."

"Those painted apes aren't my friends any more than they are yours. If the news weren't so bad in New Orleans, I'd be ready to go back."

"Is it bad?"

"I heard from Lanney when he sent money for the rental of our house. It was a bad winter. An early autumn freeze ruined the fall crops. His warehouse is empty. The Natchez are still raiding, and other tribes are rising in sympathy."

"It all seems very far away and unreal."

"It is certainly far away. His wife had a child last August, by the way, and is expecting another."

Marie looked at the black king on the board. So Henriette had a half-brother. And the warehouse was empty. If Marie were there, she'd foreclose, but what on earth would she do with a warehouse? And how would she explain it to Henri? She moved her bishop cautiously.

"Hm. What was the meaning of that move? Ah, yes, I see your strategy. We should be thinking of another child ourselves, Marie."

"I suppose so."

"You don't want another?"

She shrugged. "I don't know. Yes, I suppose I do." Perhaps she would feel differently about a child that was Henri's. She hoped so.

At first she could not believe the relief it was to have Henri away. She enjoyed his absence in a dozen little ways: having the bed to herself, a hurried breakfast and off to the atelier, the evenings to go over her work with a critical eye, to sit in her nightdress before the fire.

But after a few days she regretted not having gone

with him. One night she could not sleep because he was not in the bed beside her. She got up, wrapped herself in a fur-lined robe, and sat by the coal-banked fire to write to him.

Never before had she written to him, never before written a love letter. How was it done? Did one write as one spoke, or was there a certain form to be followed? No matter. It all came pouring out. How foolish she had been to let him go alone. How large and empty the bed was without him. How she had dreamed that he was there, kissing her in all the ways he did, and how she had awakened, trembling, eager for him.

It was true, but in the dream the face had kept changing from Henri's to Paul's, and though she had awakened saying Henri's name, the hands holding her had been Paul's hands. In the dream she had seen them plainly, the long, bony fingers with paint under the nails.

"Please come back soon, Henri, my love . . ." she wrote.

Save me from Paul. From myself.

Often Sheba and Eloise came to gossip with her while the children frolicked around the room on their fat, unsteady legs. Henriette was weaned now, but Marie had grown fond of Eloise and Guy and delayed sending them back to La Rochelle. Nor did Eloise want to go. "La Rochelle, madame, after I've seen Paris? No hurry, and I'm sure my mother would say the same. Besides, there's Joseph. What a man."

Joseph was one of Maman's footmen, who was courting Eloise.

"Don't get yourself another baby," Marie cautioned.

"Oh, I won't be such a fool this time. Anyway, he's afraid Mme. de Nemour would dismiss him if I did. He'd marry me in a minute if it weren't for Guy. He doesn't like to be reminded that there was a man before him."

"Do you want to be married?"

"What woman doesn't? A man to cook for, a man in your bed every night instead of—" Her hand flew to her mouth. "It's difficult for lovers, madame."

"I know."

Aside from her fellow art students, Eloise and Sheba were the only company she had these days. Maman had taken advantage of Papa's absence to go into religious retreat to give thanks for the recovery of Henri and Henriette.

"Belated, of course, but I think the Lord understands."

Nevertheless she emerged from the convent every few days for a sustaining meal. "We are not allowed even an egg, let alone a fish, Marie. I shall lose weight, which should be a compensation, but I can't believe hunger is good for one. The nuns are the color of wax." She added, "And my knees. There is such a thing as too much praying, Marie. But never mind, I am doing it for the little one and for Henri."

"Tell me about Henri when he was young, Maman."

"When he was young?" Maman's eyes took on a dreamy look. "He was the most charming of my children. Laure was always independent, and Nevil and Raoul and George busy collecting rocks and toads and unspeakable insects which invariably got loose in the house. But Henri—ah! I spoiled him, of course. One does spoil one's favorites. I was almost glad when the girl he was to marry died, God forgive me. I knew I'd be jealous of her. Such a sweet thing too, but no match for Henri."

"Are you jealous of me?"

"You are exactly what I would have chosen for him."

"Why is that?"

"Because he loves you! Arranged marriages—well, they are not always the success they should be. Love is so much nicer. And you keep him amused, which is good for him."

"Do I?"

"Of course. Your art classes. Refusing to go to Versailles with him. Most women would have begged to go." Maman frowned. "I hope he is behaving himself. It is a place of such temptations."

"He hasn't answered my letter."

Nor did an answer come in the days that followed.

One morning when Marie arrived at the atelier, she saw Paul's place was empty. She looked around the room, but he wasn't there. Every time the door opened, she turned to see if it was Paul entering. Finally she could stand it no longer. She went to M. Condé, who was busy with his accounts.

"Monsieur, where is Paul?" She had not meant it to come out so bluntly.

"Delivering a painting to Gersaint, madame. I had the fatherly talk with him, by the way. His—ah—sickness is far more serious than I thought." M. Condé tapped his quill thoughtfully. "Sometimes the only cure is consummation. When the dream becomes flesh, it ceases to be a dream, and *voilà*! The disease is gone."

Marie frowned. "I'm not sure what you mean."

M. Condé smiled. "I am sentimental, madame. I thought it possible the physician needed to cure herself as well."

"Oh!" Marie's face burned. "It is true, I *like* Paul—"

M. Condé nodded, beaming.

"But I—I have never been unfaithful to my husband."

M. Condé raised his eyebrows. "Is it possible?"

"I told you before, I love him. Such a thing as you hint at is impossible."

"So. So. Ah, well, poor Paul."

That evening when Marie returned home, she saw Papa's coach standing in front of the house. She ran inside expecting to find Henri, but Papa was alone in his study.

"Henri didn't come?"

"No. I came back only for tonight to fetch some papers. He is still at Versailles. He sent his love, of course."

"But no letter?"

"Letter? No. No letter. Just love and hopes that you are well."

"You may tell him that I am," Marie said coldly and went to her apartments to change.

Maman too had returned home for the evening, so it was dinner *en famille.* As Marie went to the salon she overheard Papa saying, "Devereaux is at Versailles, too. God knows what he has up his sleeve. That wife of his prances like a peahen. She flirts with Henri under Devereaux's very nose. Not that Henri—oh, Marie. Come in, my dear. I was saying the behavior at Versailles these days is a disgrace."

"I thought I heard Henri's name."

"Henri is taking care of himself. He learned his lesson long ago."

Still, it was strange he hadn't written to her. She wished she had never sent that passionate letter.

That night she could not sleep. She remembered M. Condé's words. *The only cure is consummation.* When she closed her eyes, she could see Paul's face, his broad mouth, the thick, dark lashes, the hair curling over his shoulders, a brush stuck behind one ear, the sagging hem of his smock, his shoes worn at the heels. How would it feel to hold him, to lie under him, to drain him of the passion she knew was there, waiting for her? She touched her breasts, wondering how he would touch them, and her body throbbed under her touch. She tried to think of Henri, but she could not even recall his face except for a fleeting moment.

She got up. The house was still, the fire low, the room cooling. She opened the window, and the wind blew the smell of the Seine into the room, cooled her burning body. Paris was dark, sleeping.

Consummation was not the only cure. The cure would be never to see Paul again. She must tell M. Condé tomorrow. No more lessons, no more atelier, no more the Cinder Maid. Tears sprang to her eyes. If she did that, she would regret it—regret Paul—forever. What had M. Condé said about love not interfering with desire?

But in a way she didn't quite understand she loved Paul too. Because Marie at the atelier and Marie in *le monde* were two separate people.

And she was a fool to listen to a silly old man making a living off forged Old Masters, and a greater fool to stand here on the balcony catching a cold from the night wind. She went back to bed to toss and turn until dawn.

The Pont-Neuf was more crowded than usual, and the coach stalled several times in the traffic. They were already late and would be later because she had overslept. It was a beautiful day. The Seine sparkled as if it flowed with diamonds. The trees on the riverbank were coming into leaf. Vendors of spring flowers were everywhere. The coach had come to another halt, and a flower girl thrust a bunch of violets through the window. Marie paid her and put the bouquet in the neck of her dress. The dew from the stems trickled between her breasts. She closed her eyes and tried to think of Henri, who had not written to her.

It was time to leave the coach, to become one of the poor of Paris who had no silver coach drawn by plumed horses. She always loved this moment when she became a part of the crowd, slipped off the character of Mme. de Nemour and became plain Marie. How could she have thought of giving it up?

She tossed a kiss to Paris as she turned into M. Condé's doorway. An acrobat pretended to catch the kiss and turned a somersault in the air. Marie ran up the four flights of stairs. The students all turned and stared as she closed the door and leaned against it, breathless. Paul looked not at her but at the violets and the wet stain on her dress.

"I'm late. I'm sorry, monsieur. I had a headache this morning and nearly didn't come."

"It is the smell of oil paints, perhaps. If the ache returns, you must say so. I'll send one of the students to escort you home."

"Thank you, but I'm sure I'll be all right." She really did feel very strange. She shouldn't have run up the stairs. The scent of violets and her own perfume were almost sickening.

She took out the sketch she had done the night before of Eloise holding Guy, Henriette on a blanket at her feet, and Sheba hovering like a dark spirit in the background. "I was going to start it in oil today, but I don't feel like mixing paints."

"Then let us do a little still life in watercolors, madame. Give me your violets. So." He filled a bubbled greenish tumbler with water and added the violets. These, a lemon, a pewter spoon, and a soup bowl made the composition. Marie found it uninspiring.

The shape of the glass wouldn't come right, and there was no way to correct its lopsidedness. The lemon looked like a deflated balloon. As for the soup bowl—M. Condé rolled his eyes and clucked. "I think you're not feeling yourself, madame. Would you like to go home?"

"Yes, please."

"Now who to send with you? Philippe? No, he is busy with the cavalier's hat. Ah, Paul. Have you finished the hands, Paul? Escort Madame to a carriage, please. We can't have her fainting in the street."

"I'll be all right alone." She drew her shawl around her.

"No, madame. It would not be right." M. Condé handed her the violets.

"I'll bring some more tomorrow. Perhaps I'll feel better by then."

"One hopes so, madame." His eyes twinkled.

Paul led the way down the stairs, which were too narrow for them to walk abreast. They stopped at the landing, where the tenant behind a greasy door seemed eternally to be cooking cabbage soup.

"Are you all right, madame?"

"I am called Marie." She had not realized how tall he was until she stood beside him.

He smiled down at her. "Marie. Marie. Marie."

With no warning he put his arms around her and kissed her. At first she stiffened, then she melted against his hard body and opened her mouth under his. Time, in the dim light of the stairwell, flowed around them, carrying them in its current beyond the real world. They pulled apart only when the soup maker dropped a pan and cursed.

"Marie. Oh! I'm afraid I crushed the violets."

"It doesn't matter."

"Come, I'll buy some more." He took her hand and led her down the next flight, stopping halfway down to kiss her again. This time it was she who, standing on the step above, was the taller, she who smiled down and kissed his fierce dark eyebrows, his eyelids, his cheeks, while his lips opened, waiting for hers, and his hands groped under her shawl to hold her breasts.

"Come!" He jerked away from her, and they ran down the last two flights. Once outside he paused, frowning, looking around as if searching for something.

"What's wrong?"

"It's hopeless. I can't take you to my room. It isn't suitable for a lady."

"It's more suitable than lying under the Pont-Neuf as some lovers do."

He gave her hand a squeeze. "True. I couldn't—undress you there." He led her through a labyrinth of filthy alleys to a tall house hanging crookedly over the street. "I am on the top floor. I'll carry you because—if I don't have you soon I'll go mad!" He picked her up and almost ran up the stairs. "You weigh no more than a kitten. Do you scratch as well?" She dug her fingernails into his neck in reply.

He kicked open the door of his room and dropped her on the pallet which served as his bed, then flung himself beside her.

Between frenzied caresses they managed to undress. There was no need for the play of love. The act was rushed, frantic, almost violent. Paul was no longer the gentle, awkwardly shy, and humble student but a man taking the body he desired and spending his passion on it. Marie bit his shoulder to keep from crying aloud as they rocked together in a long shuddering climax.

Then they were two again instead of one. She stroked his back, kissing him gently, while he touched her hair, her face, her shoulders, her breasts, as if to make sure they were real.

"Darling Marie, you are really here."

"I am here."

"Your headache—?"

"You cured it."

"How did I ever dare? But you wanted it too, I think."

"All last night I didn't sleep, thinking of you."

He leaned on his elbow and looked at her. "Truly? And it is as you thought?"

"Better."

He sighed, smiling. "I'll get you some wine. Lovers always have wine. It's not so fine as you're accustomed to but—" He got to his feet and looked around his room appalled. "My God, it's a sty! How could I have brought you here?"

Marie sat up. She too was appalled. Discarded sketches littered the floor, canvases were stacked against every wall. The bedclothes were dingy. The window was broken and the sill splattered with pigeon droppings.

"It *does* want cleaning." *It could be charming,* she thought. *A world of its own. A place to paint.*

"Yes, it does, and I am always too busy. But let me show you something." He beckoned her to the window and pointed out. "I look right down on Saint-

Germain-des-Prés, my favorite of all churches. That makes up for everything. And I do keep the skylight clean, so my light is good. Here, I want you to see these while I fetch the wine." He began pulling out canvases and sketch books for her inspection.

He *was* good. M. Condé was right. One day he might be great, become a court favorite. Some noblewoman would support him in return for his favors.

"And these." He pushed a sketch pad into her hands. All the pictures were of her. Marie mixing paints, Marie painting, Marie frowning critically at a picture while M. Condé gestured with his plump, expressive hands, Marie being handed into the silver coach.

"You have followed me."

He nodded. "And this." He pulled out a large canvas, the beginning of an oil. It was his studio in all its squalor. Marie lying on the pallet. The nude body barely outlined. "Because I didn't know you that way yet. And the face—I didn't know then how you would look when you desired—someone. It was a dream, you understand." His eyes were on the picture, his voice a whisper. "It will be my masterpiece, for now I know all that your body contains, the passion in it."

"Do you want me to pose for you?"

"Will you?"

For an answer she assumed the position on the pallet of the body on the canvas, legs wantonly apart, head back, lips parted.

"Wait, let me think. The violets! Here." He tossed them to her. "Between the breasts."

He worked rapidly for a while, then put down his brush. "Painting your body only makes me want it again. Marie?"

She held out her arms to him.

The light had changed. It was late. "I must go."

"Stay the night with me."

"I can't. The coach will be waiting."

"Tomorrow then? Please say tomorrow."

"Tomorrow. What will you tell M. Condé?"

"He'll give me his blessing."

"He said you would be cured after this."

"M. Condé has never been in love."

The next day the floor had been swept, the bedclothes washed, the table scraped and scrubbed, and on a wooden plate was a loaf of bread, a sausage, and cheese, along with a bottle of wine and a fresh bunch of violets.

Sometimes during the three days that followed, Marie felt a twinge of guilt, but she told herself this was a part of her that had nothing to do with Henri. This was a different happiness, a world that might have been. The days had a dreamlike quality, a magic intensity, as if a whole lifetime must be lived in a single moment and all passion spent in that time.

Between the love-making, which was sometimes gentle, sometimes so impassioned they were left exhausted, Paul sketched her, filling pad after pad, as if to capture her for a lifetime. He drew Marie naked at the window, the violets in her hair, feeding a crust of bread to a pigeon; at the table, her shawl covering one breast, an empty glass and an empty wine bottle beside her, the violets held to her nose, her eyes downcast looking at them; her back as she combed her hair, holding in her hand a tiny mirror which scarcely reflected her face.

"Will you ever complete them all?" she teased.

"It will take me years. I'll still be working from these sketches when I am very, very old."

Old. The word tolled in her mind like a bell. Long after she had gone back to Henri, when she too was old, the young Marie with her violets would lie in the sketch pad, unchanged, unchanging, in this bleak, drafty room.

"Paul, hold me."

He carried her to the bed and for a long while sat looking at her, touching her, kissing and memorizing her body. Slowly he made love to her until her passion hurried his. She closed her eyes so he would not see the tears.

They dressed and drank a bottle of wine, threw bread to the pigeon who came every afternoon to eat. Marie pretended to the end that their time together was not running out and wondered if Paul was pretending too. They even laughed on their way back to the atelier, where Marie would meet the footman. Paul made jokes about the portraits waiting for him to complete their hands.

"Poor King Charles would rather have been without his hands than without his head," Marie said. Then the laughter froze. Waiting outside M. Condé's door was Henri. "Paul, there is my husband."

She broke free of Paul's hand and ran to Henri, as if released from an enchantment. Somehow she had known it was over, but she had not expected this. "Henri, Henri! You've come back."

He lifted an eyebrow, his lips curled in distaste. "Your letter asked me to come. I thought to surprise you—and I see I have."

"It isn't what you think, Henri." But he had seen them together and couldn't know that for her the end had come and she had been pretending to avoid hurting Paul. Though the hurt must come.

"Isn't it? Do you always hold the hand of the young man you accompany to deliver a painting? M. Condé *said* you were delivering a painting because the fumes of oil had given you a headache, and he thought the air would relieve it."

"Yes. We were delivering a painting. I held his hand to please him."

"How generous. Shall we go to the coach?"

"Yes." She looked back, feeling like Lot's wife. Paul stood where she had left him, looking after them, his face drawn with sorrow. She hoped she had not destroyed him. "When did you return, Henri?"

"At noon. It was a lengthy delivery. Where did you take the painting? To Versailles?"

"We stopped to sketch along the river. Oh. Paul has my sketches. I forgot them when I saw you, I was so surprised."

"So I observed."

"Henri, it is not what you think."

"So you said."

When they were seated in the coach, she took his hand and leaned forward to kiss him. He drew his hand away and pulled back from her. "I never thought to see you look at another man the way you looked at him."

"It was a harmless flirtation, Henri. As harmless as I hope yours was with Mme. Devereaux."

"Mme. Devereaux?"

"Papa said she was at Versailles flirting with you under her husband's very nose."

"To disguise the fact that she was sharing her bed with—never mind! You've no cause to worry about Minette, Marie. Ever!"

"I'm glad. I missed you, Henri. I love you."

"Do you? I continue to wonder. I'll believe you because I want to believe you, but it seems to me you smell of your student, of love, of bed, of his body. Perhaps I imagine it. I hope so."

She was silent, wondering whether to insist that it was his imagination or to admit everything and ask forgiveness. She looked out the window, tears running down her cheeks. The trees on the riverbank were now in full leaf. Less than a week ago she had bought the first bunch of violets.

"I suppose it was inevitable," he continued, half talking to himself. "I should be glad it was a student. I'm sure his affection was sincere, not amusement. But our reunion wasn't what I had expected. My vanity was injured."

She had not wanted to hurt him any more than she

had wanted to hurt Paul. She loved them both, in different ways, in different lives.

"You understand, Marie, there is no question of your going back to M. Condé."

She imagined the stir Henri's appearance must have caused in the atelier, the students staring, whispering together, M. Condé all aflutter trying to explain her absence.

"No, I cannot go back." It would break Paul's heart. She realized now she couldn't have faced life with him in the foul-smelling old house where the *pot du chambre* overflowed in the hallway privy, the rats scuttled out of the way as they mounted the stairs, and pigeons flew through the broken window and snatched the bread off the table. Love, if indeed she did love Paul, would not be enough.

La Violette

It was Henri's decision to move to the château, where, he warned Marie, she would be his prisoner.

"With pleasure. You know I didn't want to leave last year." She didn't add, "If we had stayed, none of this would have happened."

Henri made no more allusions to Paul. Marie's art work had never been unwrapped since it had been sent home from the atelier with a polite note from M. Condé, which Marie threw into the fire. That episode in her life was over, receding like a dream.

They settled into life at the château as if they had never been away. Marie tended Maman's garden. Maman was busy in Paris with her new hotel and would not move to the country until late summer. Eloise chose to stay in Paris to be near Joseph, but they took little Guy with them.

If we adopted him, Marie thought, *Eloise could marry her footman.* She would suggest it to Henri when the time came.

The days drifted by. May bloomed and turned into June. They sculled on the river. Henri took the children wading. He read aloud to Marie. They played chess. And, almost defiantly, she painted. On warm days they took their meals in the garden or picnicked in the grove, where Henriette and Guy tumbled in the grass until they fell asleep.

One evening was so warm they stayed on after dark. The servants swung paper lanterns from the trees and brought chicken hot from the spit and cool wine for their meal. Marie ate with such relish that Henri teased, "You'll grow fat, my dear, and I'll leave you for a courtesan."

"I'll grow fat whether I eat or not. I'm pregnant."

He smiled, but the shadow of the lantern on his face made the smile grotesque. "I've wanted another child. But—is it mine?" His voice was suddenly harsh.

"Of course it is yours."

"I wonder."

Marie wondered too. She forced her voice to be calm, light, almost teasing. "I did it to please you, and you're spoiling it."

The next few days Henri treated her with aloof suspicion. One evening he said casually that he had business in Paris. He left at dawn without further warning. The sound of carriage wheels rumbling over the bridge awakened Marie. He had not said good-bye. She touched her face, but if he had kissed her, no trace of the kiss remained.

The château was empty without him. Marie had the feeling that all the servants were whispering about Monsieur's absence. Sheba sulked and, when Marie reproved her, said, "You be careful or he'll tell us to leave. He'll send us back to Céline. Then what?"

"He won't send *me* back to Céline. I don't know what he'll do with you. The way you act around him, he'll probably keep you to lick his boots."

They glared at one another, but then Sheba laughed. "I remember when first you came to Mme. Céline, meek and frightened. Now"—she wagged her head admiringly—"you'd speak up to God."

Marie's anger subsided. "No, I wouldn't. That's the trouble. Not to God and not to Henri. I'm still frightened. I thought everything was going to be all right. Why did he go?"

"You know why."

She did know. Each time she had been unfaithful, God had punished her with a pregnancy. She didn't want this child any more than she had wanted Henriette, but she hoped they would get on better than she and Henriette did. Only occasionally would Henriette consent to allow Marie to pick her up or play with her. Only occasionally would she sit on Marie's lap to hear a story or the Scottish nursery rhymes Marie had learned from her mother. She gave the impression that she tolerated Marie, and that was all.

The days became a week and the week two weeks before Marie heard a carriage rattle over the bridge and roll to a creaking halt. Her impulse was to run to him—if it was Henri—to go on her knees and ask forgiveness. She ached for his affection, for their old relationship. But some perversity she scarcely understood kept her sitting in the garden. If it was Henri and he wanted her, he would find her.

Nearly an hour passed before he strolled into the garden. She got to her feet, but he didn't offer to kiss her or come near her. "Well, Marie. You are still here."

"Where else would I be?"

"I thought with me out of the way you would go back to Paris. To Saint-Germain-des-Prés."

"My God, don't start that again."

"No? Will you come to my room, Marie? There's something I want to show you."

"Of course. With pleasure." Obviously he was still angry. It would serve him right if she threw herself in the river and drowned amongst the reeds like Ophelia.

Instead of going to their apartments in the turret overlooking the river, Henri led the way to the opposite end of the château. His luggage was there and his clothes, which had apparently been removed from their rooms. His man was in the process of putting them away.

"That will do for now, Jacques."

A large flat parcel leaned against the foot of the bed. As soon as Jacques had left them, Henri removed the wrappings and turned the painting in the heavy gilt frame toward Marie. "There, Marie. Behold, La Violette!"

"Oh, no." She moaned and sank into a chair, covering her face with her hands.

"I see you recognize her. I see my suspicions weren't imagination, after all." Henri paced the floor, kicking at the wrappings each time he passed them. "There are three of them. In one La Violette stands naked at a window feeding a pigeon. In another she sits at a table eating bread and cheese. But why should I tell you? You know what they are." He stopped in front of her. "Don't you, Marie? Well, answer me! *Don't you?*"

"Yes . . . they were charcoal sketches when I saw them. He must have finished them later."

"Oh, yes, he finished them. He is a comet. Famous overnight. This is the only one where the face is fully shown and recognizable. The others—I know your body, Marie."

"Why did you buy it?"

"Why? *Why?* Should I have left it on the market to be viewed by everyone in Paris? Become a laughing stock because my wife posed naked like any common whore from the Opéra? You ask why? God's name!"

"What is the difference between being a common whore from the Opéra and a common whore from New Orleans?"

"You were not a whore."

"Not until you and Céline dealt with me."

"There is a difference."

"I don't see it."

"You refuse to see it. That was private. This is public."

"It's all the same in the eyes of God."

"But not in the eyes of *le monde.*"

"Damn *le monde*! There's not a person in Paris whose morals couldn't be condemned. I would spit on them, but they aren't worthy of my spit."

"I wonder if you are worthy of theirs?"

"What about the other pictures?"

"They've been sold. They're the sensation of Paris.

Everyone is wondering who La Violette is and where she can be found. Your body has made your lover famous, Marie. He already has commissions at court."

"Poor Paul. That will be his ruin."

"When I left you to go back to Paris, it was to find him and kill him. On my way to M. Condé's atelier I passed an art shop, Gersaint's, and saw this."

"And did you kill him?"

"You heard me say he has commissions at court. Bah! To kill a nobody is nothing. To kill an artist who is now painting a portrait of the king's latest mistress, dressed as Diana, would be a scandal, and the secret of La Violette would be exposed."

"I see." Somehow she got to her feet and went to the picture. She could almost smell the violets. The luminous flesh seemed to tremble, the eyes, dark as the flowers, burned with longing. It was the masterpiece Paul had said it would be. "Destroy it."

"No, Marie. I have seen you look at me that same way. Perhaps in time I'll be able to forget you were looking at him." He went to the window and stood looking down at the garden. "Tell me one thing and tell me truthfully, for it no longer matters now that I've seen this. Is it his child you're carrying?"

"I don't know." He wanted the truth. The truth he had.

She left the room, trying to walk with dignity, but it was difficult to be dignified with the bulging belly that was her disgrace.

The remainder of the week was hell. Marie hadn't the energy or the courage to attempt to bridge the rift between them. Henri made no move to do so. After a week of stiff conversation in the presence of the servants and angry silences when they were alone Henri left again without warning or farewell.

A few days after his departure Marie went to his boudoir and locked the door behind her. The picture hung above the alabaster mantelpiece.

She studied it as she had not been able to do with Henri watching her. There were things she had not noticed before. The gleam of a drop of water on her flesh just below the stems of the violets. The lace bodice on the floor beside the bed. A charcoal sketch pinned to the wall above. The hands—Paul specialized in hands—the fingers of one curled in her pubic hair. The other outstretched, beckoning.

It was the most sensual picture Marie had ever seen, and it recalled all the passion she had felt. The odor of the bedclothes, of Paul's body, the bitter wine they had drunk, the need of their flesh.

She had no idea how long she stayed there staring at the picture, remembering, making a hundred different plans, imagining a hundred different dialogues between herself and Henri, between herself and Paul. Paul, who was now painting the king's mistress.

He'd have no time for Marie now. Or would he? She looked at La Violette again. There was something there she had not noticed before, something more than desire. Love. That was why Henri was angry.

In mid-July Maman and Papa arrived with their entourage, including Eloise. Henri, they said, was busy at Versailles with affairs to do with Louisiana and New Orleans in particular. Perrier was being recalled, and it was rumored that Bienville might be asked to serve again.

Throughout July and August Marie lounged in the garden while Maman pruned the blossoms and Henriette toddled after her, gathering fallen petals. Guy attached himself to Papa, imitating his walk, his lighting of a cheroot, his presenting Marie with a brandy or liqueur "for strengthening."

Laure and her husband came for a week. As usual Laure was a fount of gossip. Henri was being lionized at court, but, she said, "Don't be concerned, Marie. He treats every woman who dares to approach him as mud to be wiped off his feet."

There was a new artist, Paul Grillet, who was the rage of Paris. Everyone was scrambling to be painted by him, outbidding one another to own one of his La Violette series. "There are six now, and a rumor that there's a seventh. An early one. No one knows who owns it, and M. Gersaint was sworn to secrecy by the buyer. He admits it was the best of the lot. There's no doubt Grillet will be awarded the Prix de Rome, though how the royal mistresses will fare without him, God knows. There isn't a bed in Paris that wouldn't be open to him. But they say he is like a monk, faithful to La Violette, whoever she may be. Some trollop from the Opéra, I suppose."

Laure described each painting in detail. Marie remembered each of them. The child was active in her now, but no matter how many times she counted on her fingers, she couldn't decide whether it belonged to Henri or to Paul.

Maman and Papa tried to persuade Marie to return to Paris with them, but she refused. "I want the child to be born here. The journey might bring on another premature birth." Mostly she could not face Henri.

"But you must have a physician, a midwife," said Maman.

"That can be arranged," Papa said. "I like the idea of the child being born here. We'll send our own physician when the time comes."

Maman lingered after Papa's farewell, fussing about whether Henriette's swaddling would do for the new child and whether Marie was sure she would be all right. Despite Marie's reassurances, she continued to fidget about the room. Finally she said, "I don't know what quarrel you and Henri had, and I know it is not for me to interfere. I hope before the child is born you will mend your differences. When I see him, I'll urge him to come back here and be with you and cease acting like a fool."

"Don't, Maman. Let him come back when he is ready."

"I don't promise, but I'll try to keep still. Perhaps he'll come to his senses. But I shall certainly pray. You have no objection to that, I hope?"

"None at all. Light every candle in the church, set fire to it, if it will help."

"You do love him, don't you, Marie?"

"Yes, Maman."

Maman sighed. "Then I don't understand what the trouble is."

"Perhaps he no longer loves me."

The weather turned sultry, and the children fretful. Flies swarmed everywhere, and clouds of mosquitoes hung over the river. The water smelled stagnant, sour. After three breathless days a storm broke with a flash of lightning that crackled over the roofs of the château, blanching the landscape. A deafening explosion of thunder followed, splintering a window and showering Maman's favorite carpet with glass. A moment later the rain came in blinding sheets.

For a week it beat against the walls, crushed the garden, tore leaves from the trees, and spoiled the harvest. Waves lapped against the foundation and the stones of the bridge like angry tongues. It was cold enough for the fireplaces to be lighted, but the fires did little to dispel the dampness.

Trapped in the house, Marie was in low spirits. On a dull, dark morning the house steward told Marie one of the housemaids had asked permission to speak to her.

"She refuses to tell me what it's about, madame. They are high and mighty these days. They think themselves invaluable—and it's true. The girls from Paris don't like coming to the country, so one who is willing to stay *is* invaluable. She should bring her complaints to me first, of course, but no. It's you or no one, madame."

"Oh, for heaven's sake! If she wants to speak to me, I'll speak to her. Sometimes women prefer to speak to their own sex. Naturally if it's anything you should know about, I'll inform you."

"Certainly, madame. She's just within call, and I'll wait outside the door in case you need me."

So he could eavesdrop. "There's no need for that. I'm sure she means no harm. What is her name?"

"Charlotte, Madame."

"All right. Send Charlotte in."

She came, curtsying every step of the way, so Marie finally snapped, "That's enough. I'm not royalty, you know."

"No, madame. That is, yes, madame."

She was a tall girl with skin like cream and pale gold hair and eyes as dark as the center of daisies. Marie recognized her, remembered seeing her staggering under armfuls of sheets still hot from the iron, hurrying from suite to suite, changing beds, and sometimes singing at her work when she thought the family was out. She wasn't singing now. She looked unhappy, puffy-eyed, as if she'd been crying.

"Well, Charlotte?"

The girl twisted her apron with shaking hands. A gust of wind blew smoke down the chimney and slapped a poplar leaf against the window, where it clung, green and heart-shaped.

"Madame, I am pregnant."

Well, so am I, Marie thought. "That's not so bad, is it?"

"I'll be dismissed. *He* said so. He said when he hired us, the other girls and me, no brats or out we go."

"You aren't married, is that it?" The girl nodded. "Who's the father?"

"I—I'd rather not say, madame. You see, he—well, he has a wife, and I wouldn't want her hurt."

Marie was surprised. This was a rare girl. "That's very thoughtful of you, Charlotte. Is there some young man here who would marry you if we provided a dowry?"

"I'm from Paris, madame. I don't want any of these peasants."

"Being from Paris isn't going to help unless you have a young man there. Do you?"

"No, madame."

"There's an old saying, beggars can't be choosers."

The girl began to cry silently.

"Do you want the child, Charlotte?"

She hung her head. "Oh, no madame."

"Do you know how to get rid of it?"

"No, madame."

"Neither do I, or I'd help you. Someone around here must know. Some peasant wife."

"It's a sin, madame."

"Nonsense! It happens all the time. No one admits to it, that's all. There must be someone we can ask. The locals who bring eggs, the milkmaids, the laundress. That's it. It would be easy for you to speak to her."

"But if she gossiped–"

"Let me think a moment." She was beautiful, lovely enough that any man would want to bed her. Marie wondered who it was. Perhaps the house steward himself, oily old thing. "I could have Eloise do it. I don't think she'd mind. She can pretend it's for herself she's asking. Everyone knows she's been carrying on with Joseph and stayed behind only to help with the children during my *accouchement*. And don't worry. I won't allow you to be dismissed."

Charlotte's tears turned to sobs, and she dropped to her knees and kissed Marie's hand. "Thank you, madame. You're an angel. I don't know how Monsieur can treat you so–"

"What do you know about how Monsieur treats me?" Marie demanded.

The sobs died in Charlotte's throat. She looked as if she thought Marie were going to strike her. "The servants gossip, madame." She stared at the floor, twisting her apron again.

The silence hung between them broken only by the sound of the rain. Marie's temples throbbed, and she felt sick.

"I know servants gossip. Charlotte, who was the man?"

"Madame, I can't tell you. Please, don't ask me, don't. Don't!"

"Was it Monsieur?"

The girl groaned, rocking back and forth on her knees, her hands covering her face. "I didn't want to, madame. I had taken fresh linens to his room—"

"I don't want to hear the details. When did it happen?"

"Every day he was here, that last time. Never before, madame. I swear to that. And it wasn't me but you he was thinking of the whole time. Sometimes he said your name."

Marie put her hands over her ears. "I don't want to hear about it. Damn him, damn him, damn him!"

"I'm sorry, madame. I didn't want to tell you."

"Never mind. It wasn't your fault that I guessed." She felt as if some terrible weight were crushing her. "We must act quickly. He's been gone how many weeks now—seven, at least. Yes, we must be quick before it's too late, too dangerous for you."

"You still mean to help me even though you know? You won't turn me out, madame?"

"Of course I mean to help you! Do you think I want you bearing his child?" Marie's voice quivered with rage.

The girl shrank back as if she'd been struck.

"It's him I'm angry at, Charlotte. Not you. Sit down. We both need some brandy. You can't go back to your duties with your face stained with tears." Marie went to the commode and poured two large drinks into the fragile glasses and handed one to Charlotte. "Sit down. You need to compose yourself."

"Madame, it's not right that I sit with you."

"For God's sake! If you're good enough for Monsieur's bed, you're good enough to sit with his wife." She gulped at the brandy. "I wish the laundress could help me too."

"Madame, don't even think of it. You're too far gone."

"I know, Charlotte. I know."

The rain had stopped, leaving the countryside shrouded in ground fog, which Marie found no less depressing than the storm. She sat for hours at the turret window staring listlessly out at the white sea.

As much as she loathed Henri for what he had done, she had to admit she deserved it. But it was unforgivable that he had taken out his anger on an unwilling victim who had not dared to refuse him. Marie's act with Paul had been one of love and insatiable desire. Henri's was one of revenge.

She would go away, but there was no place to go in her condition, and thanks to that damned Edmund and her own trusting innocence, she had very little money of her own. Very little money and few friends. She longed for Céline's biting scorn, her shrug, even her calling Marie the little fool that she was; for Mimi's quick understanding and tears of sympathy. But they were far away, and there was no one else.

Charlotte's child had been aborted by the laundress, and she was back at her duties. It was not the girl's fault, Marie told herself repeatedly, but she found it difficult to meet Charlotte in the halls, and she tried to be out of the room when Charlotte came to do the bed.

Marie knew she looked haggard these days. She was always tired. Her sleep was troubled, and by day her thoughts scurried round and round like gray rats scuttling along the wainscots, gnawing at her. Not even at her parents' graveside had she been as unhappy and hopeless as she was now.

Her limbs were swollen, her feet so puffy no shoe

or mule would fit. This child was far more active than Henriette had been. It was as if Marie had a tempest trapped within her.

The mists cleared. One warm, hazy autumn day followed another. Barefoot, Marie walked the garden paths longing for release from everything. It was she who should have had an abortion as soon as she learned she was pregnant, but foolishly she had thought it would not matter.

She left the hiring of a wet nurse up to Eloise, who commented, "A pity I'm not in the same condition so I could take care of this one too. Perhaps Joseph and I will be married by the time you have another."

"There won't be another."

"There will be if I know Monsieur."

But Eloise didn't know him. Not as Marie did. She wondered if he would ever return. She wished she could make him understand that no matter whose child it was, it was Henri whom she loved. The affair with Paul had taught her that.

The child, a girl, was born in early December before the physician arrived from Paris. The woman who had aborted Charlotte's child had been called when labor began. She was a cheerful young woman with strange notions about such things as cleanliness. She washed Marie all over, especially her private parts, with lye soap and scalding water. She insisted on clean sheets, removed the hangings from the bed, and wouldn't let Sheba or Eloise in the room until they too had washed. She brewed a strange-smelling herbal tea that dulled the pain and made Marie feel lightheaded but no less able to obey the commands the woman gave to make the birth easier.

To Marie's surprise it *was* easier, far different from Henriette's, just as the child was different. Henriette had been all blond and rosy-red and round. This was a dark gypsy of a child with a mop of black curls and eyes like blackberries. She was long and thin, with large feet and hands that were always in motion, as if trying to express some secret thought.

She seldom cried but gurgled as if laughing. The wet nurse said she had never known such a child. "It's as if she was born under a lilac star and will be happy forever."

When it was time for the christening and Marie's churching, she quelled her pride and wrote to Henri asking him to be with her. He didn't reply.

The priest's mother stood as proxy for Laure, who was to be godmother, and Marie herself named the child. Désirée. As they came out of the chapel a chill wind was blowing.

Overnight, frost had laced the bare trees and crumpled the fields. White mist rose from the low-lying land, wreathing the course of the river. Damp again pervaded the house, and Marie was so lonely she dreaded each new dawn. She felt as old as the stones of the château, and it frightened her to think she was only fifteen, and a lifetime yawned before her. Then bitterness against Henri, Céline, and Edmund would poison the day for her. They had made her an old woman before her time. They might as well imprison her and be done with it. Only Paul had loved her—and unwittingly betrayed her.

Often she put her hands over her ears to shut out the laughter of Henriette and Guy and the happy shrieks of Désirée. She walked in the frozen garden until she ached with cold. She ate so little the chef threatened to return to Paris. Ten days before Christmas there was a stiff note from Henri saying it would please the family if she and the children would join them for the holidays. It was signed, "Your obedient and affectionate husband." How else, Marie asked Sheba, would it be signed? He was following protocol, and neither obedience nor affection were intended to be taken seriously.

By the same post there was a letter from Maman:

My dear daughter Marie,

Both Papa and I are hoping you will join us, leaving as soon as you receive this letter, which is being written in great haste so the coach will not leave without it. We are longing to behold our new granddaughter as well as to see you.

We pray the New Year will bring about a change in your affairs. Papa is very angry with Henri and says he is bound to be at fault for whatever happened. We must learn to forgive, even when it is not our place to do the forgiving.

Your affectionate maman,
Eugénie de Nemour-Fréjeau

It was Maman's letter that decided her. If someone was to make the first move, it must be Marie herself. She had reached the end of her endurance.

Her return reminded her of her first arrival in Paris. There was Sheba, a wet nurse, and a new baby. The difference was that Eloise sat where Henri had sat, holding Guy, while Sheba held Henriette.

Maman rushed out the instant she heard the coach, and embraced Marie. Then she took Désirée away from the wet nurse and exclaimed, "But—she is the picture of Henri! This is the child who should have been named for him."

She turned to Papa, waiting as before in the doorway. "My love, will you look! Is it not like time turned back?"

Before Papa admired the baby, he kissed Marie. "Welcome back, my dear. I've missed you." Then, "Well done, well done. Another dowry to be provided, Henri. This one is indeed a de Nemour. Henri too was born looking like an Egyptian, with enough hair to make wigs for the entire family."

Marie could not resist throwing Henri, who had been hovering like a specter in the background, a triumphant look. He came forward then and kissed her with cold lips. He gave the baby little more than a glance but swung Henriette into his arms and whirled around with her while she squeaked with joy and tugged his wig askew.

Alone with Henri in their apartments, Marie said lightly, "I wish my welcome had been as warm as Henriette's." She removed her cape and went to Henri, who was standing by the window.

"Do you? Do you think my parents' exclamations vindicated you and convinced me?" He seemed to find the view of the Seine too engrossing to look at her.

"I don't need vindication, but you do need convincing. Henri, she *is* your child."

"Last summer you didn't seem so sure."

"Now I am."

He didn't answer. After a few moments she moved away from him, defeated. She had hoped everything would be mended. Nothing was, except that she was back in Paris.

"Marie, it pains me to say it, to acknowledge it, but you are as great a whore as Minette Devereaux or any lady in *le monde* whom you disdain."

"If I am a whore, you know who made me a whore, Henri. But what I did—or did not do—with Paul has nothing to do with my feeling for you. I love you deeply, unendingly."

"A pity you didn't discover it sooner."

"Perhaps it took Paul to make me discover it. Henri—what do you want me to do? Leave you? I will, if you say so. I don't know where I'll go, but I'd rather leave you than tolerate your disdain, your rejection, your coldness."

"You need not leave. For appearance' sake we'll share our apartments, but I'll be damned if I'll share your bed."

"No doubt you have another open to you."

"That I do not. I'm as celibate as a monk." He began to pace the room, still avoiding her.

"Are you? And do you find celibacy tolerable? *You?*"

"It is no problem."

"How fortunate, since it's what you've chosen. Are we to live the rest of our lives this way?"

"Time will tell. Meanwhile we'll tolerate one another for the sake of Henriette." He looked at her in amazement as she burst into hysterical laughter. "Marie, you are overwrought."

"Overwrought? What do you expect, Henri? In God's name, what do you expect? Tolerate one another! My dear, it is you who are intolerable, and I wonder why, *why* I love you!"

Throughout the holidays they maintained an uneasy peace. Henri did not speak to her any more often than necessary. Marie put on a brave face and pretended nothing had happened. They resumed their social life—the salons, the suppers, the opera and ballet, the musicals and theater, the coffeehouses, the balls. Marie had been so starved for companionship and amusement that she found she enjoyed it all. She could hold her own now. Exile had sharpened her wits.

She soon had a gaggle of admirers with whom she flirted while keeping them at a distance, which they found all the more challenging. Henri, still playing the skeleton at the feast, remained in the background, resisting the advances of the ladies, who found his sardonic aloofness enchanting.

Early in the year Marie had a letter from Céline. The handwriting was atrocious, but it read as if Céline were speaking.

Dear Marie,

At last I write to you. Christ's bones! I had thought to see you back long before this. Though why would anyone leave Paris to come here un-

less they came in chains as I did? Do they still hold a fair in Saint-Germain? Does Gertrude Boon still do her sword dance? Throw her a coin from Céline.

There are thirteen companies of infantry here now, thanks to the Indian troubles. So you can imagine how busy we are despite crop failures, droughts, floods, a hurricane, and near famine—whatever God decides to do to amuse Himself. I have a new girl. Eglantine. It is not her real name, but if she wants to call herself that, why should I object? She thinks herself very fine, but her tongue is straight from the gutter. We are still shorthanded, or bodied.

Mimi has left us. Married a sous-lieutenant. *He decided it would be cheaper to have her as a wife than as a whore at fifty sols for fifteen minutes. He was so besotted with her that his fifteen minutes often became an hour. And you know I do not give anything away. You pay for what you get at Céline's. This is a business like any other.*

I'm still a long way from owning a grand house with a crystal chandelier and a gambling room. Yes, yes, I know gambling is forbidden, but there are ways around that just as there are ways around everything. Oui? Oui.

I hear M. Lanney is going to France soon, and not taking his wife. Things have not gone well for him due to the droughts and floods. You know what I mean, of course. They have two children now, and she is bulging again.

And do you have another too by now? I did well by you no matter what you think, Marie. It is better than being a governess.

I am sorry I didn't write sooner. I was glad to hear about your daughter born in France. Of course it was the voyage that made her arrive too soon. It was wise of you to name her for her fa-

ther. I mean, since it was not a son to be named for him.

Greetings from your affectionate
Céline

Marie read and reread the letter. It made her homesick for New Orleans. She was glad about Mimi. Now they could be friends openly instead of having to meet in secret. As for Edmund, it was obvious he had not been making his payments. That was bad news. Marie had been counting on that money to start the house on Lake Pontchartrain. If she and Henri ever made peace . . . If they went home . . . If . . .

She approached Maman about a wedding gift for Mimi. "Will you help me choose something? And shop for a crystal chandelier for a friend who wants one for her house?"

Maman was delighted. "There is no need to buy a chandelier. I ordered one for the reception room in the new hotel, and now I find it is too small—or perhaps, as Papa says, the room is too large. If it would do for your friend, we will send it."

It would do very well. It would make Céline's own reception room incandescent, and the wind blowing through the open windows would set the crystal tinkling.

They went shopping for the wedding gift, and while they were out Maman insisted on stopping by the new hotel to see how work was progressing. "I cannot stay away from it," she confessed to Marie.

The workmen greeted them with sweeping bows. "Ah, madame, you missed your artist by minutes. He has put the finishing touches on the panelings in the large salon. Very amusing, madame. They'll be the talk of Paris."

Maman hurried Marie over parquet floors into a room of such breathless height it was like a cathedral. The walls were pale lilac with decorated panelings.

When Marie saw them, she gasped and put her hand to her heart.

There they were, just as Maman had planned, little creatures aping men, dressed in the height of fashion, except for one, a supple and beautiful little cat wearing nothing but her fur and violets. The little cat on a tossed bed, languorous, sleepy-eyed, with a bunch of violets beneath her chin. The little cat, paws on a window sill, violets between her ears, watching a pigeon eat. The cat at a table eating daintily of a mouse, milk in a wine bottle, and the inevitable violets. They went on and on—while a shaggy dog in an artist's smock and worn clogs painted her, so there were pictures within pictures within pictures. Monkeys dressed in court fashion cavorted, posed, observed, smirked. And the dog, seated before the fire with his pipe, saw the little cat in the flames, not the battles Maman had imagined.

"Maman . . ."

"Isn't it clever? You see, Grillet mocks his own paintings. It is so amusing! And I was so fortunate to get him. I had to wait until he finished painting that woman's portrait. Dressed as Diana! Most appropriate. She hunted the poor king until she got him into her bed. But there, she won't last any longer than the others. My dear Marie, you're very pale. Little one, why are you crying?"

"Maman, I must tell you something. You may hate me for it." The burden of her brief relationship with Paul threatened to crush her. "I—I was—I was La Violette. I knew Paul at the atelier."

Maman looked at Marie. "But of course you were! How can I have been so blind? That is why Henri is angry."

Marie nodded.

"Poor Henri. He was so sure of you. What a blow to his vanity."

"I was a fool to risk losing him. I don't even know

now why I did it. Maman, do you hate me too? Are you angry?"

"Hate you! What an idea! Dear little Marie, I could never hate you. I'm sure Henri doesn't hate you either. It is his pride," she said. "It's not as if you deliberately hurt him."

"No, Maman, of course not!" Marie dried her eyes. "There is another painting of La Violette. One you've never seen. Like—like the little cat on the bed. Henri bought it. That is why he thinks Désirée is not his child."

"*Mon Dieu!* He thinks that? What a fool he is. She is the picture of him. I shall speak to him." Maman put her arms around Marie. "Come, no more tears. Already you've lost one of your patches."

"Please don't tell Papa about La Violette. He told Henri there were to be no affairs."

"I do not promise. This is different, you see. An artistic event. Besides, I don't see how any woman could resist Grillet. Such charm, such modesty, such gentleness and simplicity. They all want him in their beds, you know. It must be tiresome to try to please the little apes. The way he has depicted them, you can see he has no stomach for them. Yet his dislike only whets their desire. But the cat! Ah, the little cat. That is love."

"He said I was his first. He loved me very much." Marie walked from panel to panel, remembering. What a pity one could not be two persons, live two separate lives. "Poor Paul."

"Nonsense. He's growing rich and famous because of you and La Violette. He'll love someone else one day as much as he loved you." Maman gave her a quick look. "That makes you sad."

"Perhaps, but it is what I would wish for him."

Two days later at a family dinner Papa laid a bunch of violets at Marie's place. "The first violets of spring, Marie. They reminded me of your eyes." His own eyes were twinkling. With a nod of his head he indicated

Henri, who was scowling at his plate, and almost imperceptibly he winked.

"Thank you, Papa. They're beautiful."

"So are you, *ma petite*. Henri is a lucky man."

Marie tucked the bouquet into her bodice. As the moisture trickled between her breasts she smelled the paint again, the cabbage soup, M. Condé's atelier, and Paul himself. No matter how angry Henri was, she was glad all of it had happened.

Maman and Papa moved to the new hotel directly after Easter. Henri refused to move. "And we know why, don't we?" Maman whispered to Marie. "The paneling." Henri and Marie remained in the old hotel in the Marais.

It was nice to spread out. Henriette was too lively to be restricted to one small nursery. She would have taken over the entire house if she had been permitted. Even the garden was too small for her tastes, and Henri often took her to the Tuileries with him. She adored him and screamed in protest when she was returned to Eloise's care after one of their outings. He could not bear to see her tears and would kneel at her feet, embrace her, whisper endearments, promising her everything.

Désirée he ignored as fervently as he heaped affection on Henriette. It did no good for Maman and Papa to point out that Désirée had all his facial expressions and gestures, that the shape of her eyes was his, as well as her protruding lower lip, which gave her smile a pouting piquancy. He would lift his eyebrows in disbelief and say, "I don't see it myself."

To Marie it was a complete irony that the child who was not his should be his favorite. "It is because Henriette is so like you, Marie," Maman said. "He loves you in spite of the way he's acting." The way he was acting could best be described as politely indifferent.

One evening he returned from a dinner at Mme. de Tencin's, whose Tuesday evenings were always entirely male, and knocked at Marie's door. She was in bed but not yet asleep, the candles still alight in the sconces. He sat down on the edge of the bed and looked at her for a long while. Once, twice, he opened his mouth as if to speak, then thought better of it. Marie waited.

"Well, Marie . . . there's no need for me to say it. We both know I've been a fool. I'm learning there isn't a lady in Paris who wouldn't have sacrificed her reputation gladly to have been the model for La Violette. Nor is there a lady at Versailles who wouldn't seduce Grillet, given the chance. When I count the number of ladies who have not one lover but two or three, I have to admit that I am fortunate you have had but one."

"And that one very briefly."

"If you say so. I have tried to dislike you. I have tried to interest myself in other women. I can do neither. Like Papa, I am a singleminded man. I loved you the first time I saw you at Céline's when you were still a child, and I love you as a woman. I created you, and my pride was hurt when you acted on your own. But I cannot continue to live the way we have been living, avoiding one another, hating one another."

"A pity you didn't discover this before you took Charlotte and made her suffer as well as myself."

"Charlotte? Who is Charlotte?"

"Holy Mother!" She flung back the covers and sprang from the bed and began striding up and down the room, her eyes burning like dark coals. "*Who* is *Charlotte*?" She stopped before him and shouted into his face. "That helpless maid at the château whom you forced into your bed and left pregnant. Left for me to deal with. Who is Charlotte, you ask! Oh! That you could have so little concern for another person!"

"Good God! I never supposed—I thought any girl in hire would know enough—Marie, she meant nothing."

"She is a good girl, Henri. You seem to hold goodness very lightly. But you always have." She walked away from him to her chair by the fire.

The fire was nearly out, but Marie didn't know whether she was shivering from anger or the cold. She wished she had her negligée, but it was on the bed. To fetch it she would have to make what would seem like a conciliatory gesture. She felt far from reconciliation. If she had had anything at hand, she would have thrown it at Henri as once she had thrown a gris-gris.

The gilt clock on the mantel struck midnight, and the enameled nymphs moved in a circle around its base, pursued by a satyr.

The candles flames were long. One sputtered and went out, leaving a ghost of smoke spiraling to the ceiling.

"Get out, Henri. I want to go back to bed."

He came to her on his knees. She was appalled to see that he was crying. He took her unwilling hands and pressed them to his face. "Is there no hope we can take up our lives again as they were before? I have learned I can't live without you. I need you, and I beg you to need me."

"Oh, I need you, Henri. I have had no other choice than to need you. I even grew to love you." She wasn't blameless herself. Henriette. Désirée. Was she Henri's child, or did Maman imagine it?

"Then there is hope?"

She longed to take him into her arms, to belong to him again, but she steeled herself. "On one condition. That you will try to love Désirée." Her eyes hardened. "Yes, love her. I am sure she is your child."

"Very well. I'll try."

"Henri . . . I've missed you so."

Later, lying in his arms in the darkness, she said, "Henri, let's go home. To our home. To New Orleans."

He was quiet a moment, then said, "Not until I've seen Edmund Lanney and talked to him. He's due in Paris any day now. He arrived in La Rochelle a month ago."

Edmund in Paris

Edmund had come to France out of desperation. Everything seemed to have conspired against him, and none of it was his fault. The Natchez uprising had been only the beginning. Settlers crowded into New Orleans, leaving their land and crops unattended. Even the supposedly friendly Choctaw weren't above scalping an isolated family and reclaiming the land.

No one among the early colonists could remember worse weather. There were four years of alternate floods and drought. One year the crops would turn to brown ash to be blown away by the wind; the next they would sour under a foot or two of water. A hurricane devastated the city, lifted the roof off the warehouse, and ruined a rice crop awaiting shipment to France. Edmund had to make good the loss. The bottom fell out of the tobacco market, ruining the small planters. Even shipping was in a bad way. Too many ships had to sail back to France empty but for ballast because the colony had nothing to ship. Now they refused to put in at New Orleans at all. Not even Léon would come, though Edmund promised his brother that anything he brought would fetch top prices. The necessities from France that the colony depended on were in short supply.

The specter of Marie and the money he owed her haunted Edmund. There was never enough cash to make the payments. Even if there had been, there was no way he could account to Annette for its absence.

Sometimes he wished she didn't have such a head for business.

Once he had passed Céline in the square, and she had said, "Shouldn't I be hearing from you, monsieur, for *ma petite* Marie?"

He had rushed on without answering. After that he had avoided her street for fear she would dash out of her house and accost him.

Marie in France was on his mind more often than Marie had been in New Orleans. He could not forget the way she had appeared at his wedding and his sudden, unexpected, shaming rush of desire. When his child, Pierre, had been born, Edmund's first thought had been to wonder whether Marie's child had been a boy or a girl and whether de Nemour had any suspicion that it wasn't his.

He wasn't unhappy. Annette was a good wife, doing all she could to please him. But she expected to be pleased and coddled in return, especially when she was pregnant. It had begun to seem to Edmund that she was seldom any other way.

She complained of the time he spent at the warehouse or conducting business. It was true he found excuses to be away more than necessary. The house was always full of Arnolies. Annette's sisters had moved in during the early Indian scare, and the three of them frolicked like children. Claudine was courting, rather than being courted by, Captain Leclerc, and he was at the house whenever he wasn't on duty, usually with some fellow officer to amuse Angela. Naturally they preferred Edmund's food and wine to what they were served in quarters. It mattered little to them if Edmund went broke catering to them.

At least once a week Mme. Arnolie came. She inspected the kitchen, angering Calla; gave Annette advice about a hundred trifles; clucked over the grandeur of the de Nemour furnishings; and wondered endlessly about Mme. de Nemour's antecedents. "I know of no one who knew her before." Edmund had nightmares in which he blurted out the truth.

It was his father-in-law who was instrumental in Edmund's going to France. Edmund hadn't wanted to go. It had been pointed out to him that it was his duty.

"Your father's a deputy to the Council of Commerce," Arnolie had said. "Your one brother's a slaver, the other a shipper. Your sister's married to a Parisian banker who could arrange for loans. You talk to them. Tell them what our situation is. Government reports, military reports, official reports aren't worth the paper they're written on. Nobody in Paris bothers to read them. But a report from the people, delivered in person, that's what's needed. You talk to your father. He'll know what to do."

Edmund's protests had been overruled. The colony was verging on ruin due to the Indian troubles, the alternate droughts and floods which caused crop failures, the lack of slaves, and the lack of shipping facilities. There was nothing to do but to go. At best his father might make him a loan that would pay off Marie and tide him over until business improved.

"While you're at it," Arnolie had said, "take a look into the land grants, mine and de Nemour's on Pontchartrain. Sometimes, because of careless map-making or confusion, the lines overlap. Who knows—half of what he claims may belong to us." Arnolie winked. "It's a choice spot."

Edmund's father proved to be a flattering audience, listening without criticism or objection to his son's news of New Orleans.

"It's very helpful to have first hand information. The Indian wars have proven to be so costly that the Company of the Indies wants to get rid of its charter. It's trying to give the colony back to the crown, which isn't sure it wants it. Yes, all this is very helpful. I know some men who will want to hear you."

Edmund preened himself. "There's someone else in

Paris you should hear, father. Henri de Nemour. He left when the Indian troubles first started, but he knew more about what was going on than I. He had been there longer."

"You see him first. Renew your friendship and bring him up to date."

Edmund could not refuse.

Fortunately Marie was out when he called. Henri was cordial, anxious to hear all that had happened in New Orleans since he had left and hopeful about the city's recovery and its future. When Edmund asked if Henri intended to return, he nodded. "Eventually. Madame wants to return. She thinks of it as her home."

Damn. "How is Madame?" It was only decent that he ask.

"Very well. We have two little daughters, Henriette and Désirée."

So it had been a girl. At least Annette had produced a son. Why did he think *at least*? It was as if he thought she couldn't do anything else properly. He forced his attention back to Henri.

"You must dine with us. I'll have Madame arrange a date and send a message around to you," Henri was saying.

But before the dinner could be arranged, both Henri and Edmund were summoned to Versailles to report to the crown on conditions in the colony. It would be a lengthy process. Henri predicted gloomily that the hearings would drag on for weeks, possibly months. Apartments had been assigned to them, and he was taking his family. He asked Edmund to ride with them in their coach.

Edmund excused himself by saying his luggage would take up too much room, but Henri said it could travel with their own luggage, which was coming in a separate coach. "We'll be in caravan. One carriage for the children and their nursemaids, one for the luggage, my man and Madame's maid, and one for ourselves. As you can see, there's more than enough room."

To Henri's surprise Marie hadn't objected when he told her he had invited Edmund to ride with them.

"That should be interesting. I can see why the crown wants to hear from him, but I can't imagine what you can report, having been away so long."

"How it was when I was there. My opinion of its future."

"Which is?"

"That it will be a great city one day, but not in our lifetime. Not unless money and arms are poured in, not until the problems of shipping and labor are solved, a better levee is built, the marshes are drained–"

Marie interrupted. "Is it worth it?"

Henri was thoughtful. "Yes. I think so. But I'm not sure the crown and the financiers can see beyond the walls of Paris except in terms of the taxes they collect. To expect them to see beyond the Atlantic is to expect a miracle."

"Won't M. Lanney's report be very pessimistic?"

"That's why the Company of the Indies is eager to have him as a witness, to help prove they can no longer support the colony. I am to be used as persuasion that in the long run the colony will flourish and therefore the crown will benefit."

"So that's the way the world is run. One man shakes his head no; another nods yes. The two are weighed, and our destinies depend on which tips the scale."

Henri smiled. "You are becoming a philosopher, my dear."

The morning of their departure Edmund found himself at the Hôtel de Nemour. He had the same apprehensive feeling that preceded the onslaught of seasickness, but he need not have worried. There was such a flurry of confusion that Marie's greeting was hurried and casual, and she smiled as if she didn't really see him.

He scarcely recognized her. She was elegant and more beautiful than he thought it possible for anyone to be, but it was a studied beauty, like a portrait. Everything was too perfect: the fall of a curl, the placement of a patch by her eye, the color of her lips—which was undoubtedly artificial—the matching green of her gloves and shoes, the ribbon at her throat with the tiny ruby stud. Paris had changed her, and he couldn't imagine her ever going back to New Orleans.

To Marie, Edmund looked older. The laughter had gone from his eyes along with the boyish look and the aura of well-being and enthusiasm. Edmund the man was handsomer in one way but less appealing. It was foolish to go on hating him. It surprised Marie that after all this time she still felt such bitterness. The hurt was still there like an icy core in her heart. A wise woman would have forgiven and forgotten. Marie was older but no wiser.

She could see that she made him nervous and that he could not keep his eyes off her. Fortunately they were all distracted by Henriette. When the child discovered she was to ride in a different coach from her father, she began to shriek, bringing the servants into the streets. Marie would have thrashed her soundly, but Henri softened.

"Let her come with us. We can't have every traveler from here to Versailles reporting us to the guard for murder or abduction."

"From what I've seen of France they'd simply look the other way. Very well. Let her come, but it's shameful to give in to her."

Henriette clasped her pudgy arms around her father's neck and refused to sit anywhere but on his lap, leaving Marie to sit by Edmund, who pressed himself into the corner to avoid any contact with her. As if she had the plague! What a fool he was.

They rode a little way in silence, then Marie, feeling she should make polite conversation, asked, "How is Mme. Lanney?"

"She is enjoying your house. She cares for it as if it were her own. Here sisters have been with us during the Indian troubles."

"I remember them." Silly little girls. One of them running after some army officer who looked as if he'd like to escape.

"Have you children?"

He looked at Henriette covering her father's face with kisses while Henri tried gently to free himself of her embrace. "Two. A son Pierre—we call him Perri—and a daughter, Amalie. By the time I get home there will be a third."

"Dear, dear. Your wife must be glad of her sisters' help. Babies are so difficult." She reached out and tapped Henriette's ankle with her fan. "Sit like a lady or you'll go ride with Sheba. That's quite enough kissing. You'll muss your father's coat. Do you want him to appear before the king looking like a beggarman?"

Henriette turned a baleful eye on Marie. "I love Papa."

"Then behave like a lady."

Henriette looked at Henri, who nodded. She released her embrace and slid down beside him. He put his arm around her, and she leaned against him, holding his hand.

"She is enchanting," Edmund said. Her resemblance to Pierre was startling. "Would you sit on my lap, Mlle. Henriette?" He stretched out his arms to her.

"*Non, non, non!*" she shouted and buried her face in Henri's coat.

Marie laughed. "You see, M. Lanney, she adores her papa. She is my greatest rival."

Did he imagine it, or did she stress the word *papa?* He had a sinking feeling she hadn't changed and would soon be asking him for money.

* * *

Marie hated Versailles. The luxury, the gossip, the intrigue, and the idleness revolted her. "When I think of the poor people of Paris who are supporting all this, I get sick. I wish I hadn't come with you, Henri. Get your business over with so we can leave."

"You're living in one of the most beautiful palaces in Europe, the center of civilization, and you can find nothing kind to say about it?" Henri teased. "An unpredictable woman."

"It's pagan. Look at that bed! It's like an altar. All that's lacking are the priest and acolytes. We dare not lie in it together without offending God."

"I suspect God is offended regularly at Versailles."

"I'm sure He is. The people here have no souls. They're empty. Papier-mâché puppets in a lewd puppet show. They'd be better off pulled by strings in a theater in the square of Saint-Germain. The servants are so overdressed I can't distinguish them from the courtiers. The halls are so cold and drafty I wonder that the orange trees in their stupid silver tubs survive. The rooms are so overcrowded and hot and stink so of bodies that someone is always fainting or being sick."

"You'll have to spend all your time in the gardens if you want to avoid that."

"Gardens! You call those precise beds *gardens?* They're lifeless as well. Oh, yes, there are flowers. So many flowers the fragrance is overpowering. All those trees and shrubs clipped and contorted into unnatural shapes. All those gardeners snipping and raking away in case a leaf should fall! All those ornate fountains, empty because there isn't enough water for them all to flow at once. I'm sorry, Henri, but Versailles is not for me."

"Our friend Lanney is certainly enjoying it."

"Is he? I wonder how many times he's been seduced during the two weeks since we arrived?"

"Marie!"

"He was ripe for it. Didn't you notice his behavior in

the carriage? He turned red as beetroot every time I spoke to him and sat squashed into the corner as if touching me would make him randy."

"My dear! I noticed him admiring you, but I'm accustomed to that. I must admit he hasn't been behaving like a monk, but I think you exaggerate. He's more attracted by the gaming tables than by the flesh he's offered."

"Where does he get the money to gamble? To hear him talk about the hard times in New Orleans one would think he needed a crippled leg and a begging bowl to feed his family." If he could afford to gamble, he could certainly afford to pay off a part of his debt. She must find an opportunity to speak to him alone.

But Edmund had taken up with a different clique and seldom appeared at the same events as Marie and Henri. Marie suspected that he was avoiding them.

A month passed, and still he and Henri had not been summoned to speak. Life wasn't dull. There were dozens of different entertainments every evening, and the king made an appearance at all of them, if only briefly. Henri too had to make an appearance, as his absence "would be noted by someone of influence." So he and Marie attended plays, concerts, masques, balls, and did a bit of gambling themselves.

Marie longed for a quiet evening, but that was seldom possible. They did not even see much of the children. At Versailles children were hidden away like necessary but embarrassing accidents. Often when Henri and Marie did go to their apartments, the girls were already asleep. They looked weary and defenseless, as if the court were slowly draining their vitality. Frequently Henriette's face was tear-stained because she had fallen asleep before seeing her father. Désirée merely looked pale under her luxuriant hair.

Marie sometimes took them for walks, but she did not enjoy it. Henriette and Guy had to be restrained from picking the flowers as they did in their *grandmère*'s garden. Désirée, who was not yet one and still unsteady on her feet, crawled behind them and accosted every man they met, be he gardener or courtier, saying, "Papa?" Eloise and Sheba acted as if it were Marie's turn to take all responsibility, and Marie was glad when it was time to return the lot of them to the nursery.

Henri took Henriette to see a performance of *Beauty and the Beast*, setting a new precedent. The appearance of a child in public caused a buzz of shocked astonishment among the court. Henriette outstared everyone and behaved with such dignity that Louis himself came over and kissed her hand.

The incident apparently reminded the king of the reason for Henri's presence at Versailles. Two days later he and Edmund were summoned to testify at a hearing before the crown and the Company of the Indies.

Henri and Edmund's part of the hearing took two days. Henri explained the potential of the colony, and Edmund the obstacles to developing this potential. The Company of the Indies had already submitted their papers and figures. The representatives of the crown retired to consider the matter. It was now only a question of a final nod from the king. The nod was given. Louisiana became a crown colony.

The night before Marie and Henri returned to Paris, they received invitations to a masked ball. Marie didn't want to go, arguing that if it were masked, no one would know whether or not they appeared. Henri insisted it was important that they attend and bought Marie a gold wig and mask as an inducement. The wig was almost a foot high and decorated with bluebirds boasting real feathers and a garland of silk roses. The mask completely covered her face and was encircled by a stiff gold lace ruffle. Her petticoat was gold, her overskirt blue, and her bodice the rosy red of the bluebirds' breasts. Wide blue ribbons pleated at her shoulder formed mock wings.

Marie considered it a ridiculous costume, especially

after the children were brought in to behold her splendor. Désirée had an attack of giggles every time she looked at the wig. Henriette, of course, wanted it and was carried off howling, stretching out her arms to grab it. Her cries echoed down the corridor long after she was taken away.

"I suppose I could have given her a bluebird or a rose."

"Now who is giving it to her? At the price I paid for those bluebirds I'll not have you giving them away, not even to my Henriette."

Once she was there, Marie enjoyed the ball. She liked dancing, and she didn't lack for partners. But the room was stifling with the heat from the thousands of candles in the gold chandeliers and the crowd of sweating guests. She took every opportunity to stand by one of the open windows for a breath of air. She had lost count of the number of whispered proposals she had received so far that evening and thought she was about to receive another. A Pierrot who had already danced with her several times had followed her to the window.

"Madame, you are so beautiful, so enchanting, so full of life and passion, I can't stay away from you. You remind me of someone I once loved very much. You set my blood pounding in my temples, just as she did. My body aches with longing for yours. I beg you, grant me a moment, an hour, a night to be with you."

Marie laughed. "After all these years, Edmund?"

He reeled as if she had struck him. "Sacred God! It's you. No wonder—"

"That I remind you of a lady you once loved? That's an interesting confession considering the vilification you called down on me at the time."

With shaking hands he removed his mask and wiped the sweat from his face. "That vilification was well deserved. My God, what a scene you made. What a fool you were to think I could marry you."

"You needn't remind me that I was a fool. I am reminded of it every time I look at Henriette. When are you going to pay me, Edmund?"

"I wondered when you'd get around to that. You always do. I need time. The last few years have nearly ruined me. I'm damned well not going to take food out of the mouths of my children to pay *you.*"

"How much have you taken out of their mouths here at the gaming tables?"

"That's my affair."

"As you are in my debt, it is also mine."

"Will you stop hounding me? I'd rather have a bitch cur snapping at my heels. I wish to God I *could* pay you off and be free of you." He turned abruptly, pushing his way through the crowd, past the dancers.

Marie watched him thoughtfully. She should feel triumphant that he had confessed that he had loved her, to know that her body could still excite him—until he had learned who she was. Instead she pitied his weakness and pride and was saddened by it. She would be as glad to be free of him as he would be to be free of her. If they went on like this, their torment would never end. An idea formed in her mind, and she hurried after him.

The hall of mirrors glittered with light, and she was dizzy seeing reflections of reflections of reflections of herself, her ribbon wings fluttering, her petticoat pressed against her legs.

The Pierrot was far down the hall, heading for the great gaming hall. Marie and her reflections ran after him. "Edmund, Edmund, I must speak to you."

He looked over his shoulder, his face as frightened as if he were pursued by Satan. He started to turn away, then stopped and waited for her. "What in the name of the devil do you want now?"

"I have a proposal. One that will rid you of me. Come, sit down."

Suspicion flared in his eyes, but he followed her to one of the ornate gilded love seats. He refused to sit but stood in front of her, glaring down into her face.

"All right. Perhaps I'm being played for a fool, but I'll listen to any proposal that would put an end to this."

"Good. I propose a duel—don't interrupt! Listen. A duel, yes, but not with arms. I couldn't handle a sword, and I don't like pistols, nor do I want to lose my life. A duel by gaming. As I am challenging, you may choose the weapon. Hazard, faro, backgammon, chess . . . The stake is not honor but your debt. If you win, the debt is paid. I promise that. If I win—" She paused and smiled. "If I win, Edmund, the warehouse is mine. It is anyway, you know."

"You're mad."

"It's a fair proposition. Think, if you win, you'll no longer have me snapping at your heels. If you lose, you're still free of me, for the debt will have been paid."

"If I lose, where will it leave me?"

"I've thought of that too. You can continue as manager, foreman—I'm not quite sure what to call it—of the warehouse. Only we two need to know who owns it. You see, I'll even save your reputation. I remember you were always very concerned about your reputation."

He began to pace the floor, creating an army of mirrored Pierrots. "Whoever said Lucifer was a woman was right. You are Lucifer incarnate."

"I offer you freedom, and you answer with insults. I loved you once, Edmund. I loved you so much I would have given you anything you asked, done anything you required of me. I couldn't bear to attend your wedding celebration for fear I'd betray myself. I loved you so much I hesitated to see you here in Paris for fear some of the affection remained."

He stopped in front of her. "And—does it?"

"No. All I want is my pound of flesh." She stood up and replaced her mask. Edmund caught her arm.

"All right. I accept. Let's go to the tables."

Her pulse was racing by the time they reached the

gaming room. She wondered if this was the way men felt when they went to the dueling grounds. Honor, luck, life depended on chance. She had little to lose. It was unlikely Edmund would ever repay her anyway. That had been an earlier gamble, and the stake then had been love.

"There's a table!" Edmund dragged Marie after him through the room. Sweat trickled down his cheeks, and it was only by fanning herself rapidly that Marie kept from fainting.

They sat opposite, eyeing one another. Edmund smiled grimly. "Do you know what you're doing, Marie?"

"Yes. Do you?"

"It's worth the chance. Let's get it over quickly. Hazard. The first call wins."

"Not two out of three?" she taunted.

"The less I have to do with you, the better."

The croupier looked from one to the other and gave an almost imperceptible shrug. "Madame?"

"Five."

The dice rattled in the silver box and clinked onto the table. "Too bad, madame. Monsieur?"

Edmund blotted his forehead. "Nine."

"Ah! Too bad, monsieur."

Each lost chance after chance. Never had Marie seen the dice so unlucky. The silver dots on the ebony cubes danced before her eyes so she could not even count them before the croupier called the loss. Edmund's face was dripping. His suit clung to his damp body.

Marie's scalp crawled under the heavy wig. Trickles of sweat inched from beneath it. At last she threw a chance. Edmund groaned. What was it Henri had said when he had taught her the game? "The sweet little dice always fall the way I want."

She had called for an eight. The croupier lifted the silver cup and smiled. "Congratulations, madame." A double four lay on the table.

Edmund pushed himself away from the table, knocking over his chair. "So! At last you've succeeded in destroying me! I may as well finish the job." He rushed out of the room, shoving people aside, stumbling over chairs, upsetting a table, moving like a drunkard.

Marie ran after him and careened into Henri as she went out the door.

"What the devil is going on? First Lanney comes dashing out and nearly knocks me off my feet, then my own wife—"

"Where is he, Henri? Which way did he go?" She searched the crowd in the hall. "We have to find him. Hurry!"

"What is it, Marie?"

"We've been gambling. I won the warehouse. Oh, I forgot. It was to be a secret." She laughed nervously. "I know it sounds absurd, but that was the stake, Henri, and he lost. And I'm afraid he's going to do himself harm. He said I had ruined him or destroyed him or some such dramatic thing and that he might as well finish the job. I think we should try to find him. Do you know where his apartments are?"

"This way. How could he have been such a fool, and how could you have been a party to it?"

"It seemed harmless enough. What would you have done?" She was breathless, trying to keep up with Henri's long strides.

He smiled. "The same as you did. If Lanney was fool enough—but fools should be protected, not taken advantage of, Marie."

"I very nearly lost. Then I remembered that you called them the sweet little dice. I thought of them that way. Are these his rooms?"

As Henri pounded on the door an explosion within echoed his knock.

"Holy Mother! He's done it, Henri, and it was my fault!"

They forced the door open and burst into the room. Edmund's pistol was on the floor. He was sprawled in a chair holding his shoulder, his velvet coat staining with blood. He grimaced. "I can't even succeed in killing myself."

Henri laughed heartlessly. "If you had really wanted to die, Lanney, you'd have blown out your brains."

Edmund groaned. "It would have looked so unpleasant."

Yes, Marie thought, *it would have ruined your handsome face, you vain popinjay.* All her sympathy vanished. He had never been worthy of her, and she didn't regret taking the warehouse from him.

Pontchartrain

They went back to New Orleans in the spring of 1735. Henri made jokes about their returning as bread cast upon the waters. Their original party of three had increased to six with Henriette, Désirée, and Guy.

Guy had been adopted and Eloise married to Maman's footman, Joseph. Eloise had cried when they said good-bye but between sniffles said, "He'll have a better life with you than I could give him, and I'm not sure he knows the difference between us, madame. I mean, you're as much his mother as I am, just as Henriette's partially my daughter because I fed her."

The sea was like lacquer, but Marie suffered headaches, queaziness, and giddy spells. They were six weeks at sea before she realized she was pregnant. This time there was no possibility that the child was any other's than Henri's.

Marie had not wanted another child. The only consolation was that now they would have to build on the land at Pontchartrain. "The house on Chartres Street will never hold all of us."

"We shall see, my dear."

There was no "we shall see" about it as far as Marie was concerned. It might cost a fortune, but she had no doubt it would be built. She reminded herself of Maman and the new hotel.

The remainder of the voyage she spent propped up in her berth drawing sketch after sketch of the house as she visualized it, trying to remember the plans she had drawn before. She was glad now of the treasures they were bringing with them from France. Satinwood tables, fine china, crystal candelabra, silver sconces, an entire section of decorated wall paneling, carpets, a writing desk inlaid with mother-of-pearl, sheets bordered with Belgian lace, paintings, and best of all, a chaise and four horses.

The day they dropped anchor, she felt as if she had never been away. The sky was burnished gold, and the town wavered in the heat waves. The familiar smell of earth and water, the odors of the market place, of foliage and flowers, were heavy on the motionless air. The river still ran tawny with silt. Buzzards circled above the distant fields. Beyond the ramparts the cypress swamps shimmered, the fir trees stood dark and tall.

Marie felt a rush of love for it such as she had never felt for Paris. But Henriette, standing between her and Henri, began to cry. "It is not beautiful like Paris. There are no towers. It is flat and ugly. I hate it. I do not wish to stay."

"Don't be troublesome, Henriette. It is your home, and you must learn to love it."

"Papa will take me away."

"Papa will do no such thing."

"When I am a lady, I'll go back to Paris."

"Good!"

Edmund had returned on an earlier ship and moved Annette and his family back into the warehouse, so the house on Chartres Street stood empty awaiting their return. Baptiste met the ship. He was as tall as Henri now, with strong shoulders and long arms and legs. He balanced a bag on his head and took one in each hand and swung along the street with an easy rhythmic stride. He was handsome, and there was none of the sullen resentment he had displayed when they had left. No use wasting him to pull a turkey feather fan now. Marie would put him in charge of the garden when she built on Pontchartrain.

She would have liked to find fault with the house,

but she had to admit it had been well kept, thanks to Calla. It seemed cramped, low-ceilinged, and crude after the hotel in the Marais and the château. It smelled of mildew even though the walls had been freshly limed for their return. New linen gauze had been put in the window frames. Sweet-smelling grass mats were on the floor. The old feathers in the fan had been replaced. A new shuck mattress was on the bed.

"We'll be crowded." Marie sat down and surveyed the room critically. "The dining room will have to be partitioned so we can build *cabinets* for the children. You can see, Henri, it would be more sensible to start on the house on the lake front at once."

"My dear, give me time to remove my traveling clothes and have a glass of wine before you start sawing and hammering."

"I am determined, Henri."

"I know you are, Marie."

"Also we must fetch our cases from Lanney's warehouse—*my* warehouse, that is."

"Marie, are you really going to insist on his honoring that gambling debt?"

"Certainly I am. If it had been money, wouldn't you have taken it?"

"That's a different matter. To take a man's property—"

"He put it up as a stake."

Henri lit a cheroot and looked at her through the haze of smoke. "Willingly? I've never questioned you about it since it happened. You went into such a rage when I asked, and he refused to discuss it when I tried to talk to him. Of course he was in too much pain with his shoulder wound to be interested in discussing anything."

"Pity he didn't kill himself," Marie said under her breath.

"But I have never understood how the wager came about or why." He watched her thoughtfully. She fanned herself, refusing to meet his eyes. "Do you want to talk about it now, Marie?"

"No. I do not. You know yourself he'd been gambling heavily, like everyone else at Versailles. My God, those young men. If they aren't up to their ears in debt, they think they don't qualify as gentlemen. He had nothing else to wager. Come, let us unpack our things and try to make some order. We must find beds for everyone. You and Baptiste must go to the warehouse and fetch our belongings, as I said before." She started for the stairs.

"Marie!"

There was a battle of looks between them, then Marie shrugged and came back. "All right. He owed me money, with interest. I asked him for it, and he said he couldn't pay. We decided to gamble for it. I won the warehouse. There. Now you see why I intend to keep it." She turned and started for the stairs again.

"When did you lend him money? When we were at Versailles?"

The house seemed to sigh during the stillness that followed. Marie sighed in echo.

"Before that. Long before that. He—oh, well, you may as well know the truth. He came to Céline's when you were ill. Oh, not to wench. To take shelter from the storm. The hurricane. Do you remember it?" She was talking hurriedly, feverishly now. "We were all huddled in there together, expecting the house to blow down any moment, and I started talking to him. Rather, he talked. Heavens, how he talked. He told us his life history. All about his family, how he had to succeed to prove himself, about the plans he had, the warehouse he wanted to build, the merchants' exchange so he could act as middleman between the planters and the ships' captains. I had all that money you had given me and the money from my father's house and—well, I thought I'd be clever and invest it. I gave it to him."

"So that's where he got his backing!" Henri whistled

softly. "No wonder he was so close-mouthed about it. He couldn't confess to having been in a bawdy house."

"Oh, not he! Now you know why I hate him, have always hated him. He's no businessman. He as good as stole my money. He's made almost no payments, and every time I tried to collect, he called me a whore. What else could he think, considering where he had met me? But I want my money back so I can build our house on Pontchartrain, and if the only way I can get it is by taking the warehouse, I'll have it, and I'm damned if I'll give it back—no matter what he thinks of me or what you think is fair. I'll run it better than he can, and I'll make it pay. I'll let him stay there and manage it and play the part of a sniveling, cock sparrow gentleman, but I'll keep the books, and I'll tell him what to do, and the first time he tries to cheat me, I'll hand him a pistol and let him properly do the job of blowing off his head!" She stopped, choked by tears.

Henri got up and put his arms around her. "Dear little Marie, you've kept this from me all these years. You have let me tease you about being as tight-fisted as a peasant when you wouldn't spend your own money for something, and all this time—"

"All this time my father's money box was almost empty. I couldn't tell you, because I had been such a fool and felt as if I had cheated you as well."

"It's all right now, Marie. It was your money, and I remember that Lanney was a convincing young man in those days. It wasn't an unwise investment. It has simply taken time to pay off. It will still take time, Marie. The colony's in a bad way. Bienville hasn't been back long enough to cure its ills. But keep the warehouse, yes. It's yours whether you won it on a throw or took it as repayment. I'm sorry for Lanney and for his wife. She'll probably have told her parents. It will be no secret, but I'm sure he'll recover. It won't be the first scandal New Orleans has seen, and it certainly won't be the last."

Edmund's loss of the warehouse was not the disgrace Marie and Henri had imagined. Edmund's father-in-law had actually laughed and clapped him on the back.

"I didn't know you were such a plunger, my boy. Better men than you have taken lesser chances and been ruined by it. The business is still virtually yours as long as you are managing it. You'll be in a position to pull the strings"—he tapped his nose and winked—"while all the headaches belong to someone else. I'd have done the same. Tell Annette to stop sniveling. She's lucky you were only winged instead of killed in that duel. How is the shoulder?"

"It aches when it rains." Edmund had no more been able to confess to the sin of attempted suicide than he had expected his lie about having been wounded in a duel to turn him into a hero.

His father certainly hadn't been pleased with the loss of the warehouse or the report of a duel. He had called Edmund a complete ass, a milksop, a feeble-minded bungler, and the fool of the family. Edmund had been glad to leave Paris. M. Arnolie's confidence and approval were a salve. He was convinced that it had been Edmund's testimony that had persuaded the crown to accept the charter from the Company of the Indies. "Things will improve now. France will take care of us." Edmund's modest protests would not convince him otherwise. Edmund hoped he wouldn't be blamed if things didn't improve and France let them down.

Annette approved of nothing. She was furious that he had dueled. She was furious he had lost the warehouse. She was furious that the de Nemours were coming home, forcing her to choose between living in the warehouse and living in her parents' home. She didn't want to live in either place.

Claudine and Angela had married their officers and were living at the plantation. Claudine already had a huge, husky, noisy baby, and Angela was due in a few months.

The warehouse wouldn't be safe. New Orleans was an armed camp. The Natchez and Chickasaw refused to let themselves be conquered. Soldiers of fortune, Indian hunters, woodsmen, and militiamen swarmed the streets, drunken, brawling, thieving. Even after Edmund had added another room to their living quarters in the warehouse and put wrought iron bars over the windows, Annette still hated it.

When Marie and Henri came to the warehouse to look over the books and discuss business matters with Edmund, Annette had been prepared to have nothing to do with them, or at best to be cool and distant. But Edmund invited them to have coffee, and she decided if he could be gracious when they had bilked him out of his business, she could be too.

It pleased her to see that Marie de Nemour was pregnant. No matter how elegant her Parisian clothes, they could not hide the fact that she was uncomfortable, tired, and feeling the July heat just as badly as Annette herself. Annette too was pregnant again, the second time since Edmund's return. The first had resulted in a miscarriage. Sometimes she thought all Edmund had to do was remove his breeches and she was with child.

Marie also was determined to be pleasant. She noticed Annette's condition at once. "You too," she sighed sympathetically. "And in this weather. I feel it after Paris. Ah, but you have a river breeze. How lucky you are." She actually sounded sincere. "And a view of the river. I envy you that. I wouldn't be able to tear myself away from the window. How do you get anything done?" Marie moved to the window and stood there, fanning herself and looking out. "I'd sit here all day. What a lot of building has been done on the other bank. I remember when there was nothing there but the king's plantation." She was chattering like a parrot, trying to overcome her nervousness. She turned and smiled at Annette, who forced a smile in return. "You've made this room very charming." She stroked the back of a cypress wood settee. "This is nice. I never appreciated our New Orleans-made furniture until I sat on some of those ornate and uncomfortable chairs in Paris. They're beautiful to look at, but to sit in them is another matter. It's as if they resent it. They just want to stand there on their four legs and be admired."

Annette didn't believe her for a moment. She had seen some of those ornate chairs in the shipment the de Nemours had brought home. If they were so uncomfortable, why had she bought them?

At that point the men joined them. Annette felt a pang of envy when she saw that Henri de Nemour had a small girl by the hand. She was a golden, dimpled child, unlike poor little Amalie, who was already yellow with swamp fever and so puny Annette sometimes despaired of her living to grow up.

Perri had been playing quietly. Now he looked at the little girl and smiled. She broke away from her father and ran to him. "Pretty boy. I love you." She knelt and kissed him.

The adults laughed. Henri said, "Love at first sight. They're sweet together, aren't they?"

Marie and Edmund exchanged a look. To Marie they looked like brother and sister. Perhaps it was because she knew.

"You have a daughter too, don't you?"

"Yes. Amalie. She's feverish today."

"She must be about Désirée's age. When she's better, bring them to play in the garden."

Henri gave Marie an approving look.

"You were very gracious, Marie," he said afterward.

"Why not? They're our employees."

He laughed. "Incorrigible as ever!"

* * *

"There, that wasn't so bad, was it?" Edmund asked Annette. "Everything is in order, and they're going to treat me very fairly. You can buy yourself some lace if the ship's captain has any left."

"If she likes the view so much, why doesn't she live here herself? Then she could really manage things."

Edmund sighed. Women! They saw everything from a narrow point of view.

"Try to be friends, Annette. It will be easier for me. It will be worth it to take the children to play in the garden, won't it? Perri misses the garden, don't you, Perri?"

"She's pretty," Perri said.

"Yes, she's a beautiful little girl."

"Not the girl. The lady."

Annette felt like slapping him.

One of the first things Marie did after they were reasonably settled was to visit Céline. There was new furniture to go with the silk carpet and chandelier Marie and Maman had shipped from France, and the walls were covered in pale green silk.

"How grand! Where did you get those gilt chairs?"

"Mobile. Didn't you hear about the smallpox epidemic? It wiped out half the population. You could get anything you wanted because there were no survivors to claim it."

"Are they safe? You can't get pox from them?"

"Not that kind, little Marie. I hope not the other kind either. But some of the men we have to take these days!" Céline rolled her eyes. "There's a Missouri itch going around. It doesn't last long, but for a few days it's pure hell.

"No, I've had the furniture long enough to know we can't get smallpox from it. Your house is the gambling room now. Gambling's still against the law, but what man doesn't like it? It's good for business. I've never understood the connection, but there's something about it that makes them riggish as goats.

"If I had enough room, I'd take on a black and an Indian. They think it changes their luck, like betting on black after losing all your money on the red. Well—" She shrugged. "Eventually, when I have my large house. Speaking of being grand, your friend Frank Goodacre has changed his name. He's François Bonarpent now."

"How ridiculous! Does he think it will turn him into a silk purse?"

"Oh, I see. The sow's ear. Yes. Well, actually, Marie, maybe not a silk purse, but a leather one. He's making money from his bricks. Which reminds me, he brought a packet for you. I've had it so long I'd forgotten. He's built himself a better house, bought some land. He told me when I get ready to move my establishment, he'll give me a good deal on bricks."

"You're serious about moving?"

"Do you think I want to nest like a rat on the waterfront forever? Not Céline. I have my eye on a piece of property on Rampart Street, but there's no way they'll let a whore buy it. Old Bienville hasn't mellowed that much. Just because he's not capable anymore, he doesn't want anyone else to do it. Everyone was glad to have us in the old days. We were needed then."

"Surely you're needed now with all the troops."

"To hear some of the officers tell it, there isn't a woman in New Orleans who won't give it away. That's an exaggeration, of course, but there's plenty of hot blood around. Tell me about Paris."

Marie did, including the affair with Paul. "Henri has the picture hanging in our bedroom. I didn't know whether it's a warning to behave myself or masochism on his part."

"And who fathered this one?" Céline gestured at Marie's figure.

"Henri, and no doubts about it. Where's Mimi? I want to see her."

"Her man was transferred to Biloxi. She'd rather be back here. She said it's like the jaws of hell in summer and so cold in winter the water freezes in the glasses. I said, so drink wine."

While they talked Marie had been counting the money from Frank Goodacre. "Well! Can you believe it? He's paid the debt in full."

"I told you he was doing well. In a way, you gave him the start, Marie."

"Not willingly, Céline, but it's worked out for the best."

Now that Marie had the money from Frank Goodacre, she was anxious to start building. Henri had to admit that they couldn't delay much longer. "Even Bienville is on your side, Marie. He told me to put the land grant to use or surrender it. Between the two of you, I'll end up living on the lake whether I want to or not."

Now that Marie knew the house would become a reality, she worked on her plans in earnest. She spent hours poring over her drawings, planning fireplaces and windows, galleries and balconies, taking a few feet off this room to add to another, making the staircase to the upper story first a spiral, then a long, sweeping one with an interior balcony off which the bedrooms opened, circling the entire upper floor.

Money from the estate in France had come on a recent ship. Even the warehouse brought in a little income, although the colony was still recovering from the years of alternate flood and drought and wars.

"Once the land is put into cultivation, we'll have that money too," Marie said. "What are we going to plant, Henri? Indigo, rice, mulberry?"

"There's plenty of time to think about that."

"How can you be so—so maddeningly calm?"

"It's your project, Marie, and I'm not obsessed with it the way you are."

It was true she was obsessed. She never stopped

thinking about the house, and at night she dreamed about it. One day when Henri was busy elsewhere, she and Baptiste rode out to the lake. The trees had grown, the underbrush was thicker and more tangled. It looked like a jungle and was just as noisy with the sound of small birds and doves and parrots and the occasional drumming of frogs and the chirp of tree toads. Clearing to build would be a larger job than Marie had realized.

"Oh, Baptiste, I didn't remember how wild it is. It will take years before the house can be built."

"Maybe not, madame. How big is the house going to be? Where will it sit?"

"On that knoll, facing the lake, with a garden in front going right down to the shore. I want to keep as many trees as possible—" Except that oak where she had lain with Edmund. "Let me show you the drawings."

Baptiste's understanding and appreciation of the plans surprised her. He cut stakes, stepped off the size of the house, hacking aside the undergrowth, and drove stakes at what would be the four corners of the house. "I'll come back and do the job right and tie cloth on them so we can see them." He cleared a path down to the lake. "You'll want a driveway too, for the chaise. There'll be roads here one day instead of trails. It's better to plan for them now. The drive should go right up to the front of the house, then circle 'round to the back so the horse can draw the chaise to the barn. We'll dredge shells from the lake bed and crush 'em to surface the road and the paths."

"That's a wonderful idea, Baptiste."

"You'll need a lot of slaves, madame."

"We'll get them."

"What I'll do is, I'll come out here and start clearing. I'll bring a sack of rice and salt meat and sleep right here. That way it'll save time."

"Will you be safe?"

"Nothing and nobody'll get Baptiste. I want to see the house grow. I want to see the land flowering."

"So do I." Marie thought that with his enthusiasm the house would soon take shape.

Henri didn't approve of Baptiste's plan to go to the property alone. He argued that it was too large a job for one man and that it was too soon to begin clearing. "It will all be overgrown again before we start to build."

But Marie was adamant. "Baptiste is really interested in the house, Henri. Trust him and trust me. The sooner we start, the sooner we'll be finished."

Henri gave in. "All right. I'm too tired to argue. I've had a wretched headache all day. I'm going to lie down for a while before dinner. And—Marie, I don't want you going out there alone. The mercenaries have too much freedom, and I wouldn't trust them not to rape a lone woman."

"Even a pregnant one?"

"Even a pregnant one."

That evening when she went to awaken Henri for dinner, she found him burning with fever. He tried to focus on her face, then turned his head away. "Marie, get me some water."

She ran to fetch Sheba and to dip water from the huge clay pot. By the time they went back to the bedroom, Henri was shaking with chills. He vomited up the water as soon as he drank it.

"It's swamp fever again," Sheba said. "You better stay away, pregnant like you are. You sleep with the children. I'll stay with him."

Marie went downstairs, hugging her body where she carried the child. What would happen if Henri died? She would be left alone with the children, Sheba, Calla, and Baptiste all dependent on her. She would never have the house on Pontchartrain. She knew the house shouldn't be important with Henri lying ill, but it was. She wanted that house because—

because Edmund and Annette had wanted to build there. Because she still hated them.

But it was difficult to think about the house or anything else when Henri was out of his mind with fever and she was half out of hers with worry and fear. She paced the floor, putting her hands over her ears to shut out the sound of the children's laughter. She lay awake at night, waiting, listening for any indication of change in his condition.

Why did it always take a catastrophe to make her realize how much she loved him? And even if she could have risked entering the bedroom to tell him that she did, he wouldn't have heard her in his delirium.

He survived the first week, and she knew he would not die. Still, it was another week before she dared sit beside his bed to take care of him or leave him long enough to go out to Pontchartrain to see Baptiste's progress.

The tall grass had been scythed down. The house was outlined with stakes, each waving a red cloth, and the rooms marked off with smaller stakes topped with blue. The trees which had been cut down were stripped and cut into logs. He had left the liveoak standing. "That old tree, it's too handsome to cut, and the girls will like making a playhouse under the moss."

"Yes, I suppose they will."

"You tell Monsieur, soon as he's well, we can start to build."

"I'll tell him, but I think we must wait until after the baby is born. I want to be here every day. To see the dream grow."

As she was about to leave, Baptiste caught hold of the bridle and stopped her. "Madame, I just remembered something. A man was here a few days back. I was working and didn't notice him at first. Then I saw him watching me. I waited for him to speak, though I wanted to ask why he was on your land. He asked me what I was doing. I told him, clearing the land for

Madame's house. He said, 'So she's going to build.' He walked around looking at the stakes, pacing off the lengths. It was not my place to stop him, you understand, madame, but I stopped work to watch him as if I was resting. After a while he went away without so much as a nod to me."

"Was he a soldier? An officer?"

"No. He dressed like all planters dress. He was an older man."

"That's strange. If he comes back, let me know, and if you recognize him when you are in town, you must tell me."

She worried about it all the way home, telling herself it was probably of no significance. She could not tell Henri, ill or not, for he would know she had disobeyed him by going out to the property alone.

Henri recovered more rapidly than he had in Paris, and by the end of October the fever was completely gone. Sheba and Calla scrubbed the bedroom and boiled the bedclothes. The walls were relimed and a new mattress stuffed. Every effort was madc to erase the last traces of fever in readiness for Marie's lying-in.

The last month she was listless, anxious for the ordeal to be over, and resentful of every hour she had to spend away from the plans for the house. She had to let Henri go out to the land without her and was in a state of nervousness until he returned.

"Well, Henri, what do you think?"

"I approve of it. You and Baptiste have done wonders. Now, what can I do to help?"

"Nothing. As you once said, it is my project. I want to be in on all of it, and I want nothing done until I can be in on it. If this child is one day later than he need be, I shall hold it against him forever."

Louis was born on a cold morning near Christmas when a north wind smelling of snow drove tall white caps down the river and formed a thin layer of glittering frost on the roofs.

To Marie's disappointment he wasn't a golden child like Pierre Lanney. His eyes were dark hyacinths like Marie's own, and his hair was nearly as dark as Désirée's.

No wet nurse was available, and Marie was forced to feed him herself. She did not have enough milk, and Sheba had to concoct a supplement of sugar syrup, rice water, and cow's milk. Louis thrived on it.

Henriette, full of the self-importance of a seven-year-old, was so jealous of the baby that Henri scarcely dared show any interest in him. Désirée treated him like a toy to be played with and cast aside. Marie, not without some guilt, considered him more of an interference than a joy. She was happy when he no longer needed her constant attention and she could turn to her other affairs.

One blue and gold day in February Marie had Baptiste drive her out to Frank Goodacre's brick kiln. The Goodacres' new house stood nearby. As the chaise drove up a woman came out of the house and stared, mouth agape.

It had been years since Marie had seen Faith Goodacre. She had become gaunt, toothless, and gray. Her clothes hung on her bony frame. Wisps of hair which had escaped from the knot at the nape of her neck blew around her face. Even after she retreated into the house, Marie was aware of her peering through the window.

She wondered how Frank could stand to be around her. There was no need for Marie to punish him. His punishment was there, in his woman and his marriage.

The kiln was astonishing. Whites and blacks worked side by side, crushing, mixing, pouring, and firing. Some of them Marie recognized as Frank's sons. The youngest wasn't much older than Henriette. They were no longer scrawny little animals. They were tanned, husky, well-fed, and aside from the brick dust they were clean.

Frank had changed too. His clothes were dusty, but they were good clothes, serviceable and well cut to suit his big frame. He had put on weight and lost his shambling gait and hangdog look. His beard was neatly trimmed, his mustache waxed, and his hair worn in the current fashion.

He recognized Marie before she spoke and exclaimed in English, "By heaven, it's Mary Macleod. That is, Mme. de Nemour."

"Yes, Mr. Goodacre. Or should I say M. Bonarpent?"

"Yes, I've changed my name, Mary. I heard you were back. I've seen M. de Nemour several times at the warehouse. I understand it's yours now."

"Yes. M. Lanney owed me money too."

A slow flush spread over Frank's face. "I'd hoped my debt was paid off now."

"It is. That isn't why I came to see you. I think we should speak French so my man here can understand us. We're building a new house, and I want you to give me a good price on bricks. I have a copy of the plans here. You look them over, and when you're ready to go out to the site, Baptiste will take you. We want to start as soon as possible, before the colony recovers completely from the slump, while prices are still low and before someone decides to buy our grant."

"Somebody like me, Mary?"

"What do you mean?"

He grinned slyly. "You haven't heard? I bought a grant to a plantation early on in the Indian scare, Mary. Got it for almost nothing. The owner was glad to be rid of it and move into town. I mean to build on it myself one day."

And it was her father's money which had given him this start!

"I'll give you the bricks on credit, Mary, as a special

favor for what you and M. de Nemour have done for me."

"That won't be necessary. And what I did for you, as you put it, was not my doing. You stole that money."

He shuffled his feet, once again becoming the old Frank Goodacre. He rubbed his hand across the fine white dust which had settled on the chaise. "I've always felt bad about that, Mary. I won't say I'm sorry I took the money, but my conscience hasn't been exactly easy. But I've been sorry about the way Mrs. Goodacre treated you that night. I would've have done differently if she'd allowed it."

"I was angry for a long time. I'm still angry when I remember it."

"I know that." He switched to English. "Why did you have me pay the money I owed you to Mme. Céline, Mary?"

She hesitated, then her eyes flashed. "Because she took me in when your wife wouldn't. She didn't make a whore of me. Don't think that! She sent me to the convent. For a long time she was the only friend I had."

"I always wondered how you knew about my going there."

"She charged you double and gave half the money to me. She was the one who discovered you had stolen from me."

He went slack-jawed, then slapped the side of the chaise and laughed. "That beats damn-all, Mary! A man hasn't a chance against a woman. I always said so. Don't think I begrudge it, Mary. I got my money's worth. You got yours. It all worked out in the end. You'll be building a house with my bricks. By damn, that's a strange twist of fate, all right. I'll send you an estimate, Mary, and I'll do it fair and square and at a good price. I've changed, Mary. I hope in time you'll come to forgive me."

For years she had wanted to crush him as she

would a roach or a scorpion. Now all she felt was dislike mingled with reluctant admiration for what he had done to better himself. Not yet a silk purse, as Céline had said, but a good leather one.

Late in the spring another war broke out with the Chickasaw.

"I'm sick of Indian wars," Marie said. "I suppose you'll tell me we'll have to delay building until it's settled, and after I've contracted for all those bricks."

"Bienville isn't so busy with the war that he hasn't reminded me that the land has to be put to use. Apparently he has had inquiries about the possibility of buying my grant. The sooner the house is built the better."

Henri bought two male slaves to help Baptiste and hired some men from the German colony up the river who were familiar with *briquette entre poteaux* construction. The foundation was laid, and the walls began to climb. Marie was so fascinated she couldn't keep away. One day as she sat on a pile of bricks watching the work M. Arnolie rowed along the lake and pulled ashore. Baptiste saw him, put down his tools and hurried over to Marie.

"Madame, it is the man who was here before. Do you remember? The white man who came when I was clearing?"

"Yes. I remember. It's M. Arnolie, Baptiste. His land adjoins ours. I suppose he was curious. It's all right. Go back to work." She stood up, suddenly defensive. "How do you do, M. Arnolie."

"That's quite a house you're putting up, madame." He jerked his head toward the building.

Marie nodded.

"What's the size of it?" The question was bluntly put.

"Sixty by eighty. Sixteen rooms plus a vestibule."

"Versailles seems to have given you some grand ideas, madame. Or are you planning a large family?"

He chuckled and looked sideways at her out of his piggy eyes.

"What I plan to do with sixteen rooms is my affair, M. Arnolie." She dropped a curtsy. "I must start back to town." She waved to Baptiste and untied her horse. M. Arnolie hurried over to help her mount.

"Madame, I meant no offense."

"I'm not angry." But there had been something in his manner, some wiliness that had irritated her. "My husband would tell you that I've heard enough about my sixteen rooms not to need to hear any more from a—" She refused to call him a friend. "Future neighbor." She gave a curt nod and rode off.

She told Henri of the incident that night. "Stupid peasant. He's never got over our refusing to sell the property to him for his precious Annette."

"It was probably nothing but neighborly curiosity, Marie. You've no cause to carry over your vendetta against Lanney to the Arnolies." He added teasingly, "You must admit sixteen rooms for one small family *is* pretentious."

"I'll make it twenty, to spite him."

"You'll do nothing of the sort, my dear. I promised not to interfere, but I draw the line at sixteen rooms."

A few days later Henri returned home with a worried frown. "Marie, you were right and I was wrong about Arnolie. We are going to have to stop building."

Marie, who was trying to paint a picture of Louis on Sheba's lap, spoke through the paint brush she held in her mouth while using a finer one for a different color. "What makes you think I'll stop?" She removed the paint brush and asked, "What's he done? Set mantraps for our men?"

"Brought a claim against us. Produced a map of his grant showing that ours overlaps it to such an extent that the house is on his land."

"Ridiculous!"

"I'm not so sure. There have been several such errors about overlaps. Those old maps and grants were carelessly drawn."

"Surely not that badly."

"I don't know."

"Why didn't he produce the map before, when he wanted to buy?"

"It seems he had Edmund look into it while he was in Paris."

"And he is just now getting around to producing the map after all this time! That man is up to no good." She began to scrape her pallet viciously. "You can go, Sheba. I can't paint now, and the beastie doesn't seem to like sitting for his portrait anyway. You *must* do something, Henri."

"I intend to do something, but it will take time. I have to search out my papers. In fact, I think Papa has them in France, since it was his arrangement. When I have them, they must be handed over to Bienville and the council for investigation, then have a crown decision."

"It sounds as if it will take years!"

"It may."

"Damn the Arnolies to hell! I hate them all. Yes, damn them, damn them, damn them!"

Throughout the last months of summer the trumpet vines climbed the half-finished walls of the house and festooned the window frames. Moss grew on the chimneys, crepe myrtle sprouted in what was to have been the dining room, and bird droppings stained the timber. A coral vine covered the stack of unused bricks, and lizards were everywhere.

Marie fumed and wondered if the house would ever be completed or would stand an empty shell, or, worse, be completed by Edmund and Annette.

In August the expedition which had marched against the Chickasaw straggled back to New Orleans in defeat. One hundred men had been lost, among them Angela Arnolie's husband, who had been killed outright, and Claudine's, who was among thirty others taken captive and burned at the stake.

The Arnolie family went into deep mourning. Marie refused to put on black and pay a call of condolence. "They can weep their eyes out without my help. I want no part of them."

Henri went alone.

September and October were hotter and even more humid than usual. The house in town was like a kiln. Sometimes the family took a picnic to the lake and the children played house within the empty walls.

"It's probably the only time they'll ever play here," Marie said bitterly.

Early in November a ship from France brought the papers showing the original land grants. They were submitted to Bienville and the council. "There is nothing to do now but wait," Henri told Marie. He was gone every day, and every evening when he returned, Marie had but to look at his face to know there had been no decision.

It was fortunate she had preparations for Christmas to keep her busy, but she was so irritable that she scolded the girls unnecessarily, making Henriette cry, and once slapped Désirée when she wanted to go play with Amalie Lanney, who was her friend at the convent school.

It was Christmas before the matter was settled. When Henri and Marie returned from mass on Christmas Eve, he told her she could resume building. M. Arnolie had withdrawn his claim.

"We've matched our maps and come to an agreement. An old land contour line was mistaken by the mapmaker for a property line. Actually the overlap is only about fifty feet and comes nowhere near the house. And since we will be living on land adjoining theirs, Marie, I hope you will try to forgive them."

"Humph! I'll try for your sake, not for mine." Would

she never be rid of these people? Must she forever be plotting revenge? She would have it one day. "I suppose it isn't easy to have two widowed daughters on your hands and another who does nothing but get herself pregnant. Annette *is* pregnant again, in case you hadn't noticed. She complains about being crowded in that warehouse, and all she does is her best to make it more so. You'd think she'd have more sense."

"It would resolve our differences if Henriette and Pierre Lanney made a match, wouldn't it?" He laughed. "Don't look so horrified, Marie. I know how fond you are of Perri. It seemed to me an ideal arrangement."

Marie put down her glass. "You are as bad as Papa. Henriette is not yet nine. Who knows who she will take it into her mind to marry? She's so wilful that she'd reject anyone I chose just because I'd chosen him. She listens to you, I know. But I see no point in discussing it now."

"Shall we have a game of chess before we go to bed?"

"At two o'clock in the morning?"

"It's Christmas Day, my dear. Everyone is sleeping, and we are alone, the way we were once long ago. Do you remember our first Christmas, Marie?"

"We were on the ship on our way to France. The stars were shining, and there was nothing but sea and sky all around us." She stopped suddenly. "That wasn't our first Christmas, was it? Our first—you came to Céline's after mass and awakened me." She refilled their glasses. "I hated you in those days, Henri. I hated you for corrupting me, because I had to be obedient to your wishes. Because, in spite of hating you, my body liked what my mind rejected." *It wasn't until I had Edmund that I learned the relationship between physical and emotional love,* she thought. "I've shocked you, haven't I? I'm sorry. I shouldn't have told you."

He had been setting up the chess board, but he

stopped, his fingers tight around a piece. "Do you hate me still?"

"I love you! Surely you know that by now." She took the piece from him and set it on the board. "Come, darling. We don't want to play chess. We want to go to bed. Bring the wine and cakes. I'll go ahead and light the candles."

BOOK II

Henriette and Désirée

Henriette never forgot Paris. She remembered her *grandpère* and *grandmère* and her *tante* Laure, all of whom she could mimic to perfection. She remembered the château, the stiff gardens of Versailles, and both the hotels de Nemour. At thirteen she still spoke French with a Parisian accent, and long after they had moved into the new house overlooking the lake, she vented scorn on New Orleans.

Once she overheard her mother suggest to Papa that Henriette be sent back to Paris to attend school. She had held her breath until she heard his reply: "Deprive me of my Henriette? I won't allow it. You know she is the joy of my heart."

Henriette skipped away before she was caught eavesdropping. She felt strangely relieved. For all her talk, she didn't want to leave Papa. If she was the joy of his heart, he was the joy of hers. There was a special relationship between them which Désirée and Louis did not share.

Désirée wasn't the joy of Papa's heart. Sometimes Henriette caught him looking at Désirée, his eyes narrowed, his upper lip caught between his teeth, as if he didn't know who she was. Désirée didn't care that she wasn't his joy because Désirée didn't care about anything or anybody but herself. She was never solemn or sad. She never cried, not even when the sisters at the convent beat her for laughing at the psalm about "He shall cover thee with his feathers."

"Imagine God having feathers! What is He? A big

bird? I think He is a parrot all green and red and blue . . ."

She had laughed every time the cane cracked on her bottom while all the other girls had cringed. She had laughed during the hurricane in 1740, when everyone else had been cowering under the big cypress dining room table and the shutters had broken loose and banged at the windows and the air had been filled with flying debris. Désirée had run to the window, looked out at the lake, and cried, "It looks like the sea!" And before anyone could stop her, she had run out the door, leaving it to bang like the shutters. The wind had knocked her over at once. Baptiste had had to go out and bring her back, and he had said, "She was lying there laughing."

That same year there had been an epidemic. Many people had died. Every day they heard the church bell tolling another death, and another. Papa and Louis had been sick, and the house had been very still. Henriette had knelt outside Papa's door praying that he wouldn't die. Désirée didn't laugh, but she said, "I guess God will do what He wants no matter how much you pray, Henriette." Henriette knew better, for neither of them had died.

When they had gone to the funeral for Mme. and M. Arnolie, who had died of the fever, Désirée had to stuff her handkerchief in her mouth to keep from laughing because Amalie Lanney had looked so funny. Her black dress had been too big for her and was made of some stiff material that didn't move when she did but sort of caught up with her afterward. Amalie had looked funny anyway, with her eyes and nose all red from crying.

The iron bells had tolled, and it had rained heavily. Henriette said it was because God was crying. That had made Désirée laugh too. In spite of the fact that Maman didn't like the Arnolies, she had cried at the graveside when the coffins wouldn't sink and the grave-diggers had had to stand on them to make them go down. Maman had gone white and was sick afterward. She had cried all the way home and had still been crying when Papa had carried her upstairs. He had kept saying, "It's all right, my darling. It's all right." He had stayed in the bedroom with her a long time.

Henriette wished she and Maman loved each other the way she and Papa loved each other. Maman was the most beautiful woman in New Orleans, Henriette thought. All the other ladies copied everything she did, and Maman didn't care a biscuit for them. When they had first returned from Paris, all Maman had cared about was building her house. It had taken almost a year and after it was finished, all she cared about was decorating it. It was a beautiful house, and once she had it furnished the way she wanted it, she started giving lots of parties, which enlivened New Orleans society over the next few years.

Before Sieur de Bienville was sent back to France, all yellow with fever and sad-looking, she gave a farewell party for him, and she gave a welcoming party for the new governor and his wife, the Marquis and Marquise de Vaudreuil. Henriette was thirteen by then, and she was allowed to attend the party. She had danced with Perri Lanney six times.

Most girls in New Orleans were married by the time thcy were thirteen. Henriette wished Perri would ask her to marry him, but though he spent a lot of time at their house, he didn't ask. Désirée, meanwhile, chased everything in breeches, and Perri's sister Amalie was engaged. Henriette was miserable because she thought she was going to be an old maid.

After the elder Arnolies died, Edmund and Annette moved to the plantation. The Lanney family had grown. Besides Perri and Amalie, there were three younger children. Marie's children saw a great deal of them, riding, hunting, boating, and picnicking, but Marie was not inclined to have much to do with her neighbors. She seldom had anything good to say about them. She scoffed at Angela and Claudine for having married into the military again.

"I never saw two unhappier widows, yet here they are remarried to cannon fodder. And pregnant, of course. I wonder if the Arnolie girls ever put their legs together."

Henri laughed and scolded, and warned her she would be punished in the next life.

"It will be worth it."

When Amalie was married to Cadet André le Sueur, she chose Henriette and Désirée as her attendants.

"I look quite grown up, don't I?" Désirée preened herself in front of the long gilt-framed mirror in the hall. It was a winter wedding, and the cranberry red dress suited her dark complexion.

"No, you don't," Marie said. "You look exactly what you are. Twelve years old. If Mme. Lanney hadn't insisted, you wouldn't be taking part in this wedding at all. But they had to please their Amalie, who seems to look upon you as"—she almost said sisters, but she looked at Henriette and said—"special friends."

Henriette said it for her. "Almost like sisters." Her dress was holly green, which made her eyes look all the greener. "Poor Amalie, we'll look so much prettier than she will. Her complexion's too brown to wear white."

"She'll look plain ugly," Désirée said. "I don't know what André le Sueur sees in her."

"He sees a home and a meal ticket, you little goose," Marie said. "It costs those young cadets five hundred livres a month to eat, and that's without wine. Even Amalie's father knows that. For all le Sueur's big talk about his family's château in France, he owns nothing but his cape and his sword."

"And his underdrawers?" Désirée giggled. "I hope he owns his underdrawers."

Marie gave her a playful slap.

"I'll be fourteen next year, Maman. Can I be married then?" asked Henriette.

"No, you may not. It's far too young, even if the Lanneys are allowing Amalie to be married at thirteen. You're still a child."

"How old were you, Maman?"

"That's my secret. Mine and Papa's."

"A secret like the picture of you in your bedroom?"

"How do you know about the picture in the bedroom?"

"You forgot to draw the curtain over it one day. Was that before or after you and Papa were married? Were you a model, Maman? Was that in Paris? Is the artist the one who taught you to paint?"

"Were you in love with him?" Désirée asked. "Did you make babies with him?"

"What do you know about making babies?"

"Perri told Amalie what André le Sueur will do to her." Désirée twirled and admired her reflection over her shoulder. "She's so afraid. It's more than just kissing. She went crying to her mother, and Perri got into trouble. Her mother said it was true, just the same. She said Amalie mustn't cry or yell or try to run away, but to let him do whatever he wants and that after a while she'll like it and have babies. I wonder if I'd like it."

"I would if it were Perri," Henriette said. "Amalie and André get to spend a whole week in their bedroom and have their meals brought to them and everything."

"Imagine a whole week with nothing to do but make babies. Except I don't think I'd want the babies," Désirée reasoned. "I wonder if I could do it without having the babies? Perri told Amalie it's sort of like connecting your bodies."

"You're both disgraceful, and I don't want to hear any more such talk. What would Papa say? Fetch your capes. It's time to go." Marie walked down the stairs, her brow drawn in a frown. She had hoped Henriette would outgrow her attachment to Perri. Instead the relationship seemed to be intensifying.

Guy and Louis were already in the coach, and Henri was pacing the gallery waiting for the ladies. "You look very beautiful, Marie, but why so solemn?" he asked.

"The girls. Henriette's demanding to be married, and Désirée's discussing the most intimate details of marriage as if she were about to go out and try them. I wish to heaven the Lanneys hadn't decided to marry off Amalie."

Henri helped her into the coach and leaned against it, waiting for the girls. "I suppose I must make up my mind to lose Henriette soon. There are plenty of young men who would marry her. Perri Lanney for one."

"I won't have it."

Henri sighed. "Edmund seems as dead set against it as you, Marie. He said he didn't think a marriage between two people who had known each other since childhood was a good idea. I don't hold with the theory myself. I should think it would be ideal. I suspect the real truth is that the Lanneys think with Perri's good looks he can do better. The Beaufort girl, for example. I don't know how many times he has told me Beaufort has five hundred slaves and his own silk factory."

"Where do the Beauforts live?"

"Somewhere beyond the Baton Rouge."

Désirée and Henriette rushed breathlessly out the door in a rustle of silk. Désirée stopped, struck an attitude, then pirouetted for her father's admiration. Henri bowed.

"My word, Marie, they are charming. We created a couple of beautiful daughters, my dear."

Louis gave a brotherly snort. "And don't they know it!"

Henriette and Désirée admitted afterward that Amalie looked almost as beautiful as they did. Excitement had put a flush in her cheeks, her dress was creamy instead of white, and against her three attendants in their deep colors, for her sister, Jeannine, wore a deep rose, she looked like a pearl. Her doe eyes never left the bridegroom's face throughout the ceremony. He felt her eyes on him and blushed and once or twice gave her a kindly, reassuring smile.

"That's not going to be a happy marriage," Marie whispered to Henri when they were on their knees.

"Nonsense. She adores him, even though she's frightened half to death."

"But does he adore her?"

Louis nudged his mother to silence.

As they drove to the Lanney's plantation after the ceremony Marie smiled at Henri. "Here are we again. Do you remember, Henri? What a long time ago it seems."

"Very well. Thank heavens you weren't so reluctant this time."

"What are you talking about?" Henriette asked.

"We came to the wedding celebration of Amalie's parents. Your mother didn't want to attend because she was pregnant. We very nearly quarreled about it. She was the most beautiful woman at the party, just as she is now."

Henriette looked at her critically. "Yes. I know what Perri means when he says since he can't have my mother he'll have to be satisfied with me."

Oh, dear God, Marie thought.

She didn't manage to speak to Edmund until late in the evening, after the bridal couple had been sent to their bed and the party had settled down in earnest. Henri was playing faro, the children were dancing—Perri and Henriette as partners, naturally—and Annette was trying to persuade her youngest to go off to bed. He hung on to her skirts while his black nurse tugged at him. Edmund was on his way to the rescue when Marie detained him.

"Not gambling, Edmund?"

"You know damned well I haven't gambled since Versailles. Let me pass, please. I have to help Annette."

"Wait a moment. Edmund, I'm worried about Henriette and Perri."

Edmund shook off her hand. "You needn't be. I have plans for Perri that don't include your daughter."

"*Our* daughter. If she weren't, there'd be no cause for worry. They must be separated and soon."

"Can't you keep her from running after him?"

"No more than you can keep him from running after her."

"He won't do that much longer. He's going to France to apprentice under my sister's husband, just as I did."

"When does he leave?"

"During Lent."

"Not soon enough, but it will have to do." She enjoyed the rest of the party. Soon there would be no need to worry.

A few days after the New Year Marie was home alone reading a new novel by Voltaire which Maman had sent for Christmas. She heard a horse come up the road and saw that it was Pierre Lanney. Watching him dismount she thought, He's not a child anymore. He's already a man.

He had been a beautiful child, and he was handsome now. His long, curling copper-gold hair was tied back with a black ribbon, except for a few tendrils which escaped and framed his face like a halo. His eyes changed color from green to aquamarine, but they never ceased to sparkle. He was taller than Edmund, more rugged, and in spite of the ruffled shirts and full-skirted velvet coats that were the fashion these days, he was one of the most masculine young men Marie had ever seen. He should have been a hunter, a frontiersman, a privateer, something requiring strength and daring and reckless courage. No wonder Henriette was smitten.

Marie went to meet him. "The young ladies aren't here, Perri."

"I know. That's why I came." He kissed her hand, then turned it over and kissed her palm, sending a quiver up her back. Quickly she drew her hand away, shocked at herself.

Perri smiled teasingly. "That was wrong of me, wasn't it? May I come in?"

"If you behave yourself." She led the way into the sitting room.

Perri closed the door and leaned against it. "I'll behave, madame, but there are times when I regret I am no longer the child you used to put your arms around and kiss." He smiled again, making Marie feel uncomfortable. She sat down. "There is something I must talk to you about, madame. Do you know what it is?"

"I don't know what you are thinking, Perri, but I am wondering what you have come to discuss."

"My father is sending me to France."

"Yes. He told me."

Perri paced the floor a moment, then came to sit at Marie's side. He took her hands in his. "I've come to ask your advice. I want Henriette. She is so like you, so alive, so beautiful, so forthright. I want to ask for her hand. I want us to be married before I go to France. Otherwise I may lose her. She loves France," he hurried on. "She'd go with me, I'm sure. Why are your hands trembling?"

"Have you spoken to your father about this, Perri?"

"Not in so many words. I've hinted at it, but all he says is that he was eighteen before he married, and as an apprentice I'm not to think of marriage for a long time. I'm not sure he knows how strongly I feel."

"If your father won't give his permission, how can we?"

"I've thought of that. If you and Monsieur can't talk

him around, perhaps you could send Henriette to France, and once she's there, we'll manage the rest."

"You're sure this is what you want, Perri?"

"Very sure."

"And if Henri should refuse?"

"He won't. You've seen yourself that he encourages us. But if he should, I'll persuade her to elope with me."

"And she would agree," Marie said bitterly. "I know Henriette." Now it was she who began to pace the floor. Perri followed her with his eyes, a puzzled frown on his brow.

"I thought you'd be pleased. You've always liked me. I thought you would be on our side. That's why I came to you first."

"Perri, you're both young. You've grown up together. You've been closer than most young people. How do you know you won't meet some young lady in France–"

"I'm old enough to know what I want."

"Are you? In any case it's going against your father's wishes that worries me."

"He'll come 'round if you and Monsieur pressure him."

She moved to sit beside him and took his hands. They were square, solid hands, and warm, responding quickly to the pressure of hers. She realized suddenly that she was jealous of Henriette. She wished it were feasible for this young man, young enough to be her son, to take her in his arms and touch her breasts. She was also deeply worried.

"Perri, my dear, let me think how best to handle this. Don't speak to Henri yet or to Henriette. Promise me. I'll do what I can. All right?"

He raised her hands to his lips and covered them with kisses. "I knew you would. Thank you."

His visit had ruined the day for her. She should not have given Perri hope, but she needed time to think. She threw on a shawl and went to walk in the garden.

The lake rippled under the morning wind, lapped on the white shell beach. The camellias were in full bloom, and the green leaves of the irises she had brought from France speared the edge of the walk down to the shore.

She loved this house even though she had built it as revenge on Edmund and Annette. Now the revenge was turning against her. Secrets will out. Nothing remained hidden forever.

Why, oh, why, hadn't she had the "little operation"? That had been Céline's doing. Her whole life had been decided by a whore. Damn Céline!

Yet, in fairness, it had been Marie herself who had defied Céline and taken Edmund as a lover, betraying Henri. God had been a long time in punishing her. And one of the worst punishments of all was her reaction to the touch of Perri's hands.

She sat on the stone bench at the lakeside, feeling its damp chill through her skirts. She gripped the gargoyle head which decorated the armrest as if to strangle it. But neither stone nor the truth could be strangled. Henriette and Perri must be told that they were half-brother and -sister, and marriage for them was impossible. It was the only way to bring the courtship to a conclusion and prevent them from doing something foolish like eloping. The important thing was that Henri should not learn the truth.

That evening at dinner Henri said, "Edmund told me he is sending Perri to France."

Henriette went pale. "Oh, no, Papa! It can't be true."

"I'm afraid it is, my pet. He's going to La Rochelle, where you were born, to learn the business from his uncle."

"But what about me?" Her eyes swam with tears.

"I should have broken the news more gently. I thought possibly Perri had told you himself."

She shook her head. "How long will he be gone?"

"Four years."

"*Four years?* I can't bear it." She threw down her napkin and pushed her chair back from the table. Henri held out his hand to her.

"Perhaps he'll speak for you before he goes, my pet."

"But if he's gone four years, I'll be an old lady when he returns."

"Scarcely that, Henriette. Are you so anxious to marry and leave your papa?"

"Oh, no, but—Papa, if he does ask, you will say yes, won't you?"

"The parents will have to have a meeting first, but I think I can promise—"

Marie interrupted. "Promise nothing until you are sure you can keep your promise. Perri was here today, looking for you, Henriette," she added hastily. "He said his father doesn't want him to marry until after he has served his apprenticeship."

"Papa can persuade M. Lanney, can't you, Papa?"

"I don't know why you're so anxious to get married," Désirée said. "All you have to do is look at Amalie to see what marriage does to you. Ugh! She's already started a baby—"

"Désirée! Such things are not discussed in the presence of gentlemen."

"She has, Maman, and she vomits every morning, and her husband is sick of her."

"Désirée, leave the table."

"He is. He told me so himself. She won't go riding with him anymore, and she won't let him touch her. All right, Maman, I'm going. I don't see why it's so bad mentioning babies. Are we supposed to think she's like the Virgin, and Gabriel came and announced it to her? Or should we pretend not to notice she's gaining weight all in one spot and faint with surprise when she comes out with a baby in her arms one day?"

"Désirée, if you do not leave the table this instant, I shall have your father punish you."

Désirée flounced out of the room, and they heard her run upstairs and slam her bedroom door. Henriette was crying into her plate, and Louis was looking from one to the other of his parents. Guy pretended to be absorbed in the dissection of his roast pigeon.

"You should tell Désirée to stop flirting with Amalie's husband," Louis said. "She does it all the time, and he flirts back. She's terrible!"

"André's no saint himself," Guy said.

Marie put down her fork. "I've no appetite left. Henriette, you may be excused. I'll send up your dessert."

"I don't want it. I don't feel like eating." She got up, and before she was out of the room she was sobbing.

"Shall I go to her?" Henri asked.

"No. Let her cry. Louis and Guy, you may leave too."

Louis said, "I don't want to leave. I haven't finished eating."

"All right. There are no secrets in this house anyway." Except her own. "Henri, Perri made it very plain that his father isn't in favor of his marrying until after his apprenticeship in France."

"Couldn't we persuade him to reconsider?"

"Is it wise? Henriette would be very lonely in La Rochelle. No family, no friends, Perri busy all the time, and Maman and Papa a long way off in Paris."

"You've always been against this marriage."

"I admit it. I don't know why. It just seems wrong."

Henri sighed. "Let's discuss that later, shall we? I had another idea which I was going to broach before Henriette's outburst. I think this would be an opportune time for Louis to go to France. He and Perri could travel together. Perri could look after him on the trip. We could arrange for Laure to meet the ship in La Rochelle, and Louis could live with them and have a French education."

"I don't need anyone to look after me. Will I like France?"

"Like has nothing to do with it. You should be educated in France. Besides, there is the château. You've seen your mother's paintings of it. It will be yours one day."

"What do you think, Maman?"

"It's your father's decision, not mine. I'll miss you if you go, but it will be an excuse to come to France to visit you."

"Now who is making unwise promises?" Henri asked.

The next two days Henriette appeared puffy-eyed and sniffly. She cried if anyone so much as looked at her, toyed with her food, and gazed pleadingly at her father, who tried to pretend there was nothing wrong. Late one afternoon they saw Perri coming up the driveway. Henriette's tears vanished, and she ran upstairs to bathe her face.

Marie was left alone with Désirée to greet him. "Désirée, I want to talk to Henriette and Perri alone. And no eavesdropping! In fact, I shall take them into the garden so there will be no chance of it."

"Don't you trust me?"

"Not for a moment."

"You treat me like a child!" Désirée stomped up the stairs.

Marie turned to Perri. "You look very glum today."

"You haven't heard. It's to be sooner than I thought. My uncle Léon's ship cast anchor at La Balize last evening. He never stays long once he arrives here. He's afraid of hurricanes. Have you had time to think about the problem?"

"I've thought of almost nothing else."

"You sound very solemn."

"You'll find what I have to say is very solemn. I had hoped never to have to say it to anyone. I'll wait in the garden."

She sat on the bench near the water's edge remembering the day she and Edmund had picnicked there.

The oak tree where they had made love was hidden by the wing of the house. When the children were small, they had used it as a playhouse. It had always made her uncomfortable to have them in there.

Perri and Henriette came down the path, arm in arm, his head bent as he talked to her. They were so much alike Marie wondered that Henri did not see it. A stranger meeting them for the first time would take them for brother and sister. It was amazing the secret had not leaked out long before this.

"I've told her," Perri said, "that I appealed to you the other day and you said you would try to help us."

"I didn't say that. I said I would think about the problem. I have thought about it, and I have come to a conclusion. The marriage is impossible." Henriette wailed. Marie held up her hand. "Listen to me. I want you to give me your oath that you will never reveal what I am going to tell you. Not to anyone. *Anyone.*"

"But Maman—"

"Do you promise?"

Perri looked very serious. "I promise. Henriette does too, don't you, Henriette?" She nodded. Her eyes were again full of tears.

"The marriage is impossible for a very good reason." Marie paused, then forced herself to continue. "Before I was married to your papa, Henriette, Perri's father and I were lovers." Perri stifled an exclamation and looked from Marie to Henriette. "Yes." Marie gave a wry smile. "You see the resemblance now, don't you, Perri? You and Henriette are half-brother and -sister."

Henriette went white and gave a choking cry. "Maman." Her voice was a whisper. "I don't believe it. It isn't true. Please, *please*, say it isn't true."

Marie gestured helplessly.

Perri frowned, troubled rather than shocked. "I think it—must be true, Henriette. She wouldn't say it otherwise."

"But—I don't want it to be true. It's terrible! It's wicked." She began to twist her scarf in her hands.

"Love is never wicked unless it hurts someone."

"You're hurting me! You're hurting Perri. And Papa. What about Papa? Do you think it doesn't hurt him?"

Marie struggled to keep her voice calm. "Your father doesn't know, Henriette, and I don't want him to know. He loves you and thinks you are his own. He doesn't know about Edmund and me."

"He doesn't know you're wicked! He doesn't know everything about you is a lie!"

Perri took Henriette by the shoulders. "Henriette, *you* are hurting someone. Your mother. You mustn't say things you'll regret."

She twisted away from him and struck out with her fist. "Don't touch me, Perri! You're my brother, and I wanted to *marry* you. Marry my brother! I let you kiss me. Oh!" She wiped her face and lips as if to wipe off the memory. "It is horrible! It's sickening and disgusting. I feel as if I'm covered with mud and swamp slime." She looked at her hands, turning them over, amazed to find them clean.

Marie leaned on her elbow and covered her face with her hand. She was the one who felt sick and dirty. She had not expected such a scene. How would Désirée have taken it? Somehow Marie thought she wouldn't have been shocked. She might even have laughed, the way she laughed at everything.

Perri said quietly, "Henriette, you're making far too much of this."

"Too much!" Her voice rose hysterically. "Too much, Perri? It isn't your mother who was a—a bad woman. Who betrayed my darling papa"—she began to choke with sobs again—"who isn't my papa at all. I can't bear it that I'm not his child. I would rather have him as my papa than her"—she looked at Marie with loathing—"as my mother."

In spite of her efforts Marie's voice shook. "Then

you must go on pretending that he is, for his sake as well as your own."

"*You* needn't tell *me* what to do. I'll be as kind and loving as I can be to make up for what you have done." Her sorrow was turning to icy anger. "As for you, Perri, I'm glad you're going to Paris. I never want to see you again, ever, ever, ever."

"That's foolish, Henriette. Just think what friends we could be. Closer than friends, because we have a special bond."

"I don't want any special bond with you!"

"Perri's right, Henriette." Marie held out her hand in supplication. Henriette ignored it. "But don't you see how much more wicked it would have been if I hadn't told you? If I had let you marry? What can I say to heal the hurt except that you'll understand later, when you fall in love again—and you will, Henriette. Or when you marry. Papa will find a nice husband for you—"

"I don't want a husband! I'll never marry. I'll enter the convent. I'll drown myself in Pontchartrain. I'll never understand anything but that you are a wicked woman who did sinful things, and I hate you!"

Perri tried to restrain her, but she ran to the house sobbing. He looked after her, then came to the bench and sat down beside Marie.

In the silence a bird sang. The air smelled of rain. Since Marie had sat here a few days ago the irises had edged up another inch. They would bloom soon. She sighed.

"Well, Perri?"

"I'm sorry for what Henriette said. She didn't mean it, I'm sure."

"Oh, she meant it, Perri. My sins have caught up with me."

"And it is my fault. I've been so blind. I should have seen it long before this. Has no one else ever noticed the resemblance?"

"No. You see, everyone assumes she's Henri's

daughter. When you assume something, you see what you expect to see, just as you saw Henriette differently when I told you the truth. Thank you for taking it as you did."

"It gives me a special bond with you too." He said it almost shyly.

"Does it, Perri?" She wondered in what way. "You don't think I'm wicked?" She forced a tired smile.

His eyes filled with adoration. "I think you're wonderful. My father was a very fortunate man. Why didn't he marry you? Didn't he know about—Henriette?"

"He knew. I wanted him to marry me. He refused."

"He was a fool."

"He wanted to marry your mother."

The explanation that Perri had allowed his father to convince him to put off marriage until his return satisfied everyone. To Henri it explained Henriette's tears. To Désirée it pointed out that if Perri cared that little about Henriette he wasn't worth crying over. To Annette it showed how sensible he was, though they could have used the dowry.

Henriette clung to Henri for comfort. The only thing that puzzled Henri was her anger at Marie. "It's because I agreed with Perri," Marie said with a shrug. "She wanted me to plead her cause, and I refused. I'm not going to have the Lanneys saying I was begging them to have my daughter."

"I admit I'm glad she won't be leaving us. It will be lonely enough with Louis gone, but to lose the two at once . . . I'm getting old, my dear."

"Are you? So am I."

Henriette didn't take the veil or drown herself. After the first awful days of weeping, she subsided into an icy calm. She had never understood what people meant by heartache, but she understood now. Hers ached with a hard, tight pain. It was almost impossible to breathe. Only Papa, who was not her papa at all, could strengthen and comfort her. She avoided her mother, who had brought this pain, this shame onto her. She knew now why Maman loved Désirée better; Désirée was Papa's child, and she was not.

When Perri came to say good-bye, she found nothing to say to him but stood there with tears running down her cheeks. When the families stood at the dock waving good-bye to Perri and Louis, she looked at Edmund and thought, *He is my father.* She didn't want him for a father. She wanted Papa.

Désirée tried to comfort her, but it did no good. Désirée's idea of comforting was to say rude things, call Perri a milksop who did what his papa wanted him to do, a flirt who made girls fall in love with him, then jilted them.

Every time Maman tried to speak to her, Henriette walked away. Once, after everyone had gone to bed, Maman came to her room. She sat on the bed and put her hand on Henriette's shoulder. "Dearest child, you must listen to me."

Henriette wrenched away. She scrambled out of bed and retreated to a corner of her room like an animal at bay. "Don't touch me! Don't come near me! I will not listen to you and your lies. Just leave me alone!"

Marie did not try again. She didn't exactly ignore Henriette. She just acted as if nothing were wrong.

Papa said, "You'll feel better soon, darling. Love that's not fulfilled dies eventually. By the time he comes home, you'll be in love with someone else."

"No. I won't. Not ever. I don't want anyone but Perri."

Poor Papa. He didn't know the real reason she couldn't have Perri. She hoped he would never know. It would break his heart.

That year there was going to be a carnival on Shrove Tuesday. Maman had told them about Carnival in Paris, how at midnight the music stopped, the lights went out all over Paris, and the church bells tolled, echoing up and down the Seine. For days Maman and Désirée talked about nothing but the costumes they would wear. Henriette said she didn't need a costume because she wasn't going. Not even Papa could persuade her.

"You're being selfish," Maman said. "Now someone will have to stay home with you and miss the fun. We promised everyone they could go."

"No one has to stay home with me. I'll be safe."

"It's not that you won't be safe. It isn't proper."

Guy offered to stay behind. Even though Guy was only a milk brother, fed at Eloise's breast just as she was, he seemed more like a real brother than Perri. Henriette could see he really wanted to go to Carnival. He had a crush on Jeannine Lanney, even if she was not quite twelve. She was as coquettish as Désirée and a tomboy besides.

It ended with one of the house maids being ordered to stay. She gave Henriette an angry look and didn't answer Marie when she told them to keep the doors locked.

Everyone left early, the family, the house slaves, the field hands, all dressed in costume. The city was being transformed into a gigantic ballroom where slaves and masters, Indians and militia would all mingle together. There were to be fountains of wine, music, dancing, gaming, contests, cockfights, a parade, everything one could wish for.

The silence when everyone was gone was eerie. Henriette had never heard it so still. Yet it was still in a strange way. The birds were louder. She could hear the wind in the trees. She could hear the lake lapping on the shore and the rope that tied the skiff to the landing squeak as the boat pulled at it.

At noon the maid brought her lunch and slammed the plates down on the table. Then she stood, arms akimbo, glaring at Henriette.

"You're a nasty girl, and I hope your papa doesn't give me to you to be your slave when you get married. If you ever find a man to marry you once you been jilted. Just because you wanted to stay home and cry yourself ugly, *I* had to stay home. I had me a costume, and I was going to meet Ben from Lanney's plantation. Now he'll find himself another woman, and it'll be your fault. You can't have your man, and I can't have mine."

No slave had ever spoken to her like that before or used that tone to any member of the family. Henriette turned red, partly from anger and partly because the girl hated her.

"I'm sorry. It isn't my fault. It's my mother's."

"It's your fault because you wouldn't go. You wanted to stay home and sulk and ruin my good time because you aren't having none. I got me a costume—"

Henriette got unsteadily to her feet and mustered all the dignity she could. "Look here, girl. You don't have to stay to take care of me. If you want to go to town, go. Go!" She pointed at the door, feeling foolishly dramatic.

"Yes, and if I go, what'll Madame say?"

Henriette didn't want to think about what Maman would say. "I'll tell her I gave you permission. I'll take full responsibility. Now get out and stop ranting at me."

She sat down and continued eating her lunch, not because she wanted it. She had to force herself to swallow. She felt the girl glowering at her, but she didn't raise her eyes. After a while the back door slammed. Henriette waited a few minutes, then she pushed her food away and went upstairs.

She saw the girl, dressed in one of Désirée's best petticoats, a tablecloth draped around her as a shawl, and her hair powdered, probably with flour, set off down the road. It was obvious she was singing, for she danced every few steps, moving from side to side as she went. Once she twirled and stuck out her tongue and raised her finger in a voodoo sign at the house.

Henriette stuck out her tongue in reply, but of course the girl couldn't see it. Henriette sat down and took up her sewing; not that there was any point in embroidering pillow cases now that she wouldn't be marrying Perri, but she could give them to Désirée when she got married, as Dés surely would.

Every now and then she put down her sewing and listened. She had never noticed how the house creaked even when there was no one to walk in it. As the minutes ticked by she began to wish she had gone with the others. She wouldn't have had a good time, but it would have been better than enduring this stillness which wasn't stillness. She wondered what time it was and when they would come back home. Probably not until late. Not until after dark.

Henriette wondered if anyone was at home at the Arnolie place. Maybe Amalie would be there since she was pregnant. Or the nursemaid with Mme. Angela's newest baby. It was a long, lonely walk, but it would be better than sitting here, listening.

As she got up to change to shoes more suitable for walking she glanced at the window and drew back, almost choking in an effort not to scream.

A man stood by the cook house. A black man, naked except for a ragged scrap of cloth hanging in front like the breech clouts the Indians wore. He had a musket like the militia men carried. He stood there, listening, looking around, glancing over his shoulder. Then cautiously he pushed open the door of the cook house and went inside.

A runaway slave from the looks of him. Or a maroon. One of those slaves who had never been broken and had run away to the forest to live like a wild man. Calla's husband, Baptiste's father, had done that, Papa had told them. That's why Calla couldn't be married to the man she lived with now. That's why Papa never wanted them to go to the forest alone. Sometimes at night the maroons raided the outlying plantations. Henriette had never heard of one coming during the day. She had never known one to come at all.

The minutes passed so slowly it was as if the world had stopped turning. A fly soared round and round the room, thudding against the mirror and the wall. Finally she saw the man come out of the cook house with a sack bulging with the food he had stolen. He stood for a long time, his head tilted as if listening, still as a statue except for his eyes. The fly buzzed angrily. The man took a cautious step toward the house.

Henriette remembered she hadn't locked the door after the maid had left. She felt sick, and tears gathered in her eyes.

He had moved so close to the house she could no longer see him. She too stood still as a statue, listening.

For a long time nothing happened, except that she knew he was moving from room to room downstairs. Then she heard the bottom step creak.

The staircase went straight up from the front of the house to the back in a long, graceful slope. Maman always looked beautiful coming down it when there was a party, her skirts rustling and trailing behind her, like an angel descending from heaven. At the top of the stairs there was a landing with two steps to the left and two to the right where the hall divided and went right around the staircase. The bedrooms opened off on either side.

She heard the man reach the landing and stop, as if trying to decide which way to go. She was too frightened to pray for him to go to the other side, but he did. She heard him open the door to Guy's room and go in. After a while he came out again. He opened the door to Louis's room, but he didn't go in. What was the use? It was practically empty since Louis was gone. Then he opened the door to Maman and Papa's room. Henriette heard him laugh.

Cautiously, her heart pounding with fear, she

opened her own door and tiptoed out into the hall. She had almost reached the top of the stairs when he came out with Maman's pearls around his neck. Henriette screamed as he raised the musket and fired. The wall splintered behind her. She threw herself down the stairs, falling most of the way. She heard him thudding after her.

Her skirts were a terrible tangle. The gun thundered again, and a chair in the hall fell over as one of its legs was blown off. Somehow she got to her feet, somehow she got the front door open and slammed it almost in the man's face. Screaming, she ran down the path and collided with a young man who was running toward her. They collapsed together. He was first on his feet.

"Are you hurt? Are you all right?" He bent over to help her to her feet. She pushed him away.

"Get him! He has Maman's pearls!"

The maroon was running along the lake front, the heavy bag banging against his legs. Before the young man could take up the chase, they heard more shouts and shots. Then Calla's man, Judd, came roaring around the house and attacked the young man, knocking him down on top of Henriette.

"No, no, Judd. It's the maroon! He went along the lake."

The young man groaned and sat up feeling his jaw. Blood was oozing out of his temple. "You're hurt. Oh, I am sorry." She knelt and examined his head. "We must wash it. Come in."

Now it was she who helped him to his feet. He was taller and broader than Perri and burnt dark by the sun. His clothes were plain, as if he weren't quite a gentleman, but his face was handsome. He gave her a funny, crooked smile. "I've had bricks fall on me, but that slave of yours is worse than any load of bricks."

"I'd like to know where he was when I needed him. Can you walk?"

"Nothing wrong with my legs. Just shaken up, that's

all." He was struck by a sudden thought. "The skiff. I'd better make it fast. I jumped out when I heard you scream and the shots. My boots are full of water." He walked unsteadily toward the shore, where his skiff was bumping against the one Papa kept tied to the landing.

Just then Judd and a man Henriette recognized as a stablehand came back. Judd had Maman's pearls. "Lost him, Mademoiselle Henriette. But here's Madame's pearls. They caught on a branch as he ran. Some of 'em may be lost, but most are there."

"Go tie up that young man's skiff for him. His head's bleeding. There was no call to knock him down. He was trying to help me."

Judd jerked his head at the stablehand, who went down to the lake. He gave the young man a nod. "Sorry, Monsieur. We heard Mademoiselle Henriette holler. And the shooting. And here was a stranger . . ."

"You've been here all the time?" Why hadn't Papa told her he was leaving men on the place?

" 'Course we been here. You didn't think the master'd leave the place unguarded with all the free liquor flowing in town."

"Where were you? That man robbed the cook house and came right into the house. Goodness knows what else he got away with besides the pearls."

"We were having a little game of hazard in the barn, see."

"And a little of Papa's brandy, from the smell of you."

"I expect he'll flog us when he gets home," Judd said sheepishly. "Come on, you, we go look for the other pearls. Probably trampled in the ground."

Henriette turned to the young man. "Come. You can bathe your head in the house."

He stopped at the steps and sat down and took off his boots to empty the water out of them. The gesture was so natural, so unembarrassed that Henriette found it endearing. Perri would have excused himself for such gaucherie, but all this young man said was, "I hope you don't mind feet. Since my mother died my socks aren't worth wearing. My sister Lottie hates to mend."

"I've seen feet before. My brothers and sister and I used to go wading in the lake."

"Did you? I didn't suppose rich folk ever did things like that. My name's Jacques Bonarpent. You're one of the de Nemours, aren't you?" He pulled his boots back on.

"How did you know?"

"It's our bricks built your house. I delivered a lot of them out here myself."

"That's impossible. The house has been here for almost five years." She led the way into the house and scanned the room. Maman was going to have a fit about that chair. The shot had ripped the cloth so that all the stuffing was bulging out, and one leg had broken as well.

"I'm eighteen. So I was thirteen when it was being built. Our father made us work from the time we were old enough to stand on our two feet."

"Oh. Well, come upstairs. You can go in Guy's room to wash. I'll try to find something to put on the cut."

The banister was shattered at the top. The shot must have just missed her. She poured water into the basin for him, showed him where to find the towel, then went to find Maman's medicine chest. Henriette wondered what would have happened to Perri and Louis if they had been made to work from the time they were old enough to walk instead of being taught to hunt and ride and dance. She turned over the bottles and tins of salve, wondering what to put on a cut. While she was pondering, the young man came out of Guy's room and grinned at her.

"Don't bother. It's only a surface cut and not as deep as it looks. Surface cuts always bleed a lot."

"I don't know what to put on it anyway," she confessed.

He grinned again, and Henriette couldn't help smiling back. "How come you aren't at Carnival?"

Henriette's smile faded. "I didn't want to go. It seemed—stupid. Why aren't you?"

"Same reason. I came out for a row on the lake to take a look at your house. From a distance," he added hastily. "I wasn't going to come ashore. I just wanted a long look. I figured nobody'd be home. Then I heard you scream, and the shots."

"I'm glad you did. Thank you."

"I didn't do anything. Your blacks would've saved you."

"I'm glad you're here. Would you like something to eat?"

"I can always eat, thank you."

She led the way to the dining room. Her meal, almost untouched, was still there, with the wine pitcher, the plate of cold sliced meats, the rice salad with prawns, the brandied fruits, the seed cake. "Please sit down. I'll get a plate and glass."

Maman wouldn't have approved of his table manners, but Henriette rather liked him for that very reason. He was obviously hungry and ate with relish. Watching him, Henriette felt her own appetite return, and she finished her almost untouched meal.

Jacques Bonarpent gulped down the bite he had just taken. "Did he interrupt your dinner?"

"I wasn't hungry. I was upstairs."

"Not hungry! I guess that's why you're so thin. I've been hungry all my life. Not that we don't have enough to eat now, but we didn't used to have."

"We always have too much."

They smiled at each other.

"Do you think, as long as I'm here, I could have a look around? You see, my father's going to build a new house. He got some land a few years back during the Indian trouble, and he wants to build on it. We didn't do it before because my mother never wanted to." He stopped to choose a piece of cake.

"My mother was obsessed with building. It was all she ever thought about when I was growing up."

"Well, all women are different, no matter what they say about when their skirts are—" He turned scarlet. "I'm sorry. A gentleman wouldn't have said that. Not even thought it."

Henriette blushed, but she couldn't help giggling. "Go on about your house."

"Yes, I'd do better talking about that, wouldn't I? My mother died in the '40 epidemic, but one way or another we never got around to building until now. I'm going to design the house. That's what I really want to do. Not make bricks. Draw designs, make rooms." The slice of cake had disappeared. Henriette pushed the plate toward him, and he took another piece. "Not that I'm going to live in it, see. I get the old house if I want it. I don't want to live with my family. There were always too many of us. I like my privacy."

"So do I," Henriette said, surprised she had never thought of it before.

He grinned at her again. "I don't suppose you made this."

"Made what? Oh, the cake? No, I didn't. I think I could learn." She said it slowly, because it was a new idea and it pleased her.

"Then you'd better start learning." He gave a nod and a wink and turned as red as he had when he made the remark about the skirts.

"All right," she said meekly. "Tomorrow. Tomorrow I'll ask Calla to show me how."

The afternoon passed quickly. Henriette couldn't believe they had so much to say to each other. She had never talked that much with anyone. When Jacques finally decided he should leave, he made her find Judd to tell him that Jacques was going and to please keep an eye out until the family returned home.

She walked with Jacques to the lake front and watched him untie the skiff.

"Look, Henriette." No *Mademoiselle*, just Henriette, as if he had known her all his life. "I'll be back, if your mother will allow it. I don't think she likes my family much, but maybe if you tell her I helped you today, she'll let me call."

"I hope so. If she doesn't—I'll meet you somewhere."

"That wouldn't be right. It's got to be done right, see." He took her hand and looked at it as if he had never seen a hand before. "You're awfully dainty. I'm not sure you can learn to make cake." He gave her another wink and leapt into the skiff. As it drifted away from shore he blew a kiss.

"Oh, Jacques, I hope you can come back."

The suffocating misery, the leaden unhappiness had turned into suffocating delight and joy. How could she ever have thought she loved Perri?

Jacques

"Many are they that rise against me," Marie quoted. She was propped up in bed waiting for Henri to finish undressing.

Henri looked amused as his head emerged from his nightshirt. "Why do you say that?"

"First that unsavory affair with Perri, and now Frank Goodacre's son. And Henriette alone with him in the house, unchaperoned, the entire afternoon. All because that wretched girl reviled her, and Henriette had no better sense than to let her go off to Carnival. In Désirée's best petticoat at that."

"There was nothing unsavory about the affair with Perri except your attitude and Edmund's, my dear. And Henriette swears Jacques was a perfect gentleman."

"He wasn't born a gentleman, and changing his name to Bonarpent doesn't make him one. She might have been raped."

"By Bonarpent or the maroon? We're fortunate, you know. She wasn't harmed, and we lost nothing but some food, some wine, and a trinket or two. Judd found all your pearls."

"We have a ruined chair and splintered railings. They should all be beaten, including Henriette."

Henri yawned. "Not tonight. We'll consider the matter further tomorrow." He put out the candle and drew Marie down beside him. "Did you notice how different Henriette looks? It's the first time she's smiled since Perri left."

"She needn't smile over a Goodacre boy. I won't have it."

"I doubt if your forbidding it will stop the smiles. I'm glad to see her happy again. Here, don't pull away from me. I may be too old for Carnival, but I'm not too old to make love to you."

"Oh, Henri, I do love you so."

It was Henri who gave Jacques permission to call to be formally thanked for his assistance to Henriette.

"You're asking for trouble," Marie told him.

"Let's look him over, Marie."

"I don't have to look him over. I know his family."

Marie watched, annoyed, while Henriette tried to decide on a gown. Her eyes shone, and she almost trembled with excitement. "There's no need to go to all that trouble for the son of a peasant, Henriette. Don't get any ideas."

"Too late, Maman. She already has ideas." Désirée bounced on the bed.

"Maman, you will be nice to him, won't you? Don't go all grand and look down your nose. Be the way you were with Perri. He's nice, Maman. Really he is."

Marie gave Henriette a hopeless look and slammed out of her room. As she went down the stairs it flashed through her mind that this house had brought them nothing but trouble. Had she not built it so close to the Arnolie plantation that the children had too much contact, Henriette wouldn't have fallen in love with Perri. Had she not used Frank Goodacre's bricks, that son of his wouldn't have come to look at it. Had they still lived in town, Henriette could have stayed home in safety. The son of Frank Goodacre. One of the little animals!

She heard him talking to Henri on the gallery. The days were warm, so the door stood open to allow the breeze off the lake to flow through the house. She went softly so she could listen. It was a shy voice, slightly accented, and he made no grammatical errors. It was almost too perfect. She wished she could find fault with it.

They were talking about the maroon. "I think he was more frightened than she was, monsieur. I don't think he would have harmed her, though of course it was lucky the shots went wild. He thought he was alone in the house. All he wanted was to get away. I'm glad I was nearby. I—" He stopped as Marie came onto the gallery. He stood up and bowed, not awkwardly, as she had expected, but with casual ease. "Madame, thank you for receiving me."

She inclined her head. There was little of his father or mother about him. He had his father's build, of course. Perhaps his mother would have had that coloring if she had taken care of herself. It was an honest face, guileless, and he did not shift his gaze the way his father had used to do. He was modest but sure of himself. It was difficult to find fault with him, except that he was the son of people Marie disliked. He was even handsome.

"Thank you for the help you gave our daughter." She was being the grand lady despite Henriette's plea. She couldn't help herself.

He blushed. "I think I must apologize for having stayed so long when we weren't chaperoned. It wasn't proper, I know, but she seemed so frightened I didn't like to leave her."

"No, it wasn't proper, but she assures me no misconduct took place."

His blush deepened. "Madame, I wouldn't have—" He gulped. "I hope you don't think that of me."

Marie thought she wouldn't have trusted Perri alone in the house with Henriette. Was there something about this young man's simplicity that had restrained Henriette?

"I'll call my daughter," she said.

Marie waited at the foot of the stairs, and Jacques stood in the doorway. Henriette had chosen, finally, the simplest dress in her wardrobe, a flowered pink cotton petticoat with a pink and blue striped overdress which she usually wore to help her mother garden. She wore no jewelry but a ribbon around her throat with a silk forget-me-not pinned to it. She looked so demure Marie wanted to laugh. Henriette almost ran down the stairs, her lips parted in a smile, her eyes dancing. Halfway down she called out, "Jacques, Calla's teaching me to make seed cake."

"What?" Marie exclaimed.

"Yes, Maman. I thought you knew. The first one was terrible. We had to give it to the chickens."

Marie looked helplessly at Henri. He was laughing.

Marie hadn't visited Céline for a long time, but she went to see her now. Governor Vaudreuil had shut down many of the houses of prostitution and gambling dens along the waterfront. He had even succeeded in destroying some of the so-called nests of vice. With or without his blessing Céline had moved her place of operation. She had six girls now, two gaming rooms, three slaves, furniture that would have graced Versailles, and a reputation for elegance.

Marie left her chaise at the warehouse and walked to Rampart Street. She wore a dark, simple dress and a veil and hoped no one recognized her as she waited for the door to be opened.

Céline was at her desk in her private room, her account books open in front of her. The smoke from her cheroot layered the air, bees hummed in the honeysuckle outside the window, and every now and then Céline gave the overhead fan a yank to send it swaying.

She kissed Marie and waved her to a chair. She looked older under her paint, but Marie reminded herself that she probably looked older too. How many years had it been since she had collapsed on the doorstep? Sixteen? No. It was seventeen.

"Well, Marie? How goes it?"

"Better for you than for me."

Céline's eyes narrowed. "What now?"

"Henriette wants to marry Frank Goodacre's son."

Céline's astonishment turned into laughter. She laughed until Marie was ready to shake her.

"I don't know why you find it so funny. If I had known you were going to laugh, I wouldn't have told you."

"I would have found out when it happened."

"What makes you think it will happen? It won't if I can help it."

"Can you stop it?"

"I don't know. Why did you laugh?"

"Because all our hatred, all our manipulation, all our anger in the end comes to nothing. What did your hatred of Bonarpent get you? Money to build a house on the lake."

"His son on my doorstep."

"Jacques is a good boy."

"What do you know about it?"

"He's never been here."

That was something. "His father is a thief and his mother a slattern. She's dead, by the way."

"I knew that. A long time ago. And his father is a thief who paid his debt to you." Céline pushed a glass of wine toward Marie. "What does Henri think?"

"Henri thinks whatever his precious Henriette wants him to think. He was pushing for a marriage between Perri Lanney and Henriette because they thought they were in love."

"You managed to break up that one."

"I had to tell them the truth. Henriette hated me for it. Perhaps she does still."

Céline gave the fan a pull. "Perri came here a few times. Rather, Edmund brought him."

"To gamble?"

"Not to gamble, Marie. My God, be realistic. Edmund educated the boy. Perhaps to save him from 'educating' Henriette."

Marie got up and looked out into the garden. "What shall I do? She'll hate me all the more this time."

Céline lighted another cheroot from the glow of her last one and looked at Marie through the smoke. "Marie, do you remember where you were when you met Henri?" She tapped the papers on her desk. "With Céline. Do you remember who stood beside you at the grave of your father and mother? Who arranged for the burial, ordered the coffins? No—" She waved aside Marie's protest. "Never mind the money. That is beside the fact. Frank Goodacre. Bonarpent. Do you remember your father's house? Scarcely more than a mud hut, was it? Do you ever look at the picture of yourself which I've never seen—the one painted in Paris—and remember how it came to be painted? Do you ever face God honestly?"

Marie swung around to face her. "Do you?"

"I remind Him every Friday at confession that I am a harlot."

"You think I should let them marry." It was not a question but an accusation.

"I think you should let it take its course."

Marie did not go home immediately. She walked along the levee thinking of what Céline had said. The river was busy these days. Boats came down the river all the way from Illinois loaded with flour, grain, and furs. As the boatmen rowed they sang songs Marie had heard in the streets of Paris. The words were different now, the names changed.

She had come down that river herself, long ago. What had happened to Mary Macleod? What had changed her?

Anger, pride, lust for revenge, covetousness. Nor should she forget envy. Envy that Annette had won Edmund. Not that she wanted Edmund now. That, thank God, was over. Now there was Perri. She felt shame remembering how she had responded to his touch. Soon enough, too soon, he would forget her in the beds that would open to him in La Rochelle. Just as Paul would have forgotten her by now.

She had not forgotten him or the simple happiness she had known with him. Perhaps that was what Henriette was reaching toward. Perhaps she was more like her mother than Marie knew.

Paul had been a peasant too. Now he was famous and a gentleman. Jacques wanted to be an architect. Henriette had persuaded Marie to show him the plans she had drawn for the house and the pictures of Henri's château. To Marie's surprise he had discussed them intelligently. He had asked questions about the construction of the château which Marie hadn't been able to answer. He had wanted to hear about Versailles, and Marie's comment had been that one either froze or suffocated there.

"The fault of the plans or the builders?"

"I don't know. Perhaps you can see it one day."

He had looked at her, his eyes shining as if she had given him the gift of hope. "Oh, madame, I should like that. I want to study in Paris. The French architects are famous. Hardouin-Mansart, de Cotte, Boffrand, both the Gabriels, Servandoni. I dream one day my name might be mentioned with theirs." He had laughed self-consciously. "My father said I should keep my mind on making bricks."

He and Henriette had exchanged a smile.

"Let it take its course," Céline had said.

It seemed to Marie that it was taking its course whether she interfered or not. Better to let them meet at home, where she could watch them, than under some damned oak tree, where the affair might take a very different course. Frank kept Jacques busy enough so that his visits weren't as frequent as Perri's had been. And Henriette was learning to cook. It was more than Marie knew how to do.

She looked down at the church, its steeple shimmering under the hot sun. She thought of the dark, hot interior and the day she had waited there for the priest, the day she had fainted on Céline's doorstep. Céline who reminded God of her sins on Friday nights.

Marie didn't need to remind God of her sins. It was she who needed reminding.

When she got home, she went through the house searching for Henriette. She found her in Henri's study writing in a little book. Henriette put her hand over the page and waited, almost apprehensively, for Marie to speak.

She's frightened of me, Marie thought. *She still hates me because of Perri and Edmund.* Between Henriette's fingers she read, in neat script, *Gumbo Poulet.*

"Henriette, I can't live with your anger and your sorrow any longer. If you want Jacques Bonarpent, I won't stand in your way."

Henriette stood up, and her voice trembled. "Do you really mean it? I do want him. I love him far more than I ever thought I loved Perri. Jacques is so different. He is so real."

Paul had been real too.

"Perhaps now that you are in love with Jacques you will begin to understand about Edmund and me."

"It's how I feel about Papa—"

"You should feel no differently than you did before," Marie said sharply. "You must understand, I love him as much as you do."

"But you must have been in love with M. Lanney to—to let him do that to you. It's—wicked unless you're married, isn't it? Like bad women."

"I loved him in, well, perhaps in the same way you thought you loved Perri. I don't remember anymore. And I thought he *was* going to marry me. He married Annette instead."

"That's why you dislike her! I see now." Henriette nodded wisely. "We seem to be very involved with the Lanney family, don't we? As if we were woven together in a web."

"Not anymore."

"No? I feel much more like Papa's child than, you know, *his*."

"And so you should. Now about your marriage, Papa and I will discuss your dowry and meet with M. Bonarpent about the settlements. Eventually Jacques must go to Paris to study. You can live with Grandpère and Grandmère or in the old Hôtel de Nemour in the *quartier* Marais. You must try to be a good wife and be patient with his work. He may be poor for a long while to come."

"I won't mind that as long as we're together. Thank you, Maman, for finally agreeing."

"Well . . . I want you to be happy."

Marie went out, leaving Henriette to her recipes. There. It was done. When she went upstairs she pulled back the curtain which covered the painting of La Violette and stood looking at it for a long time.

On one point Marie was adamant. The young couple was not to live with her or with the Bonarpent family. They were to be settled in the old house on Chartres Street. It shocked a good many parents, Annette Lanney among them. Girls should live at home the first few years of marriage, until after they were acquainted with their husbands, until after the first babies were born and the bride had learned household management.

"She'll learn better on her own," Marie said ruthlessly. She could not admit that she didn't want Jacques in her house, where his family could visit whenever they wished. If Henriette could tolerate them, she could tolerate them in her own house, not in Marie's.

Actually the arrangement pleased everyone. Jacques said he had lived in a large family too long not to like being on his own. Henriette was delighted to be out from under her mother's eyes. And in the fall, after the hurricane season, they would be going to France if it was possible.

Territorial war had broken out between France and England, and shipping was unsafe. English privateers patrolled the Gulf and were seizing French ships. As usual when hostilities with England broke out, the Indian troubles erupted too. Fortunately the city had thirty-seven companies of soldiers now, so there was little need for worry.

One morning late in July Marie had taken Annette and her son, little Gustave, into town with her in the chaise. She hadn't been anxious for Annette's company—she never was—but this time it had been unavoidable. Amalie's confinement was drawing near, and Annette had remembered some baby clothes packed away in the warehouse. "I didn't give everything to Angela and Claudine," she said. "I wanted some things left for my grandchildren. I could have gone to town alone, but I'm afraid to these days. There are so many drunken troops, and they're worse since the war started."

"Are they? It seems to me they don't drink so much as sell the liquor they buy to the slaves and the Indians. They're the ones I worry about. Some of the slaves actually carry guns. Not that *I* expect to get shot."

"You're so brave, Marie."

"Am I? It's just that I have other things to think about."

She left Annette at the warehouse and went around to see Henriette. She had baskets of fresh vegetables and fruit from the plantation gardens, a bottle of brandy, two of wine, some eggs, and a freshly killed chicken.

"I don't know why I bother with you," she said, handing Henriette the baskets. "You and Jacques should provide for yourselves, but we have more than enough."

She gave Henriette a sharp look. At least she had

had sense enough not to have gotten pregnant yet. Poor Amalie Lanney must have started a child the night of her wedding, and she had been miserable ever since.

"Do let's sit in the garden, Maman. Isn't it stifling? Everything is littered with Jacques's drawings. He worked until all hours last night. I wish his father gave him more time to work during the day."

Marie followed Henriette. "I needn't ask if you are happy. I can see you are."

"Oh, Maman, I didn't know it was possible to be so happy. I wish I could tell you!"

"You don't have to tell me. I know how it is to be in love. Now if we could get Désirée settled—"

Henriette made a fist of her two hands and looked hard at them. "Maman, you must speak to Désirée."

"What must I speak to her about?"

"Oh, Maman, are you blind? Haven't you seen how she flirts with André? Amalie has noticed. That's why she's so miserable. It's not just because she's pregnant."

Marie's temples throbbed. "That's monstrous!"

"I tried to speak to her, and she laughed at me. You know how she is. She said André had preferred her to Amalie all along and that—oh, I shouldn't tell you, but I think I must. That at least she knew enough not to make a baby."

As Marie stared at Henriette in disbelief there was a tremendous explosion, causing the house to groan and the walls to shake. It's God's wrath, she thought wildly. We're all to be destroyed. But of course it couldn't be. That was foolishness.

Henriette was on her feet, her face white. "What was that? What's happening?"

The thunderous sound came again, and the trees bent under the rush of wind. The house shuddered, creaked.

People began to shout, the banquette thudded with

running feet. Another rumble, this one low, growling, expanded into a crash, and again, the rush of wind.

"It's a cannon. What can be happening?"

"How do you know, Maman?"

Marie shrugged as another blast splintered the air. A cloud of black smoke drifted across the sky.

Marie and Henriette went into the street, which was crowded with curious people. Smoke hung over the levee, acrid, choking. A drummer beat the way for a crier who ordered the people back into their houses. No one would obey until they were told what was happening. At last they were advised that three English privateers had come up the river during the night and were engaged with two French merchantmen tied up in the harbor.

"Stay away from the levee! Don't go near the levee!" the crier bawled, which only served to send the crowds flocking to see the battle.

"Shall we go, Maman?"

"Into the house, yes. What would Jacques and Papa do if we were hurt?"

They went back to the garden, because the house rocked so violently with every blast that Marie expected it to fall down around them.

It was impossible to speak, almost impossible to think, with the noise. Marie's thoughts came and went in scraps and snippets. Was Henri safe? He had gone to the merchant exchange early that morning. Would Annette have sense enough to come here to Henriette's? Not Annette. She would huddle by her husband, expecting him to save her. And Désirée. She couldn't think about Désirée now. Henriette had exaggerated. Désirée said things to shock her. She loved to shock, to tease.

"You aren't afraid, are you, Maman?"

"What makes you think that?"

An explosion made it impossible to answer at once. "You're sitting there, drinking wine and eating cake as calmly as if you were at one of Mme. de Vaudreuil's afternoons. You don't even flinch when there's a roar."

Marie looked at the table set between them. If Henriette hadn't told her, she wouldn't have known she was drinking wine and eating cake. She had tasted neither.

"I'm not afraid either," Henriette said. "But I'm glad Jacques is out at his father's plantation instead of here. He'd insist on going to the levee to watch. This way, I don't have to worry."

The battle continued for two hours. The sudden silence, when at last it came, was eerie. A cheer went up. The bells began the Te Deum.

"It's over, Henriette. We've won. I must go see if Henri is safe."

"I'm coming with you, Maman."

They pushed their way through the crowd. A man stopped them to say, "The river saved us! Good old Miss.' The English couldn't maneuver against the current. We hit them broadside every time. They won't be back in a hurry!" Smiling, he went on his way, accosting everyone he met saying, "The river saved us . . ."

"The river isn't always so kindly," Marie said. "Not when it overflows and drives us to our rooftops."

Henri met them outside the warehouse, his face grave. "I was coming to get you. Annette is badly hurt. We've sent for the priest."

"What happened?"

"Little Gustave wanted to see the battle, so she took him to watch. The current caught one of the English ships, and their cannon missed the mark."

"How stupid of her!"

"My dear, Gustave is dead."

"Oh," she said more quietly. "And Annette? Where is she?"

"Inside. A surgeon is with her. Henriette, stay with me. Let your mother go."

Marie didn't need to be told Annette was dying. The bandages on her chest were soaked with blood.

Her breath was shallow and blood trickled from her mouth, making a bubbling sound in her throat. Edmund knelt beside her, tears running down his cheeks.

The surgeon looked at Marie and shook his head. "Take her hand," he directed Edmund. "It will comfort her."

This was no place for Marie. Why had Henri sent her in here? But she couldn't make herself move until the priest came. Then she fled.

"There's nothing I can do in there," Marie told Henri. "I doubt she can even take the Sacrament."

"Someone must be with Edmund and the family when he breaks the news. You don't mind, do you, Marie? Take him in the chaise. I'll stay here and start making arrangements."

"Why should I do it?" Her voice was harsher than she had intended. Henriette was staring at her, her eyes like cloudy green water.

"Because you're a woman. A situation like this needs a woman. Think of Amalie. The shock may bring on an early birth."

"Her aunts are there. Well, of course it will be a shock to them too."

"Shouldn't I go too, Papa? Amalie is my friend."

"We'll follow shortly, Henriette. Hush. Here he is."

"She's gone." Edmund looked helplessly at Henri.

"Marie is taking you home, Edmund."

"Thank you." He noticed Marie for the first time. "Yes. I guess that is best. I must go home."

He followed her like a sleepwalker. Smoke still hung in the air, turning the sun red as death, drifting like a current down the river.

As they were about to leave, Henriette ran after them, put her arms around Edmund and held him a moment, then kissed him.

"Thank you, my dear. Thank you."

They rode through the town without speaking. Now the bell tolled the deaths, each note falling heavily through the heat.

"Two sailors were killed as well," Edmund said abruptly.

"She shouldn't have been on the levee, Edmund. Why didn't you stop her?"

"I didn't know she had gone."

They turned off the levee road onto Tchoupitoulas, leaving the sound of bells behind.

"Do you know what Henriette said to me?" Edmund asked.

"I didn't know she said anything."

"When she kissed me. She said, 'Be brave, Papa.'"

Marie looked away.

"I didn't know she knew. When did you tell her?"

"How do you think I kept her and Perri from marrying?"

"I see. It was kind of her. I found it comforting. But I won't try to claim her, Marie. I should tell you, Annette said—" His voice broke.

I'll wring Henri's neck for putting me through this, Marie thought.

"Annette said to tell you she forgave us."

"Forgave us for what?"

"For Henriette. She guessed a long time ago. She said to tell you she understood."

Marie sighed. She didn't want Annette's forgiveness, but it was too late now to reject it. Henriette was right. Their family and the Lanneys were webbed together, caught like flies.

Marie decided not to tell Henri what Henriette had said about Désirée. She felt certain Henriette was imagining the whole thing. During their calls of condolence and at the funeral and the dinner afterward Désirée behaved with perfect decorum. Cadet le Sueur seemed oblivious to her existence. Toward Amalie he was tender and solicitous. He comforted Jeannine and her younger brother, Léon. He supported Edmund like a true son.

If there were any clandestine meetings, they were

too cleverly arranged for Marie to discover them. She delayed speaking to Désirée. Henri had his annual bout of swamp fever, and by the time he recovered, Marie had put Henriette's warning out of her mind.

Despite the war, the steady, deadly rise of prices, the shortage of money and supplies from France, and growing dissension among the officials, the social life continued at a frantic pace. Flour might cost 365 livres a barrel, but there was no shortage of cakes and sweet breads at the entertainments. Wine might cost five hundred livres in Spanish silver or eight hundred in paper, but its consumption increased. Money depreciated, but gambling increased. For every cabaret the governor ordered shut down, a new one opened.

The white population grew steadily and with it the need for housing. Frank Goodacre owned three brick kilns now, and Jacques was doing well as an apprentice builder. He complained that he was seldom allowed to use his imagination, but he was making money and saving it to see him through the time when he would study in Paris. That plan had been put aside until the shipping lanes were safe again. Henri would not allow his daughter to risk capture on the seas by privateers.

Jacques and Henriette were an accepted couple in New Orleans society. Jacques had learned to dance, and Henriette took part in the theatricals the governor's wife was fond of producing.

Marie entertained less frequently these days, and then gave only small parties, picnics, or early supper parties on the gallery. But her heart wasn't in it. The ceaseless talk about the war, the cost of living, the loss of another ship to the English privateers, the latest rumor about the Indians all wearied her.

The business with Perri, losing Louis, Henriette's marriage, Annette's death, all weighed more heavily on her than she would have thought possible. She felt guilty about Annette and half-angry at Edmund for having told her Annette knew. She found herself thinking of Perri and felt guilty for missing him. And she had been unfair to Jacques, but it wasn't too late to remedy that. She liked him in spite of herself and even relented enough to invite Frank Goodacre to one of her suppers.

But she was tired. When news came from France that Papa de Nemour had died, it was the last straw. Marie took to her bed for a week. Her body seemed to melt into the covers, the days and nights merged into one another. Time ceased.

She opened her eyes one day to find Henri standing by the bedside. "If you are ill, I think we should send for a surgeon."

"No, no. I'm tired, nothing else."

"Do you feel like discussing something?"

"What now? What's happened?"

"Lanney wants to buy back the warehouse."

"And I suppose he demands an answer within the next ten minutes. That entire family is so impetuous."

"It's you who are impetuous, Marie. I don't want him to change his mind."

"You want to be rid of it?"

"I'm tired of its problems, tired of being a middleman between greedy sea captains who think they can charge the earth because of the shipping hazards, the French merchants who don't want our worthless money, and the local merchants who can't meet the prices and so drive their own up. Lanney likes that kind of thing. He enjoys every triumph he brings off. I hate it. I've been doing it only because your game of chance forced it on me."

"I suppose he wants it cheap because goods are scarce and half the ships don't get through."

"You aren't so ill you aren't ready to press a bargain, are you, my dear?"

"As far as I'm concerned, you can give it to him. We've made enough out of it. As you say, I won it by a throw of dice."

"For money that was owed you."

"Yes. Do whatever you like, Henri. I don't care."

She didn't care about anything. Even after she was up again, she could find nothing worth doing. Henri was home more often now, and they resumed their chess playing, but even the more complicated games which Henri set up bored her. She no longer felt like the white queen, but rather like a pawn of small importance.

With Baptiste's help she planted a grove of magnolia trees, but it gave her small satisfaction. "It will be years before the trees bloom. I may be dead by then."

Perhaps it was Papa's death that had made her feel old. But twenty-eight wasn't old. There was scarcely any change in the reflection she saw in the filigree mirror between the Mary who had first looked into it and the present Marie. Old inside, that was it.

The days slipped away between her fingers, like water. Each night she went to sleep thankfully in Henri's arms. At least he was there, though another day was gone. Christmas came and went. A grand ball at the governor's mansion welcomed the New Year. Another Carnival turned the city upside down. It was time to think of arranging a betrothal for Désirée but that too was put off from day to day to week to month.

In August the Lanney family emerged from their year-long mourning. Poor little Amalie was pregnant again and her first not yet a year old.

"She's going to be like her mother and pop them out like a hen laying eggs," Marie said to her daughters.

Henriette looked shocked, but Désirée giggled. Marie shook her finger at her. "You shouldn't laugh. It encourages me. As it is, I shall have to confess my naughty words."

"She's awfully bony for a hen. She wouldn't make a very good meal."

"Désirée, you're horrid. Amalie is your friend, and you shouldn't talk that way about her, even if Maman does."

"Oh, pooh. I don't mean it. You know yourself she was never pretty, and that baby's just like her. Always spitting up so it smells. The other day it spit up on André's coat, and you should have heard the fuss. He needn't have carried on so. He's its father. Poor thing."

Marie wondered whether Désirée meant the baby or André was the poor thing. André le Sueur was a *sous-lieutenant* now and very proud of his new uniform.

"Don't you go flirting with him now that Amalie's pregnant again, Désirée," Henriette warned.

"Flirt? Who flirts? That's not flirting. It's just teasing. He does rise to the bait so beautifully. If he were a fish, he'd have been caught long ago."

"He was caught," Henriette said sharply. "By Amalie, and don't you forget it."

Marie was bewildered. She remembered now Henriette's warning, but Désirée had dozens of beaux at every ball and dinner they attended. Why would she want that pompous young man who, as far as Marie could see, didn't have so much as a feather for a brain.

Andre le Sueur

Désirée herself didn't know why she wanted him, but want him she did. She had wanted him before he had married Amalie and had wanted him ever since. When he looked at her, her blood turned to water and her bones to Mississippi mud. When they danced together, her nipples hardened and she had a funny feeling between her legs. Several times she had looked so deeply into his eyes that she felt as if she were going to fall in to them and drown. He felt the same, for he had said, "Oh, God!" It was as if something had torn between them when he had looked away.

During Amalie's first pregnancy they had met secretly several times. The first time it had been an accident, but after that their meetings had been arranged, although neither would have admitted it, for that would have been admitting they were being dishonest and disloyal. André made up for it by being more attentive to Amalie, who was pleased and bewildered by this new surge of passion.

Amalie confessed to Désirée she wished his attentions would stop with kisses. "I hate it. It's so nasty, like animals, and he's too big, and it hurts, and whatever I'm supposed to feel, I don't. He keeps asking me if I have, and I say yes, but I don't know what it is."

Désirée knew what it was because she had felt it. It happened while the Lanneys weren't attending parties because they were still in mourning. There was a masked ball at the governor's which Maman and Papa had declined to attend, so Désirée was going to stay overnight in town with Henriette and Jacques. André told Amalie he was on duty that night. Instead he arranged to meet Désirée.

It had been so easy to slip away from the party, to meet André outside and go through the dark, empty streets to Henriette's garden. They were scarcely inside the gate when he began to kiss her face and eyelids and neck and the roundness of her breasts above the tight bodice. He had knelt in the grass and pulled her down to him. She didn't stop him when his hand went under her skirt, up, up her thigh to the place no one should touch. She didn't care that it was wrong. She wanted it as much as he did.

It had been strange and wonderful, all her energy and her entire being centered in one throbbing beat, and André saying, "Désirée, darling, darling, darling, you're glorious. I made you do it just by touching you. What would it be like if we were really together and I was really inside you?"

She hadn't even been able to answer. She couldn't imagine why Amalie didn't like it. It was the most wonderful thing in the world.

Later she had been worried. What if she were pregnant? Could she get pregnant just because her body had done that? Could she get pregnant by his kisses and his hand stroking her there? She had worried about it a whole week and finally found the courage to ask Guy. He had laughed so hard he had made her feel a fool.

"Just you watch out, Dés. Next thing you know it'll be something bigger than his finger. Then you'll have something to worry about."

After that it had been more and more difficult for them to stay apart, and more and more difficult to stop where they did. Then André had told Désirée that Amalie was pregnant again. Désirée was furious. It was if he had been unfaithful to her, although she knew very well it was Amalie to whom he was being unfaithful.

For a while she was distant and refused to meet him. She had relented because she couldn't stand it any longer. Still, she wouldn't let him do everything. He said he respected her for it. He didn't know it was because she was afraid of having a baby.

It had been a relief when his company had gone off on patrol. The Choctaw tribe had split into two factions. One was loyal to the French and the other to the English.

"Don't get killed," Désirée begged him.

"Not yet. I can't die until I've had you."

She thought it was bad luck to say such a thing.

When Papa told her he had arranged a marriage for her, she had been glad. She didn't particularly like Michel Vatrin even if his father did have two hundred slaves and she and Michel would be rich. If Maman complained because André didn't have any brains, what couldn't she say about Michel! All he could talk about was indigo and the price of olive oil and spices. He was like an old man.

But it didn't matter because after she was married to Michel she could still meet André in secret. All sorts of ladies in New Orleans had lovers, and everyone knew it. Then, if she and André made love and she had a baby, it would be all right. Everyone would think the baby was Michel's.

Maman fussed over her trousseau, and there were boring family dinners with the Vatrins. Michel's sister gave her a baby dress, which Michel looked at stupidly and said, "What's that for?" Michel's father clapped him on the back and said he'd soon know.

When André's company came back, Désirée managed to meet him in the Place d'Armes. She told Maman she was going to see Henriette, and she told Henriette she was going to church to pray to love Michel more than she did.

"Yes," Henriette said. "I think you should. He really is nice, Désirée, and it will be easier once you're married. He's probably as sick of his family as you are, and once he's away from them, he'll turn into a real person."

"I can't imagine what I'll find to say to him."

"You'll find lots to say. Jacques and I talk constantly."

Désirée fidgeted. "Jacques is different. Well, I must go."

"You'll come back, won't you, before you go home?"

"Maybe."

"Oh, please do."

André was sitting on a bench in the Place d'Armes. They caught one another's eye, then Désirée slipped into the church and knelt in front of the Virgin.

She thought he would never come, but then suddenly he was beside her, whispering how much he loved her, how much he had missed her, and that he wanted to touch her breasts and kiss them.

"André, I'm to be married."

"What!" The word exploded like a musket in the silence.

"Hush!" Désirée looked around nervously, but the church was empty. "To Michel Vatrin in three weeks."

"You can't! I won't have it. I'm in love with you. How can you marry someone else?"

"I certainly can't marry you. Do you expect me to be a spinster?"

"I expect you to be my mistress."

"I can be after I'm married."

"He'll never let you out of his sight. Not that a gelded bull like him would know what to do with you when you're lying naked before him with your legs wide open."

"I'll show him," Désirée teased.

André was shaking with rage and jealousy. His face had gone white and wavy in the flicker of the votive candles. "I won't have it!"

"There's no way to stop it." She began to cry. She hadn't known until now how much she loved André and how much he loved her. It would have been easier if the Indians had killed him. Then she could have married Michel and been sad about André forever.

"Désirée, listen, my father-in-law is sending a ship to France a week from now. It's carrying a rich cargo—deerskins, tobacco, indigo, and a fortune in letters of exchange and piastres. Because of the English privateers raiding the Atlantic a company of soldiers is going along to help protect it. I'll volunteer with the excuse that I haven't seen my parents in France for a long time. Amalie'll be glad to have me out of the way. She hates me to—bother her when she's pregnant. And any other time as well. You come to the ship to see us off, and I'll get you aboard and hide you somehow. By the time we're at sea, it will be too late to do anything about it."

"You mean *sail* with you? What about when we get to France? They'll arrest us, won't they?"

"We won't go to France. The ship puts in at Havana to take on fresh water and supplies. We'll get off there and disappear. Well, what do you think?"

"I don't know. Do you think you could really hide me? What would we do when we got to Havana?"

"I've some money to keep us for a while. Then I'll join the Spanish army. France and Spain are allies, so it won't be like turning coat."

"Oh, never mind that. A soldier is a soldier. I just don't want to starve or be put in prison or be sent back here in disgrace."

"They'll never find us. Say yes, darling. Think how happy we'll be. Dés, there's no one in the church. Give me your hand. There, there, darling. You see how much I love you, how much I want you." He placed her hand on his groin.

It was a terrible thing to do in church, but lovely too. She wished she could see what it looked like when it was all hard and bulgy like that. Amalie was a fool.

"All right, André. I'll go with you. Yes, I'll go."

After he left, she continued to kneel, staring at the

fluttering flames. She tried to pray, even if she was all sticky between her legs. "Holy Mother, tell me what to do. Holy Mary, pray for me. Mother of good counsel, guide me. I love him. Help me."

She waited. No small voice answered her. The Virgin, clutching her Son in one arm, her other raised in benediction, her head tilted to one side, smiled at Désirée. But it was a smile as bland and meaningless as the plaster of which she was made.

Wedding presents began to arrive. The trousseau was finished, as well as the wedding dress and the dresses for the attendants. Maman went around frowning slightly, and Désirée couldn't sleep nights because she couldn't decide what to do. Every morning when she looked in the mirror she saw that the circles under her eyes were darker than ever.

One day Maman said, "Why don't you and Guy ride over to the Lanneys? You look as if some fresh air would do you good. And Amalie feels so badly she can't be an attendant. It would be kind of you to call."

"Since when have you cared about Amalie?"

"Maybe I'm getting older and kinder—and wiser."

"You aren't old, Maman. Why, you're not much older than Jacques. I'll bet you could have lots of lovers if you wanted."

"Lovers are too much trouble." Marie smiled.

The day was dull and wet and windy. It did make her feel better to be out in it. It made her decide not to go with André no matter how much he begged her. It was too chancy.

"Have you been meeting André?" Guy asked.

"There hasn't been any chance."

"You'll forget him once you're married. It must be difficult to be a woman and not be able to play a bit before you're married."

"I don't think Michel Vatrin would know whether I had played or not."

"It's better not to play with someone else's husband.

Go easy Dés. You've only got a couple more weeks."

Désirée hadn't expected André to be at home. It was getting to be more and more difficult to face him in front of Amalie. He and Amalie and Jeannine and Léon were playing faro. They were delighted to see Désirée and Guy.

The candles were lighted, and a fire crackled in the fireplace. A pot of chocolate was keeping warm by the fire. Jeannine poured them each a cup, and André laced Guy's with brandy.

Amalie wanted to talk about the wedding. "Jeannine said her attendant's dress was beautiful. I wish you could have waited until after the baby was born so I could have been an attendant too."

"I had nothing to say about it. I'd just as soon wait forever."

Jeannine laughed. "You could run away."

Désirée stared at her.

Jeannine laughed again. "Don't stare so. I didn't mean it. Girls can't run away. Where would they go?"

"André's running away." Amalie put her hand on his. "Papa's sending a ship to France, and André's going on it to help protect it from the English. He won't be here for your wedding, will you, André?"

"'Fraid not. I'm off in two days time."

"You see, it will give him a chance to see his family in France. He won't be here when the baby's born either, but I don't mind that so much. I know how I'd feel if I hadn't seen my family for years." She bit her lip and wiped away a tear. "He won't be back until spring."

He won't be back at all if I go with him, Désirée thought.

"When do you sail? We should see him off, shouldn't we, Guy?"

"Wednesday, just before dawn. I go aboard the night before and stand watch with the seamen."

"If you sail before dawn, you won't have me there to wave you off. I like my sleep," Guy said.

"Too bad." Désirée gave a shrug in imitation of Maman.

"There's a mystery aboard," André said. "You know not many people are traveling these days with the war on. The cabins are empty. But one is reserved this time for an unknown lady. It's rumored she's running away from her husband. My captain fixed it up, and he told me about it. We're great pals, he and I."

"Who can that be?" Amalie asked. "I can't imagine anyone we know doing such a dreadful thing."

"Oh, I hear she's quite old," André said carelessly. "A touch more brandy, Guy?" As he stood behind Amalie he gave Désirée a nod.

When they were ready to leave, Guy said, "Well, we won't be seeing you for a while, André. Bon voyage. And watch out for the English." They gave one another a hug and a kiss on each cheek.

Amalie said, "André, you should kiss the bride. Give Désirée a kiss for luck."

Désirée thought she was going to burst into tears. After he kissed her, he shook her hand, and in his was a piece of paper. She didn't have a chance to read it until she got home. It said, "The cabin is for you."

Désirée had a nightmare that night. She dreamed she was standing on the wharf and the ship with André on it was slipping farther and farther away from her. He reached his arms out to her, and the water between him and the shore grew wider and wider. She sobbed until she couldn't stand up, and she sank down on the wharf crying and clawing at the earth. He called to her, "Désirée, Désirée, Désirée . . ."

"Maman?" Where was the ship? Where was André?

"You were having a nightmare. I heard you crying all the way in our room. Are you all right?"

"I think so." In two days the ship would be going, and she wouldn't see him again. "Maman, did you love Papa when you were married to him?"

"Yes, of course."

"I don't love Michel, Maman."

"He's a nice young man, Désirée, and very rich. It's a good marriage."

"I don't even like him very much."

"Is that why you were crying? Was that your dream?"

"Not exactly."

"I'll get you some wine. It will help you go back to sleep." Her mother took the candle, leaving the room in darkness. It was raining outside. The air smelled of it, and Désirée heard it dripping down the shutters. How could anyone be as miserable as she was?

Maman came back with a little silvery tray. On it was a glass of port and a piece of cake. She lighted the candle by Désirée's bed from her own. When she leaned forward, Désirée saw she didn't have her nightdress on under her negligée. She wondered if she and Papa had been making love the way André wanted to do with her.

"No more bad dreams, darling." She kissed Désirée and gave her a hug.

"You're beautiful, Maman."

"So are you, darling."

How could she leave Maman and Papa? How could she take André from poor ugly Amalie?

But the next day she packed a little bag, just in case she decided to go. She went to the storeroom under the eaves and found the veil Maman had worn to Annette's funeral. It would hide her face when she went aboard the ship.

There were several wedding gifts she wanted to take. They'd be useful to sell in Havana. She wished she could say good-bye to Henriette and Guy, but there was no way.

The Vatrins came to supper, and Michel tried to hold her hand under the table. His hand was big and clammy with sweat, and Désirée imagined it touching her breasts. Big, wet hands all over her, and his big wet mouth slobbering on hers. She knew right then that she couldn't stand it. How could Maman and

Papa have done this to her? It was their fault she was leaving.

When they went to bed, Maman kissed her and said, "No bad dreams tonight." The bad dreams would come if she was married to Michel.

She waited until the house was still, forcing herself to stay awake. Then she dressed, put on her heaviest cape, covered her head with the veil, and took the little bag. She left a note on her bed:

I have gone to France with André le Sueur. I love him and cannot bear to be without him.

The house was very still. She felt her way down the stairs. As she opened the door the wind caught her cape and blew it back so the door closed on it. She had to open and close it again. It was as if the house were trying to keep her.

A fine drizzle blew in her face. The world was cold, and unseen things scurried in the ditches beside the road. Once something squeaked, and there was a wild threshing in the grass.

It was a long walk into town. She lost all sense of time. She imagined arriving too late to see the ship leaving and the water widening the way it had in her dream. Finally she reached Tchoupitoulas Road. Mist, white in the blackness of night, wreathed the river. She could hardly wait to find the ship and take off her shoes and go to sleep.

The lanterns glowed like ghostly haloes through the mist. A soldier challenged her on the wharf. At first she didn't know what to say, then it came to her. "Let me pass, please. I have a cabin reserved on *L'Oiseau.* I am Madame—" What name was she supposed to give? Stupid André, not to have told her.

"We're expecting you, madame. This way." He led her up the gangplank and turned her over to André, who bowed elegantly over her hand, saying, "I'll see you to your cabin, madame. You'll meet the captain in the morning after we're at sea, but only if you wish it. He appreciates your desire to remain unknown."

It was a tiny cabin. André folded back her veil and kissed her. Then he took her in his arms, his body hard against hers. "Darling, Désirée, I knew you'd come." There were tears in his eyes.

Désirée was happy. Day after day she had the sea around her, the sea she had come to love as a child on the way back from France. Night after night she held André in her arms. It was more wonderful than she had ever imagined. Their bodies were made for each other, their passions equally matched, inflamed by the touch of a hand, a glance, a smile.

Not once did either of them regret what they had done or mention what they had left behind. They were together, and that was what mattered.

Three days out of Cuba a sail was sighted. Three-masted, square-rigged, it was soon identified as an English man-of-war, and it gave chase. To Désirée, huddled in her cabin, the battle was both frightening and exhilarating. She responded to it almost sexually, as if she were the one under assault. The ship reeling under the cannon fire, the rattling and splintering of wood, the thunderclap of each explosion was horrible and thrilling. Acrid smoke seeped under her door, making her cough and weep. The ship shuddered and squealed as if it were alive.

An explosion made her ears ring, almost deafening her. A thunderous crash followed, knocking her off her feet. The ship lurched, sending her sliding from one side of the cabin to the other. She tried to get up but was knocked over again. Now she was frightened. The ship did not right itself but listed so badly she had to walk uphill to her bunk.

André pounded on her door, shouting frantically. She tried to open it, but it was jammed.

"Stand back, I'll ram it."

He threw himself against it again and again, but it would not budge. Outside the porthole the sea rose like a wall against the ship. Again Désirée wrenched at the door, tears streaming down her cheeks.

An ax split the door apart, and she squeezed through. She started to embrace André, but he jerked her by the hand. "There's no time for that. Come on."

The havoc was terrible. The mainmast was down, men were mutilated and bleeding, and the ship was almost on its side, the sails sagging over the water.

André dragged her to the rail. Below, far below, a small boat filled with soldiers was pulling away from the ship.

"They didn't wait for us," André said in a dazed voice. "The bastards didn't wait. Come back! Come back!"

The soldiers waved farewell.

They looked at one another, tears filling their eyes. For the first time Désirée noticed André was hurt. His arm hung at a strange angle, and blood soaked his coat.

"A ball hit me. It'll be all right." His face was livid and in spite of the cold, perspiration poured from his brow.

The ship lurched, sending them sliding down the deck into the sea, where the sails filled with water as they had once filled with wind. The ship creaked and squealed and groaned like a mammoth animal dying. Hatches and cargo and splintered masts floated all around them. André managed to grab a piece of mast, and they clung to it.

Désirée nearly let go when the sea churned as the ship turned over like an old turtle, then slowly, very slowly, went down.

The waves, white-tailed and steep, kept breaking over them. Désirée's arms were numb, but she didn't say anything because André had only one arm to use. They bobbed on the sea for what seemed like hours.

"Dés, I'm sorry," André said.

"It isn't your fault. I wanted to come."

After a while she closed her eyes for just a moment.

When she opened them, the sun was setting in a gray sea. André was gone. At first she couldn't believe it. She screamed his name until she was hoarse, then she began to sob. There was no feeling left in her arms. She didn't know how she had held on in her sleep, but she knew she couldn't hold on much longer. Soon it would be dark, and in the darkness no one, if there was anyone, would find her.

Still she clung to the mast as she had once clung to André. She leaned her head against it and in spite of her efforts fell asleep. When she awakened, the mast was no longer in her arms, and her skirts were dragging her down into the black water, black as the pits of hell the nuns had told her about.

Perri

". . . we entreat Thee on behalf of the soul of Thy servant, Henri, whom Thou hast this day bid to pass out of this life . . ."

I cannot stand it, Marie told herself. I cannot stand to see the coffin sink, the bubbles rise. What a hideous way to bury our dead.

She put out her hand as if to stop the priest. Guy took it in his firm grasp. Her son, but not of her flesh. Steadfast Guy, who had been with her throughout Henri's final bout with fever, made arrangements, comforted her, kept her world turning when she would have willed it to stop.

It had been she who had comforted Guy five years ago when Désirée had gone. He had blamed himself. He had seen, should have guessed, should have warned them. Henriette had warned Marie, and she had not listened.

". . . we who are alive who are left, shall be caught up with them in the clouds . . ."

She looked across the grave where the Lanneys stood. Amalie had worn mourning ever since André's elopement, as if to reproach Marie for what Désirée had done.

Warned or not, who could have stopped them? How could anyone have known they would be so selfish, so foolish? There was an old proverb, "The heart of a maiden is a dark forest." Marie had never known what was in Désirée's heart. They had been punished. God had seen to that. Let them rest.

". . . from the pains of hell and from the deep pit . . . from the jaws of the lion . . . the black gulf . . ."

"Webbed together," and the web still unbroken. Guy was still determined to marry Jeannine, against Amalie's wishes. Amalie wanted no part of any of them. Henriette had tried to see her before she and Jacques had left for Paris, after the peace treaty of '48 had been signed and the seas were safe again. But Amalie had refused to face her.

It was surprising that Amalie was here today. Did seeing dead the father of her enemy give her some macabre satisfaction?

Marie cast her handful of earth and turned away. She said to Guy, "Take me home."

The house was stifling. The shutters had been closed to darken the house to the dead. The smell of the sulphur and pitch torches they had burned to destroy the poison of the fever lingered still. Marie opened the shutters, slammed them back to let in air which did not smell of fever and decay.

The table was laid. The breads and cheeses, the cakes and cold meats, the deviled chicken and brandied fruits waited under tents of netting. The gumbo, the fish stews, the rice boiled in the kitchen. A black child turned the spits with the huge roasts as the first chaise rolled up the drive.

Soon a purple sunset streaked the sky. Baptiste lighted the chandeliers, moving from room to room with the long pine taper, setting the crystals tinkling and turning to rainbows. Guests filled the house, eating and drinking their fill, speaking in hushed tones behind masks of grief. After a while, their mourning done, they filtered into the dining room for a game of hazard.

Marie went into the garden. Rose and shades of mauve melted together on the surface of the lake. A bird sang among the long dark buds of the magnolias.

Tomorrow she would write to Louis, to Henriette and Jacques, to Maman and Laure. That was the last remaining task. Then a different life would begin. Life without Henri.

A man came down the path. Marie braced herself for more hushed sympathy. It was Edmund.

"I'm leaving now, Marie. Will you be all right?"

"Of course." Why should he ask that after twenty years?

"I believe you will be. You are so strong. You have always been strong."

What did Edmund know about her strengths and weaknesses?

"You should think about remarrying eventually, Marie. You are still young, still beautiful."

"There's no one I would want to marry."

"I have always regretted that I didn't marry you. I was a callow youth, wasn't I?"

"We've been better off this way."

"I wonder. We'll never know, will we? Let's see one another from time to time, Marie. Amalie is no longer as bitter as she was."

"I should think five years would have cured that." She regretted her words. It had taken her longer than five years to forgive Edmund and Frank Goodacre. François Bonarpent.

"I wish she would marry again. She needs someone."

"I wish she would stop wearing mourning. It's not becoming and no longer appropriate."

"Jeannine has tried to persuade her. Perhaps Perri will be able to. She was always very close to Perri."

"Is he coming home?"

"I thought you had heard. He should be here within the month. I'll tell him to call. He was fond of you."

The stars were coming out, thick and silver so the sky and lake were alight with them.

They walked back to the house.

There were no supper parties on the gallery now. Marie didn't mind the solitude, but she wished Henri were there to share it with her. They had become extensions of one another. She moved toward him in the bed at night and awakened when she remembered he wasn't there.

The house was too large, too silent. She had never really wanted to live out here. It had been to spite Annette. She should move back to the house on Chartres Street, but the plantation needed her, and the house standing empty would be taken over by spiders and the dampness.

For a week her mourning wardrobe occupied her. A black silk embroidered with jet beading. A purple gauze with violet panniers and ruching across the low bodice. Two mulberry India cottons with loose, airy sleeves. She tried them on, one after the other, and approved her reflection in the mirror. She was still beautiful, but there was no one to admire her, unless—unless Perri called.

She was a fool to look forward to his return. Would he find her old? Would he have a wife?

Every day she dressed carefully, expecting him. One day Sheba told her he had returned. The servants always knew what was happening before anyone else.

"Blew in last night on the big wind." Sheba laughed at her own joke. "He's grown tall and handsome and full of Paris. Enough trunks for six people. Guy'll be telling you about it." Sheba never called any of the children by a title, even though they were grown. She was free. She didn't have to.

"What does he plan to do now he's home?" Marie sipped her café au lait and looked at Sheba over the cup.

"He's supposed to run the merchant exchange for his papa, but it sounded like he's not in a rush to do anything. Ask him yourself. He'll be coming over. He said so."

Her hand trembled as she put down the cup so it rattled in the saucer. If he had brought home a wife, Sheba would have mentioned it.

Why was she such a fool? Why should she remember a young man kissing her palm years ago?

It had started to rain again. The house was oppressively hot and muggy. Marie was sitting on the gallery watching the rain roil the lake. It was too hot to do anything. She wouldn't even have bothered to dress if it hadn't been for the possibility that he might come.

He rode up the driveway, bareheaded, carrying a package under his cape. She stood up, then clung to the back of her chair for support. Her heart pounded like that of an infatuated girl.

He hesitated, one foot on the step, his eyes taking in everything about her. She touched her hair uncertainly, moistened her lips.

He had matured, grown handsomer. His eyes were the same clear peridot green as Edmund's. But his face was stronger than his father's, his body more solid, broader, and, it seemed to Marie, full of strength and restrained passion. But she had slept in a lonely bed for two months now.

"Welcome home, Perri." She held out her hand.

He put down the package, took the hand, and drew her forward, his gaze so intense, so piercing that she lowered her eyes. He pulled her, almost roughly, into his arms. The jeweled buttons on his coat pressed into her breasts. The wind blew his cape around him, and he enfolded her in it.

At first she melted against him, then as quickly drew back and kissed him lightly on each cheek. She struggled to be free of the folds of his cape, but he held her, laughing at her struggles. "You're as beautiful as I remember. Perhaps more beautiful." He put his mouth on hers in a long kiss.

Roughly she pushed him away. "Perri! You mustn't kiss me like that."

"Why? We're old friends, aren't we?"

"Is that the sort of behavior you learned in France? You know very well that is not the kind of embrace or kiss that old friends give one another." She pulled her hand away before he could take it again. "No!"

"You *are* glad to see me, aren't you?" His voice was soft.

"Yes. I'm glad. Very glad. I've missed you as much as I miss my own children. But you must give me time to know you again."

"I'll give you time if you wish it. Time to realize I'm not the boy who went away but a man who has come home—to court you."

She gave a nervous crow of laughter. "Perri, you're absurd! First you sweep me into your arms and kiss me like a lover, then you announce you are going to court me. Court me! Perri, I am old enough to be your mother. Don't jest."

"I'm not jesting. Damn it, Marie . . ." (Marie, not Madame, she noticed.) "Every day of the voyage home I thought of you. How you would look, what we would say to one another, of touching you."

"Long days at sea give one too much time to brood and dream and imagine impossible things. Don't the poets call it a sea change?"

"It wasn't a sea change. Scarcely a day passed in the five years I was gone that I didn't think about you and look forward to coming home. Why can't you take me seriously?"

"I'll take you seriously if you stop talking romantic nonsense. Come, tell me about France. Did you see Louis before you left? And Henriette and Jacques?"

"Yes, I made a point of seeing them. Except that Louis has your eyes, he is so much like Henri it is amusing. The same mannerisms, the same elegance. You would laugh to see him."

"I wish I could see him. And Henriette?"

"Happier with Jacques than she would have been with me. They are wonderful together. She admires him, is proud of him, encourages him, delights in everything he does. She would never have felt that way about a warehouse and an exchange merchant. And she wouldn't have wanted to come back here. She is a true Parisienne."

"And you?"

"I couldn't wait to come back. I love this place. Home-sickness is hell, Marie."

"I love it too."

"But I had one thing which helped. Let me show you."

He unwrapped the package he had brought. Marie was reminded of a package Henri had once unwrapped. This was smaller, little more than two feet square, and Marie gasped when she saw it.

"Ah, you recognize it. It appeared in Gersaint's gallery two years ago, and I bought it at once. They say Grillet turns out a new La Violette every few years. You see, he now puts a little violet above his signature. The real model is still one of Paris's mysteries . . . but I knew who she was."

She sat with one elbow on the table, the violets thrust into the low, square-necked bodice of blue homespun, the hair tied with a ribbon the color of her eyes, which gazed lovingly at the unseen artist, the lips open in a smile which was almost a kiss. In the background were the skies of Paris, the roofs of Saint-Germain-des-Prés.

"She hung beside my bed and gazed at me every night. You see, Marie, you have never been far away from me."

"Perri—you are unrealistic."

"I am in love."

She put her hand on his lips. "You promised, no nonsense. You are in love with a portrait. A woman you created in your imagination. You don't know me. You don't know anything about me, about the way I think or react or feel. I assure you, you are not in love with me, and you'll soon learn it now that you are home. What are your plans?"

He shrugged. "To become a partner in the business,

to run the plantation, to help New Orleans become a great city."

"Your voice lacks enthusiasm."

"I'm enthusiastic enough, but after one evening at home I've learned how much opposition I'll have. My father seems to live in dread of floods and droughts and lack of shipping. No one has taken the slightest interest in the plantation. Not more than half of it is still in cultivation. All Léon is interested in is hunting and horses. There won't be any game left at the rate he's killing it off. And he doesn't give a damn about affairs here, because he'll soon be marrying one of the Beaufort girls and moving to Natchez. And then there's Amalie. She's like a specter and just as cheerful to be around."

An uncomfortable silence fell between them.

"I'm sorry," Marie said finally. "I can't apologize for what Désirée did. Is that heartless? Henriette and Guy warned me, but even if I had believed them, I don't think I could have stopped her."

"I don't blame you or them. God knows she and André paid for what they did. Anyway, that's past. Yes, I have plans if I'm allowed to carry them out. I've made arrangements with my uncles in France for slave shipments, ships to carry away our exports, for distribution and merchandising. My grandfather will do all he can—God knows how anyone gets anything done at that rotting court at Versailles."

"I remember feeling the same about it years ago."

"What about you, Marie? I was sorry to hear about Henri."

"I suppose I'll go on living here. Guy is still with me, and he handles everything very well. I miss Henri. I miss the comfort of having someone I love nearby. I hope if Guy marries he'll bring his wife here, and there will be laughter and children again."

"Is he planning to marry? He should. He's as old as I am."

Marie considered how to answer. "He would like to

marry your sister Jeannine but . . . Amalie stands in the way. She won't hear of it, and Edmund seems to be afraid to cross her."

"Ah, that explains what Jeannine meant when I teased her about marrying. She said if she couldn't have the man she had chosen, she'd have no one. I thought there was a rather ominous silence after that. Then Léon broke it with some jest about women being chattel and having no right to choose their husbands. Jeannine and Guy? Why not? I'll talk to my father."

"It won't do any good. He's afraid of reopening old wounds."

"Amalie rubs salt in her wounds to keep them open."

"Five years does seem overlong to wear mourning."

"Do you know, it's doing me a world of good to talk to you. I've a million things to tell you. May I come again? Often? My mother is no longer alive to be jealous of you."

"Your mother had to put up with a painful memory. It seems she knew about your father and me."

"Perhaps she was afraid of history repeating itself."

"Nonsense! I'm sure such a thing never crossed her mind."

"It crossed mine." He grinned as she held up a hand in warning. "All right, Marie. No nonsense. No kisses. We'll sit across a chess board and learn to know one another."

"And dispel boyish dreams so you can build new ones."

"Any new dreams will include you. Nothing I will learn about you can make me change."

"You're talking nonsense again, Perri. But we shall see."

He got up and carefully rewrapped the portrait, then fished about in the pocket of his coat. "I have something for you. I meant to give it to you in a more romantic way, but I think you wouldn't approve."

It was an egg-shaped cloisonné box. "It's beautiful."

"You can thank me later. Open it after I've gone. I'll go look for Guy now."

He kissed her hand and without a backward glance left her. He didn't turn or wave, and she thought, "He's taunting me. He claims to be a man, and he is still a boy."

When he was out of sight, she opened the box. On its velvet lining was a delicate gold chain coiled around a diamond cut in the shape of a heart. A tiny scroll of paper tied with a single red thread lay beside it. She unrolled it and read, *Mine is yours.*

She snapped the lid shut and went into the house. Sheba was polishing the banisters. Marie wondered how much she had seen and heard.

"He's grown handsome," Sheba said.

"He always was, even as a child."

"What's that he gave you?"

So she *had* seen.

"A box." Marie cupped it in her hand and showed Sheba. "A box for trinkets."

"Pretty. I heard him say he'll come again."

"Yes. I think he's lonely. I should have asked him to dinner. I'll let Guy do that."

He was there the next morning while Marie was still having her coffee and rolls in bed. She heard Guy greet him, but no one announced Perri's arrival to her. Later, as she was dressing, she looked out the window and saw the two of them walking toward the fields.

All day she expected them to come back, but it was evening before Guy returned, alone. He dropped a kiss on Marie's forehead and sprawled in a chair. "It's good to have Perri back. Like old times. He's more serious than he used to be. He's full of schemes and getting damned little sympathy for them at home. Léon has let the plantation all but return to swamp. Some of the drainage ditches have collapsed and never been repaired. Perri and I spent the day tramping over both our places. He wants to try cotton in addition to the indigo."

"Cotton's been tried before. The crops are poor, and there's no gin."

"It might grow under the right conditions. And a gin could be built." Guy got up and went to the wine cabinet. "He wants me to oversee his place. I told him I'm not sure I could handle both that and this one. Advice is about all I can spare. He's coming to dinner tomorrow." Guy paused while he poured the wine. "If he can manage, he'll bring Jeannine. He . . . thinks he can persuade his father to agree to the marriage."

"I hope he can. Would you bring her here to live?"

"With your permission. I sure as hell don't want to live in the same house with Amalie. But there's no point in deciding that until we've seen the bans posted. Then I'll believe it."

"Everything's going to be all right." Suddenly she was sure of it. She had not felt so lighthearted since before Henri had died.

Guy and Jeannine were married three weeks after Perri's return. Only Marie and Perri attended the wedding ceremony. Guy brought Jeannine home, and the house of mourning came to life again.

Perri's visits became a matter of course. Scarcely an evening passed when he wasn't there. He and Marie played chess, talked, laughed together and with Jeannine and Guy. The four were so companionable Marie had difficulty remembering that she was fourteen years older than they were. She felt like a girl when she was with them. They boated and picnicked, they played duets and danced, they played faro and hazard, losing and winning fortunes in dried peas. More and more, Jeannine and Guy made excuses to leave Marie and Perri alone together. Marie scarcely dared admit, even to herself, that she was glad when they did.

One evening as they sat alone by the dying fire

Perri said, "You have never thanked me for my heart or even worn it."

"It's beautiful, Perri, but I was afraid if I wore it you would think I was committing myself to having accepted it. As for thanking you, I did not want to thank you for something you might ask me to return. I am not talking about the diamond."

"I know what you're talking about. I've held my tongue, haven't I? There's been none of what you called 'nonsense,' has there? I don't know that I can keep up the pretense much longer."

"Perri, please don't say anything that will make us feel embarrassed with one another afterward. I want to be your friend no matter whom you may marry."

"When the devil do you think I have time to court anyone else? Why do you think I *want* to court anyone else? If you won't let me speak, I can't tell you how I feel. I come here against my father's wishes—oh, yes, he disapproves—but I come because I can't stay away. You know I wanted your kisses and hugs as a child, your admiration as a youth. My God, how I showed off for your benefit."

"Or for Henriette's."

"For yours. Now I want your adoration and devotion. Oh, I had women in France, and I know you loved Henri and love his memory still. But you've a lifetime before you, and I want you to share it with me. You said I should learn to know you. Well, I have learned, and nothing has changed. Has it changed for you?"

She twisted the peridot ring on her forefinger. She thought, *I always do this when I am nervous. When I am afraid to answer.*

"Or should I ask, have you finally grown to think of me as a man instead of that boy who sailed for France?"

"I'm not sure how I think of you."

"Then I'll give you more time."

"It isn't that kind of time I need. It's time turned

back so I could be young again. Then whatever you want might be possible."

"I don't want you young or any way other than you are."

"You've created a woman in your imagination—"

"Damn it, Marie, you are not my imagination! You are you, as I have always known you. I want to marry you. There! The nonsense will out. But it isn't nonsense. I want you more than I have ever wanted anything. Don't you see what we could do together? The life we could have?"

"It would be the scandal of New Orleans. The tongues would never stop wagging."

"The devil with scandal and busy tongues. They don't matter to me, and they shouldn't matter to you. Not if you love me. But I see I am pleading a lost cause. Good night, madame."

He left so abruptly she was uncertain he had gone until she heard the door slam behind him.

That was a Friday. By the following Wednesday Perri had not yet returned. Every day Marie expected him and hoped for him, telling herself at the same time she was a fool. On Wednesday the entire Lanney family left for Natchez for Léon's wedding.

"You should have been invited too," Jeannine said at least a dozen times. She said it again at the door waiting for the chaise. "It's shameful."

"It would have been most inappropriate, even if I weren't in mourning."

"*I* wish you were going. Weddings are stupid. I much prefer the way Guy and I were married." Jeannine drew on her gloves. "I asked Perri why he hadn't been around lately," she added, pretending to concentrate on the pearl buttons. "He told me."

"Oh?"

"I wasn't the least bit surprised or shocked. I said, 'Perri, you have my blessing.' And"—she drew a deep breath—"Guy said you have his."

"Dear Jeannine, you are as hopelessly romantic as

Perri. I was married and had a baby when Perri was born."

"Oh, pooh. I don't want to hear about it. And here's Guy with the chaise. Don't be lonely while we're gone, and do think about it, Marie. You'll have plenty of time to think until we return."

On Monday evening she heard Perri's voice in the hall. He came into the room unannounced, shut the door, and leaned against it looking at her. His clothes were travel-stained and his face drawn with weariness. Her impulse was to take him in her arms and kiss the circles under his eyes and smooth back his hair. She took a step toward him, then caught herself.

"Perri, you're supposed to be in Natchez. What are you doing here?"

"That's a gracious welcome! The wedding's over, and I was free to leave. The festivities bored me. I'm here because you are here. I traveled all night. I need a brandy, food, and—and you." His mouth was stubborn, his chin defiant.

She could fight it no longer. She held out her arms, and in two swift steps he was in them, pressing her against him so she felt the length of his body, his back powerful under her hands. Desire and passion flowed through her fingertips and through her lips. Finally they broke apart, and he held her at arm's length, the expression on his face transformed from weariness to joy. "Do you know, I had given up. I thought, If she refuses me this time, I'll never trouble her with my 'boyish dreams' again. But you want me, don't you, Marie?"

It took all her courage to say it. "To my shame, yes."

"My darling Marie, is there shame to love?"

"I'm not sure it is love on either part." Perri groaned. "Perri, it may be nothing more than desire. But a long time ago in Paris a wise old man told me that often the only cure for desire is consummation.

Perhaps—after tonight—you'll look for a younger bride."

Consummation was not a cure. It convinced Perri that what he had dreamed was reality. It plunged Marie headlong into love. She was willing to marry him, if at the end of her mourning he would still have her. She could not imagine being without him ever again.

Sheba guessed. For days she rebuked Marie with her eyes and finally burst out, "And Monsieur not yet a year in his grave."

"I can't bring him back whether it's six months or a year or six years. Do you want me to be alone the rest of my life? To lie in an empty bed? To reach for a ghost?"

"Someone your own age, it wouldn't be so indecent. His father. You loved him once. He's alone too."

"He had his chance a long time ago."

"You doing this to get back at him after all these years?"

"I'm doing this because I love Perri."

"When you're fifty he'll be thirty-six. He'll break your heart."

"I'm a long way from fifty, and he may break it long before then, Sheba."

Dawn came later in winter, and often the household at the Lanneys' was astir before Perri returned. "They're wondering who the lady is who entertains me all night. It seems I've been caught without my knowing it. Yes, darling, it's too late now to be careful."

One afternoon Marie came down from the nap she took in order to be fresh for Perri and found Amalie standing by the fireside.

Amalie had not been in the house since Désirée and André had run off. Her years of mourning had not been kind to her. She looked like a pinched, bitter old woman. The white pleating at her throat made her skin look yellow. Unless she did something about herself, she would never find another husband.

"Amalie, what a nice surprise. Please sit down."

"No, thank you. I don't think you will find it nice when you hear what I have to say." She shook her fist in Marie's face and screamed, "Can't you leave my family alone? First my father, then my husband, now my brother. Are you and your daughters shameless?"

"I don't know what you mean, Amalie." Marie kept her voice soft, gentle.

"Don't lie. You and my father—my mother hated the sight of you—"

"Did she?"

"Désirée, whom I loved and trusted, took my husband, killed him! And now you're corrupting Perri. Can't you leave us in peace? Must you suck every drop of our blood?"

"Have you spoken to Perri, Amalie?"

"I tried. He's mad! You've enchanted him. You've put a spell on him. He wants to marry you. Marry you! An old woman, and he wants to marry you!"

"There is no such thing as a spell, Amalie."

"Don't tell me there isn't. One of your slaves probably got it for you. Went to the obeahman and got a love potion. Blinded Perri, so he sees you as something you aren't."

"Amalie, listen to me. Perri thinks he has loved me all his life. He'll change. He'll grow out of it, given time. Let it take its course. If you don't fight it, he'll forget more easily."

"Meanwhile all New Orleans will be gossiping."

"About me. About Perri. Not about you."

"No, they've had their gossip about me. About me and your whore of a daughter."

"You shouldn't know such words, Amalie."

"I know the word, and I know one when I see one."

"Amalie, get out of my house." *Oh, Edmund!*

"Not until you promise to leave Perri alone. Bar the

door against him. Break the spell you've put on him."

"Get out, Amalie."

Amalie drew a knife from her sleeve, held it above her head, and ran at Marie. Marie moved in time, so the knife crashed against her shoulder.

Amalie was strong for so frail-looking a creature. Marie had all she could do to grab her wrist and hold the arm out of striking distance. They swayed to and fro, Amalie struggling to be free. They crashed to the floor as Perri rushed into the room. He dragged Amalie off Marie, but she swung the knife at him, grazing his cheek, before he wrenched it from her hand and threw her into a chair.

"So, when I stopped you from slashing the portrait, you came to slash the flesh and blood! They told me you'd gone in this direction, Amalie, by the old short-cut we used as children. That's how I guessed. They'd have you up for murder, do you know that? Do you know what they do to murderers?"

"I'd be proud to die."

"Oh, God!" He turned to Marie who was holding her shoulder, the blood flowing out between her fingers, down her breast. "Darling, you're hurt."

"Take her home, Perri. And don't come back. She's right. I've done enough harm." Marie left the room before he could protest. She heard the door close behind them.

She awakened at midnight, her shoulder throbbing, the bandages soaked. Perri sat beside her bed. "Sheba let me in. I came before dark to see how you were, and I'm never leaving you again. I've spoken to my father, and while he didn't exactly give me his blessing"—Perri made a rueful face—"he said I should do as I please."

But that was not what Edmund said when he came to see Marie the next day. His first words were, "I'm shocked."

"I am too, Edmund."

"He's demented."

"So Amalie said."

"Why did you encourage him?"

"I thought he would tire of me more quickly if I—gave in to his desires."

"Tire of you! I remember what you were like in bed. You cast spells with your body."

"You and Amalie do go on about witchcraft, don't you? Any spell I cast over you, Edmund, you broke easily enough. It was your own hunger that was the spell. Perhaps when Perri has had his fill, he'll find someone else to marry, just as you did."

"He wants to marry you."

"Don't worry, Edmund. I'm not such a fool. I won't have him."

The banns were posted a year to the day after Henri's death. The gossip which no one had quite believed was now fact. New Orleans society talked of nothing else. The marriage settlement and dowry were discussed in shocked, delicious detail: the Arnolie-Lanney plantation went, in joint ownership, to Guy—"her *adopted* son, my dear"—and young Leon Lanney. The de Nemour property would be Perri's along with the merchant exchange and the warehouse—"so in a way she comes into her own again"—the house on Chartres Street Perri and Marie were keeping as a *pied à terre*. She had signed everything over to Perri—the house, the slaves, the indigo and vats, everything except her jewelry.

There was no fool like an old fool, they said, and no fool like a woman in love with a man young enough to be her son. She was thirty-five if she was a day, and Perri Lanney was only twenty-one.

As she put her signature on the papers and shoved them away Marie could not resist saying, "So, no doubt Annette would be pleased. The property she wanted has finally come into Lanney hands."

Edmund glowered, but he had been glowering

throughout the proceedings. "This isn't the way she would have wanted to gain possession of it. She would never have dreamed of or tolerated such a possibility."

"I agree. But it's Perri's now."

She had signed it over because she no longer wanted it. It reminded her of the past, or her pride, of what she had done to Annette, what Désirée had done to poor sick Amalie. She wanted to close the door on the past.

She went into debt redoing the interior of the house. Chairs, sofas, armoires were sold, thrown away, or relegated to the house on Chartres Street. The walls were painted pale lavenders, aquamarine, and rose, the tones of the reflections on the lake at sunset. The heavy brocaded curtains were discarded, replaced by ruffled cotton, filmy as silk. The gilded chairs were painted white, then rubbed down so only dull gold shone through. She had them recovered with home-dyed, homespun cottons. "I want it to be like a French country house, simple and open and comfortable."

"How much have you spent?" Perri asked.

"You've no right to question that until we are married, my love."

"Are you aware that the price of indigo has dropped to five livres?"

"Has it? I'll be soon through. It will all be ready by the time we're married. Perri, you haven't changed your mind and are too kind to tell me?"

"My darling, I am so happy I'm afraid it's a dream."

"If it is, let's hope we never awaken. Sometimes I am so afraid. You know how they're gossiping. I *am* old, Perri. We must look very foolish together."

"I don't give a damn for their gossip, nor should you. And in my opinion we're a handsome couple." He grimaced. "I wish my father thought the same."

"It bothers you that he won't give you his blessing, doesn't it?"

"He gave me the warehouse, which is more profitable than his blessings. I think he did it only because he knows I'm running it more efficiently than he ever did, and of course he retains his partnership until he dies. We're a bit strained when we're together. My happiness annoys him. He'd prefer to think you set traps and seduced me. I told him it was the other way around, but he looked down his nose at that."

"Perri, I don't want you to regret anything, not even your father. Or most of all, your father."

"The only thing I regret is that you made me wait so long."

The wedding was simple with only Guy and Jeannine as witnesses. Afterward they had supper at home with Céline, at Marie's insistence, as a guest. Guy and Jeannine were puzzled by her presence, but Marie had told Perri all about her early life, and he agreed that as long as he and Marie had set about to be the scandal of New Orleans, they may as well go all the way.

Laughter and brandy flowed freely. Toward midnight Perri whispered to Marie that he couldn't wait much longer to take her to bed.

"It's not as if you haven't taken me to bed before," she teased.

"Not as my wife."

"Does that make it different?"

"It does to me, and it had better be different for you."

"It is different already. I don't have to be afraid that you will change your mind. My God! What is that?"

No one had heard the carriages arrive. A cacophony rocked the gallery, horns blowing in discord, drums thudding unrhythmically, hammers beating on buckets, spoons rattling in tin pans, rachets, and a howling, hooting mob screaming obscenities.

"The devil!" Céline said. "I heard a rumor there might be a charivari, but I didn't think the fools would go through with it."

Guy pushed back his chair. "I'll drive them off."

Céline caught his arm. "Ignore them. They'll wear themselves out if we pay no attention. Marie, no, don't look out the window."

But she had already seen. Dancing up and down, leering through the window and shaking false bosoms, was a man made up as a hag. He wore a bridal veil, and painted wrinkles lined his face. He dragged with him in his dance a bewildered boy of eight or nine, obviously the worse for drink, who waggled his tiny penis at his bride.

Marie put her head in her hands. "Perri, what have I done to you? What have I done? Forgive me!"

She was a fool, an old fool, just as all New Orleans was saying. She saw the marriage now as another attempt to get back at Edmund. She would never learn to let go of her hate, to forgive. The worst of it was that she loved Perri, would always love him, not just with her body but to the depths of her soul.

"Don't cry, darling. Don't let them see you cry. We know what we did, we did it for love. Our friends know it. There is nothing to forgive."

"It's jealousy," Céline said. "I've heard talk. I always do. There's probably not a man in New Orleans who wouldn't like to spread your legs, Marie. Sorry, Jeannine. You're a lady and shouldn't hear that kind of talk. There's not a one doesn't envy Perri just as they envied Henri. You've got that look about you, Marie. I doubt there's a woman who doesn't wish she looked as young and could snare a younger man. Christ's bones, they do make a hell of a noise, don't they?"

"Perri, I've ruined you. It doesn't matter whether I'll ever be received again, ever be able to walk in New Orleans with my head held high. It's what I've done to you. In time you'll come to hate me."

"What you've done to me has made me the happiest man in New Orleans by flouting their talk and becoming my wife." He put his arm around her, drawing her close. The hoots became jeers. Marie shoved him away.

"For God's sake, don't make it worse by letting them see you embrace me."

"Marie!"

"I can't stand it." She went boldly to the window and looked out. "All New Orleans must be out there trampling my garden." She gave Perri a twisted smile. "Even your father, Perri. Even Edmund."

"He was one of the instigators," Céline said.

"Damn him to hell! My own father!"

Guy got slowly to his feet. "Marie, I think you should face up to them. Ask them in. Treat them as if they had been invited. Laugh at them. They'll admire you for it."

She drew a deep breath, wondering if she had the courage to face them. "May I, Perri?"

"I'd rather drive them off the land with a musket. But perhaps Guy is right. It's your house, darling."

"No longer. It's yours."

They went arm in arm to the front door, fixed smiles on their faces. As they opened it and called, "Come in, come in," the noise died away. The false bride fled, tripped over his skirts, and sprawled down the steps, dragging the boy with him. They ran off in the night, the boy's crying echoing back. A few people hurried after them, Edmund among them. Gradually the others shuffled into the house, offered shamefaced congratulations, clapped Perri on the back, demanded a kiss from the bride, even accepted food and drink.

The noise had roused the servants, who, sensing what would be required of them, were already preparing more food, making punch, passing among the guests with trays. The horns and drums made music now, and Perri led Marie in a hornpipe while the onlookers clapped and cheered.

The party lasted until eight in the morning. Breakfast was served on the gallery as the sun glistened on the lake. Marie gradually lost her fear of their ridicule and was the gayest of them all, going from guest to guest to see that each cup or glass was filled, the food to their liking. Then she and Perri toasted one another. He picked her up and carried her over the doorstep, calling back, "It's time I bed my bride."

Glasses were raised as the crowd watched them ascend the long flight of stairs. Within an hour or so the last guest was gone. Marie was asleep in Perri's arms.

In time people grew accustomed to the marriage. There were other newer scandals to discuss, though they never ceased to exclaim that Perri grew older and Marie grew younger. It was difficult to remember that he was—how many years? Fourteen?—younger than she. A few eyebrows were raised when she produced in rapid succession three healthy babies. She was not so old after all if she could do that. And they were all boys: Gavin, named for Marie's father; Edmund for Perri's, which did nothing to soften the elder Edmund's attitude; and René for Perri's grandfather in France.

Their house parties, their dinners, their hospitality became famous. They were among the first to entertain M. de Kerlerec and his entourage when Kerlerec replaced Vaudreuil as governor. Two hundred guests were present, and the house was turned into a fairy forest with garlands and foliage, a miniature lake and perfumed fountain, while musicians on painted gondolas sernaded the party from the Pontchartrain.

The warehouse and plantation had never been run so well. Perri curtailed Marie's extravagance gently but firmly. He was an ardent lover. There was no longer any need for caution, and he refused to use the silk sheaths or to allow Marie her chemicals. By the time their third son was four months old, Marie was pregnant again.

"I'm too old to have all these babies," she protested. But she loved him too much to refuse him anything.

She would bear children for him until she dropped. Strangely she seemed to get stronger with each birth and not only stronger, but younger-looking.

The months flew by. The fourth child, a girl whom they named Mariette, was born. Marie was so oblivious to the outside world that it shocked her to learn that France and England were at war again, fighting over possession of the upper Ohio Valley.

"But it is too far away to concern us," she said.

"It does concern us. Shipping is in trouble again."

"Perri, shipping to and from New Orleans was in trouble before you were born. It is always in trouble."

"We can't export our indigo. The stores and warehouses are empty. The Choctaw are threatening—"

"They always threaten when there's war with the English. Be happy and don't worry, my love."

When Marie became pregnant again just months after the birth of Mariette, she began to worry about being able to deliver a healthy child. Céline who up until now had been amused by Marie's succession of pregnancies, was aghast. "Marie, you're forty. It's time you stopped. Can't that man leave you alone?"

"I don't want him to leave me alone, but I'll admit I don't want any more children. When I remember all I said about the Arnolie girls! It's just punishment."

Until now the births had been easy. But with the fifth child the labor lasted three days. The surgeon told Perri he could save neither mother nor child. The priest was sent for, the windows were shrouded, work on the plantation ceased.

Perri was on his knees sobbing as the priest administered the last rites. Marie put her hand on his. She wished he would go away. He was making it more difficult to die, to leave him.

She did not die, but there would never be another child. This one was born as Marie was sinking into unconsciousness. It was a girl as pretty and perfectly formed as a doll. Marie named her Flora.

Marie was happy as she had never been before. Except for the inconvenience of the blockade, the war, which was so far away, scarcely touched them. Perri took care of everything. Marie had nothing to do but attend parties, give parties, play with the children and watch them grow, and worship her man. It was indeed a dream from which there seemed to be no awakening.

The one flaw was that Edmund had never entered their house or acknowledged Marie as Perri's wife. She knew this pained Perri, and she had made several overtures toward Edmund, which were rebuffed. She had long since given up trying to mend the rift.

The war dragged on for seven years, but another year passed after it had ended before New Orleans learned the terms of the peace treaty. Perri came home livid with shock. New Orleans had been ceded to Spain as compensation for its loss of Florida.

"But why?" Marie asked. "What must the court at Versailles be thinking of to do such a thing?"

"I don't know, and I don't know yet what it will mean. Every coffeehouse in town is crowded with irate citizens drawing up petitions and delegations and letters of protest. When Versailles sees how we feel, they may relent."

But the treaty remained unchanged, and the Spanish governor arrived, uncheered and unwelcomed.

"We may as well start learning Spanish," Marie said. "I suppose it will be easy for the children, but not for me. I've spoken French too long. I'm not sure I want to be Spanish."

"I refuse to be! I'm still French no matter what flag they hoist in the Place d'Armes. Life isn't going to be easy. They've already refused to redeem our paper money. They've passed an edict forbidding ships to unload cargo without the governor's permission. And French ships are required to have a passport in order to dock or trade with our own—French—colonies. Not only that, the bottom's fallen out of our market for pelts, tobacco, indigo, sugar—everything. Spain can get all she needs from her own colonies."

"It sounds like the end of everything. We'll be poor, won't we?"

"Everyone in New Orleans will be poor except the damned Spanish, who are determined to bring us to our knees."

"Can't something be done?"

"Something will be done." He said it so grimly that Marie felt a premonition.

He took to coming home later and later. Often Marie and the children had dinner alone, and she would be ready for bed before he arrived, flushed with excitement. She sat in her negligée at the table with him while he ate his cold supper, which he seemed scarcely to taste, and scarcely spoke to her.

"Perri, what *is* going on? I must know. Have you another woman?"

He looked at her as if she had gone mad, then burst into laughter. He took her hand. "It's not a woman, Marie. You should know by now there is no woman but you. It's—oh, damn, I've been sworn to secrecy, but I suppose I must tell you. It's a band of patriotic citizens drawing up a plan to drive out the Spaniards. We're led by the attorney general himself, and every important man in New Orleans is in on it. Men who served under Bienville, our Swiss troops, the German settlers, the Acadians, every planter up and down the coast."

"I don't like the sound of it. I almost wish it *were* a mistress. This sounds dangerous."

"Desperate causes require desperate action, Marie."

The worst of it was that Gavin, young Edmund, and René were as excited as their father. They decorated their rooms with the fleur-de-lis. René had Baptiste help him fashion a wooden sword. They were full of talk about the right of the people to decide their own welfare and the shame of being sold like slaves to a foreign nation.

"You're parroting your father," Marie scolded them. "You don't even know what all those words mean. My father, your grandfather, Gavin, for whom you were named, backed a cause he thought was right and was exiled for it. Right doesn't always succeed, and vengeance also harms the avenger. I wish to God your father wouldn't bring his politics home."

Many nights he didn't come home at all. He was traveling the countryside, speaking at secret meetings, inciting men to strike for liberty and throw off the Spanish yoke.

He grew tense and hot-tempered. He muttered in his sleep at night, flung his arms about, and didn't once touch Marie in love, as if all his passion were being spent on the cause of France.

In mid-October Amalie died. She had spent the last years of her life locked in an upstairs room, where she could not harm herself or others. Yet in the end she threw herself out her window and died of the injuries.

Perri had little grief to spend on her. "She ceased to be my sister years ago," he said. "She's been a poor mad soul, no one I knew. How do you expect me to be sad?"

The funeral party turned into a meeting of conspirators rather than mourners. They drew up lists of those who could provide muskets and powder.

"It's really come to that?" Marie asked on the way home.

"The date is set for later this month."

"Perri, you will be careful, won't you?"

"Do you think I want to die?"

The evening of the twenty-seventh he told her he had business in town. "I may not be back tonight. Don't wait up for me." He kissed her as he had not kissed her since this business had begun. The boys cheered and waved their flags as he rode away. Gavin sulked because he was not allowed to go with his father.

That night the guns at the Tchoupitoulas Gate were readied, and the next morning the insurgents took the town in a bloodless march. The troops escorted governor Ulloa, his household, and his officials to a packet awaiting them on the river, put them aboard, and ordered them to sail. Ulloa fled to Havana and from there to Spain.

Throughout the winter and the following spring an uneasy peace returned to the colony. The French flag waved over New Orleans again. They had shown the king they did not wish to belong to Spain. Surely now he would reconsider and reclaim his people. Such was the optimism that spread through the city.

Marie and Perri entertained again. The laughter and music of their parties floated out over the calm waters of the lake. There was dancing in the gardens, where the paper lanterns swung their colored shadows as the wind blew them.

One evening as Marie stood beside Jeannine on the gallery Jeannine said, "Guy told me he heard Spain is sending a military force to take possession of New Orleans. The men who were involved in the revolution have been warned to go over to the English bank for protection. How deeply was Perri involved, Marie?"

"I don't really know. I'll ask him."

She didn't manage to see him alone until after the guests had gone. As they walked upstairs arm in arm she told him what Jeannine had said. "I'd heard, Marie. There's no need to worry. Why should I flee? I was a very small fish in the whole affair."

"You're sure there's no danger?"

"The greatest danger I see now, Marie, is that when the Spanish return, we'll no longer be able to import Bordeaux and will have to drink that Catalonian rubbish instead."

"Be serious, Perri."

"I am, my dear. Come, let me undo your laces tonight. You know how I love to see your body emerge slowly from all that silk, and take possession of each sweet inch I uncover."

"You'll never tire of me, will you, Perri?"

But for a long time after he slept, she lay awake, listening to his breathing, a worm of worry gnawing at her heart.

The days passed with an undercurrent of nervous apprehension. When the news came that a Spanish flotilla had passed La Balize under the command of a Spanish general by the unlikely name of O'Reilly, one of the former revolutionaries tried to appeal to the people to oppose the landing.

"Don't listen, Perri," Marie pleaded.

"I know damned well we can't oppose twenty-three Spanish men-of-war. For once my patriotism fails me. But I think I'll take the boys to town to see the show."

René was impressed by the music, the silver maces, the glittering uniforms, and the three thousand soldiers. Edmund and Gavin cried when the French flag was lowered and the gold flag of Spain raised. They returned home in a state of hysterical excitement. Marie was angry with Perri for having taken them. "It's bad enough for you to be involved in rebellion, but for heaven's sake leave them out of it."

A few days later Perri received an invitation to a conference to be held by General O'Reilly. "Perhaps he is ready to be conciliatory. After all, with the troops he has at his command he can afford to be."

Marie spent the afternoon giving the children a Spanish lesson. They had begun to learn Spanish in the days of Governor Ulloa and dropped the project after he had fled. Now it was mandatory they learn to speak it. It was a tedious business, and her head ached with the unfamiliar words. When they heard a horse galloping up the driveway, she said, "Thank goodness, there is your father. We'll stop for today."

She went to the door to greet him. But it was Guy.

"Perri has been arrested."

Life seemed to drain out of her. She stared at Guy speechlessly.

"Lafrénière, Masan, Marquise, Noyan, Villeré, Caresse, Poupet, Boisblanc, Braud . . . it's an endless list. Perri must have been in more deeply than we knew."

"But he was invited to a meeting. I saw the invitation myself. Very grand, in Spanish."

"It was a trick. When the men got there, the room was filled with Spanish soldiers with fixed bayonets. The house was surrounded by troops as soon as the doors shut behind them. They were denounced as traitors and arrested by the order of the king of Spain."

"Where is he? We must go to him."

"I don't know. Some were taken to the Spanish frigates. Some to the barracks jail. Some are locked in O'Reilly's mansion. The whole town is in a state of fear. No one knows who will be taken next."

"It seems to me every planter on the coast was involved. Including you, Guy. Will they arrest the lot of you?"

"God knows. Do you really think you should go to town, Marie? Wouldn't it be better to wait here?"

"Do you think the Spanish are going to have an announcement of Perri's arrest delivered to me by a uniformed courier like that damned invitation they delivered to him? No, I must go to him. For your safety, I'd better go alone."

"Do you think you and Perri mean no more to me than that? Of course I'm going with you."

The town was silent, shuttered. The smell of fear was strong in the air. Spanish soldiers patrolled the streets, their boots loud on the banquettes.

Marie and Guy were kept waiting outside the governor's mansion while Marie's name was announced. Bayonets were crossed over the door to prevent their entry.

"As if we'd storm the place," Marie whispered. Guy silenced her with the pressure of his hand.

The governor refused to see her or to give her any information as to Perri's whereabouts.

"What shall we do now? Someone must know where he is. I must see him, Guy. I must!"

They went to the house on Chartres Street, and Guy said, "I'll go for Edmund."

"Must you bring Edmund into this?"

"He is Perri's father. He has a right to know what has happened."

"I suppose he does. Get him then."

She paced the floor until they returned, wondering what to do.

It had been years since she had exchanged words with Edmund. They had even managed to avoid one another at Amalie's funeral. When he entered the house followed by Guy, he looked so old and drawn that her heart filled with pity. Swiftly she went to him, took his hands, and kissed his cheeks. There were tears in both their eyes.

"It is a tragic way to be reconciled, Edmund."

"He should never have got mixed up with those patriots. Couldn't you have stopped him, Marie?"

"No more than you could have done. He wouldn't listen to me. Don't we know anyone . . ."

"Perhaps we should wait. They'll be forced to inform us eventually."

"Wait for what? For them to deliver his body to us?" Edmund's sudden pallor shocked her. "I'm sorry, Edmund. All right, I'll wait. But I'm not going back to the plantation. Not until I find him."

They spent the night at the house. The hush that had fallen over the town was frightening. There was neither laughter nor music in the streets; only the passing of the patrol every hour broke the silence.

Once Marie got up to get a glass of wine and found herself afraid to light a candle for fear the gleam falling through the shutters would invite suspicion.

Guy and Edmund were still awake, sitting in the dark, talking in whispers. She joined them, and they sat until dawn drinking.

Morning was no better. No vendors cried, no carts creaked in the street on their way to market. Marie fell into a fitful sleep, huddled in her chair. It was hot with the shutters closed, and the taste of wine was sour in her mouth. Edmund and Guy sprawled in their chairs, snoring.

Marie went to her bed and closed her eyes. Just as she sank into sleep she heard a voice in her mind.

"Céline."

Electrified, she sat up. She was alone, and there was no one there who could have spoken. But Céline would know. "Men talk when they're lickerish," Céline always said.

Marie sponged her face and dressed. She awakened Guy and Edmund to tell them where she was going. "Wouldn't it be better if I went?" Guy asked. "I mean, a woman going to a place like that."

"You might be arrested. I'll go. I'll paint my face. Perhaps the soldiers will think I'm one of them returning from a call."

The streets were deserted except for the soldiers. They looked at her curiously but made no move to accost her. One called something in Spanish, and the others laughed, but they didn't stop her.

When Marie reached the house, Céline's maid opened the door. She thought Madame was in bed. It had been a busy night.

"But I have to see her. Which is her room?"

"Marie?" The voice came from the office. "I'm here. I haven't gone to bed yet. I was writing to you."

She was sitting at her desk, a piece of paper before her. She's growing old, Marie thought, but so am I. Céline's hair was dyed a startling shade of red. Her face was covered with patches of indecent design, her eyes grotesquely outlined with color.

"Yes, I was writing to you. It never occurred to me

you'd come here. In our business you don't need a common language," Céline said. "But it's surprising what you learn in bed. I learned a little Spanish when Ulloa was here. His soldiers were obliging instructors. Most of the words wouldn't do for elegant society, but no matter. These new bastards are just as talkative. They were very excited last night. They could talk of nothing but the arrests. That and the positions in which they wanted to rut. When I heard Perri's name mentioned, I strained every effort to understand. I'm quite good at Spanish, I find."

"You know where he is!"

Céline nodded. "He's aboard the frigate lying in the river. It's possible they won't detain him, Marie."

"Did they say so?"

"No, but they have the important men. They'll be tried and found guilty and executed. I think Perri is considered fairly unimportant."

"Céline, how can I thank you?"

Céline shrugged, licked her finger, and made a mark in the air. "Another good deed to my credit when I die, eh? Be careful, Marie. Why don't you wait and see if they let him go?"

"I'll think about it." But by the time she got back to the house, she was determined to try to see him.

"If they don't think he's important, they may be willing to release him. Especially to his wife," she told Guy and Edmund.

"Not without O'Reilly's orders, Marie."

But nothing they could say would stop her.

She was thankful for the years of living on the lake. She could handle a skiff, even in the current of the river, which was low and sluggish in July and August. If it had not been for the errand on which she was bent, she would have enjoyed the morning, the smell of the water, the bright ripples, the reflections.

She pulled alongside the frigate and caught one of

the lines. The sentinels were at first astonished, then they waved their arms and ordered her away.

She summoned every word of Spanish she knew. "I come for my husband, Señor Lanney, who is prisoner. His arrest is a great mistake. Release him in my care, please, and I promise we will do no more harm to the Spanish governor or Spanish law."

"Go away, señora, or we will be forced to shoot."

"I will not go away. I want my husband."

"Señora, I must warn you, we will shoot."

She was never sure what happened next. There were scufflings, shouting, the sound of running feet, and the crash of bodies. Perri leaned over the rail above her.

"Go away, Marie, darling, go away!"

"Jump, Perri!"

But as she spoke the sentinels closed in on him. There was the flash of a bayonet in the sun. Perri's mouth opened, soundlessly. His grip loosened on the rail, and he slid from her view.

A soldier's face appeared beside the sentinel. "Eh, señora, you're happy now, I think? Your husband knocked down his guard and tried to escape when he heard your voice. You should have obeyed us. He escaped, yes. He is dead. Here is proof." He tossed a bloody cloth into the skiff, and while she stared at it he cut the line. The skiff drifted down the river.

It was Perri's shirt, the elegant shirt he had worn to the meeting, with lace at its throat and sleeves, and Perri's blood where the bayonet had gashed it. She had killed him as surely as if she had thrust the bayonet herself.

Back at the warehouse she sat in the skiff waiting for the blood to dry. She heard a splash and looked up at the frigate. They had thrown his body overboard. She watched it sink and rise, sink and rise, turn like a log as the current carried it down toward the Gulf.

* * *

No one reproached her, which was worse than recrimination. The family was stunned, but they scarcely dared to display their grief. Edmund bolted the warehouse and the exchange. They closed themselves up on the two plantations and waited to see what would happen.

The trials of the leaders, accused by secret witnesses they never saw, dragged on for two months. In October the verdict was reached. Some were sentenced to six years imprisonment, some hanged, and some executed in the barracks' courtyard. All their property was confiscated.

Marie was the first to receive word that the plantation was forfeit to the Spanish government. She had signed it over to Perri when they were married, and therefore it was his. The warehouse and exchange, which Edmund had settled on Perri at the same time, were also forfeit. The officials went to Edmund and demanded the keys.

A Spanish lady and her husband came to inspect the house. They walked through it, commenting to one another, twitching the curtains, patting the chairs, peering into the cupboards, inspecting the bedrooms, opening armoires, counting the linen.

Marie was given two days to vacate. It no longer mattered. The house had brought misfortune. She wished she could have died in Perri's arms, but she had to go on living for the children.

Half the string of Maman's pearls bought passage for her and the children to France. The Spanish lady questioned who the rightful owner of the jewelry now was. She took Marie's hand and twisted the peridot ring. Marie produced the settlement papers proving that her jewelry was her own, that all she was taking with her belonged to her. She also had to produce the paper showing that Sheba was free. She was sorry now that she hadn't freed Baptiste and Calla.

She cut the two paintings of La Violette out of their frames and rolled them and packed them among her clothes. Grillets would fetch a good price in Paris. She could live comfortably, provide dowries for Mariette and Flora. She could live at the château with Louis in her tower room, or with Henriette and Jacques in the new hotel—no longer so new. When all the children were married, she would move to Saint-Germain-de-Prés, to some drafty garret room and begin to paint again.

Edmund came to see them off, tears streaming down his face. "I wish you would stay, Marie. I need you. You were my first friend when I came here. It took me years to realize I love you. Stay with me. Please."

"There's nothing here for me anymore, Edmund."

"I need you. I too have lost everything."

"You have Jeannine and Guy and their children."

"But not you."

"You didn't really want me, Edmund. If you had, you would have taken me. It's like the time you tried to kill yourself. You didn't want to die."

"It would have been better if I had."

"But you did not. And I did not die with Perri. We have to go on. *Au revoir*, Edmund. If you ever come to France, I'll be glad to see you."

The ship cast anchor. The current took it. Edmund waved from the levee. The sun gilded the roofs of the city and the steeple of the church where Marie had first seen Céline.

California
Woman
Daniel
Knapp
The first novel
in a new series